EVOLUTION

BOOK III OF THE DARK MATTER TRILOGY

TERI TERRY

Charlesbridge TEEN

First US paperback edition 2021
2020 First US edition
Copyright © 2020 by Teri Terry

At the time of publication, all URLs printed in this book were accurate and active.
Charlesbridge and the author are not responsible for the content or accessibility of any website.

Published by Charlesbridge Teen, an imprint of Charlesbridge Publishing
9 Galen Street, Watertown, MA 02472
(617) 926-0329 • www.charlesbridgeteen.com

First published in 2018 by Orchard Books
An imprint of Hachette Children's Group
Part of The Watts Publishing Group Limited
Carmelite House
50 Victoria Embankment
London EC4Y 0DZ
An Hachette UK Company
www.hachette.co.uk
www.hachettechildrens.co.uk

Library of Congress Cataloging-in-Publication Data
Names: Terry, Teri, author. | Terry, Teri. Dark matter trilogy ; [3]
Title: Evolution / Teri Terry.
Description: [First U.S. edition]. | Watertown, MA : Charlesbridge, 2020. |
Series: Dark matter trilogy ; book 3 | Audience: Ages 12+ | Summary: Shay, her manipulative father,
    Xander, and the other survivors are hiding out at the secret Multiverse compound in Scotland,
    where Shay still hopes to find some trace of the real Callie, her boyfriend's missing sister, and heal
    the breach between herself and Kai—who remains her best chance to escape her father's clutches
    and stop the deadly contagion.
Identifiers: LCCN 2019033825 (print) | LCCN 2019033826 (ebook) |
    ISBN 9781623541385 (hardcover) | ISBN 9781623541392 (paperback) |
    ISBN 9781632899125 (ebook)
Subjects: LCSH: Epidemics—Juvenile fiction. | Human experimentation in medicine—Juvenile fiction. |
    Genetic engineering—Juvenile fiction. | Missing children—Juvenile fiction. |
    Fathers and daughters—Juvenile fiction. | Scotland—Juvenile fiction. | Science fiction. |
    CYAC: Science fiction. | Epidemics—Fiction. | Genetic engineering—Fiction. |
    Missing persons—Fiction. | Fathers and daughters—Fiction. | Scotland—Fiction. |
    LCGFT: Science fiction.
Classification: LCC PZ7.T2815 Ev 2019 (print) | LCC PZ7.T2815 (ebook) |
    DDC 813.6 [Fic]—dc23
LC record available at https://lccn.loc.gov/2019033825
LC ebook record available at https://lccn.loc.gov/2019033826

Printed in the United States of America
(hc) 10 9 8 7 6 5 4 3 2 1
(pb) 10 9 8 7 6 5 4 3 2 1

Display type set in S&S Amberosa Sans by Gilang Purnama Jaya
Text type set in Stempel Garamond by Adobe
Printed by Berryville Graphics in Berryville, Virginia, USA
Production supervision by Brian G. Walker
Jacket and map art by Sarah Richards Taylor
Designed by Sarah Richards Taylor

Each of the seven stages of evolution can only be investigated from the one before, stepping backward in time . . .

—Xander, *Multiverse Manifesto*

PART 1
MICRO-EVOLUTION

Random changes that give a survival
advantage are perpetuated within a
species: the fittest survive and pass
on their traits. But what if the changes
aren't random? This is the moment
humankind will truly evolve.

—Xander, *Multiverse Manifesto*

QUARANTINE

CHAPTER 1

LARA

MY FEET TAKE ME TO THE VERY EDGE OF THE WORLD.

There is nothing beyond this place if I look at it straight on—the woods, the path, and even the sky above them disappear, lost in a white mist. If I turn my eyes far to the side, I can almost see ghostly images of trees and hills, spread out below. So maybe the world does go on, and a part of me somehow knows that it must. But it's the edge of *my* world.

If I think about it ahead of time, I can't come here. I can't decide to walk to this place; I can only do it as if by accident. If I'm upset enough and just *walk*, without planning to go anywhere in particular, I end up here. It's a reflex, like my leg jerking up if my knee is hit just so with a hammer.

Why was I upset? My thoughts veer in a direction they can't take, and slip away.

I lean forward, tilting into the world that vanishes beyond and below—arms outstretched in a sort of *Titanic* moment—and close my eyes. Can I lose my balance and tumble forward down this hill, out of this place?

Maybe I could if I fell asleep. No one can control where I go in my dreams—not even me. I shiver, my thoughts dragged back to last night. To . . . to . . . *well*. Whatever it was has vanished from my thoughts. Calm washes through me once again.

Unable to stop myself from trying, I lift my right foot and step forward. But when I open my eyes, it's the same as always: I've turned and gone the other way, away from the edge. I sigh and lean against a tree.

Roots stretch out near my feet, twisted and exposed. If my foot caught against a root, just *here*, could I sprawl and fall forward then? But no, it's too late: I've thought about it now. I can't trick my feet into a trip that formed in my thoughts.

Maybe next time.

Then I hear the summons, deep in my mind—

Lara, come.

And it's another reflex that has me instantly running, back the way I came, with direction and purpose—

Obedience.

The sort that is blind.

CHAPTER 2

SHAY

THE PLANE LURCHES AGAIN, and I grip the arms of my seat tight.

Elena sits terrified in the row in front of me; Beatriz, next to her, isn't bothered at all. Maybe when you're eight years old like Beatriz, you're not scared; you can't be. But the usual assumption with that would be that you're not scared because you don't understand you could really be hurt, or what death even means. That doesn't apply to her, right? Beatriz has seen her whole family—and many more—die from the epidemic. She saw survivors like us, too, die around her in the fires of the vigilante survivor hunters, Vigil. Beatriz knows what death is, what it looks like, how it feels to watch someone you care about die screaming. To be flooded with their last thoughts if you touch them after they're gone. Maybe after all that, flying into a storm seems tame.

Chamberlain has hitched a ride too, and is half on the seat next to me, half on my knees. The tip of his tail twitches almost imperceptibly, like he is annoyed but not deigning to let it ruffle his cool cat persona.

His front claws are embedded in my jeans, holding on and scratching my leg underneath now and then when the plane pitches or drops— the feline version of the brace-for-your-life position? I stroke him as much to reassure myself as to reassure him, and I try to concentrate on here, now, on my fear and his warm weight and claws. But it isn't anywhere near enough to take my focus away from the agony inside.

Kai closed his mind.

He turned his back to me and walked away.

I feel as if I'm draining away, my essence leaving me, drop by painful drop.

Hang on, everyone, we'll be through this in a moment. Alex broadcasts the thought to all of our minds from his seat up front: he's the one at the controls, flying this thing.

Alex—Xander, I mean, as that's how he is known by everyone here. *My father.*

Not that he's ever been that to me.

Fairness makes me admit he never had the chance—not when Mum left him and never told him about me. But now he knows I'm his daughter, and the thought makes me uneasy. Mum didn't want him to know, did she? Now that she's gone, I can't even ask her why.

Xander isn't scared, at least not that he lets any of us see. None of his followers on the plane with us are either—they are calm, serene, even—and somehow I know that Xander's reassurances were more for Beatriz, Elena, and me than anyone else. The others trust him completely.

Who are these people, really? They are all members of Multiverse. It's like a cult, Iona said—one that worships truth. They worship Xander too, by the looks of things. The day Iona read something about them in the newspaper on the school bus and then told me about it seems like a million years ago, and remembering that day, one of our last ordinary days together, fills me with longing to be with her. My best friend—is she all right? What would she make of Xander? I hope she never has the chance to find out.

As if Xander controls the sky and weather as much as this plane and all of our lives, our path evens out soon after his reassurance.

The plane glides smooth, safe, but Chamberlain's claws continue to hold on like the tumult inside me. I fix my eyes out the window, mental barriers up—not wanting any stray thoughts to leak out to those around me. I struggle to control the tears that threaten, but one spills down my cheek and I flick it away.

Kai, how could you shut me out?

I agreed to go with Xander to try to find Kai's sister, Callie, but Kai wouldn't listen to *why*. All he saw was me leaving with his ex-stepdad, a man he hates; all he heard was that Xander is also my father, something I hadn't told him. I knew I should have ages ago, but couldn't bring myself to say the words. At first there were too many other things for him to deal with, then the longer I kept quiet, the harder it was to explain why I hadn't told him before. But the way it came out—Xander being the one who told him—made everything worse.

And Kai didn't believe me that it wasn't Callie's ghost who had been with us all along, that instead it was Jenna, an imposter. That it was actually Jenna who was destroyed in the bomb blast—Jenna who gave up her existence, such as it was, to save me. More pain twists in my gut. We went through so much together, and now, because of me, she's gone.

But it all adds up to this: Kai's sister, Callie, a real girl who lived and breathed and may do so still, could be out there somewhere, and only Xander can lead me to her.

Worse than everything else is that Kai didn't believe in *me*.

Xander said he knows how much it hurts to be different, to lose somebody because of it. He lost Mum because she sensed the difference—a *wrongness*, she called it—inside of him.

I'm scared she'd think the same about me now.

Is that the real reason behind Kai's rejection?

He's always struggled with how I changed when I survived the epidemic that killed so many—the one he is immune to. The way I can talk in his mind, and manipulate auras—to heal, to kill. The latter may have only ever been to defend myself, but his horror when he knew . . . He couldn't handle it, could he?

By shutting me out of his mind, Kai left me with no other way to reach him than through a message—one I had to pass hurriedly to his friend Freja. She knew I spoke the truth; I'm sure of that. When you speak directly into somebody's mind, survivor to survivor, it's hard to do anything else. And she said she'd tell him what I said.

Please, Kai: believe Freja. Even though you wouldn't believe me.

The plane soon starts to descend, and I glance across the aisle at these followers of Xander's. Gold glints at their necks like it does at mine. The pendant, a gift from Xander, is a model of an atom—the mark of Multiverse—and although the chain hangs loosely, it feels like a noose slowly tightening around my throat.

One of his followers must feel my gaze; he turns and smiles. There is respect for me that wasn't there before, now that he knows I'm Xander's daughter. Like the rest of them, he seems calm, gentle—kind, even. But I know they killed easily enough when they rescued us from the army. There is something about that combination—casual violence with a smile—that makes me shiver.

Admit it, Shay, if only to yourself. You're scared.

I want to step back in time to get away from these people, but I *must* find Callie. It's the only way to make Kai see I'm doing all of this for him.

CHAPTER 3

LARA

I OPEN THE DOOR, breathless from my headlong dash through the woods back to Community. Cepta is at her desk. Her dark hair covers her face as she leans over whatever she reads, and I know there is no point in rushing her.

Time ticks slowly by. Just as I'm wondering if she'd notice if I left again, she looks up and smiles. Despite the way she made me run and then wait, the warmth of her smile makes me happy.

"There you are, Lara," she says, her soft voice gentle and chiding. "Where've you been?"

"Nowhere. I went for a walk."

She nods. Her eyes are careful. "Where did you go?"

She knows. She always knows. Why does she ask? "To the edge."

"Why do you go there?"

"I don't know. I'm telling the truth!"

Her eyebrows go up slightly; she tilts her head to one side. "I know,

Lara. At least, I know you think that is the truth, but there is more behind both my question and your answer. Come here."

She holds out a hand, and I step forward. Her hand closes over mine. Her skin is warm; the soft white sleeve of her tunic brushes my arm. The gold of her necklace—the mark of Multiverse—glints in the lamplight and holds my eyes. I used to have one, but she took it away.

"You know I'm only trying to help you." And as she says it, I know it's true, and yet . . . and yet. What?

"Have you been practicing your mindfulness while you walk? Before you sleep?"

"I try," I say, and that much is true.

"Try *harder*. Earn your place among us. You can do it."

But she doesn't really believe that, does she?

She knows that I am tainted, that I will fail. And so do I.

Later I'm sitting upright, cross-legged on the floor. I breathe out slowly, feel the air leave my lungs, then breathe back in slowly too. I am here. Like the floor, the air, my lungs. No before, no after, only now. Thoughts flit through my mind, but I don't have to let myself get tangled up inside them. I breathe, in, out, and any tension left in my body drains away.

Cepta's light touch on my mind is approving, but then nothing ever changes, does it? I never change.

Negative thoughts are only mental events. Cepta explained they don't define me. I accept and acknowledge them, and they drift away as I breathe out once again.

Soon Cepta judges I am ready, and I rise, slip into bed. I focus on the feel of the cool sheets on my skin, the weight of the blanket, each breath, in and out.

Sleep well, Lara, Cepta whispers inside my head, and then she's gone.

CHAPTER 4

SHAY

I ALWAYS HATE THAT FEELING of deceleration when you're coming in to land; it just feels plain *wrong* to slow down in midair.

Xander is good at this, though. We touch down with barely a bump. Out the window it is still dark, but it is that moment of hushed stillness that comes just before dawn.

I unclip the seat belt and stand, lifting Chamberlain in my arms. He's one heavy cat. Xander waits at the front of the aisle like some sort of flight attendant.

"That was a difficult flight. Is everyone all right?" he says, aloud this time.

Elena has lost her fear now that he is looking at us. "Of course," she says. "Never had any doubt that we would land safely."

He laughs like he knows how scared she really was.

"I'm fine," Beatriz says, "but I wish Spike were here too."

I've been so consumed with thoughts of myself, of Kai, I haven't been thinking of Spike, and I'm stricken. He's part of us, part of our group, and he's not here. He's not *anywhere* anymore. And it's my fault.

Elena must catch my thought or read my face, because she takes my hand. She knows that Spike pushed me to the ground, away from the army bullets that ended his life. *Spike wouldn't have been who he was if he hadn't done everything he could to save you, would he?* Her silent words, said in my mind.

But she doesn't understand; she doesn't know what I did. I'm a coward. I hide it down deep so she won't see it.

We climb down the steps to the runway, if you can call it that. It's grass and not much wider than the wingspan of the plane. Xander must really know what he's doing to land here.

The sun is just creeping up, casting first light on tall trees at the edges of the field. Low houses are built in their shadows, the sort with living roofs: plants and grasses grow across them. Maybe to obscure them from anyone flying above? Chamberlain squirms, and I bend to put him down. He rolls on the earth in delight. Oh, to be a cat.

"Where are we?" I ask.

"Scotland. A remote highland community we built a few years ago; none but us know where it is. We've managed to stay isolated from recent events."

"Do you mean the epidemic hasn't found it?" Elena asks.

"Yes. It's stayed clear."

So. They've built a place in the woods, complete with an airfield that looks like a meadow, that no one has found or infected. It must have been hard to stay hidden to start with, no matter how remote. Clearing most of the country with the epidemic has likely made it easier—it has suited them.

"How many people live here?" I ask.

"In the inner community, about a hundred. Outlying, almost two hundred."

Is one of them Callie? I say to Xander, and only him.

Patience, he answers the same way. His eyes move from mine to the trees above us; someone is approaching—a woman.

"There are over two hundred now—two hundred and nine," she

says when she reaches us, her voice soft and lilting. "We've had a few more join us since your last visit, Xander." *Welcome*, she adds to all of us, silently—she's a survivor.

Dark hair cascades down her back, and her aura is one of the brightest I've seen, save perhaps Beatriz's. It pulsates and shines. She wears a white tunic and dark leggings, a Multiverse necklace around her throat, and a wide smile that is all for Xander.

"Cepta," he says, his voice warm. He bends to kiss her cheek, and there is a sense of a quick, silent exchange between them—one they don't share with the rest of us.

He turns to us. "This is Cepta. She is Speaker for this Community." He introduces Elena and Beatriz, and then there is a dramatic pause as Cepta looks at me and wonders who I am.

He puts his hands on my shoulders.

"And *this* is Shay. My daughter."

Cepta's surprise is complete. "Your daughter?" She looks between me and Xander and back again, wonder in her eyes. There is another swift, silent exchange between them.

She turns to me and smiles widely. "Welcome, Shay." She bends to kiss my cheek now too, and she's shining clean and smells lovely and makes me feel like an unkempt rat fresh from a night in the sewer. The marks of blood, death, and battle stain me inside and out.

"Come," Cepta says. "I've prepared a guesthouse for the three of you—even though Xander never told me who it was for!" She laughs.

"I like to keep anyone as curious as you in suspense," he says, but he looks at me as he says it. Was that comment meant for me?

He links his arm in Cepta's as she leads us to one of the houses. They leave Beatriz, Elena, and me at the door, saying that today we should rest. Tonight at sunset there will be dinner and a meeting. Xander and Cepta leave us and walk off hand in hand.

On the other side of the door, everything in the guesthouse is simple, and so clean and white that I'm afraid to touch anything. There's food set out on a low table. Beyond are three small bedrooms—I sigh in relief when I see the shower in the bathroom. I start to ask if anyone minds if I go first, but Elena just shakes her head and pushes me toward it.

11

I'm inside, door shut. There's no lock, and I wish I could lock it, even though there is no sense of danger or that anyone would intrude. Besides, Elena and Beatriz are out there. If anyone came, they would let me know. I make do with moving a freestanding towel rack in front of the door.

I strip off and kick my clothes into the corner, hoping there will be other things to wear when I'm done. I never want to touch mine again—they're dirty, stained by the day, like I am. A day I can't keep out of my mind any longer.

Spike: he pushed me down to the earth when he was shot. He saved me, and he died. Spike, my friend: gone. I'd tried to rub his blood off my skin, but it is still there; I can wash off what I can see, but it will always be there. Then I see the soldiers I killed, so many of them, using my mind—their blood didn't touch my skin, but I still feel its mark.

The water is hot, and there are old-fashioned, big bars of soap—I scrub and scrub my skin red-raw. With the shower still running, I sit down underneath it and draw my knees up to my chest. I rest my head on my knees.

So many died. Then Jenna came, and she protected me—her cool darkness flowed over me and Chamberlain and stopped the bomb from killing us—but it destroyed her. I still can't believe she's really gone.

And all of this was too much, way too much, to bear.

But then Kai came, and somehow I found I could bear it as long as he was close. These lips, Kai kissed. These hands, he held. These arms were tight around him, and now all I hold inside them is myself. The water is hot on my back, my head, but I'm trembling.

Tonight will come. I'll have to go to this meeting, whatever that is about. Tomorrow will follow too. I'll be strong then. I'll gain Xander's trust; I'll find Callie; I'll find a way out of here for both of us.

But not now. Now, I let my tears fall: I cry for Spike—I could have saved him, but I didn't. I didn't want to kill to help us get away, and then what happened? More death. I cry for Jenna, who we thought was Callie—she saved my life, mine and Chamberlain's.

And I cry for Kai most of all, for the empty arms that are mine—now and tomorrow and tomorrow's tomorrow. The days stretch

12

before me in unending loneliness, and I have to accept that it may be this way forever. Even if I find his long-lost sister, will he forgive me for all the things I never told him?

Later, somehow, I will find hope—I'll have to, or I won't be able to go on. But right now all I am is despair.

CHAPTER 5

LARA

A SMALL SQUARE ROOM, *windowless and dark.*

No, not again: I can't bear it.

I struggle against the restraints that strap me to the chair, even though I know there is no point; I can't help myself. No one can.

One wall starts to glow.

Beads of sweat break on my brow.

I know I'm dreaming; I know this isn't real. I should be able to change what happens, like Cepta has been trying to teach me—my subconscious is in control. Isn't it?

Flames erupt from the wall.

I imagine the door bursting open—firemen, hoses. The ceiling magically sprouting a major sprinkler system. Or even getting beamed out of here to a starship in the sky at the last, crucial moment.

But no matter what I try, nothing works.

I'm burning, my flesh is burning, I'm screaming . . .

SCREAMING

There is no help, no way out, no rescue . . .
What am I screaming?
WAKE UP.
A command, straight to my mind.

As I open my eyes, tendrils of the nightmare fall away, cobwebs that I push through until they're gone.

I sit up, throwing off a sense of uneasiness. I frown. There was something unpleasant in my dream— horrible, even. What was it?

Lara, come. It's Cepta, and there isn't just the usual impatience coloring her thoughts this morning; there is some sense of anticipation or excitement.

I get up, throw the curtains open. Last night's storm is gone. The world is washed and shiny new under bright morning sunshine.

And something else is new: a plane has landed on the airstrip on the field below.

CHAPTER 6

SHAY

SHAY, ARE YOU ALL RIGHT? It's Elena—from the other side of my bedroom door.

It's just a headache, I lie. *I'll be out in a minute.* I do have a headache, but it's that dull heaviness that comes from too much crying rather than anything being medically wrong. If the world would just leave me alone, I'd stay in this bed and not move again forever.

Chamberlain bats my cheek with a paw, and I open my eyes. He rubs his head against my chin.

Well, maybe not *forever.* I reach out a hand to stroke him.

Is there anything I can do? Elena's concern washes over me, but sometimes someone being nice is the last thing you need—it's like being granted permission to stay in bed hugging a pillow, whimpering, for eternity. Mum always knew, didn't she, if it was time for a hug or a push. An acute stab of missing her fills me again. Right now I need a push.

Shay? Elena again.

No, there's nothing you can do; I'm fine, I answer.

I make myself sit up, and my headache intensifies. I put my head in my hands. Am I up to this? I need to have my wits about me. Xander isn't easily fooled: I can't let him see that the only reason I'm here is to find Callie and take her home. I need to make him trust me.

Maybe I could beg off this meeting thing and stay behind . . .

No. Fix it, Shay. *Reach* inside, find the pain, and fix it. Not the Kai-shaped pain—that's beyond what can be dealt with this way, or it should be, anyway. But how my head feels, now that I might have a chance with.

I close my eyes, focus, and *reach* within—to travel along with my blood, swirling and rushing through my body. Like it always does, this takes all my attention—so that weirdly the most inward-focusing thing I can possibly do eases my attention away from myself, or my feelings, at least. Just the act of *reaching* out calms the emotional maelstrom inside and leads me to another sort of storm: I spin with blood cells, molecules, atoms, particles—particles that become waves, waves of healing. I soothe and ease swollen sinuses, sore nose, puffy eyes; even out red and blotchy skin; edge my mind and body toward awareness, wakefulness, readiness. And—as an afterthought—I make a slight adjustment to neurotransmitters, bumping up my serotonin levels a little. This'd be a great skill for a psychiatrist: no antidepressants needed. They could just fiddle with your brain a little instead.

By the time I open my eyes, I'm ready to face the world. Or this weird corner of it, at least.

I stand and pull a fresh tunic over my head. After my endless shower, I'd been relieved to find clean clothes had been put out for me, but the uniform could get boring: white tunics and black leggings, along with the cool feel of gold hanging around my neck.

I open my door, and there, waiting in the hall, is Xander—dressed more or less the same way, but his tunic is a deep blue that brings out the color of his eyes. No sign of Elena or Beatriz?

"They've gone ahead with Cepta," he says, answering my unspoken question.

"Am I late?"

He shakes his head. "No. I thought we should have a moment on our own."

"Oh. Okay."

"I know the last few days have been difficult. And that it was hard for you to leave Kai behind."

"Yes. It was."

"But apart from that, is being here—is everything all right?"

"I don't know," I say, answering him honestly. "I don't know how I feel about anything right now."

"Is there anything I can do?" The same question Elena asked, but the effect is different: he's not someone who would be a good shoulder to cry on, and that's not what he means anyway. He's asking for something specific to fix the unfixable.

Though there is one thing. He could answer my questions, especially the most important one: where is Callie? But that look he gave me earlier, when he said he likes to keep anyone curious in suspense—it means no. Asking won't help. It might even make it harder to learn what I need to know. I shake my head, hold my tongue.

"Time to go, then." He holds out his arm, and I take it. He pats my hand and holds it closer to his arm. He's warm and I'm cold, and there is something about that simple gesture that touches me inside. I don't understand how I'm feeling, but I can't think about why or what those feelings mean when he is close like this; he'll read it. I have to save it for later.

"It'll be all right, Shay," he says. "You belong with us. You'll see."

The stars are out. They cast just enough light to see the path, our surroundings. The houses are scattered under the trees. As I saw when we arrived, they all have plants growing on the roofs. As we go by and I look closer, I see details I didn't before: most of the plants are herbs, lettuces, other things that can be eaten, but all are planted in a random way—not in neat rows. Is that to blend in under the trees if anyone looked down from the sky above?

The buildings almost feel like tree houses the way they are arranged, but built under the trees instead of in them. Or maybe with their living roofs, they're more like hobbit holes. Where do they get power, water? Do they have phone lines or cell reception? Internet?

It's nothing like any community I've seen anywhere before, and there is a sense of *rightness* about it. *Mum would have loved it here*—an involuntary thought. She always yearned to be close to the earth, the trees. And this is what he built.

My footsteps falter, and Xander pauses too. He looks at me, waits.

"What went wrong with you and my mother?"

"I loved her." He speaks truth. "Part of me still does." There is an intense sadness running through him and his aura.

"You were a survivor back then too, weren't you, like Kai said. How?"

"There was an accident. At Desertron, in the US—have you ever heard of it?"

I shake my head.

"It was a particle accelerator complex, built in Texas before CERN existed. Officially the project was canceled before they'd finished construction. In reality it was completed, but that was covered up after the accident. Others died; I survived. No one realized what happened to me in the process."

"When was that?"

"1993. A long time ago now. I've been alone a long time."

"From what I've seen, there are always people who want to be around you."

"Not ones like me. And you." He regards me seriously. "We have much to learn about each other, and I'm sure you have some hard questions for me, as you should. But know this: I've always done what I thought was right. Things may not always have worked out the way I wanted them to, but I've tried. No matter what your mother or Kai may have said."

He tugs my arm a little, and we walk on. *Me too*, I say in a small voice, only to myself. I do what I think is right—like when I thought I was a carrier and left Kai in order to turn myself in to the air force—but I was wrong that time. I was wrong not to believe Kai when he told me Xander had been a survivor for many years. I was wrong not to tell Kai that Xander was my father. How can I judge someone else for making mistakes when I make them all the time?

Though the consequences of Xander's mistakes—well. Mine mostly hurt me; his have killed many thousands, perhaps millions by now.

There's a larger structure ahead, and this is where we are going. There's a low hum of voices. Faint lights through shaded windows.

Xander reaches for the door, holds it open, gestures for me to go first. He follows behind, shuts the door, and stands beside me. The room is full of people sitting on benches by long tables. They were chatting as we came in, but now all talking in the room ceases as everyone turns toward us.

Could Callie be here?

My eyes scan the room quickly: there are men, women, and children of all ages, Elena and Beatriz among them. But no one looks anything like Callie.

Everyone is still looking at us, and it feels like too many eyes focused too closely. But as if Xander senses I'm about to pull away, he takes my hand. I'm trapped.

"Greetings," Xander says. "It's been too long since we joined together, and there is much to talk about tonight. We'll enjoy dinner in a moment, but first, I want to introduce you to someone." He pauses and looks at me, smiles, drawing it out. "Everyone, this is Shay—my daughter."

Ripples of surprise fill the room. I'd have thought because some of them knew about me that they'd have told the others by now. Though I'm getting the feeling Xander likes a stage. His followers obviously know it, so they don't spoil his fun. Then there are smiles and nods all around, and murmurs of "Welcome."

I feel like an idiot and want to escape, but don't know where to go—there aren't any empty spaces near Elena and Beatriz—and everyone is still looking at me, waiting. Do I have to say something?

I swallow, mouth suddenly dry. "Ah, hi. Thanks."

Xander leads me to a small head table—one set for six—at the end of the rows. Cepta is already there, and three others; I wonder if someone got evicted for me? There are two empty seats, one next to

Cepta, and I'm expecting Xander to sit there. But he takes the other chair, leaving me between him and Cepta's quickly hidden displeasure.

I scan the room again in case I missed Callie somehow, but no. There are about a hundred people here tonight; perhaps this is the inner community Cepta mentioned, whatever that is. Everyone is in charming white and black apart from Xander and Cepta—they are both in blue tunics, though she wore white earlier—and there's not much difference between men, women, and children. They all have a gold necklace like mine around their necks—Beatriz and Elena do now too. And the only survivors' auras in the room are Xander, Cepta, Elena, Beatriz, and me. Until we arrived, Cepta was the only one. Is that why she is Speaker?

Cepta rings a little bell, and a door opens at the back. In come others bearing food and drinks to each table. They're dressed differently, in more ordinary clothes, with variations of color and style.

A woman puts a plate of what looks like a vegetable-and-bean pie in front of me, and as she does, I see there's a mark on her hand, like Xander's: *I* for *immune*. His is false, but since nobody knew he was a survivor from that accident so long ago, they must have assumed he was immune when he didn't get sick. Others bringing in food have the mark too.

"Most of our food is grown or gathered here, or traded with other communities like ours," Cepta says. "You'll find we're all strictly vegetarian. I hope you don't mind?"

I shrug. "When in Rome," I say. And I'm remembering that Dr. 1's place in Shetland where Kai and I stayed had only vegetarian food—not that we were invited guests, or that we knew back then that Xander was Dr. 1. Does Xander even know we were there?

"Have you still been eating meat?" Xander asks me, a note of surprise in his voice. And now I'm realizing that the whole time at his place in Northumberland we didn't have meat either—I'd just assumed it wasn't available, rather than that it was a deliberate choice.

"Um, yes—when it was there."

They exchange a glance. "As survivors we find that eating animals when we can sense their auras and feelings so strongly is quite . . . distasteful," Cepta says.

21

"We grow our own food here, ourselves," Xander says. "So if we raised and then butchered an animal, we'd experience their death."

"Of course, I get that," I say. I hadn't thought of it before, and it makes me have more enthusiasm for bean pie than previously. Though not everyone here is a survivor? To be fair, the food is good and plentiful enough, if a bit bland. I hadn't wanted anything earlier, but now that it is in front of me, I'm starving.

Okay over there? It's Elena, hailing me silently.

I think so, I answer the same way.

I was worried about you, Shay, Elena says, *but you look amazing. Get real.*

Look. She shows me what her eyes see. My skin is positively glowing—maybe I overdid the healing earlier? Through Elena's eyes I can secretly study Cepta next to me too, and she's stunning. She actually looks a little like Mum did when Xander would have known her, going by photos from years ago. Does he have a type? Slender, long dark hair, too young for him by twenty or thirty years.

I'm not sure about her, Elena says.

"Shay?" I turn to Cepta. She's looking at me, waiting, amusement in her aura. Did she say something to me?

"Sorry?"

"It's time." She nods and rings a little bell, and everyone stands. The door opens, and the servers come back in, clear the dishes and then the tables away; the benches are repositioned around the edges of the room.

People stand and chat in small groups, and I take the opportunity to escape to Beatriz and Elena. As I walk toward them, people gently move to the side, making room for me—watching me.

"Hey, how're you?" I say to Beatriz.

"I don't know. Why didn't we sit with you?" *The people we were with were boring,* she adds silently.

Sorry about that. Xander's seating plan, I think.

I tried to talk to one of the people bringing dinner, and they wouldn't answer.

That's weird.

22

People are starting to move to sit around the edges of the room, and I take Beatriz's hand firmly. *I'll sit with you now.* No one objects.

Cepta stays in the center of the room, smiling, while everyone sits down. "Welcome to all, and welcome back, Xander," she says, and her smile widens as her eyes reach his. "And welcome to our new members, Beatriz and Elena. And Xander's daughter, Shay." She gestures toward us. "I won't keep you tonight; I know we're all waiting to hear from Xander." She sits down, and he stands, walks to the center of the room.

There is a sense of anticipation in everyone. Cepta's face is flushed, and she stares at Xander like his very presence is precious to her.

But he doesn't say a word. Instead, he closes his eyes and *reaches* out to each survivor in the room. And he shows us newcomers—Elena, Beatriz, and me—what to do. To focus inward, and then outward: so we are *reaching* in and out at the same time. First we *reach* out only to each other, until we are in sync completely. Then we *reach* out to every other soul in this room: the non-survivors too.

To begin, everyone starts to breathe together: inhale, exhale, slower and slower, until all are synchronized. Then our hearts beat in sync too—the chambers contract and expand as if linked by the same electrical impulse—until finally we are all joined as if each person here in this room is part of me.

The rush of warmth and joy is so complete I almost let go unconditionally. But I can't do that. I can't let anyone know why I'm really here. I throw up walls, keeping part of me separate and alone, and hide that I'm doing it. And joined as I am with every mind and soul, I can tell there are two others who are partly shielded: Xander and Cepta.

We breathe as one, our hearts beat as one, and even with part of me held back, there is still a deep, aching peace, a salve to my bruised soul—one I've never experienced before.

And then it's not just us, the people in this room. We *reach* farther—to the trees, to the buildings with their living roofs, to the creatures of the forest, even birds and insects. To Chamberlain too. And to the fields and gardens, with their chickens that lay our eggs and cows that provide milk, butter, and cheese.

I see now why the people here can't countenance lamb or veal or any other meat. When you know the soul of the calf so completely—and his mother too—you just can't have him for dinner. This is why they are all vegetarians.

There is such a sense of peace and belonging to each other, the earth and all its riches; it almost makes me want to cry.

We are filled with wonder at what is happening, and not just the three of us who are new to this experience—I can tell this is more than has ever happened here before. Having more survivors take part has allowed our joined minds to gather in more of the world that surrounds us.

Later we begin to separate, one by one, and go off to rest, to sleep, but as each person leaves, they still retain the sense of *community*—the name they give this place I understand more completely now. Survivors—Xander, Cepta, Elena, Beatriz, me—stay to the end, holding the links in our minds that make this possible, and we separate last of all.

We stand together, slowly coming back to here, to now, and open our eyes. Elena's face is wet with the tears I resisted.

That was as you predicted, Xander, Cepta says. Her eyes are shining. *We* reached *farther and for longer than ever before.*

Yes. Imagine what this will be like when there are more of us.

Could we link to other Communities? Cepta asks. *Could we* reach *far enough?*

We can try. And then? Our entire planet—joined as one. And then beyond, to the stars. But now everyone must sleep.

As he says the words, I feel the fatigue deep inside. *Reaching* so widely, for so long, has worn us all out.

We file out the door into the night, Xander last behind us. The moon has moved across the sky: we've been in there for hours.

Xander's hand touches my shoulder. *Now you truly understand,* Xander whispers inside of me, and only me. *You're one of us now, and you always will be.*

When I'm back in my room, alone, I want to stay in that same frame of mind. Even now that we've all separated, the aftereffects—both of joy and of a bone-deep tiredness—are so strong that I feel like I've been drugged. I have to force myself to shield, withdraw, and consider what happened tonight.

I'd wanted—*longed*—to be with everyone fully, not holding any part of myself back.

And Beatriz was so happy she was glowing inside and out. It was the first time I'd ever seen her smile in a way that was all of her.

But I wasn't the only one not fully in the joining: Cepta and Xander held back part of themselves also. They must have secrets they don't want to share too. I wonder what they are.

If I know this about Xander, then he will know it about me as well: he will be wondering the same thing.

When we walked alone together earlier, and he told me how much he cared for Mum, we shared the same pain of having lost her. It felt *real*.

Earlier I resolved I had to make him trust me, but I was doing such a good job of fooling him about how I feel that I was fooling myself.

This is *pretend*. I can't trust him, not when so much is at stake.

I must remember who and what he is—or at least work that out more fully. So many people died in the epidemic because of him—including Mum. He might not have meant for any of that to happen; he might have thought he was doing the right thing, like he said earlier, though it's hard to see how. But if Callie is here—and the things he says and doesn't say imply that she is, or that he at least knows where she is—then he stole a child away from her mother and brother. *Nothing* can make that right.

And there's another issue. Xander wanted us to imagine what this will be like when there are more of us: but what about the cost? So few people survive the epidemic that makes us the way we are. It would have to keep spreading for more people to survive it; for those survivors to link and join around the earth, the epidemic would have to precede them.

Many people would have to die for a few more to live like this.

CHAPTER 7

LARA

I'M **WAITING IN THE HOUSE** around the hill—the one that is hidden away on its own. Cepta brought me here yesterday and told me not to go out. That she would come for me.

I was bored and did try to leave at one point, but I couldn't find the door. It wasn't where it usually is, and I was puzzled.

Why am I staying here? I usually sleep in my own room, in a small house near Cepta's that is just outside the ring of Community. It is closer to Community than the places below the hill where the servants and field-workers live, but it's not quite part of it either.

Me being hidden away now *must* have something to do with the visitors—the ones who came in the plane while I slept.

Lara? I'm coming. Cepta's words in my head make me jump. *And Xander is too; he wants to talk to you. We'll be there in a few minutes.*

Xander is here, and he's coming to see me? But that can't be why I've been moved; he visits now and then, but I've never been hidden away like this before.

My heart starts to beat faster, and I feel Cepta's light, calming touch—my heart rate eases.

Then the door reappears, and I consider making a break for it—but no, there's not enough time. They step through the door.

Xander smiles, and he is only ever kind to me, but there is something about him—I don't know what—that always makes me want to run.

"How are you?" he says.

"I'm fine."

He looks at Cepta, and the way she looks back at him says they must be talking silently inside their heads. The slight twitch of Cepta's lips says she's annoyed. Abruptly she leaves.

The door shuts behind her, and my heart thuds again in my chest. This time Cepta doesn't ease it.

"It's all right, Lara. I just want to talk to you." Xander sits down. "Are you still having nightmares?"

When he mentions my dreams, I remember them again in a rush of pain and fear. I feel the blood drain from my face, and nod.

He gestures, and I sit next to him on the low sofa. There is a space between us, and he doesn't move to fill it, but I sense the disappointment in him that I didn't sit closer.

"How are you getting along with Cepta?"

I raise my eyes in surprise. They flick to the door and back.

He half smiles. "It's all right. She's not listening."

I'm startled. She *always* listens: not at doors, nothing as obvious as that—she doesn't need to. And that's when I realize her light touch on my mind—one that is nearly always there, to the point I almost don't notice it anymore unless she says something to me—is gone.

"You mean I can think anything? Say anything?"

"Of course," he says, and I can tell that he means it too. When Cepta asks questions, you know what you are supposed to answer, even if it isn't true.

"Well, we get along okay, I guess."

"But?"

"I . . . I don't know. I don't feel right most of the time."

"In what sense?"

27

"It's like I feel okay, but it isn't really me who feels that way. It's like I'm sleepwalking."

He nods, his eyes thoughtful. "Perhaps it is time to try something different. Did you sense the joining last night?"

I shake my head but say nothing. When they talk about sensing things that I don't sense, I never know what to say.

"May I?" And I know what he's asking, but I'm surprised. Cepta never asks, and I wonder what would happen if I said no. But for some reason, I don't want to.

I nod, and there is another touch on my mind. Different from Cepta's—deeper, darker, richer.

I should hope so, he thinks, and he's amused. He gently sifts and sorts through my memories of the weeks and months since he was last here, but it doesn't take long; not much happens in this place.

You're sad I'm bored? I'm surprised again.

I want to make things better for you. I want you to be happy, he thinks.

Am I unhappy? I puzzle over that. *What does* happy *mean?* And he's even sadder now. His touch withdraws.

"Can we practice together?" he asks aloud.

"All right."

We sit on the floor. Eyes closed. We breathe, focus on our lungs expanding, filling slowly with air. Air is slowly easing out. Again and again. His mind is there somehow, but it's not touching mine anymore, so how do I know it is there?

Acknowledge thoughts; let them pass through. Breathe.

He stays a long while, and I almost feel like I'm in a trance. I'm so relaxed that I forget I'm not supposed to be thinking. *Am I happy now?* I ask him, then start to apologize for losing concentration.

It's all right, he says. *And you're getting there.*

But he's not happy. He's sad.

CHAPTER 8

SHAY

"XANDER AND CEPTA SEND THEIR APOLOGIES; they've had to attend to a few matters. They will be back this afternoon." The woman at the door smiles shyly, and I know her name: Persephone-who-likes-to-be-called-Persey. She's in her early twenties, maybe. After the joining last night with everyone in Community, somehow now I find I *know* them, and not just their names. If I focus on her open face, there are details spilling into my mind—not the boring stuff, like shoe size or grades in school, but the deeper details. She's a botanist and a poet; she sings poems to the plants in the greenhouse to make them grow.

"They suggested I show the three of you around Community some more this morning—if you like?" Persey says, and after a quick internal exchange with Beatriz and Elena, I agree.

Soon we are trooping after Persey with Chamberlain trailing behind. She shows us the small farm and the houses of Community. She shows us the solar panels and waterwheels that provide our power. She points out the entrance to a research center and meeting rooms but says they are mostly hidden underground. She adds that Xander wants to show that to us later himself.

And finally she takes us to the library.

What an amazing space—for only a hundred people? Shelves are crammed with books on everything you could think of—almost all of it nonfiction. There are tables and computers too. Beatriz starts scanning shelves, and Elena tries out the computer facilities. They both want to stay here, but I'm restless and want to wander on my own.

I head outside again; Persey follows. Am I not allowed to be alone? Would she go away if I asked her to? Though maybe this is an opportunity to learn a few things. I hide my initial annoyance and smile.

"How long have you lived here?" I ask her.

"About two years now."

"So since before the epidemic."

"Yes."

The epidemic is a horror that seems remote from this place, as if this corner of Scotland is in a bubble that protects it.

"Who are the other people who served dinner and stuff last night, then left?"

"Some are friends who would like to join us. But most are the immune who fled and needed help, a refuge. It isn't what we are here for, but we couldn't turn them away. Some may later join Community if they wish to and are suitable."

"What do you mean?"

"Well, you know last night, how Community joined together? That."

"So not everyone can do so?"

"There is a degree of skill with mindfulness required; not all can achieve this. Also, they have to be welcomed by Cepta and the group."

"Who is welcome and who isn't?"

"We have to know they aren't sick. That they won't taint the group."

"What kind of sickness—what do you mean?"

"Well, that their minds aren't tainted."

"Do you mean if they are mentally ill?"

"That isn't quite the same thing. Sometimes a mental illness is a bar, sometimes not—it depends on their spirit. Joining may heal them in some cases. But in others, even if they are healthy by the views of most, they can't be allowed to join, as they may damage the connection among us all. Also, not everyone is *able* to join—as in, able to bring themselves to surrender to the group. There is a degree of loss of self in the joining; some people don't like that." Persey is appalled anyone could feel that way; it's all over her aura.

"But what about me? And Beatriz and Elena? Did the group decide to welcome us?"

"Of course. You came with Xander."

"So Cepta and the group as a whole—or Xander—can allow someone to join?"

"Well, I suppose so. But we would always agree with Xander, so it is kind of the same thing."

"The people who served us dinner last night—why didn't they speak?"

"They're not part of Community."

"So they can't speak to us?"

"No."

"And they can't join with us either, even though things like grass, trees, animals, birds, and insects can?"

"Well, no, they can't. It wouldn't be right."

I half frown to myself, decide to leave that one for now and see what else I can find out. "Are you immune?" I ask.

"I don't know," Persey says.

"So Community hasn't been infected?"

"No, we've been safe here."

"Except for Cepta and Xander. Since they're survivors."

"Near the beginning of the epidemic, Cepta caught it on a trip to Edinburgh. She stayed there until she was well and then came back to us."

"And there are other places like this one?"

"Yes, quite a few. Though the closest to us is several days' walk away."

"Do they all have their own Speaker?"

"Yes."

"Are Speakers always survivors?"

"I don't think so. They had Speakers before the epidemic, so they couldn't be."

"What about Xander?"

She's puzzled at my question. "He's always been as he is. He's Xander."

"Does he have any other family?"

"We're all his family."

"But are there any children here that are actually his? Like me; I'm his daughter. Does he have any others like me?"

"There've been rumors." She looks shocked at her words.

"Rumors? It's okay; you can tell me." I *will* her to tell me, soothe her aura to remove any inhibition about doing so that she may have.

"Well, it has been said that some of the younger children born here might be his." Her eyes are wide and dreamy, like having his child would be the best imaginable thing—and she must be, what: forty years younger than him? *Ick.*

"No older children?"

"No."

"Does Cepta have any children?"

"All of the children here are her children."

"Did she, you know, give birth to any of them?"

"No. At least, not that I know of."

Frustrating conversation, but through it all I could sense Persey's thoughts and see the truth in her aura: she's not being obstructionist, she just looks at things differently from me. There's part of me that's appalled—it's as if she's been brainwashed and this is some kind of weird cult, like what Iona said ages ago. There's another part of me that marvels at how happy and well-balanced Persey seems to be; the way all of Community seems to be.

Stop questioning what you can sense and see, Shay: they don't just seem to be—they are. You can't be joined up like that with all of them without knowing it as a certainty.

But what about the others that work for them that are not part of Community—the ones that are not allowed to speak? It's hard to believe. Cepta said there were over two hundred of them versus a hundred in Community: they must live somewhere, but Persey didn't take us anywhere near them on our tour. I'm itching to wander off and see for myself.

I go to read at the library, and eventually Persey says she must leave to attend to the greenhouses. I wait a short time, then go for a walk.

Soon another member of Community is there, smiling. Jason is his name. He walks alongside me.

Am I not allowed to walk around alone? Or maybe I'm just such an object of curiosity that I can't be resisted. Either way, it'll soon be annoying.

I give up and head back to our house, saying goodbye to Jason and then closing the door in his face in case he was thinking of following me inside. Not that any of the doors lock. At least I'm alone now, apart from Chamberlain; he's asleep on my bed but stirs when I go in.

I wonder if Chamberlain would be followed too?

I rub the soft fur under his chin, and he purrs, his eyes opening to slits, then closing again.

"Fancy a walk?" I say, and his eyes open wider. I hold his with mine and *reach*. And it's different from when I've looked through the eyes of spiders or mice or birds. It's almost like doing this with a person, even though he's a cat.

His feelings are ruffled, as if he knows what I just thought.

Most gorgeous, lovely, intelligent, amazing cat—ever. Which makes you a few notches above the average human.

He approves.

I picture where I'd like him to go—wander out the door, out of this ring of Community houses. Beyond and below. And then I show him Callie: the one I seek.

He yawns and gives one of those all-body stretches only cats can, sits and regards me, like he's thinking it over.

Please?

He goes.

I curl up in bed in the warm place where Chamberlain was sleeping a moment ago and keep my light touch on his mind—watch out of his eyes. He jumps out of the kitchen window, and the view lurches, then rights itself, as he walks down the path.

I've never tried this before—to ask something as unlikely as a cat to go where I want—and can't quite believe it seems to be working.

Something moves in the grass, and he stops, intent, then suddenly springs forward—but misses. A butterfly flutters out of reach over his head.

He jumps onto a roof at the edge of Community—stops to wash his face, because grooming is important. Through the trees, far below, his sharp eyes catch movement. People?

Investigate, Chamberlain?

He jumps down, walks through the trees. There are faint paths. He follows along, sniffing the air; his nose tells him there is meat. He walks faster. Vegetarian cat food isn't impressing him very much.

In a clearing are several caravans and lean-tos made of sticks and canvas. There is a central barbecue of sorts, or a fire, at least, with a spit over it. There are too many people here for so little shelter; they must sleep on top of each other to get out of the rain. Not everyone looks that clean or well-fed, and there are voices and clatter. The whole scene is chaotic, almost the opposite of the calm order on higher ground.

"Cat!" A small child sees Chamberlain, grins and points. He starts to toddle over, but Chamberlain has spotted the one who seems to be in charge of the cooking. He runs over and winds around her legs.

He's a good judge of cat people; she leans down and strokes him.

"Oh, it is that great cat that came with *his* daughter. He's probably starving, poor puss. Don't worry, we've snared some nice, fat rabbits—we've enough to share today."

So, even though I've seen very little of them, they know who I am, who my cat is.

Chamberlain's annoyed.

Sorry, didn't mean to say you're mine, or anything like that.

He's soon feasting on scraps of rabbit, and I can tell he thinks even secondhand rabbit is pretty good after weeks of the likes of beans.

Tummy full, he's of a mind to nap in the sun, but I persuade him to have more of a look around. He wanders down the path, finding

cting pats here and there,
dly.
the woods. How do they
e epidemic? It could dec-

rd to imagine that Xander

d and lose the connection
n thoughts. I get up from

CHAPTER 9

LARA

THERE'S A FACE AT THE WINDOW looking in at me. It's a child—from outside Community—with a thin, solemn face and dirt on his clothes. When he sees I've noticed him, he moves as if to run away.

"Don't go, you're not in trouble," I call out, and smile, an idea in my mind. Cepta's touch hasn't returned, but I still can't see the door . . . maybe he can help?

He hesitates, steps back. Poised to run.

"Would you like something to eat?"

He has a hungry look about him, one that sharpened when I asked. "Wait a sec," I say. I turn back, gather a plate full of cookies, cheese, and fruit, then hold it so he can see through the window. "If you open the door for me, it's all yours."

He hesitates, his eye on the food. He disappears from sight, and then the door opens. I hold out the plate; he snatches it and runs.

I stand in the open doorway and breathe in deep. Not that it was stuffy in there—the windows opened a little, just not enough for me to climb out of them—but having been trapped for so long, I felt like it was.

Dare I step out of the house?

I could just leave the door open and know that I can leave if I want to. Cepta will be furious if she comes back and I'm gone.

But the temptation is so strong. I take one step out of the house, then another, and then I walk quickly away from it, as fast as I can now in case anyone is coming to check on me.

I want to know *why* I was stuck in there. There must be a reason: who came when Xander did?

I want to find out.

I skirt the edges of Community, staying just out of sight of its windows and paths. Members rarely venture beyond their boundaries; they don't seem to care where the edges may be, not the way I do.

I avoid the others too, those on the fringes—I go the long way around their places. They're not likely to say anything to Cepta or anyone in Community if they see me, but Cepta can see what they know if she asks them, and why take any more risks than I am already?

As I walk, I concentrate on breathing. If Cepta checks on me, she might think I'm practicing mindfulness and not realize where I am so long as I stay calm. If my emotions flare, she always seems to know, to pay more attention, and then I'm sunk.

There is a particular tree I'm heading for. It's easy to climb, and the leaves are dense, and once I'm perched up there, I can watch the entrances to the library and the underground place next to it. This is where most of the Community members come and go—I don't know what happens down there. I did ask Xander about the library once, hoping for something interesting to read, but he said I wasn't allowed to go there. He brought me some books, but they weren't the sort of thing I wanted to read, and he seemed so disappointed when I didn't read them that I didn't ask again.

I reach the tree and clamber up quickly, just missing being spotted by a few people coming out of the library. I climb a little higher and settle myself on a good branch where I can watch the doors and path below, and unless someone looks up in exactly the right spot, they are unlikely to see me.

Time passes. People come and go, but they are all people I recognize. My legs are stiff, and I adjust them now and then.

I watch and I wait.

CHAPTER 10

SHAY

XANDER TAKES ME ON A TOUR of what he calls their research center. It looks like a small house at ground level, but inside there are stairs going down, and the place is huge underground. There are laboratories, computer rooms, conference rooms. As we go, he points out Community members and their work.

We pass a windowed door, and I glimpse Beatriz inside and step back to look again. She's cross-legged on the floor, with her eyes closed.

Hi, B, I say, but she doesn't answer.

"What is she doing in there?"

"It's a quiet room. One you can't *reach* out of—like the ones in the air force facility hospital."

I shudder. I'd hated it there, the feeling of being cut off from all life. Not even a spider could get in. "But why have one here?"

"Cepta has been trying to find a way to *reach* through it. The authorities know this can be used to block our abilities, so we're trying to find a way around it."

"Yes, but why Beatriz?"

"I assume Cepta enlisted her help. Beatriz has remarkable clarity and concentration."

"I know that, but she is also a child. Shouldn't she be at school or playing games or something?" I shake my head.

I knock on the window, and she opens her eyes. I open the door and, as I do, realize it was locked from the outside.

"Hello, having fun?"

She makes a face. "It's creepy being in here. Cepta said I had to think my way out before I could leave."

I hold out my hand. "Come on; I'm breaking you out."

Cepta appears in the hall, irritation through her aura. "You've interrupted my experiment."

Tough. "Xander, didn't you say each member of Community decides for themselves what they want to study?"

"Yes."

"Is Beatriz a member of Community in her own right?"

He's surprised. Considers. "Yes, of course she is," he says, and Cepta is *not* happy. Xander is amused.

"Well, Beatriz, what would *you* like to study?"

She doesn't even have to think. "Joining more and more—farther—at greater distances. Around the whole world, and then the stars! Like what we talked about last night. And then Elena and me talked about it some more. Could we do that?"

"Wow. Nothing like a little ambition. High five?"

Beatriz jumps to high-five me, then races off to find Elena. Cepta flounces down the hall.

"Xander, seriously, no matter what her brain can do, Beatriz is still a child. She needs boundaries. She needs looking after."

"Beatriz *is* fascinating . . . the youngest survivor we've found. She seems to instinctively do things we have to painstakingly learn. But I do actually agree with you.

"How about this: there is an outlying Community, remote and small, mostly just farming and agriculture. The Speaker there is grandmotherly, but she won't stand for any trouble. We could send Beatriz and Elena there. Beatriz could try her long-distance communication at increasing distances on the way."

"She won't want to leave us."

You mean you don't want to let her go. But see—and he shows me the place he is thinking of sending them. It's like a family farm with all the animals, and she'll love it.

"Now come. I'll show you more of what is being studied here," he says.

Community members are investigating everything from alternative sources of fuel to genetic manipulation. Xander's face is animated as he tells me about their work and that there are other branches of Community around the world. Members everywhere are concentrating on finding the answers to many more questions—and he is the leader of them all.

I study him as much as listen to his words. His eyes have a hunger—the hunger to know all that can be known. And this intense curiosity, the desire to know everything about the world around us, is one I share. I've always been this way, but am I more so now, since I became a survivor? I think so, though exactly why is less obvious. Maybe because I can understand and see connections between things in a way I couldn't before.

But there are limits to what I would do to learn; I'm not sure Xander has any. This is the core of who and what he is.

Finally Xander takes me into a conference room and closes the door.

He gestures at a chair.

"Now it is for you to decide. What work would you like to do here?"

"What are the options?"

"As wide as the multiverse itself."

"What does that even *mean*? What is the multiverse?"

"That's my particular obsession," Xander answers. "That this universe we live in is just one of many—are they connected? How? Can you reach one from another? Do they influence each other—does an action taken here have a reaction in another universe?"

I tilt my head to one side, thinking. "If our actions create reactions in another universe, it stands to reason that actions undertaken there would have reactions here too."

He grins. "Yes, exactly. And if our every decision has a result not just here and now but also for every version of ourselves in multiple universes, each one playing out a slightly different destiny? Fascinating."

"Trying to think that through makes my brain hurt. Besides, how could you ever know?"

"It's a thought experiment: working from a premise to the logical conclusions to see the results, then finding a way to test it."

"I can't see how you could."

"Me neither . . . so far. But I will." He says it with a crazy kind of confidence; he really thinks he can work out *anything*. "So, that is mine. What is your particular obsession?"

I have it without even needing to consider. "Why are we survivors? Why do some live when most die? Why are some immune? What is different about them and us? I want to understand this epidemic, how it acts. And then work out how to stop it."

"You talked about the relationship between us and the origins of the universe before: do you think it all fits some grand evolutionary scheme?"

"Do you mean about the big bang, and trying to work out why matter was favored over antimatter? Then yes." And now I'm remembering Spike, and all of us talking this through, and I'm sad again. When I look back up at Xander, there is sympathy in his aura—he seems to know what I am thinking even though I'm sure I was shielded.

"That can be your focus. See where it takes you. It may help if you study the different stages of evolution, and consider them going backward in time."

"Back to the big bang, is that what you mean?"

"Yes. From cosmic evolution—the development of space, time, matter, and energy from nothing—to stellar: complex stars formed from chaotic first elements. Then chemical elements developed, then planets. Organic life followed, then developed into different kinds of life. The final stages of evolution—variations within a species—are usually where most focus lies in evolutionary studies, but it all goes back to what came at the beginning."

My head is spinning with the vast changes from ancient to *now*. "Looking at it that way, moving through all the different stages—everything was always constantly changing, and still should be."

"Exactly."

"I don't know that these are questions we can answer. I'm not sure it is the same one I've chosen: to find out why some people survive, and some don't. Unless—" I stop, focusing at last on the place I'm sure he was leading me all along.

"Yes?"

"Unless we are evolving, right now. Is that what is happening?"

"Isn't this fascinating? And beyond that, is there another stage of evolution, one we are·soon to experience?"

"What stage would that be?"

"The one where we *choose*. We decide the human race will evolve in a certain way. We do it actively, not passively."

"Even if we could do that, *should* we?"

"Well, if you work out how we are different, and if it follows that people can change so they will survive the epidemic, surely you want this?"

My head is spinning—again. "I guess. But isn't it like playing God? Changing people, deciding who lives and who dies?"

"Isn't that what modern medicine has been doing, or trying to do, for many years? Recent advances in genetics have made it possible to make changes in genes, to fix faults that cause illness. To save lives."

"I need to think about this some more."

"Yes! Think, and study, and think some more, and who knows where it may take you. May you have more success than I've had unraveling the mysteries of the multiverse."

And then I'm remembering Xander's house on Shetland; Kai and I broke in, stayed there. The whole house was designed around a telescope, one that tracked beautiful Albireo, a binary star pair.

"Can you see other universes in the sky?" I ask. "Is that why you're so interested in looking at the stars?"

His eyebrow goes up, a crinkle of amusement, and I realize my slip: we've never talked about his telescope or us having been there. "It's all right; I know you and Kai stayed in my house," he says.

"How?"

"From the laptop. Kai attempted to erase history in a rudimentary way, but it was set to record and track use. I saw everything done on it while you were there."

I'm shocked and think back, trying to remember everything we did on his laptop.

"I was impressed you deduced the door code," he says. "And the computer password too."

"Your favorite star system: the one tracked by the telescope."

"Yes. And it's not just a beautiful star system; it is also the event horizon of a black hole: the point beyond which the gravitational pull is so strong that not even light can escape. Could that be the way to reach other universes?"

"Doesn't everything that goes past the event horizon of a black hole disappear forever?"

"Exactly. But where to?"

"Build a spaceship and find out?"

"Perhaps one day. Did you use the telescope?"

"Yes. Sorry, I didn't know it was your house I was trespassing in then. You were just this shadowy evil figure, Dr. 1: creator of the epidemic that killed so many."

"And now that you know who Dr. 1 is, what is your assessment? Still shadowy and evil?" He grins; he likes sparring with words.

"Shadowy, yes. There is too much I don't know or understand about you. Evil? Refer to my previous statement: I don't know."

He laughs, shakes his head. "I've explained to you what we were doing on Shetland."

"Tell me again."

"Very well." He leans forward. "I can be more complete now that you know I've been a survivor for some time. I found I could cure myself of any ailment. I wanted to know if this could be used to cure diseases like cancer. We—"

44

"We?"

"Multiverse was partnered with the Special Alternatives Regiment of the army. SAR was set up to develop new weapons to be used in the war against terrorism—the sorts of weapons that might not be sanctioned if made public. They were independent and set up with a double-blind: no one knew what SAR did, so no one could get in trouble for it if it came to light. All SAR was interested in was a possible antimatter weapon. I don't think they understood it well enough. They probably thought we'd make some sort of ray gun or something—*zap!* to our enemies. But all we cared about was targeting antimatter to cure cancer."

"And Jenna and Callie—how were they involved?"

"Jenna was a cancer patient. I told you before—she was psychotic from secondary brain cancer. Such a shame, as we finally did it: we cured her of her cancer! She was our success."

"She was a survivor."

"Yes. Sadly, she died in the fires that followed the accident that destroyed the research institute. Why she told you we did that deliberately . . ." He shrugs. "I don't know. Some delusion she had?"

"And what about Callie?"

"Callie wasn't involved."

"But she must have known Jenna, for Jenna to pretend to be her. Where is Callie? Is she alive and well?"

He hesitates. "She's alive," he says.

"But not well?"

"She is physically well."

"Where is she? Tell me, please."

He's conflicted. I can see it in his aura, read his face. And I'm desperate to know, and I realize now it isn't just for Kai anymore, but for myself too. Kai and Callie share a mother, but Callie and I share a father: she's my half sister.

"I've lost so much, and she's my sister too. I need to know. *Please.*"

There is resolution in his aura; he's reached a decision. He nods. "I'll try to—" and he stops, looks to the door.

It opens, and Cepta peeks in, smiles. "Sorry to interrupt. It's time."

45

We get up from our chairs and follow her, and I try not to be obviously upset at her interruption. Xander was about to tell me something about Callie; I'm sure of it. Will he still want to once he's had a chance to think about it? I can only hope.

Elena and Beatriz wait for us at the exit. It's dusk now. I'd lost track of time in that windowless place. We start out the door, but Cepta says there is something she must do and turns back.

CHAPTER 11

LARA

IT'S STARTING TO GET DARK. I'm getting more uncomfortable perched in the tree, and I'm thinking of climbing down, going back before anyone notices I'm missing. Then the door next to the library below me opens again.

There's a girl I don't recognize, much younger than me—she walks with a woman, also one I don't know. New members of Community? I frown. I can't see why I'd be hidden from them if they are; they've never done that before.

And then out comes Xander, and with him is another girl.

I squint in the poor light. She looks a few years or so older than me; there is something about her—I don't know what it is. I will her to turn her head so I can see her more clearly, and when she finally does, I'm startled.

I know her. Don't I? I frown, shake my head. There is nothing I can think of that says why I know her, but there is a deep certainty inside: she's my friend. I want to go to her, but not under Xander's eyes.

They walk together through the trees; soon they'll be out of sight. I want to see where she goes.

My pulse quickens as I climb carefully down the tree, one foot feeling below for the next branch, then the next. I don't dare go too fast, but I'm afraid they'll disappear and I won't know where she's gone.

I'm near the bottom when a hand reaches out and clasps my ankle. It pulls hard, and I fall the rest of the way, bumped and scratched by twigs and branches, and land on my backside.

I'm yanked up to my feet.

It's Cepta.

She's furious. She slaps my face, and I hold a hand to my cheek, shocked. Tears rise in my eyes.

How did you get out of the house?

Her mind slams into mine so hard that it hurts. She sees what I did, and who I saw just now.

She pulls me by the hair.

Walk, she demands, and leads me back to the house. She pushes me through the door with so much force that I fall to the floor.

Stay here. Forget. Sleep.

Forget . . . what? I pull myself up from the floor, shaking, not sure how I got there. I hurt all over; the side of my face is sore.

I walk slowly, carefully, to the bedroom and get into bed.

Darkness falls on my mind and thoughts before my head hits the pillow.

CHAPTER 12

SHAY

IT'S TIME FOR DINNER, and then—my stomach lurches, in a good way—joining. When we get to the great hall, Beatriz smiles at me as she goes to her seat across the room. After less than two days in this place, she's flourishing. Now that I've gotten her away from Cepta, she loves it here again, and there is a part of me that does too. If only all were as it seemed to be: a bunch of lovely, happy people who join with the earth and the trees and each other, and spend lots of time thinking and trying to solve problems.

I'm struck again by how much Mum would love this, and how much I would have thought I'd have hated it if anyone had told me about it ahead of time. I shake my head and shield my thoughts. It's not as simple as that; nothing could be, with Xander in charge of it all.

Cepta hurried us along before, but now she's late. It's almost like she timed her interruption earlier to stop Xander from telling me about Callie. Though she's often late; I know this from sharing thoughts with everyone last night, as we are about to do again. Cepta finally comes through the door, walking slowly across the room. Her cheeks are a little flushed—was she rushing before she came into view? She reaches our table and rings the bell to signal for dinner to be brought.

Joining that night is even *more* than it was the first time—if that is possible. I *reach* deep inside myself, then out to everybody else. Once again we begin by breathing in sync, filling ourselves with oxygen and the breaths of each other until our hearts beat as one. There is only a thin veneer of hesitation inside of me—a layer, a barrier—that stops this from being so complete there could be no turning back.

And then we cast out to all living things around us—nonliving too, like the stones and the earth—and I can feel Beatriz leading us, taking us even farther than last night.

Chamberlain is with us too, but this time I realize that I sense him in a way that the others don't. He's flitting through the trees in the dark on some nighttime quest.

After the joining, everyone is smiling. There is a look exchanged or a small touch to a hand or a shoulder as one by one we separate and walk out into the night—alone now, but not alone at the same time. If I needed to *reach* out again, we would all be there for each other.

I'm not as tired as I was the first time, and my mind is calm, still, focused. This is the right time, exactly the right time, to begin my chosen task in Community—the official one, that is.

I'm a survivor. What is different about me?

Alone in my room, I sit on the floor, cross-legged, eyes closed. I breathe slow and even, as we did earlier, but this time I only *reach* in, not out. As my heart rate slows and my breathing deepens, I travel further inside: not through blood like I usually do, but along the pathways of my nerves. From the periphery at first—fingertips, fingers, the palms of my hands, up my arms, my throat—along each nerve and the fine branches connecting one nerve to many others, finally leading up along my spinal cord and to my brain.

I'd adjusted neurotransmitters between cells yesterday without really thinking about what I was doing, but now I go closer—further—deeper. Swirling beyond the cellular level to molecules, atoms, particles within atoms, and *there*—something is there. I've sensed it before, when healing myself. But what is it?

A dark and silent stillness. It somehow *shields* part of me, but from what? Is it antimatter? Antimatter can still be detected in survivors, but it doesn't make them sick, and they're not contagious either, so something must be stopping it from mixing with ourselves and others.

There is nothing known in our matter-based universe that can do this.

Is it something I made myself when I was ill, or something that was always there? Does everyone have it, but not everyone works out how to use it to save themselves?

How long I'm like this, *reaching* and focusing on places inside, I can't tell. But when I've finally had enough and come back to here and now, my body is stiff and aching. Chamberlain is sitting next to me, eyes wide open and looking fairly annoyed. Have I been ignoring his pleas for attention? When I'm *reaching* like that, I can't see, hear, or feel anything in the usual way.

"Bedtime, I think?" I say, and scratch behind his ears, but he's wide-awake. He looks at me, walks to the door, and looks back again.

Interesting. I *reach* out lightly to join with him. He's agitated about something out there in the night, but I can't work out what—his feline mind and memories don't work enough like mine for me to see what it is.

But he wants to show me something—of that I'm sure.

So much for sleep. Maybe a walk will do my stiff muscles some good. I stretch, go through my bedroom door, then open the one to the outside, wondering as I do if someone from Community will instantly appear to walk with me like they did during the day, but no. I think everyone here sleeps soundly after joining.

Chamberlain leads through the trees, and I sense he's impatient. I follow along more quickly, and he starts to run, then waits while I catch up.

This isn't an ordered path he's following, and it takes me longer than him to find my way through undergrowth and trees. There's a slope up—a small hill. And around the other side of the hill, surrounded by trees that nearly hide it from view, is a house. It's built like the houses of Community, but it's not part of it; it wasn't on the tour we had of the place either.

Curiouser and curiouser. *What have you found, puss?*

Chamberlain leads me to a window. There's a middling moon tonight, just enough light cast through the window to see a sleeping form in a single bed.

A girl. A girl with long dark hair.

Could it be Callie?

She's turned away so I can't see her face, can't be sure.

Earlier I showed Chamberlain what Callie looked like. Has he found her, led me to her?

Wow.

Clever cat, you are. I bend, stroke him, then walk around until I find the door. I hope this will be like all Community houses, even though it is set apart, and be unlocked. The handle turns.

I cross the front room in darkness and find the bedroom door. It's open. I don't want to scare her; I knock lightly against the door, but she doesn't stir.

I step into the room, study her face, and now I know it: I have no doubt. It is her.

"Callie?" I say softly.

Nothing.

I *reach* out lightly to her aura; she's in a deep sleep, so deep it doesn't feel *right* somehow. I adjust her consciousness a little, nudge her toward wakefulness.

She stirs; her head moves.

"Hello?" I say. "Don't be scared."

She sits up, wincing as she does so. And she looks at me with eyes that even in moonlight I can see are the blue of our father's.

"It really is you!" I smile. "So many people have been looking for you."

Her eyes are wide. "Who are you?"

"My name is Shay."

"Why would anybody be looking for me? Who are they?" Her voice is puzzled.

I step closer to her. "Your mother, of course! And your brother—Kai. And me too. I'm your sister—your half sister, that is—though we haven't met properly before."

Her eyes on mine are blank, and even though I'm sure it's her, I'm starting to doubt myself. "It is you, isn't it? Callie?"

She draws breath in sharply, pulls her knees up against her chest. She's shaking her head hard, side to side.

"Is something wrong?" I say, and move toward her. "Callie?" I say her name again, and she starts to scream.

PART 2

MACRO-EVOLUTION

If all life on Earth—plant, animal,
human—evolved from a common
ancestor, life must be able to evolve
from completely different forms.
Why would—why should—
this process have stopped now?
Change is the most constant
force in the universe.

—Xander, *Multiverse Manifesto*

QUARANTINE

CHAPTER 1

FREJA

THE STORMS HAVE GONE, and the morning is beautiful.

Kai still sleeps.

We'd driven for hours in the rain, as fast as we could, to get away from that airfield and SAR. But finally we had to rest, and we found a deserted cabin high on a road with the winding approach visible below us.

And now I've slipped outside to face the dawn.

To face myself.

I know Kai can't read my mind the way survivors can, yet there is something he has, some way of seeing things in me that I don't see myself. I need to think without an audience—telepathic or otherwise.

The sun touches my skin, but still I shiver. I hold my hands out to it and *will* the slight warmth to magnify, to travel through my body. A flush starts deep within me and grows until I'm glowing with its heat, but I still feel cold inside.

So, Freja: what have you done this time?

Looking too closely at myself makes me uneasy, but it must be done now, while I'm alone.

Shay *reached* out to me with her mind—explained why she was leaving—and she asked me to tell Kai. I withdrew from her touch and thought about what she said. I knew she was being honest and open. I knew she truly thought it was right to leave Kai and break his heart—again. To go with Xander and try to find Kai's sister, if she can even be found.

And then I went back to Shay's mind and told her I'd pass on her message.

But I didn't.

I didn't tell Kai. I didn't give him hope that his broken heart might be healed again.

Why?

There are reasons wrapped around excuses that I don't want to face, but I make myself.

Is it because I want him for myself?

No. Maybe that is true also, but I did this for him. There is one thing I know above all others: false hope is worse than none. Shay has hurt him like this before; she's done it again now. Given a chance, she'd do it again in the future. Of this I have no doubt.

Kai makes me feel . . . protective. In a fierce way, like how a cat will face any threat for her kitten. He is a broken thing that needs to be mended. Shay will not do this for him; she hurts him again and again. I feel it deep in my gut.

I will mend him.

I will be what he needs. And right now? He needs a friend, most of all.

"Freja?"

I spin around, feeling weirdly like I've been caught doing something I shouldn't. Kai stands in the doorway behind me, hair mussed, clothes creased. Still gorgeous. And the sadness in his eyes and aura somehow makes him even more so—makes me ache to reach out and hold him.

Instead I smile. "Good morning," I say. "Did you sleep?"

"Surprised myself, but yes."

"You were worn out. I'm surprised you woke up this early."

"I thought I heard something."

"Sorry, I tried to be quiet—" I start to say, but then I stop speaking when he holds up a hand and turns his head to the side. Listening. And that is when I hear it too.

CHAPTER 2

KAI

THIS ROAD WOUND UP AND UP LAST NIGHT—the extended view of it below us was part of the reason we picked here to stop. And just now on the road, perhaps a few minutes away? Jeeps, two of them, and a truck. Army. Heading this way very fast. I curse under my breath. There was no sign of anyone following us last night. We should have taken turns staying awake, keeping watch, but we were both so tired.

"Maybe they have nothing to do with us," Freja says.

But neither of us believes it. We race for the car.

We watch, wait until they disappear down a dip so they won't see us, then accelerate up the road. We're climbing; the road rises ahead of us still.

Freja turns in her seat. "I can see them again now," she says.

If we can see them, they can see us.

The road twists; there is a drop-off to the left side, one that gradually steepens.

"How about we fake an accident, then run and hide?" I say.

"I always wanted to be a stunt double."

We go on until there are some woods that climb to the right. I turn the car to the cliff.

We get out, and I reach back to wedge a map book on the accelerator before releasing the brake. The car lurches forward, catches my arm, and almost sends me flying along with it.

It catapults over the edge, bounces down the steep slope. Crashes.

I stand still, watching it fall, but they are getting closer, and Freja pulls on my arm. We run into the cover of trees off to the right just as there is a loud explosion below us.

We scamper farther up rocks and sparse trees, crouch down to hide just as the jeeps speed around the corner. Smoke and flames are rising from below, and they screech to a stop.

Figures in biohazard suits get out, peer over the edge, shake their heads. Is it working? Do they think we died in that wreck?

But then the truck that was farther behind pulls in. Another suited figure gets out, speaks to the others. Then he turns, looks around, then up at the woods—straight to where we're hiding. He speaks, gestures to the others, and they start up the slope toward us.

Some of them circle to our left, some to our right, and some straight toward the woods.

Run!

We dodge between rocks and trees, trying to stay out of sight, but then there is a shout—we've been seen—so now we just run, full tilt, uphill, clambering over rocks.

"Stop or we'll shoot," a voice calls out.

A bullet rips into the dirt above us.

We stop. Turn and raise our hands, with no certainty that they won't just shoot us now anyway.

For myself I almost don't care. Whatever happens, I feel half-dead inside already. But Freja trembles at my side; she wouldn't be here if it weren't for me.

I wind my right hand around her left one, as they are, over our heads. *Sorry I got you into this mess*, I say silently and hope she'll hear.

Soldiers, breathing hard, reach us a few at a time. The first few train guns on us until the rest arrive and surround us. But they don't seem to plan to shoot us—at least, not yet.

"Move!" one says, and they push us back the way we came, down the slope through the trees.

When we get to the road, there stands Lieutenant Kirkland-Smith.

CHAPTER 3

FREJA

I'M SICK WITH FEAR. These people—I know what they do to survivors. And I know there is something I could do to strike out right now into their auras—to kill, the way Shay and Xander have done before. But I can't bring myself to do that. I just can't.

I can't hurt anyone. I'm sorry, I whisper to Kai inside his head, and his grip on my hand tightens.

"Kai, isn't it?" one of them says, the one who told the others what to do. "But your friend I don't know."

He nods at one of the soldiers, who then grabs my arm, starts to pull me away from Kai.

"Leave her alone!" Despite the guns still trained on us, Kai strikes at the soldier who grabbed me. But two more are there, and one hits Kai. I scream, struggle. He falls to the ground.

One of them holds me while another grabs my left hand. He holds it out to the one calling the shots for inspection.

"No immune tattoo, I see," he says. "What is your name?"

"Freja. Freja Eriksen," I say, so scared I give my real name without stopping to think to give a false one.

"Freja, it is a pleasure to meet you, even under such circumstances. I'm Lieutenant Kirkland-Smith. Now. Would you care to explain why you are inside the zone, alive, but without a tattoo or a suit?"

I stare back at him, silent, mind racing. *They don't know what I am.* But what do I say?

"Well, I'll tell you what I know, and perhaps you can fill in the missing details." He gestures to another soldier, who pulls Kai to his feet and holds him with an arm around his neck. Kai groans, his eyes only half-open. Another soldier holds a gun to Kai's head—and in that moment, I almost think I could do it: I could strike out at them to stop them from hurting Kai any more.

But wait. Are they trying to provoke that reaction? Is this a test?

Instead, I let the fear show on my face, and a tear trickles down my cheek. "Please don't hurt him, please . . ."

"That is up to you, Freja. Now listen. This is what I know. We were at Alexander Cross's house when you and Kai arrived. There were a number of survivors there; there were a few . . . altercations. Some of them got away. We followed, but they took off in a plane in a heavy storm. We tracked you from that airfield and find ourselves at this moment. Is that correct so far?"

I swallow, find my voice. "Yes."

"Why were you there with Kai?"

My eyes move to Kai; his are drooping closed. Does he hear what I say? "Kai was looking for his girlfriend."

"Shay McAllister; a survivor."

"Yes."

"Was she there?"

Should I answer? They *must* know she was there: it's another test.

I nod. "She chose to leave with the others and Xander. Alexander Cross, I mean."

"And why didn't the two of you go with them? Wouldn't it have been easier to get away in the plane?"

"Maybe. Xander used to be Kai's stepfather; they don't get along. We didn't want to go with them."

"I see. And where did they go?"

"They didn't tell us."

He stares back at me in silence, and I resist the urge to say anything else.

"Are you immune?" he asks, finally.

"I must be," I lie. "I haven't caught it."

He's looking back at me, considering what I said. Finally he nods at the soldier with the gun to Kai's head, and my heart almost stops—but then the soldier moves it away from Kai.

"That'll do. For now. But know this: we will take you back to the old zone boundary where we can test you to find out if you are a survivor. So, Freja, is there anything else you want to tell me now?"

My stomach lurches with fear when he mentions being tested: have they got the scan that detects survivors? I struggle to keep it from my face. I shake my head. "No. Let us go. We haven't done anything!"

"Oh? Survivors are a threat to public health and must be reported to the authorities. Did you attempt to report them?" He doesn't wait for an answer. "And the man you call Xander—well, let's just say he has a lot to answer for regarding the start of the epidemic. I ask you again. Do you know where they went?"

"They never said! I told you: he and Kai hate each other. He was hardly going to tell us where they were going."

"You say you haven't done anything. Yet when we followed to ask you these reasonable questions, you ran away. You crashed your car down a cliff to try to evade us. These are not the actions of the innocent."

They take us to the back of the truck and lock us inside.

CHAPTER 4

KAI

FREJA GENTLY TOUCHES the spreading bruise above my eye, and I sense what she is about to do and shake my head. If she heals me, they'll know what she is.

Let me take the pain away; I'll leave the surface abrasion and bruise as they are. They won't be able to see what I've done. A gentle warmth inside me spreads, and the headache that jars with each bump on the road is soon gone. My thoughts start to feel clearer.

Thank you.

Anyway, if they scan me, they'll know what I am soon enough, she adds, and there is dark fear twisting inside her.

I put my arm around her shoulders and draw her close. She snugs her face in against my chest, and even though she's almost as tall as I am, she feels slight, fragile. Her heart beats fast. *I don't think they truly believe you are a survivor, or they wouldn't have brought you along,* I say, leaving unsaid what the alternative may have been. *Maybe mentioning testing you was a bluff to make you react? These guys are*

SAR, not regular army. I'm not sure they've even got access to things like scans.

Then why not just let us go?

I've got no answer for that.

I should have used another name. I'm wanted for murder in London. And if they find any of my It's All Lies *vlog posts about being a survivor and not being contagious, they'll know anyway.*

Didn't those posts get taken down by the police almost as soon as they went up? Look, you did the best you could. Let's hope they don't work it all out.

We bounce along in the back of the truck for what feels like hours. Freja finally falls asleep in my arms, and her lashes, so blond, curl on her cheek. The red dye in her hair is half grown out to blond now, but the crazy look suits her.

She's always seemed strong, fierce even, yet she couldn't strike out at the soldiers—couldn't bring herself to hurt anyone, even when she's so afraid. And I wonder about this contradiction between how she seems outside and what she is like inside.

I'd felt ready to give up, to die by the side of the road. It was only when that soldier grabbed Freja away from me and I didn't know what they were going to do to her that I seemed to come back to myself, to feel what was really happening.

She's here because of me. I can't let them take her. I can't let her die.

CHAPTER 5

FREJA

I'M DREAMING; I KNOW I AM. Kai's arms are around me. We're rocking—on a boat?—and I imagine the sea all around us. But then we lurch when the truck hits a pothole, and I remember where we really are and the fear rushes back.

I don't want to stir, to let him know I'm awake; he might take his arms away. Instead, I keep my eyes closed and *reach* out, around us. Perhaps I can find out something, anything, that will help.

There is a soldier driving the truck we are in; the lieutenant is next to him. There is a spider on the corner of the window, and I watch and listen from her point of view.

They are silent. The lieutenant is reading something, some papers, but there are no eyes to see them from but his, and I wouldn't dare. He's smart, that one: he might sense me the same way that Kai can, and know I'm there.

Ahead of us is a jeep, other soldiers—four of them—inside. With no superior officer listening in, they are talking. I observe them from the eyes of a fly to start with, then I'm startled when one of them swats me from the window with a rolled-up paper. I fall, stunned, to the ground before I remember to detach myself, but it gives me a small rush of anger, enough to dare to *reach* out again.

The one who swatted the fly—I touch his mind as lightly as I can and listen to them talk.

"... much farther to base?"

"Another thirty miles."

"Can't believe Lefty had us follow them out here, this far into the zones. What's the point?" Lefty: that must be what they call the lieutenant when he isn't listening.

"Enough of that," one of them says. "He knows what he knows, and even if he doesn't—do as you're told."

They start discussing something about the jeep engine, and I wonder: can I somehow make them talk about what I want to know? I think of myself, what I look like—and project that to his mind.

"She's a stunner, this girl we picked up today." He whistles low.

The one next to him laughs. "Thinking with your little brain again, Jack? She might be a witch."

Witch: they mean survivor.

"No way. She'd have brain-zapped you for sure when you had the pistol to Pretty Boy's head."

"Just as well, with Clark the one who was covering you. He'd as likely have shot you as her."

"What's Lefty want with them, then?"

"Reckon he thinks they know more than they are saying; he wants to know what it is."

"I bet I could get her to talk: pillow talk," Jack says. Crude images flash through his mind, and repulsed, I pull away.

So: the pistol to Kai's head *was* a test, one I passed. The soldier who held the gun wasn't too happy about being used this way; another soldier was covering him—one I never noticed. He must have been at a distance. And we're going to base, wherever that is, not to the zone boundary to scan me—unless the base is on a zone boundary, I guess?

There is another jeep behind us, with more minds that I try to read. There is talk about Lefty and his decisions again. They're not too happy with him just now either, about their men who died back at Xander's house. The plane that crashed. They're wondering why there have been no reinforcements.

And as I listen, a plan is beginning to form . . .

CHAPTER 6

KAI

THE TRUCK FINALLY SLOWS, THEN STOPS. Freja stirs in my arms. A few minutes later, the door opens, and we're blinking in the bright light. The sun hangs low in the sky—it's late afternoon.

"Get out." A soldier with a gun gestures at us.

Freja stumbles. "Cramp," she says, and rubs at her leg.

We're in what looks like a village—old stone buildings—no people in sight. Has it been cleared by the epidemic?

The lieutenant walks over with more soldiers. "Kai, I think it is time for the two of us to have a chat. Alone."

He gestures at one of the soldiers. "Please take our other guest to the blue room and keep a close eye on her until the doctor is here to assess her. Use near and remote detail."

A doctor? To assess her? Will he bring the scan?

Her eyes are on mine. *Play along for now,* she says. *See what you can find out.* She is led away, and I want to protest, to not let her out of my sight, but she's right. There's nothing else we can do at this moment.

"Come," the lieutenant says. He doesn't look to see if I follow, but given that there are three soldiers with guns behind me, it seems like the right thing to do—for now, like Freja said.

I follow him through the front door and into a grand sort of dining room.

He gestures to a chair. "Have a seat. Excuse me a moment," he says, and walks through a door at the other end of the room, leaving me with the three soldiers.

Minutes later he returns without his biohazard suit, trailed by a civilian with a tray of tea things. He puts it on a table and then leaves.

"I've had some sent to Freja as well." The lieutenant places a pistol on the table to his right and sits down.

He turns to the soldiers. "Leave us," he says, and they back out of the room and shut the door.

As if he's daring me to lunge for the pistol, he turns the other way to pour the tea. I'm just reckless enough to think about it, but the angle and distance are against me, plus I'm guessing the soldiers didn't go far. And I'm also curious: what does he want to talk about?

"Milk? Sugar?" he says.

"Just milk."

He adds milk, pushes a cup toward me.

"How is your head? Shall I get the doctor to check it when she's here?"

"No. I've had worse. From some of yours."

"Ah, that incident in Killin."

"The incident, as you call it, when I was beaten up and chained to a bench, to try to flush out Shay and kill her."

He takes a sip of tea and looks at me over his cup. "Instead, she killed several of my men. She's dangerous."

I say nothing to that. She did what he said, and I remember the extreme shock I felt to see it that first time—what she can do with her mind.

"Kai, let's try to put that behind us for now. I suspect you and I have something in common, and I want to ask you about it."

"Oh, really? What's that?" And this time I take a sip of too-hot tea and stare at him over the rim.

70

He smiles. "A hatred for a man named Alexander Cross."

My hands tighten on the cup. "Hatred is a strong word."

"Sometimes it fits. Let me tell you my point of view on the man. He manipulated and deceived an entire army regiment—my regiment. He falsely obtained government funds and assistance for a project and then twisted it to suit his own ends. As a result of his deception, an epidemic was created and released—killing millions."

"I'm not going to argue with you: he's a complete ass. But he said *you* were also behind the epidemic—that you were in partnership."

"We asked him to create a weapon we could target and contain. He chose to go another way, and you see the result for the country."

"He said he wanted to cure cancer."

He laughs. "Yes, he's such a philanthropist, isn't he? No. He deliberately created and released the epidemic."

I shake my head. "No matter what I think of him, *why* would he do that? It must have been an accident."

"I think not. And I was hoping you might be able to shed some light on his reasons."

"He didn't confide in me."

"No. But you lived with the man for many years; you knew him. Why would he deliberately release an epidemic? I have a suspicion—but not the reason behind it. And it's not that he's an insane, psychotic murderer. He is highly intelligent and always had a reason for anything he said or did. As much as you can say someone is sane who has done such a thing, I believe this to be true. But *why*?"

He pauses, as if he thinks I've got some insight to share with him. And despite the whole situation and fear for Freja's welfare and everything else, I *want to know*.

"Tell me your suspicion. Maybe then I'll understand what you need from me."

He pauses, then nods. "I think he deliberately set out to release the epidemic far and wide, and that he did this to create survivors."

"What?"

"Survivors occur at a very low incidence—at current estimates, perhaps one in fifty thousand who get sick will survive. What I don't understand is how he *knew* some would survive, or why he wants them. He's been collecting them from here and there—the latest that group that escaped from the airfield and went who knows where with him. But why?"

I stare back at him, mind racing. The thing I know—that Alex himself has been a survivor for a long time—is the missing piece of the puzzle. Isn't it?

"You know something," he says.

"Maybe. And I'll tell you if you let us go."

He finishes his tea. "Your bargaining position just now isn't the best. Still." He taps his fingers against the desk a moment. "This is what I'll do. If Freja is proven not to be a survivor by the doctor tomorrow, I'll let both of you go. If she is one, then only you can go."

"No. Both of us go, and go now."

"I can't do that if she is a survivor. That isn't negotiable."

"I don't understand. Why do *you* want survivors? What is this really all about?"

CHAPTER 7

FREJA

I'M LOCKED IN A ROOM—the blue room, Lefty said: furniture, curtains, all blue.

Near and remote detail, he also said, and there is one soldier in the room with me at attention, as well as two outside the door. And one of the ones outside is Jack—he of the crude fantasies.

There's a knock on the door, and a tray is brought in. Tea. Pastries. I'm famished and, despite everything, dig in. I need to keep up my strength.

I keep a light touch on the minds of those around us.

Kai and Lefty are in another room down the hall. There are two soldiers outside that door. One here, two outside—no, now there is one. The other has gone to a kitchen with the one who brought tea. The others left soon after we got here—to fetch a doctor—and my skin crawls when I think of it.

Whatever we're going to do has to be done before they get back.

I curl up on the sofa, pretend to sleep, and *reach* out to lightly touch the mind of the soldier in my room. He's the one they called Clark. He's dull, no imagination, no thoughts but guarding me and fulfilling his orders. I sigh.

Jack, outside the door, is another story. He's full of impatience, dislike for Lefty, this whole situation. He is the one who can be twisted.

I send a picture of myself to him like I did before, and soon his images are repulsive again, but this time I don't let myself pull away. I call him, tempt him: add a siren to his fantasy game.

A very dangerous game to play.

CHAPTER 8

KAI

THE LIEUTENANT STARES BACK AT ME, then finally nods. "You want to know what is the problem with releasing a survivor? All right: I'm in the mood to chat. I'll tell you a little more, and then you'll understand."

He wants to chat? It is more likely that he's trying to talk me around—to get information out of me—but I still want to know what is going on myself. "I'm listening," I say.

"I'm a cautious man. When we reached the arrangement with Alexander Cross at the Shetland Institute, I had someone on his team who reported to me. We learned some very disturbing things. Did you know in their experiments they created one survivor? A girl."

I'm twisted up inside when he says it: a girl—my sister. Callie.

But Shay said it was someone else . . . and here is someone who may know the truth.

"What was her name?"

He raises an eyebrow. "I don't know. Subjects were numbered."

"Did you know her—can you describe her to me?"

He's startled, but answers. "A young girl—twelve years old, I believe. She'd been a runaway."

"What did she look like?"

"Ordinary. Brown hair, brown eyes."

"Brown eyes, are you sure?"

"I think so."

"And her hair—what was it like? Was it really thick dark-brown hair?"

"No, not at all. Light-brown, mousy sort of hair. But why?"

I'm unable to answer, full of shock. It couldn't have been Callie, not with that description. Shay was right; it wasn't Callie's ghost who was with us all that time.

"What's wrong?"

Should I answer? I don't know. Maybe it'll make him trust me. My head drops to my hands, and I sigh. "I thought it was my sister—my half sister. Alex's daughter. She's been missing for over a year now."

"Your *sister*? Would Alex stoop that low and experiment on his own child?"

"I thought he did."

"You must hate him even more than I do."

"Yes. Maybe. And? What was it you were going to tell me?"

He takes a moment to organize his thoughts. Nods.

"They did a series of tests on the child after she survived, and found something startling—shocking, even."

"What?"

"Some of this you probably know. That survivors have certain mental abilities. But there's more: there were actual changes in her DNA."

"I'm not a scientist. What does that mean?"

"They thought maybe they'd understand how she survived if they sequenced her DNA, found genes that were different. The human genome has been completely mapped. There are individual variations to a degree that make us different from each other, but the overall sequence and parameters are known. But it wasn't just a few different sequences or genes; it went well beyond that."

"What are you saying?"

"She wasn't really even human. She was some sort of freak mutation—an abomination. That is why survivors must be eradicated."

"*What?* Are you serious?"

"Deadly serious. They're not like the rest of us. They can't be allowed to pass these changes on and pollute the human gene pool."

"This is insane."

"It's true. And the records of the studies were destroyed; the scientists died in the explosions and fires. No one is left alive who knew of it firsthand, besides me and Alex. Yet he is taking the opposite course: trying to save instead of destroy these monsters."

I stare back at him. He's sitting there calmly calling Shay—Freja too—*monsters.* Though the label fits Alex well enough.

There are still too many things about Alex that I don't understand. "How is it that Alex was working for the government at this air force institute where survivors were hidden? Didn't they know what he'd done at Shetland?"

He frowns. "No. They didn't know he was involved from the beginning."

"They didn't even know about Shetland, did they?"

"No. Not to start with. They do now. But not about Alex's role. He hid his tracks—and identity—very well."

"Yet they weren't trying to eradicate survivors at that institute, like you are. You're not actually working for the government anymore. Are you? You said they know about Shetland now. Are you wanted by the authorities for what happened there?"

There is a flash of anger in his eyes. "Alexander Cross is the criminal, yet we are the ones blamed. But that's enough of your questions; it's my turn. Tell me what you know about your stepfather."

And I don't know if I should say anything, but somehow I *have* to tell him—here, at last, is someone who believes me about Alex and the things he is capable of.

"Alex is a survivor."

"He was immune, according to official records. Of course, according to official records, he's also dead—yet we found him and the missing survivors from the air force institute at his house."

"He was a survivor. He faked being immune somehow."

"Are you saying he caught it in Edinburgh, or—"

"No. He was a survivor for over a dozen years at least, since before he married my mother. Maybe longer—that's just when I first knew him. If, as you say, he was trying to create more survivors—he knew how, because he is one."

Kirkland-Smith's hands are together—he's thinking—then he smiles, satisfied. He calls the guards in.

"Thank you for our talk, Kai. But I'm afraid you know far too much now. You will have to remain our guest. Perhaps there are other things you know that you will remember with time? As will Freja. Unless she is a survivor, in which case her DNA will be analyzed and she will be executed."

Fury is rising inside me, and there is nothing to lose, not now—

But the pistol is already in his hand, as if he knew, and the guards are there dragging me out of the room and down the hall.

They take me to an empty, windowless room and throw me inside. A lock clicks in the door. It's a standard door; maybe I could break it down, but when I peer through the keyhole, there is an armed guard on the other side.

And I'm furious—so angry—at this situation, at myself. I told him the one thing he needed to know, but he's never going to let us go, is he? He lied.

Was any of the rest of it the truth? If so, how much?

I shake my head. He said survivors are monsters. Alex I can believe. But the others? Changes in their DNA: what does that even *mean*?

It just doesn't make any sense. Until they got sick, they were normal, ordinary people.

And what about Callie? My sister. If that wasn't Callie with us as a ghost all along, then who was it, and where is Callie?

Shay said it wasn't her. I should have believed her, but would it have made any difference? Would she still have left with Alex?

At the edges of my awareness, I can feel Freja calling me to talk, but I don't let her in, not yet. I need to hold in the pain.

CHAPTER 9

FREJA

I'M PANICKING: WHY WON'T KAI ANSWER? I can sense him; he's alone in a room down the other side of the building. He seems to be okay but doesn't respond when I call him with my mind. I'm about to give up when he finally lets me in.

Sorry I didn't answer, Freja. I had to do some thinking.

What's happened?

I've been an idiot.

I mean what's happened lately.

Gee, thanks. Okay. The lieutenant wanted to know whatever I could tell him about Alex. And I thought I did all right, getting info out of him—and suggested a trade of what I know to let us go.

And?

I told him what I know, and he's not letting us go.

Kai replays the whole conversation in his memory for me, lets me watch, and shock vibrates through my system. Changes in our DNA? Monsters? Survivors are to be eradicated for the sake of the human gene pool?

Because the human race is so perfect and pure as it is, isn't it? Nice.

And now Kai knows Callie may still be alive. I'm uneasy. Will he guess what I didn't tell him?

Focus his attention elsewhere.

Lefty is a slippery character. He picked up from what I told him that you and Alex don't like each other and played you with that.

Lefty? Perfect name. Yes, thanks for pointing that out.

So the doctor comes tomorrow, and she can somehow tell if I'm a survivor. Then they'll study my DNA and that's it for me. And I'm not like everybody else—I'm dangerous.

I always knew that.

Huh. This guy must be completely crazy. Right?

Now Kai is uneasy. *DNA and tests and science—what does it even mean?* I catch an echo of his thought that he quickly hides: he wants to know what Shay would have made of all of this.

I shove down the hurt to focus on the problem. *Whatever it all means, there is one thing that I do know for sure: somehow, we've got to get out of here. Tonight, before the doctor arrives.*

I think I could break my door down if there weren't an armed guard on the other side of it.

I might have a plan to distract him.

Freja, don't do anything crazy. Tell me what it is.

No can do, still thinking. Why don't you get some sleep? I'll wake you up if anything happens.

I wait until Kai drifts off to sleep, until it is later, quieter. There is just one guard outside Kai's locked door. Potential monsters are obviously considered to be more dangerous, as I've still got two: one inside my room and one outside my door—Jack.

Lefty is a good long way away from us in another house across the road, asleep. Two other soldiers, also asleep, are at the other end of this house. I visit the sleeping soldiers in this house first, lightly touch their minds—making their sleep deepen until almost nothing could wake them. I hesitate, then do the same to Lefty. I think I'm safe from him noticing anything odd from my presence while he's asleep.

And now it's time for Jack.

What do I do? I'm sure he's the only one who'll go against what he's told. I need him to open this door. I need to get out.

I can't do anything too direct. I'm guessing that if he actually thought I *was* a witch, as they see us, he'd remember his orders.

I send images of myself to Jack: first just looking at him. But not here, not anywhere in the house; this time I'm getting into the back of the jeep, beckoning him to follow. I make him think it's all his fantasy, one that can come true, even as the thought makes me sick.

Finally he knocks on the door, then unlocks it. The soldier in my room goes to the door. I stay where I am, lying down on the sofa, pretending to be asleep.

"The lieutenant wants to interview the girl," Jack says. "He told me to bring her."

"At this hour?"

"Ours is not to reason why." He shrugs casually, too casually, and I'm thinking this guy will never buy it.

But he does.

"Lieutenant also said you're to go on a perimeter patrol."

The soldier sighs and trudges outside.

"You, get up," Jack says to me, and I yawn and stretch slowly, like a cat, one just woken, and he's nearly drooling. Pig.

I stand and start to walk for the door, but he pushes it closed.

"I thought the lieutenant wanted me?"

"And I thought you were asleep." He grins and shakes his head. "Let's just say I was hoping you and me would get along."

"Maybe . . ." I say, and smile up at him.

He smiles back, and it's all I can do not to be sick on him.

"Maybe I've got a fantasy—a soldier," I say. "Like you."

"Oh yeah?"

"A big, strong soldier . . . but not here. In the back of an army jeep."

His eyes widen. I'm ready to soothe his aura if my fantasy and his being so much the same raises his suspicions—but there are none there. He must really think he is irresistible.

He unlocks and opens the door, gestures for me to go in front of him. He slides his hand down my back, and I want to slap him, but I don't. The soldier outside Kai's door is too close. He'll hear.

We walk quietly in the dark down the hall, and the whole time I'm checking where everyone is and watching Jack's aura—where he is strong, where he is weak. I hadn't thought properly beyond getting him to unlock the door, and now I'm cold with fear. We go out the back door.

The jeep is there in the dark, and I'm trying to think, to work out what to do now, but my mind is circling too quickly. I'm scared.

He grabs at my waist and I flinch, pull away, and his eyes narrow. Before I can figure out what to do, Jack puts his hands on my shoulders and turns me so we're facing each other. He pushes my shoulders hard and slams me into the jeep. My head snaps back and hits the bar, and I'm almost seeing stars. Then he's opening the door and pushing me roughly through it, and this isn't going how I planned, not at all.

This is the moment.

The one I find there *is* a time and a place where I can hurt somebody. I slam my mind hard into his aura. Not to kill, just to hurt, but aimed to hurt him the most. He pulls away, screams. Falls to the ground outside the jeep in the dirt, curling into the fetal position. Then there are footsteps in the house—the soldier guarding Kai has heard something; he's coming—

Kai! Help me! All my panic is in the thought I send to him.

Kai is awake in an instant, and I can feel him battering against the locked door, kicking it again and again, and at the same time, I *reach* out to the aura of the soldier who is coming here, making it so he can't hear Kai.

He is here now, and his gun is drawn as he sees me, sees Jack keeled over in the dirt, just as Kai's finally broken through his door.

"Did she kick you where the sun don't shine? Probably deserved it." He leans over to help Jack up just as Kai bursts out the door and slams into him from behind, knocking him from his feet. The gun falls from his hands, and I scrabble on the ground and grab it, then stand up.

Kai is grappling with the other soldier still, leaving Jack to me. I point the gun at Jack, but my hands are shaking.

"Bitch. What did you do to me?" Jack says, and gets up, staggering, and starts to come at me.

And there is no thought, no decision—only reflex. I pull the trigger. The sound—so loud.

The gun's kickback slams my elbow painfully into the side of the jeep.

Blood: it's flooding over Jack's chest. There's a surprised look on his thick face as he falls to the ground.

Kai has dealt with the other soldier; he's lying on the ground now too, not moving. Kai stands, looks at me.

"Freja?" he says. I'm shaking, still holding the gun tight. He pries it out of my hand.

There are sounds in the distance—feet—someone is coming. Either the guard sent to the perimeter by Jack, or one or more of the others have woken up.

Kai uses the gun to shoot out the tires of the truck parked next to the jeep, then pushes me into the front of the jeep, and I want to scream at being pushed inside it again even though it is Kai.

He starts it. The tires squeal as we take off up the road even as someone appears in the distance. There are gunshots.

"Get down!" Kai says, and as I do, the back window is shot out.

Glass flies through the air; some hits me in the back, and there is another sharp pain—welcome pain, as it stops me from thinking about what happened. What I've done.

We accelerate and leave them behind.

CHAPTER 10

KAI

I DON'T DARE STOP, not until some serious miles are behind us. They'll be trying to follow, of that there is no doubt.

But Freja: she won't, or can't, talk to me about what happened—either out loud or silently. She killed that soldier; she must have—she shot him, point blank. She's hurt physically—not seriously, at least I don't think so—but that isn't the problem. She's shut down.

We're racing through small villages, towns. All look deserted; cleared by the epidemic? I find one with an auto shop, cars for sale, and park behind it so the jeep is out of sight of the road. I force a door open, find a cabinet with all the keys in it, and pick a car I can get out that has gas in it.

I pull in behind the shop. Freja is still sitting in the front seat of the jeep where I left her, face expressionless, blank. I get out of the car and open the jeep's door, then hold out my hand. She takes it, lets me help her out of the jeep and into the other car.

We race on into the night until the gas is almost gone.

Still she is silent. There are no signs of anyone behind us—at least, not yet.

I find a farm, a barn I can hide the car in.

There's a granny flat behind the farmhouse. I break into it, checking that there are no occupants, alive or dead. Then I draw Freja in to sit down on a sofa next to me.

She's shaking. I hold her hand gently, touch the side of her head. There's bruising there, and some blood on her back, and she winces. That's when I see that her top is ripped. I touch the collar, and she flinches.

"Freja? Are you all right?"

She shakes her head, looks down.

"Do you want to talk about what happened?"

"No. Tomorrow; I'll talk tomorrow," she whispers, at last—breaking her silence.

"Okay. Should we get some sleep now?"

"No. I mean, not yet," she says, her voice quiet and small. She looks up, and her eyes are full of emotions that I can't read. She reaches a hand toward me. I take it; she leans against my shoulder. I put my arms around her, and she moves closer, buries her face in my chest. I stroke her hair, and she stays still in my arms for so long that I think she must have fallen asleep. But then she pulls away a little, touches the side of my face, and kisses me.

Her lips are soft, hesitant, almost childlike, and I kiss her back once, then start to move away, but her hand moves back and catches in my hair, pulling me closer, and her kiss deepens.

And all the fear, the pain, the despair—everything we've been through, and somehow survived—disappear.

PART 3

ORGANIC EVOLUTION

Organic life evolved from an inorganic soup; animate came from inanimate. All the things we've become arose from this miracle of spontaneous generation—yes, I will call it a miracle! And once our science can explain and replicate this, we will be gods ourselves.

—Xander, *Multiverse Manifest*

QUARANTINE

CHAPTER 1

LARA

I'M BURNING, and I scream my name inside again and again:
Callie, Callie, Callie!

Trying to hold on to what I am, even as the flames destroy me.

But this time I'm not asleep, I'm not dreaming, and it goes on and on. And there is a girl here who says her name is Shay and that she is trying to help me, but there is nothing she can do. Then Xander is here too, and Cepta, and between the two of them, they finally break inside. They split me open like an egg, smashed on the pavement.

Calm washes through me, cools the flames and holds them at bay. But the fire is still there. It will always be there.

CHAPTER 2

SHAY

CEPTA PUSHES ME OUT, says I must leave—that I've done enough damage. But I hesitate in the doorway and only go when I see for myself that Callie is finally calm, still. Cepta is at her bedside, holding her hand.

Xander follows me out of the room, closes the door behind us, draws me away.

"What did I do?" I ask him, unable to understand what has happened. She sounded like she was in such pain—her screams were agonizing—but nothing I could say or do would soothe her.

"It's not your fault. You shouldn't have spoken to her without being prepared, but you didn't know."

"Prepared?"

"It was her name you said, wasn't it?"

"Yes. Callie."

"She can't bear to hear her name; it's always the same if she does. We've been calling her Lara instead."

He's in pain too—it's raw on his face, his aura, and despite who he is, I find myself reaching out to him, putting my hand on his arm. He places his hand over mine.

"I'm to blame," he says. "Both for not telling you and for interfering in Cepta's treatment yesterday." He sighs. "I thought Callie needed more freedom, but perhaps I was wrong."

"Her treatment? What are you talking about?"

"She's unwell, and has been for a long time," he says. "I don't imagine Kai has told you about this—I'd be surprised if he did, anyway. About Callie's . . . mental balance. She'd been seeing psychologists from a young age, but Kai could never accept there was anything seriously wrong."

"Why was she seeing psychologists? What was the problem?"

"There has been some debate on that. A form of dissociative identity disorder is the usual diagnosis, though she doesn't fit all the diagnostic criteria. I took Callie to see Cepta—you wouldn't know, but she's foremost in this field of psychology. Callie needed her help."

"Are you saying you kidnapped her to put her in therapy?"

"Nothing as crazy as that sounds." But there are ripples of uncertainty now in his aura, ones he is letting me see. "Not exactly. Look, Sonja—her mother—wouldn't let her get the help she needed. Sonja was into this completely medical approach; she didn't understand the finer points of the balance of the mind the way Cepta does. Callie was just going to be away with Cepta for a few days, but things went, well, wrong. Her episodes got worse instead of better."

"Why did things go wrong? Did you experiment on her in Shetland?"

"What? No, of course not. Cepta says it's her age—hormones, adolescence—that this is exacerbating her condition. Where did you get an idea like that?"

"Jenna. She said they were friends, and that they were there together."

"Jenna was a cancer patient. She was also a patient of Cepta's—she may have met Callie through Cepta. The secondary brain cancer Jenna had made her psychotic. I told you before, that crazy stuff she said about us burning her alive in a fire? That's just not true. You have to believe me. She died when the institute was destroyed—in fire, yes, but it was an accident."

As I listen to Xander, I get more and more uncertain. How can the things Jenna said—things she shared with me, when we were joined together—be so wildly different from Xander's account?

At the time I'd have staked my life on Jenna's truthfulness. All right, she knew she was the carrier and didn't tell me; she hid it from me somehow. She could be deceptive, manipulative too, but at the end—no. She didn't lie to me: I know it.

But if she believed it herself, it would have been true to her.

I don't know what to think.

"Has Callie been here all along?"

"Yes. Under Cepta's care. And she's much happier than she was, more stable. Unless something happens to set her off."

"Something like me."

"You weren't to know. Her own name distresses her so much—if she is addressed by it or even just overhears it, she reacts like she did tonight. Cepta says she's dissociated from herself to such an extent she can't bear anything that draws her back to who she was—even her name."

Xander appears so caring for Callie, and so full of uncertainty too—something I've never seen him show before.

"Oh my God. You're human after all."

"Am I?" Now he's amused.

"Yes. You don't know everything, do you?"

He shakes his head. "I *want* to know everything. But if there is one subject I'm as at sea with now as I was when I was sixteen, it's the workings of the female teenage mind—Callie's in particular."

"I've got some insights into that in a general way, I guess. But I don't understand how you could keep her from her mother and brother."

"For her sake. To try to make her well."

He believes what he is saying, completely. He believes that he's done the right thing.

Has he?

How can I know? I've never met Kai's mother; I have no idea what she was like, what their home life was like, and I'm uneasy. To be fair, Kai wasn't the most level-headed person; his emotions and reactions were pretty messed up sometimes. And he grew up in the same family.

"Look at it this way," Xander says. "If a child was being mistreated by one parent and the courts wouldn't do anything, and the other parent took the child away, would that be the right thing to do?"

"Are you saying she was being mistreated?"

"She wasn't being *treated*. What if a parent wouldn't treat a readily treatable illness that could kill a child—would you accept taking the child away to provide the treatment?"

"Probably. I think so." Though now I'm remembering Mum. She didn't believe in conventional medicine; when I got the flu that later killed her, she didn't call 999 and let the authorities take me away. She took me away herself, and we hid in the night. Would I still be alive if she hadn't?

"In Callie's case, there was a treatment she desperately needed. I took her away to give it to her."

Xander walks me to my house, then goes back to check on Callie. He says to try to sleep, that he'll be back to talk about it some more tomorrow.

The door closes behind him, and I lean against it. What a night. I found Callie—or rather, Chamberlain did—but what I found wasn't what I was expecting at all. And what do I do now?

The plan was always: find Callie, run away from Xander with her, take her to her mother and Kai. But is that even possible? Does she really need to be with Cepta? How could she go home to her old life when the mere sound of her name makes her scream like she's being tortured?

And thinking that makes me hear it again in my memory, the sound she made. It was almost inhuman, like a wounded animal—the purest expression of agony. I'd *reached* out to Xander's mind in a panic to come and help when I couldn't. He must have called Cepta.

And I'm the one who made her feel like that.

I'm so sorry, Callie.

CHAPTER 3

LARA

MY HEAD IS THICK, HEAVY. When I finally open my eyes, I wish I hadn't—they are swollen and scratchy.

Like I've been crying.

Why?

I get up, go to the bathroom, splash water on my face. There's a red mark on my cheek, and I raise one hand, tentatively, to touch it. It's sore, like I've banged my head into the door.

Or been hit.

I frown, but my memory of the day before won't come, and then *calm* washes through me.

"Lara? You're awake. Good. I've brought you some breakfast."

Cepta stands in the doorway, and something makes me want to flinch, to step back, and her eyes widen and her smile falls away.

But then a wave of peace fills me inside, and when she comes close and holds out her hand, I reach forward with mine. She clasps it in her warm one and smiles.

"But first, before breakfast, come with me."

She draws me into the lounge, pulls me to the ground to sit next to her, cross-legged. We breathe. In, out, in, out; still, calm. I feel the floor beneath me, the air as it flows in and out of my lungs, my heart as it beats.

There is a flush of heat inside me, and then the ache in my head and my cheek and my eyes goes away.

There now. Does that feel better? she asks.

Yes. Thank you. But why—

No questions. Come. We open our eyes, and she helps me to my feet.

There's a plate of fruit, rolls, and cheese, and a flash of another plate much like this one flits through my mind—one I held up to the window? And gave to a boy who opened the door?

"What an imagination you have," she says, and I see that it was a daydream—a wish for a friend in the window. But I don't have any friends, do I?

Cepta has me follow her to the fields below Community to help there in the gardens—pulling weeds, thinning plants, cutting lettuce for dinner. All tasks I've done many times before, but this time, something is different.

Cepta stays close by. Watching.

By lunchtime she's bored and has retreated to a shaded bench with a book. She could help; that'd give her something to do.

My back is aching from stooping over, and I adjust, kneel on the ground, when something soft brushes the back of my arm. Startled, I turn.

It's a cat. A beautiful gray cat—and he's huge. I reach out a tentative hand; he sniffs it, then rubs his head against it. I stroke his fur, and there's a deep rumbling purr inside him. He flops by my feet.

I always wanted a cat. I couldn't, because . . . because somebody was allergic to them. I frown. Who? Another thought flits through my head—an orange tabby, one that was mine. But no, that's not right. I never had one. Did I?

This cat reaches out a paw to bat my hand until I stroke him some more, and his purr deepens.

93

Maybe, at last, I've got both a cat—and a friend.

When Cepta's had enough boredom and calls me to go, like he knows it's best, the cat follows behind, at a distance. When she leaves me in the house, I concentrate hard on the door as she shuts it.

I still can't see the door, its outline or handle or anything at all about it. But I watched just exactly where it was, and now I reach out with my hands, eyes closed, and find the door handle. I turn it, open it a little, and look out.

Is he here?

He peeks through some trees, then runs over to the door. He winds around my legs and comes in.

I don't leave the door wide open, just ajar. So I can still see it and this lovely cat can leave if he wants to. I know what it feels like to be kept and confined; I wouldn't do that to him.

But I hope he stays.

CHAPTER 4

SHAY

IT'S EARLY THE NEXT EVENING before Xander appears, and I'm sick with impatience. He barely opens the door before the words I've been waiting to say spill out.

"She's my sister. I want to see her."

"I understand that, really I do. But I'm concerned that there will be a repeat of last night."

"There won't be. I won't use her name or say anything that will remind her who she is. I promise." And I mean it as I say it—for now. But the more I think about it, the more I wonder how it can be the right way to treat anybody—denying that who they really are ever existed?

"Cepta still thinks we should give it some time, until the memory of the incident has faded. Otherwise seeing you may trigger it again."

"But—"

"I know you are impatient to see her. But we must consider what is best for Callie."

And I remember Beatriz locked in the quiet room for Cepta's experiment, and I find it hard to trust Cepta—to believe that she'd put Callie before her own interests.

And what is she interested in more than anything else? Xander.

"Yes, I understand Callie must come first, and I agree. But—"

"Patience." He grins. "I have none, so why should you? But that is as it will be for now. In the meantime—there are things to do, to study. To think about. Come."

I follow him to the library, and he leaves me at the door. Elena and Beatriz are inside already, and he asks me privately not to tell them about Callie for now. Then he goes.

"Where've you been? What's wrong, Shay?" Beatriz asks me instantly.

"Nothing."

"You're lying."

"Nothing I'm going to tell you about, then. Come on: distract me. Tell me what you're doing."

Beatriz smiles. "We're going to leave soon to go a few miles away and see if we can still reach joining tonight. And if that works, then go a bit farther, then a bit farther." She's excited.

"Yes. Fascinating, isn't it?" Elena says—she is too. "I wonder what it will be like if it works. Will everything in between you and us link together as well?"

Nobody knows, and despite everything else, I'm curious and excited to try it too.

They leave soon after, along with some others from Community who know the way to the farm they will ultimately travel to, and who will walk with them. I'm sad to see them go—especially Beatriz. But I try to hide it from her.

I wander through the library shelves, wanting something—anything—to distract me. Something random . . . molecular genetics? And now I'm remembering how I fiddled genes that code for the curly hair protein in my hair to make it straight.

And there I was saying to Xander that I wasn't sure if we should change ourselves, even assuming that we could—and yet I've already done it. Is this change to my hair a permanent one, or as it grows will it revert? If it is permanent, does that mean that if I had any children, they'd inherit the straight hair gene from me, not curly? If that is so—well, I've already evolved to suit myself.

Intrigued, I hunt through one tome, another. I've always found genetics fascinating, and it's so much more complicated than they taught us in biology at school. Most things aren't simply coded for by one gene. It's not just one gene that makes somebody tall, for example; there are a number of genes that interact, and they're all influenced by what happens to the person in their environment as they grow, like what sort of nutrition they have. And most—if not all—complex traits are like this.

And despite not wanting to think seriously about anything right now, I get drawn back to my questions. Why are some people immune? Everyone else who is exposed gets sick, and most die, but why do a very few of them survive the illness? Are the answers to both questions in their genes?

Maybe there is something programmed in their genes that makes survivors survive. Maybe if we looked at our DNA and compared it to everyone else, we could find what it is.

I'm so engrossed that I ignore sounds of movement around me, people coming and going, until finally there is a throat-clearing sound. I look up; it's Persey, my guide from the other day.

She smiles. "I didn't want to interrupt. You looked so intent."

"That's okay. What is it?"

"It's dinnertime."

That's when I notice everyone else has left.

We walk there together. "Are we late?" I ask.

"Almost. But we aren't likely to be last."

"That'll be Cepta."

Her eyes widen. "Yes," she whispers, as if it is scandalous to notice.

Thinking of Cepta makes me nervous: I haven't seen her since last night when Xander and I left her with Callie. Has she stayed with her all day? She wasn't happy with me then. But edging out the nerves is excitement: wanting to join again tonight and see what happens.

97

When we get to the door, it is easy to see that there are fewer of us here tonight, by a quarter or so: did that many leave with Beatriz and Elena? And there are a few extra empty chairs at the head table too. When we walk in, Xander motions for Persey to come with me and join us there. She's thrilled; at Xander's urging, she sits next to him, and I sit next to Persey.

Cepta isn't here yet; she's late again.

She appears at the door last of all and walks in that unhurried way she has, even though everyone is waiting for her.

She pauses at our table, at the new seating arrangement.

"Sit here, next to me," Xander says; there is an empty seat on his other side. And her hint of annoyance turns to a smile of pleasure.

"Where are those who are not here tonight?" she says.

"Elena and Beatriz have walked several miles toward the farm," Xander answers. "To experiment with maximum joining distance."

She raises an eyebrow. "And the others?"

There is the sense of a swift, silent conversation between them now—and an icy glance from Cepta to me. Was this decision made without her input? I try to stifle my smug grin, too late; I need her on my side—to help Callie—and I promise to make myself suck up to her later.

Xander is amused, and I have a flash of insight: did he deliberately exclude Cepta not only from the decision but also from the knowledge of it? It's like he enjoys keeping her off balance, to see how she'll react.

But then he takes one of her hands in his, and the ice melts. She smiles and rings the little bell. Dinner begins.

Later, Xander, Cepta, and I, as the survivors, join together first, as always; but this time, instead of linking with those in the room next, we call out beyond for Beatriz and Elena. There is nothing at first, and our thoughts are tinged with disappointment. Isn't it going to work?

But then a familiar touch finds me: it's Beatriz. She is very faint to begin with, but then stronger as Elena joins her; as we consolidate the link here with Xander and Cepta, it is strengthened further.

Next, we gather the others. Breathing in, out; in, out; in time, hearts begin to beat in synchrony. All the members of Community—both those here and those with Elena and Beatriz—join together.

And tonight when we stretch out to the trees, insects, animals, birds, we go farther and farther. There is the rush of a river between us and Beatriz's location—a flash sense of amoebas, water insects, and fish. Animals of the forest that were beyond our reach before join us, stopping still in their tracks, wondering who and what we are.

And it is so far beyond anything experienced by any of us before, it is as if our emotions and joy are swelling with the earth and its riches.

It's so amazing I almost forget my barriers—and I think I would have, completely, but for a small intrusion, a foreign touch. It's Cepta. She wants in; she wants to know *me*—all of me. But she's shocked I caught her.

No, Cepta; it's not as easy as that.

She sends a private message to me. *I am Speaker. It is my duty to know everyone in this Community, completely*, she says, but she's defensive as she says it. I'm not like everyone else here, she knows.

Perhaps we should check that with Xander?

She withdraws.

I sigh to myself. I'm *so* not doing well at winning her over.

It feels lonely back in the house I was sharing with Beatriz and Elena. I wander from room to room, and then I pause in Beatriz's doorway. Eventually I go in and straighten her pillow.

Getting her away from here felt like the right thing to do, but I wasn't prepared for how much I'd miss her and Elena. Now I'm the only one here who isn't completely integrated into this place.

Even with Elena and Beatriz, I had to watch what I said—I couldn't risk letting them know my plans. It's been so long since I've talked with anyone with whom I could completely let my guard down, say what I think—feel what I feel without having to hide it—and I *yearn*:

For my mum, always; part of me still can't accept that she's gone. For Kai.

But maybe even more, just now, for Iona—my best friend. We could talk complete nonsense or what was most important to us at the same time. I keep wondering what she would make of this place. Is she even still alive? I don't dare try to find out, in case communications are being tracked and she somehow gets drawn into this.

Even Chamberlain appears to have deserted me.

Now that I think about it, I didn't sense him when we were joining earlier like I have the other times. I'm worried: I hope they didn't run out of rabbit in the woods and think a big cat would make a good barbecue.

I close my eyes and *reach* out: *Chamberlain?*

I find him and feel a rush of relief. He's asleep, and now he's a bit annoyed I've woken him. He opens his eyes, lifts his head. He's on the side of a bed—perhaps he's found someone who doesn't toss and turn all night and disturb him, like I do.

A hand strokes him, and he turns his head to have his chin rubbed.

Just before he closes his eyes again, I get a glimpse: dark hair. Blue eyes.

It's Callie.

CHAPTER 5

LARA

I'M HALF-ASLEEP, one arm around my cat.

My cat: something inside chimes to think that.

But suddenly he lifts his head. He sits up, stretches, and jumps to the floor.

He walks out my bedroom door.

"Please don't leave," I say, and follow him. But he's just gone to the front room and is sitting on the floor by the partly open door.

I wonder if he's hungry?

There's some cheese left on a plate from earlier, and I break it into pieces and hold a bit out on my finger for him to consider. He sniffs and takes it delicately with his rough, wet tongue.

Some more? I hold out another bit, and another.

"I must give you a name. What would you like to be called?" I ask him, but then he walks to the door, puts a paw in the gap to open it a little more, and my heart sinks. Is he leaving?

I get up and go to the door to say goodbye if he is, but through the door, I see something else, something unexpected.

Standing there is a girl, older than me. She looks familiar, but I don't know why, and there's an echo of unease. She's in the dress of Community—gold at her throat—yet I don't recognize her. They are forbidden to talk to me, but I know them all by sight. Who is she, and why is she here?

She smiles, bends down, and pets my cat.

"His name is Chamberlain," she says, and I'm shocked: she spoke to *me*? I should go in, close the door—but I don't want to lose Chamberlain.

Somehow I find my voice. "Is he your cat?" I say, and I'm sad. She'll take him away.

"No," she says. "He's his own cat. He comes and goes as he pleases. He must like you, to come here."

And I smile at Chamberlain, and at her. She smiles back.

"I'm Shay," she says.

"I'm Lara."

"Pleased to meet you." She holds out her hand, and I hesitate, then hold out mine. She shakes it, and her hand is warm and firm. She hesitates to let go but then does.

"I was worried about Chamberlain, so I came looking for him. Is it all right if I come in for a little while?"

I look nervously at the door. What if Cepta comes back? Would she be angry?

Almost like she hears my thoughts—even though there is no sense of a touch from her mind in mine, like I can feel with Cepta—she shakes her head. "It'll be all right. I promise."

And somehow I believe her. "Okay. Come in."

I switch on the small lamp, and she comes in, and this feels . . . odd. I've never had a guest of my own before, and today I've had two: Chamberlain and Shay. We sit on the sofa together, Chamberlain at our feet. He looks back and forth between us, as if sizing things up, then jumps up and sits half on Shay and half on me.

"Well, thanks a lot, Chamberlain," she says, "giving Lara the end that purrs."

I laugh and scratch by his ears, and he rewards me with a purr like she said, but he doesn't look sleepy anymore. He gets up a minute later and starts prowling around the room, looking in shadows and behind chairs.

"He might want to play," Shay says.

"With what?"

"Is there anything he can chase, like some yarn or something?"

"I think there's some string in the kitchen."

"Perfect."

I go in and find it, cut a length off with a knife. I dangle it in front of Chamberlain's face, and he looks at it but doesn't move.

"Let me try?" Shay says. I give her the string, and she dangles it by his feet, then walks around the side of a chair so the string disappears. He crouches down, intent, then suddenly springs after it. She runs around the chair and he chases the string, and I smile.

"Your turn," she says, and gives me the string. And I do the same thing, around the back of the sofa, and it works! I run around the room, dragging it over chairs and tables, and he chases me all the way. He skids on a table and falls off it and looks so startled that we can't help but laugh.

"What's going on here?" I spin around, and Cepta and Xander are both standing in the doorway.

CHAPTER 6

SHAY

I STAND BETWEEN LARA-WHO-IS-CALLIE and the two adults. She's scared for a split second, then calm washes through her—it's Cepta who does this to her, and I'm furious that she forces emotions she wants Callie to feel inside of her. I try to hide it.

"We were playing," I say. "With the cat."

"Yes," Lara says. "With Chamberlain," she adds, like she is proud to know his name.

"Go to your room, Lara, and stay there," Cepta says, but she doesn't just say it, she forces Lara to move her feet, one step after another, until she is in her room and has shut the door.

"You were told not to come here," Cepta says to me.

"I was looking for Chamberlain."

"And just happened to find him here."

"Yes."

"I find that hard to believe."

I say nothing, arms crossed.

Xander holds up a hand. "Peace. I don't care how Shay got here, or whether it was before or after the cat. All I saw was my younger daughter looking happier than she has in months with that stupid cat and her disobedient sister, and however it happened, it's obviously done her good."

Cepta is shocked—deeply. It's all through her aura.

Chamberlain also looks affronted.

"I'm sure this *stupid cat* is smarter than most therapists," I say. I can feel Cepta's fury now. "He probably hasn't played like that since he was a kitten, but somehow he knew how to make Ca—Lara, sorry—smile, and he did it."

"And so did you," Xander says. He approves. "There is another bedroom here, is there not?" he says to Cepta.

"Yes, but—" Cepta says.

"Have it made up for Shay. They can stay here together."

More silent arguments.

He shakes his head. "Make it so," he says coldly, out loud, a moment later.

Take that, Cepta. I didn't even have to suck up to you or anything. I say that silently, to myself, but Cepta's eyes narrow. Maybe I didn't screen that quite as well as I should have.

"Sofa is fine for tonight," I say.

Cepta regains her composure. "We will talk tomorrow. We have to establish parameters that you must stay within. She may have seemed better tonight, but you could easily provoke a relapse like you did before if you aren't careful."

Xander agrees with Cepta on that, so I nod and say I'll meet with Cepta to discuss it tomorrow.

Finally they go.

"Lara?" I call out at her door.

"Yes?"

"Do you want to sleep now, or come out and talk to me or even Chamberlain for a while?"

There is a silent pause. "I can't come out of my room," she says at last. "Cepta said so."

105

I roll my eyes. "Can I come in?"

"Yes!" she says, with eagerness all through her voice.

I open the door.

She's in bed. Her eyes are shining. "Are you and Chamberlain really going to come and stay with me here?"

"You heard that, did you? Yes, we are." On cue he jumps onto the bed and curls up next to her. "Didn't anyone stay with you here before?"

"No. I mean, Cepta visits me all the time, especially lately. And before that I had a small house beside hers."

"So you've been living alone?"

"Yes," she says, and starts to stroke Chamberlain, then pauses, looks at me, eyes round. "Won't Cepta make you leave—"

"No. Xander said I can stay."

"But he's not always here." She's troubled.

"But I will be. And Chamberlain too. We're not going anywhere."

"Really?"

"Really." On impulse I reach for her and give her a hug, like I would if she were Beatriz—a girl much younger and one I know a little better, maybe, but it feels like the right thing to do. She's stiff at first, like she doesn't understand the concept, then droops against me, and when I start to pull away, she holds on a moment before she lets me go.

"Maybe it is time to go to sleep now," I say. "It's late."

She obediently lies down, closes her eyes.

Stay with her, Chamberlain? I say to him, but I needn't have bothered. He likes it there.

I start to walk out of the room.

"Can you leave the door open?" she says. "I hate closed doors."

"Of course."

So I leave the door partly open and angle the lamp across the room so it doesn't cast into her room too much. I sit on the sofa, certain sleep will be a long way away for me tonight.

I had to hide it before, as much as I could—first from Xander and Cepta, then from Callie herself—but I'm absolutely *furious*.

106

I'm glad I followed Chamberlain to Callie tonight, ignoring their instructions to keep away. I'm glad that Xander could see things as they were, at least in that moment: that my being here with Callie was the right thing.

I really do think that Xander cares for her, but what was he thinking—leaving Cepta in charge of her? And I don't care what kind of nightmares Callie was having, or whatever other issues she has. It can't be better for her to be half zombie, not allowed to feel her own feelings or make any decisions at all. She's like a much younger girl than she should be—she must be thirteen by now, but she acts and talks as if she were younger than Beatriz.

And she was made to stay here, in this house, by herself? I can't believe it. I'm stunned.

I don't care if she was being monitored Cepta's way, from a distance. It's still wrong.

Poor Callie. When I got here, it was all through her aura: she's been so very lonely. A girl without a family who cares to look after her, without any friends her own age. A girl who didn't understand *hugs*.

I promise myself: things are going to change, more than they think.

But I have to take things slowly and carefully. Despite my instincts, I don't know for sure what she's been through or what is wrong. And if I upset Cepta and Xander's world order too much, they may take her away.

And I can't let that happen. She's my *sister*—half sister, that is.

I've almost been forgetting tonight that she's Kai's half sister too; they had different fathers and the same mother.

Callie may be what links Kai and me together and what could bring him back to me, but at this moment that isn't the most important thing. She's my sister: I *have* to help her.

And I've been lonely too.

CHAPTER 7

LARA

WHEN I WAKE UP THE NEXT MORNING, there is a sense of excitement, of difference. Half-asleep, I lie there and wonder what it could be.

For one thing—Cepta's touch on my mind, the one I wake to every morning—is gone. That is so startling I open my eyes wide when I realize it.

Then something moves beside me: it's Chamberlain. Has he stayed with me all night?

And then I can hear some movement outside my door. And it's not shut; it's part open, just like I asked for it to be.

I smile and get out of bed. But when I go through the door, it isn't Shay who is there. It's Xander.

"Good morning, Lara."

"Hi." I come out and try to look around without making an obvious thing of it. She's not here; she said she'd be here.

"Shay will be back soon, if that is who you are looking for; she had something she had to do. And I thought we could have a talk."

"Oh. Okay." And I'm nervous that Shay won't come back. But then I realize she'll have to: her cat is still here. I relax a bit and sit next to Xander when he gestures.

"What do you want to talk about?" I say.

"Do you want Shay to stay with you?"

I'm suspicious of this question; Cepta had a way of asking me if I'd like something before telling me I couldn't have it.

I shrug. "I guess so."

"Why?"

I frown, confused. "I don't know. I like her. She can stay, can't she? And Chamberlain too?"

"Yes, for as long as you want."

"But you're not always here."

"No. There are other Communities I have to visit sometimes, things I have to do."

"And when you're not here, Cepta says what is what."

"I see. And you think she'll change things?"

I stay silent. I know she will.

"I'll fix it. Don't worry."

"Okay."

We have breakfast together, and then he says he has to go.

As he walks out the door and away from the house, little by little, Cepta's touch moves back into my mind.

CHAPTER 8

SHAY

IT'S A GRAY. CLOUDY DAY; not raining yet, but the heavy feeling of the sky says it will. Cepta's house is lit with slender candles that cast flickering shadows on the walls and draw my eyes.

"I've always preferred softer light, but I can turn on the lamps, if you like?"

"I don't mind," I say, but I'm not being entirely truthful. Since nearly burning to death at the air force institute, I'm less than comfortable with open flames of any sort.

"Come. Sit," she says, drawing me to a chair by her desk. "We need to talk about Callie. She is still my patient, and she is still under my treatment. You need to be mindful of that and take great care with her. She's fragile." Cepta's aura is calm and exudes compassion, concern.

"If you could explain what is wrong, what she is being treated for? Then maybe I could help."

"She is your sister, and I appreciate you care. But perhaps this is beyond your expertise."

"Perhaps you could try to explain anyway."

There is a long pause, a raised eyebrow. A sigh. "Are you familiar with dissociative identity disorder?"

"I've heard of it."

"There are different types. Callie had a mild form for years, but her identity diffusion intensified with adolescence. This isn't uncommon. In simple terms, she dissociates into different identity states—Lara is one of them, and the one we promote for her welfare. Callie is, in essence, her true self, and that is what she is most afraid of. Occasionally other personalities manifest."

"But why is she afraid of herself? I don't understand."

"Until she can face this and tell us, we don't know."

"But then shouldn't we be encouraging her to be who she really is, to face whatever scares her so she can deal with it?"

"It's not that simple. The terror blinds her to thought or reflection. She needs time."

"If she needs such care taken with her, then why was she living alone?"

"She is never truly alone, day or night. She is monitored at all times. For example, Xander was with her when she woke up this morning, as you know. He's left now to move on to other tasks he must attend to, but I'm in touch with her, even now as we speak. This is important, Shay. And essential to her safety and continued good health. Xander agrees with me on this."

"Surely someone being with her physically has to be better for her."

"If that someone is you?" Cepta smiles. "Even you need to sleep. Without a mind touch to keep tabs on her, you'd have to watch her all night—to wake her from the nightmares she regularly has. The longer she stays in the nightmare, the more trouble she has coming back from it."

"Anything else I need to know?"

"You already know to avoid her real name: Callie; also avoid any mentions of the past, before she came here. Other things? She's afraid of confined places. Open flames. Also, intense emotions can trigger psychotic episodes like you saw the other night and must be avoided."

"Is that why you damp down her feelings inside?"

She raises an eyebrow, a tinge of surprise in her aura.

"I could feel your presence in her mind, and what you did."

"It is essential for her to avoid panic attacks to accept treatment. Do not disrupt this bond between the two of us, or the consequences could be severe."

Her warning is clear.

The wind is picking up as I walk back through Community, and I feel as angry and restless as the storm that is nearly upon us.

Being *monitored* isn't all that Callie needs. Lara, that is—I have to start thinking of her with that name, or I'll mess up for sure. What about Lara needing someone to talk to, someone who doesn't tell her what to feel and when to feel it? What about being tucked in at night?

And something else about all of this is troubling me.

Cepta talking about different personalities draws me back to another girl with the same problem: Jenna, who thought she was Callie. Why would these two girls have such similar-sounding conditions?

I almost turn around, go back to Cepta to ask her about Jenna: Xander said she was her patient too. But that would mean, well, talking to Cepta again. And I've had enough for one day.

The first heavy drops of rain start to fall just as I get back to the house, but I need to push myself—to do something physical, anything.

Lara is on the sofa, Chamberlain asleep next to her. Her hands are folded on her lap, and she's looking at the floor when I walk in.

"Hi, Lara."

She glances up, then back to the floor.

"Hi."

"Is everything okay?"

"Fine."

"Do you want to do something?"

"I don't know. Like what?"

"I don't know. Go for a walk, maybe?"

She glances at the window. "But it's starting to rain."

"I know! And the wind is howling too, but it's not very cold. I'm going. Do you want to come?"

When I say *I'm going*, her eyes are back on mine, fear inside them. "Yes. I'll come," she says, but *don't leave me* is all over her aura. Is that why she was being standoffish when I came back? She wasn't sure that I would.

We wrap up and head out. The wind whips our hair around; cold drops start to fall harder.

"Where should we go?" I ask her.

"I don't know."

"Is there a place you like to walk that you could show me?"

"To the edge!"

"The edge of what?"

"Of the world. Come on."

"Race you?" I say, and she hesitates, but then all at once takes off. I chase her, running in the rain, laughing, jumping in puddles, and part of me marvels at how much like a little kid she is, and another part of me is surprised how much fun I'm having too. This is something I missed out on by being an only child, maybe. And thinking of that and about growing up alone with my mum makes me ache for her, a pain that is never far away.

Lara stops by a tree, leans against it, and I catch up with her, stand next to her.

"What's wrong?" she says.

"I was just thinking about my mum. She died in the epidemic."

"Oh. I'm sorry to hear that."

"Where's your mum?" The words are out before I can think whether I should be asking this: it's probably in Cepta's no-go areas.

But she doesn't look upset, just puzzled; then she shrugs. "I don't know. She was never around, so I don't much care."

And she runs off again.

Now I'm puzzled too.

That doesn't sound the way Kai refers to their mum. Is this part of another personality?

She stops at the top of a hill, arms stretched out dramatically. A path zigzags down below us and leads to a narrow track road.

Is there movement below us? I squint and can just make out a group of people in the distance, walking this way—quite a number of them—and I'm filled with misgivings. Who are they? I connect quickly with Xander and Cepta to tell them what I saw.

"Here it is," Lara says.

"What?"

"The edge of the world."

I frown, puzzled, then touch Lara's mind lightly: what does she see?

And through her eyes, everything past the point where she stands is blank, like somebody erased it all. Why?

Can I convince her what she sees isn't real, get her to step forward?

But my eyes are drawn again to the people approaching us below: we should get away from here.

Another time.

CHAPTER 9

LARA

I'M WRAPPED IN A BLANKET, towel around my wet hair, hands clasping a mug of hot sweet tea, and a very heavy cat across my knees.

The door opens.

"Hi, Lara." It's Cepta. My eyes flick to the back of the house—Shay is having her turn in the shower.

"Hi," I say.

She comes in, sweeps toward me, and smiles, and I'm happy to see her smile, to feel its warmth—a feeling that slides through the rest of me.

"I've missed you today," she says. "What have you been up to?"

"We went for a walk. In the rain!"

"Indeed! Hope you don't catch cold. Is Shay still in the shower?"

There is the sound of a door opening and closing behind us. "She was."

"She'll be late soon; no matter. They'll wait."

Shay comes out fast, so fast that she must have known Cepta was here, and so she rushed to join us. Her hair is wet, tunic and leggings pulled on and not quite straight.

Then there is something happening—I don't know what it is—between them. I glance at Shay.

"Why not out loud? I'm sorry, Cepta. If Lara can't come to joining tonight, then neither will I."

There is real shock on Cepta's face. "It is part of your duty as a member of this Community to be there. Not a thing you can take up and put down again as you like."

"I can join from here, can't I?" Shay says. "If Beatriz can from miles away, I think I can when I'm only a few hundred feet from the hall."

"Well, apart from that. We also have to discuss the approach—" Cepta's words break off, replaced by silent ones. The approach of what?

"Tough," Shay says. "I'm sure you'll cope without me. We have an evening planned, haven't we, Lara?"

"Yes. We're telling stories," I say. "I've been making one up in my head about Chamberlain."

"I think Xander might have something to say about this," Cepta says. Cepta and Shay both defocus again, and I know what they're doing—it's like a conference call. With Xander. Emotions flit across Cepta's face. First anger. Then sunshine.

"Enjoy your evening, girls." She sweeps out of the house.

"What made her so happy all of a sudden?"

"Let's just say she's got a date for tonight," Shay says. "And I'm trying *very* hard not to think about it."

CHAPTER 10

SHAY

DESPITE WHAT I SAID, I'm unsettled by not going for dinner with the rest of Community. There is a sense of being a part of this place that I've never experienced anywhere before in my life. I mean, I was part of my family, but really that was just me and Mum, and as wonderful as she was, being connected and close with a large group of people like this—well, it's on another scale. Maybe the way we moved around when I was younger made me miss out on any sense of what it would be like, being with the same people all the time and really knowing them.

Someone comes with our dinner and to make up a bed in the other room for me—it's one of the non-Community members. I say thank you, and she just smiles. I help her set out our dinner, and then get in her way by the door.

"Hi," I say.

Her eyes glance up at mine, then down again.

"She won't talk to you," Lara says.

"Why not?"

"You're in Community."

"So? No one else can hear now."

"She doesn't understand how things work," Lara says about me, and the woman shakes her head.

"Will she talk to you?" I ask.

"Probably. But not while you're listening."

The woman leans forward, whispers something to Lara.

"She has to go now," Lara says. "Her children are alone. She's nervous of the new people."

Lara turns quickly, takes the bread and fruit that came with our dinner, and passes it to the woman. She looks uncertainly at me.

"Shay won't tell," Lara says.

The woman takes it and almost runs out the door.

"Lara, you have to explain to me. How do things work?"

"Well, it's like this. Cepta said that some of these people who are immune can stay and help in the fields and with chores and stuff, but they're not allowed to talk to Community members. If they do, they get sent away. And there's not enough food for them, but it's even worse everywhere else, so they want to stay."

"Why on earth aren't they allowed to talk?"

"I don't know."

"But they'll talk to you?"

"Sometimes. I'm not in Community, or with them—I'm neither. And only Xander, Cepta, and you talk to me—not anyone else in Community." She says it matter-of-factly, but she knows how separate she is. "That server I know—Anna. She's told me a bit about her children. There are four of them."

"Is that why you're so skinny—giving food away?"

"I'm not that hungry most of the time anyway."

I raise an eyebrow. She's lying. Sweet-natured girl.

Now she's alarmed. "You won't tell, will you? Cepta says it's wrong to waste food."

"Of course not! And if they're going to eat it, how is it wasted?"

"Cepta says it is a waste to feed those who don't feed their minds."

118

I'm uneasy. What is this place? It's this amazing feeling of belonging to each other and the earth and all the life around us—but not other actual people, ones who don't *feed their minds*. Whatever that means.

People who are hungry. Who have nowhere to go because of the epidemic. People who do menial chores for us—but aren't allowed to speak or they get sent away to starve.

Joining will be soon, and for once I'm not sure I even want to. How do I hide what I was just thinking?

"Is something wrong?" Lara says.

"Something usually is. But something is also right, and that is *you*."

A smile lights her up from the inside.

CHAPTER 11

LARA

SHAY IS GONE. I mean, she's still here; she said she wouldn't leave, and she hasn't. She's on the floor, cross-legged. But her eyes are closed, and her mind has gone to join with the others.

I watch her curiously. What is it like? I've asked Cepta before, and if she's in a good mood, sometimes she tries to explain. She says it's pure joy. If she's in a bad mood, she then adds, one I'll never experience.

But *why*? That is one question I've never understood the answer to.

What would happen if I spoke to Shay now? Would she hear me? Would everyone she is joined with hear me too?

I'm tempted to try.

This is the one time I've noticed before that Cepta's touch on my mind is almost gone. I say "almost" because I think if I screamed at her, she'd probably still hear—screamed inside my mind, that is. She's got some sort of radar on me, she said once.

But it is a time I can think about things without her noticing. At least, not until later.

"Hi, Shay," I say. Voice low.

No reaction.

I wave a hand in front of her face. There is still no response, and I'm disappointed.

"Shay?" I say, louder this time, then sigh.

I'll just have to wait for it to be over. Lucky I'm good at waiting.

CHAPTER 12

SHAY

JOINING FROM A HOUSE across the other side of Community is no different than if I were in the same room as the others.

We *reach* out for Beatriz and Elena, and tonight we get a surprise. There are others.

Beatriz is excited, and her voice is even and clear. *We've joined with another group of survivors*, she says. *There's Patrick, Zohra, JJ, Henry, and Amaya. They're traveling with us now to the farm.*

And then they join in as well, and there is a chorus of names and introductions and personalities to match each one of them. And Patrick, with Beatriz's help to extend his *reach*, sends a message to me alone.

They knew Kai and tried to help him find me; Beatriz has told them what happened, and he's sorry we've been separated. The sorrow that has been muted by everything else threatens to take me away, and I almost withdraw, but joined as we are, these people—even the ones I've just met—are *more* than anyone can ever be. They shore me up.

And Xander knew about Patrick coming already: he had been

encouraging them to travel and join us. With so many more survivors, joining is far beyond anything we've experienced before. Then Xander says we should try to *reach* other Communities in Scotland, to see how far we can go. All of us join in with him and *reach* out. We find a startled Speaker near Glencoe, another in Crieff, then on the Isle of Skye. Soon we are covering most of Scotland.

Around us the members of Community are puzzled, wondering why they haven't been joined in yet, but we strengthen the linked survivors first, then we—and the other groups in different places—as one *reach* out to those nearby us.

Initially it takes more concentration, synchronizing breathing and heartbeats with so many souls in so many places, but soon that is as automatic as breathing and pumping blood around my own body.

We are one, survivors and members of Community here and elsewhere—the earth, rivers, lakes, and forests too, and all that lives, breathes, or grows within them—all of Scotland that lives and breathes.

But it's not *all* the people, is it? What about those who work for us? Why don't they join too?

Some small part of me remembers enough about who I am as me, alone, to try something else—carefully, cautiously, a sliver of my consciousness divided from the rest so no one should notice—to feel for the others beyond us in the woods, and Lara too. But they're all blank, and I don't understand why.

Blank . . . or somehow shielded?

And something else is wrong: it's Cepta. I can't quite work out what it is. She's here, joined with the rest of us. We're all connected, and that takes effort and concentration to achieve. But there is a background note coming from Cepta; it's discordant. And it isn't her being angry or annoyed with me; it's something else.

I try a small silent whisper.

Cepta? Are you okay?

I catch a glimpse of fear, pain. One that is washed away so fast I think I imagined it. But that wasn't done by her. At least, I don't think so.

Was it . . . Xander?

Then I think, *So what?* If Xander has gotten annoyed with Cepta for some reason, it's about time.

Yet later, after we say goodbye and separate off one by one, part of me—shielded carefully—is still disturbed by what I sensed before. She was frightened—it felt real. Why?

Somehow I have to try to *reach* her again.

Cepta? A private message.

What is it? A very sharp retort, and more the Cepta I expect. *Is everything okay with Lara?*

Yes, fine.

Well? What do you want?

Nothing. Never mind.

I'm busy. You're on your own tonight.

I get a small glimpse—one I'm sure she's shared deliberately. She's with Xander, in his house, walking to him and unbuttoning her tunic, and I disconnect as fast as I can.

She's busy with my father. BLEUGH. That is just so *gross*.

I slowly come back to myself, to my body, and open my eyes.

Lara is here, watching me, her head tilted to one side as if she's been studying me and is wondering something.

"What?"

"You were making faces."

"I'm not surprised."

And now I have an idea. If Cepta is busy, and Xander is too—well. Lara and I really *are* on our own tonight.

"Is it time to tell stories now?" Lara says. "I've been waiting *ages*." Her voice is aggrieved, and I'm pleased: that she's feeling what she wants to feel. Lara loves stories—Callie loved to read, Kai said. There are no books in this house.

But I know where we can get some. Maybe . . .

"Now you're smiling in a funny way," she says. "Like you've thought of something you shouldn't."

"Oh yes. Do you fancy an adventure?"

CHAPTER 13

LARA

IT'S DARK, IT'S LATE, and I tingle with knowing we're doing something I'm completely not supposed to do.

Shay walks up to the library door, opens it. A door she's free to go in and out of, but I'm not.

She steps in and the lights go on, and I jump, sure someone has seen us and put them all on.

"The lights are automatic, it's fine," Shay says. "Come on. If we get caught, I'll say it's my fault, that I made you do it. It'll be all right."

I look all around us.

"Everyone is asleep, I promise you."

I step forward, almost shaking, until I'm standing in the doorway.

Through it, as far as my eyes can see, are books. Shelves and shelves of books.

"Are you sure?" I say.

"Yes. There's no point in me picking something for you; I'd get it wrong. You have to do it yourself."

"Cepta will know."

"I'll deal with her."

My mouth is hanging open now, and I snap it shut again.

I *want* to come in—I believe Shay when she says she'll deal with Cepta—but somehow just can't take that one more step.

"Let me help you," Shay says. She takes my hand, and then, at the same moment, something eases inside me. We step inside together.

My eyes and then my hands run over the books, wanting to take in and touch them all.

There's a lot of the boring stuff, like Xander brought me once—about stars and rocks and things I've never heard of—but then Shay finds a section with stories.

I'm pulling books off the shelves and going through them and hugging them like friends, and now Shay is laughing at how many of them I've got.

"Let me carry some for you," she says, and takes some of them, looks through them. "Really? *Moby-Dick*?" She makes a face. "Well, if you want it."

"Do we sign them out or something?"

"No. If anyone notices the fiction depletion, I'll say I took them."

We're there for ages because I keep seeing something else I want, until finally Shay stifles a yawn. "Come on. Let's go back and get some sleep."

We step out of the library, and the lights go off automatically.

We lug the piles of books back to the house. Shay turns on the lamp, and I pick *I Capture the Castle* and open it.

"You're not going to want to sleep now, are you?" Shay says.

"No. That is . . ."

"What?"

"Not unless I have to."

"You don't *have to* anything. Stay up as long as you want."

I start reading but get a sense of Shay's eyes and glance up again; she's looking at me still, a serious, odd expression in her eyes.

"What?"

"Looking at you now, I don't understand. There's nothing wrong at all; you're perfect."

126

I close the book, disquieted. "A funny sort of perfect."

"You tell me, then. What is the less-than-perfect problem?"

I frown. "My thoughts slide away when I try to think about it. About me."

"There are blocks in your mind; I can see them: they stop you from thinking certain things. Cepta's doing, I expect." She's annoyed, but not with me.

I look back at her, understanding something I haven't before. I thought that not being able to think about some things I wanted to was part of what was wrong with me. But Cepta did it? On purpose? I cross my arms, an unfamiliar feeling rising inside. "Sometimes I could just slap Cepta. If she were here right now, I would!" I mime a slapping gesture, and there is a weird feeling inside, like the idea came from outside of me—but then it slides away. "Anyway, that would be a *very* bad idea."

Shay grins. "Perhaps a less direct assault would be better." She looks at me, considering. "It would be difficult. But I could try to remove the blocks in your mind, a little at a time, in unobvious ways so they don't notice. And we could see what happens. But only if you want me to."

There are shadowy places inside me, glimpses caught now and then when I'm half-asleep or thinking of something else—like the way you catch something out of the corner of your eye at night that you can't see if you look at it straight on. I'm afraid of what hides in my edges. I shake my head.

"That's okay," she says. "Let me know if you change your mind." There is disappointment in her voice, but she smiles. "Go on, read for a while if you want to; I'm sleepy." She heads off to her room. She leaves the door part open, and the light goes off inside it a moment later.

I open my book, but at first I'm just looking at the page and not taking in the words I was so desperate for a moment ago.

Cepta does things to my thoughts. She makes me do things I don't want to do; she makes me feel things too. I told Xander I felt like I was sleepwalking a lot of the time, and it's true.

Maybe it's time to wake up.

CHAPTER 14

SHAY

LARA COMES INTO MY ROOM early the next morning. My eyes are still shut, but I'm half-awake and can feel her presence. I stretch and yawn, then sit up.

"I changed my mind," Lara says.

"What about?" I say, but I think I know. I have to stop myself from reacting too much: it'll only scare her.

"Can you get Cepta out of my head? She's there now." There is a mixture of fury and fear in her aura.

"I'll have to go into your mind. Is that okay?"

She nods, but it's jerky, like she's struggling to make that simple movement when someone is trying to take her control away.

I *reach* out to her lightly, to Lara—inside. And there she is: Cepta is coiled around her thoughts and feelings like a hidden serpent.

Cepta, what do you think you are doing?

She's startled that I see her there, then annoyed. But there is more; something is wrong, very wrong, in Cepta's world. What is it?

I'm checking up on my patient, is all she says.

She's fine, or she was before you started poking around, and now she's frightened. Stop it.

I give her a mental *push,* and just like that, Cepta is gone from Lara's mind. That was easy: too easy? Could it be because I'm next to Lara in the same room, and Cepta is farther away, wherever she is? Or maybe she didn't bother to *try.* Which doesn't seem like her.

Cepta? Are you all right?

Leave me alone. And then she's left mine as well.

Lara gasps. "She's gone."

"Can I check some more? Make sure she's not just hiding?"

"Yes."

I deepen my touch on Lara's mind, but find no trace of Cepta's presence. She really is gone. There are blocks in place still, though. I'm about to ask Lara if she wants me to try to remove them as well, but I'm interrupted by a mental call.

It's Xander. *Shay? What have you been up to?* His tone is irritated, but with who, I can't tell.

Taking care of my sister, I say. There is a pause.

We need to talk, he says.

We're talking.

Come to the research center.

I don't want to leave Lara alone. Can she come?

It's against the rules.

Whose rules? Who makes them? I'm pushing him and can't stop myself even though I'm not sure if I should be doing this.

Bring her.

I open my eyes. Lara is looking at me still with that intent way she has. "Is Cepta really gone?"

"I think so."

"Thank you."

"Xander wants to talk to me, at the research center."

"Don't leave me alone; she'll come back!"

"No, she won't; I'll watch for her. I promise. But I'm not leaving you here; you're coming with me."

We walk across Community soon after. Lara doesn't believe Cepta will stay out; she might have a point. She's scared of her, of having anyone in her mind; she didn't like agreeing to let me in and only did so that I could deal with Cepta.

But her hesitation stems from more than just that. It's almost like she's scared to think for herself too—probably because she hasn't been allowed to for a long time, and that makes me angry again.

Maybe there is a way to make her feel freer.

When we reach the research center, Lara stops at the door. I hold it open.

"It's okay, I promise."

She hesitates, and I give her a small nudge with my mind. She steps through the door.

"Lara, do you know what a quiet room is?"

She shakes her head.

"It's a room where no one can *reach* your mind."

Her eyes widen. "Not even Xander or Cepta?" *Or you*, she's thinking, but she doesn't say it out loud.

"Not us, not anybody. And there is one here. How about you wait in the quiet room while Xander and I are talking? You'll be completely safe there, I promise. You can sit and read the book you brought, or just think."

She nods, and I hail Xander, tell him I'm taking Lara there.

But when she sees it, that it is a small room that locks from the outside, she shakes her head, backs away. Cepta said she's afraid of small places, didn't she?

There's a whisper of a memory inside, of another girl who was afraid of small, confined places: Jenna. There are so many similarities between these two girls. Surely they can't all be coincidences?

"How about we stay right here to talk? And you can see us through the window in the door. Would that be all right?"

She hesitates. "Okay. But will you let me out if I knock?"

"Instantly. I promise."

She goes in, checks the room from corner to corner, then finally sits in the chair and opens her book.

"It's okay," she says. "You can shut the door now."

I shut it, watching her through the window. She looks nervous—not that I can see her aura anymore in the quiet room—but she gives me a thumbs-up just as Xander's footsteps approach.

"Good morning," I say.

"Is it?" Annoyed is right. His aura almost bristles with it.

"Can we talk here? I told Lara I'd stay in sight in case she wants to get out."

"Sure. Fine." He defocuses; I sense him telling others to stay away. His eyes turn back to me. "Cepta's furious with you."

"Oh?"

"You took Lara to the library last night."

"She was starved for something to read."

"I tried bringing her books before; she had no interest."

I shake my head. "The wrong sort of books. She wanted stories—you know, novels."

"Cepta thinks reading fiction would be bad for her, that she'll take on personas from stories and that that could worsen her identity confusion."

"Look at her, Xander. She's in there now, reading and perfectly happy—especially because she's in a quiet room, where no one can get at her mind. Cepta has been far too controlling of her thoughts and feelings."

He sighs, and I can see the indecision on his face. He's being told one thing by this woman he believes is an expert, a psychologist, and completely different things by me.

Then he glances again through the window in the door, at Lara reading her book—she doesn't seem worried about being in a small room at all.

"I'm inclined to give you some latitude in this regard. She's happier with you than she has been here before."

"What about Cepta?"

He shrugs dismissively, and there is a part of me—a very small part, it is true—that feels sorry for her.

"Can Lara come to dinner tonight too?" One last rule to break.

"Cepta thought the number of people would be too much for her. It's why she's been kept separate from Community."

"It's made her feel alone and isolated."

"Fine. Try bringing her tonight. But she can't try to join with everyone; I agree with Cepta there. It'd be overwhelming, connecting with so many different people. She can't do that without holding on to a strong sense of who she is, or she could get lost. I've seen this happen before. It's far too dangerous."

CHAPTER 15

LARA

WHEN THE DOOR TO THE QUIET ROOM CLOSED, my heart rate increased and I was sweating. But I made myself breathe in, out, in, out; focus on the chair, the air in my lungs; and gradually I calmed down. And I did it by myself; I didn't need Cepta doing it for me.

When I glance up, I can see Shay through the door. Xander is there now; they're talking. Whatever it is about looks serious. He turns his head toward me, and I look down, pretend to focus on the book in my hands.

Cepta's not here. No one can hear my thoughts?

I can think *anything*, and nobody would know. But I'm so used to not doing that—to hiding what I think and feel, even from myself, that I don't know where to begin.

And despite how I managed to calm myself this time, I still *know*.

There is danger, something that lies hidden at the edges of every room I go in, large or small. I know it is there in the shadows.

It will come for me when it wants to, and there is nothing I can do.

CHAPTER 16

SHAY

AT DINNER IT'S OBVIOUS from Cepta's aura that she wasn't with Xander last night. Her plans must have fallen through, and that's why she's been in such a state. I know what I saw so can only assume he rejected her.

Cepta is angry—frightened too—but keeping such a tight grip on it that to anyone but a survivor, it wouldn't be apparent. Externally she's as always. Contained. Calm. Maybe there are a few spots of high color in her cheeks not usually there, ones she hasn't noticed or she would have taken them away.

But Persey doesn't have the ability to control how she feels like Cepta does. She's lit up from inside—smiling at Xander in absolute adoration, in a way that must be obvious to everyone. ICK. He touches her hand when she sits down, and she literally almost swoons. Until now, that was something I thought was made up in romance novels.

Do the others notice Cepta's demotion?

They must. He's changed where everyone is sitting. Now Xander is flanked on one side by me, then Lara, and on the other side by Persey, then Cepta. And he leans toward Persey in a way he didn't with Cepta. His chair is closer to hers too.

What is she: maybe twenty? She's not that much older than me. This is just so totally *disgusting*.

Anna is one of the servers, and when she sees Lara at the head table with me, her eyes widen slightly. I smile when I see that she gives Lara an extra-large portion of everything.

When dinner is finished and the tables cleared away, it is time for the main event of the evening: joining. Should I go back to the house with Lara and join from there? I ask Xander, but before he can answer, Lara shakes her head.

"I know the way," she says. "I'll walk back on my own."

"Are you sure?"

"It doesn't matter if you're there or not when your mind is off away; you're just a solid lump when you're like that. I think the house could fall on your head and you wouldn't notice."

"Sorry," I say. "But I'll take you back."

"No, you won't." She heads for the door, and people part slightly, leaving a space around her.

"She seems to be recovering her teenage attitude," Xander says.

"A good thing, don't you think?"

"Just not *too* much."

"I thought you'd be used to being around teenagers by now." I glance at Persey.

He raises an eyebrow; his face goes cold. "That is not your concern." And I shiver under his rebuke, a reaction that feels like a physical hurt.

Be careful, Shay, Cepta whispers in my mind. *Don't think being his daughter changes this truth: you can be out of favor as easily as in it.*

I ignore her, even though I'm uneasy—but not in the way she might think. Why did I react like that? Why did it *matter* so much when he was displeased with me, even though what I said—well, he totally deserved it.

There is something about him that makes you want him to smile at you. In the short time I've been here, I've begun to like being one he favors, one he listens to.

I feel eyes on me and glance up. Cepta has a knowing look, as if she could see exactly what was in my mind.

The survivors—me, Xander, and Cepta—must begin the joining process together, and I wonder how it'll be, with what seems wrong between the two of them. But when we begin, it is much as always. Though maybe Cepta is shielding more than she usually does?

Then she flinches, and she is more open—as if she'd been pried like an oyster shell. And she is hurting, but Xander is disdainful.

What you are—where you are—is only because of me, he says to her. *Remember that.*

Yes, Xander, she whispers.

And I'm shocked—both at this exchange and that he let me see it. Then I'm remembering what Cepta said before. Did he do that deliberately, to give me the same lesson?

And then these uneasy feelings between us are gone as if they never existed. Cepta is as strong and clear as always; she and I are equal with Xander as we *reach* out to Beatriz, Elena, Patrick, all the other survivors. I see now that they've spread out to different places, so we are covering even more of Scotland in our joining tonight. It wouldn't take that many more of us to bring the entire country along.

And it is so *beautiful*, peaceful and vibrant with life at the same time: I belong to Scotland and Scotland belongs to me, both at once.

I'd give *anything* to feel this again.

Everything.

CHAPTER 17

LARA

"HI," SHAY SAYS.

I look up over my book. "Hi. How was it?"

"Joining? It was . . . well. Pretty awesome."

I raise an eyebrow.

"Sorry. Is that like being told the best chocolate in the world is on the shelf but you can't have any?"

"In a way. But maybe . . ." I pause, thinking. "Maybe it's like it's the best chocolate in the world, and I'd love to eat it, but I know I'm allergic. I want it and don't want it, at the same time." Somehow I *know*: it'd be a step I couldn't back away from.

"There's something I want to talk to you about." Shay is uneasy, and I'm alarmed. "I kind of have a confession to make," she says.

"What is it?"

"You know how I asked you about taking blocks out of your mind. Well . . ." She's squirming a little, like she's uncomfortable with me looking at her. "I kind of had done some of it already, before I asked you. If I hadn't, you wouldn't have been able to make yourself step into the library or the research center: they were blocked. Also, if I hadn't, you wouldn't have been able to ask me for help, like you did the morning after the library. You weren't able to use your own will enough to do so."

"So you fiddled around in my brain and didn't ask first. Just like everybody else always does."

"Yes. But only so you could make choices yourself."

I'm upset; I can feel it welling up inside me. "I thought you were different."

"I am! And I won't do it again unless you ask me to, I promise. Do you understand what I said—why I had to do it?" Shay looks distressed, and I think that I do understand, that I will forgive her.

But this is an important point I want to make.

So not just yet.

That night I can't sleep. I'm uneasy. Things are changing; I can feel something coming as if I'm vibrating with a storm that will be here soon. I wander through the house barefoot and trip on the edge of a chair. It goes over with a crash, and there are tears in my eyes from stubbing my toe.

I hear Shay get up in her room.

"Are you all right?" she starts to say, but then stops. There is a sound outside in the night.

"Who is it?" I ask her, knowing she has ways of working out who people are even when she can't see them, like Cepta can.

Before she can answer, someone knocks quickly, then opens the door—it's Anna. She's holding a candle in her hand. Her face is frightened in the flickering light.

"What's wrong?" I say.

She looks at Shay but then just blurts it out, loud enough that Shay can hear her too. "The new people that arrived yesterday; they're staying below our camp. They're sick. Some have died."

"Sick?" Shay says. "Do you mean . . . ?"

"They've brought the epidemic." She looks at me. "I wanted to warn you, Lara—to run. Hide. Save yourself."

I hear her words, but they are distant, fading, and my eyes are only focused on the flame dancing in her hand.

Shay is saying something.

Anna leaves; she must take her candle with her.

But it is still here, growing and twisting and hot—

held in my eyes—

and I try to see the world as it really is, not this nightmare—

but I can't stop it—

I can't—

it's here—

the edges—

the shadows—

they're growing—

the fire—

it's here.

CHAPTER 18

SHAY

"LARA! LARA? WHAT'S WRONG?"

She's shaking; her face is white, then red. She drops to the floor, rolls up into a ball, to the smallest she can be.

"Lara! Answer me."

But then she starts screaming—a high-pitched sound that tears into me—like she did the other night when I said her name, when I called her Callie.

This time I am *not* calling Cepta or Xander. I'm not letting them crack her open, forcibly soothing her—like crushing her spirit into a straitjacket. No.

There are ripples of black pain all through her aura when I *reach* out as gently as I can. *Lara, can I help you?*

NOT LARA!

Who are you?

CALLIE, I'm CALLIE! And now she's screaming her name over

and over again, and I'm seeing what she sees, what she feels, and it takes all my strength of will not to withdraw in horror and fear.

Was it Anna's candle that brought this on now?

She's burning, on fire—like I was, when I nearly died . . .

And this is how Jenna *did* die—the first time. When she was cured in fire.

Did Callie hear about this, then imagine it somehow?

No—it isn't just that; it can't be.

It *is* Jenna: this is exactly her memory, one she shared with me before. How can Callie have Jenna's memory? How is that possible?

Callie stops screaming; she collapses against me. "Jenna?" she whispers, out loud—did she hear my thoughts when I was *reaching* out and trying to help her? "Jenna," she whispers again. "She was Jenna—that was her name. Part of me died with her."

And Callie is out of the memory, or dream, or whatever it was now—and she's crying, not just a little but the complete gut-wrenching sobs that take over every part of you. I'm rocking her in my arms. "Shhh, shhh, Lara, I've got you; nothing can hurt you."

She shakes her head. "I'm *Callie*," she says between sobs.

"Okay. Callie. Nothing will hurt you ever again, not while I'm here. I promise."

But even as I say the words, I don't know if this is a promise I can keep. Anna said the epidemic was in the woods below us. Without Jenna around anymore to spread it far and wide, it can only pass from person to person, but they are so near. Has Callie been exposed to it before? Ninety-five percent of people die—five percent are immune. Very, very few are like me and get sick but survive.

Can I really protect her from this?

Completely exhausted, Callie finally lets me half carry her to her bed, and she falls asleep almost instantly, her hand still clinging to mine. I keep expecting someone to come—to have heard her screaming and come to investigate—but no one does.

I watch her as she sleeps, unwilling to take my hand away in case it disturbs her.

How did she experience Jenna's death? She was *there*—I know she was—every detail was exactly the same as the memory Jenna shared with me before. And Callie said part of her died with Jenna?

I can't think of any way this makes sense.

But this mystery will have to wait for another day.

I *reach* out to the woods and beyond. I seek out birds, other animals, any eyes I can spy through—to see if I can find evidence of the epidemic, like Anna said. There's a small hope inside me: maybe she was mistaken. Maybe they've got an ordinary flu or some other illness.

But it doesn't take long to find a rat sniffing at a body. Dead. There's no doubt it is from the epidemic: there is blood in the open, staring eyes. And then I see there are more who are ill, who are dying, even now.

The epidemic has never found this place before.

Community: they aren't immune; they aren't protected.

Is Callie?

I *reach* out with my mind, this time to find Xander, panic leaking through my thoughts.

CHAPTER 19

CALLIE

THE NEXT MORNING I WAKE UP SLOWLY.

I'm alone—no, Chamberlain is here, asleep by my feet. There's a note on the table by the bed:

Please don't leave the house—it's important. I'll explain later. I'll be back as soon as I can. Love you, Shay.

I touch her last three words with my fingers, feeling as though the warmth these words carry stayed here in the paper for me to feel.

She didn't put my name at the top of the note. Maybe she was unsure whether it was a good idea, if I'd gone back to being empty Lara.

No: that won't happen. I'm Callie. I know this now. I never want to be Lara again.

I also know there are many other things I've forgotten—or been made to forget. I want them back.

Last night when I saw the candle in Anna's hand, the edges moved in, surrounded me. The thing of shadows was here, and we writhed in pain in the flames together.

But this wasn't like before—all those other times. Although I could never remember my nightmares after I had them, when it happened last night, I remembered them all. Was it different this time because Cepta's influence was gone?

I was still terrified and screaming, and there was pain, but I was also *aware*. I knew it wasn't a hallucination or a nightmare; it was real. It really happened. Not to me, but to other-me: the one who has lurked on the edges of my life for as long as I can remember. She's been silenced lately by Cepta's tricks, but she's tired of being ignored.

Shay was with me last night, but instead of pushing other-me away like Cepta would have done, she stayed with me, helped me deal with this memory—because that is what it was. She knew what it was because she saw it herself.

And she knew her, recognized her: other-me.

It's Jenna, she'd whispered, words full of amazement, in my mind.

Names have power. Jenna thought she was me back then, in her memory of fire and pain, much like sometimes I think I am her. Our lives are so entwined the edges are blurred, but once I had her name, I could see her for who she really was.

Callie has power too, and it's mine:

I claim it.

CHAPTER 20

SHAY

I RUN ACROSS COMMUNITY to Xander to tell him face-to-face what he was resisting from a distance.

"Xander! There you are. We all have to leave right now. Maybe it isn't too late to escape the epidemic."

"No," he says. "We must stay and fight."

"Fight? What on earth do you mean? You can't fight this thing. People will die—most of them here, if not all, will die."

He shakes his head, his aura tinged with sadness, and something else—something I can't read. "We stay and fight, because that is all we can do."

Xander takes me to the hall. The place where we joined last night is now where our sick are being brought. There are five from our Community—ill, in agony, on makeshift beds on the floor.

Five so far.

It's too late to flee.

I'm terrified for Callie. I *reach* out to her, to see if she is still okay.

She says she's fine, that I should stay to help if I can, and she promises to stay where she is. I'm thankful for once that she has been kept apart, that her house is the one away from all the others.

She's brave. She doesn't think she'll get sick, and I can only hope she's right.

It was me who arranged for Callie to come for dinner with everyone last night. What if she caught it then, before we knew it was coming to us? I'd never forgive myself.

Cepta is fiercely trying to take their pain onto herself—to ease them—and I have respect for her I didn't have before. She is their Speaker; these are her people. She will do anything she can for them. She broadcasts her will: *They are mine. They cannot die. I won't allow it!* But more become ill, and more. And soon the first ones die despite her raging against it.

What can I possibly do to stop this?

When I first learned how to see auras, I had just read about them—in Xander's books in his Shetland cottage. My own aura matches the hues of a rainbow: the books said this is the sign of a healer, a star person. And while I didn't know what the latter meant then and still don't, *healer* is obvious. A healer makes sick people well. But how? I'm scared.

I want to run away, but instead I kneel next to a girl—Megan. She's no older than Beatriz.

"It hurts so much," she says, gasping, and I *have* to help her. I have to try to find a way to stop this illness.

How does it cause pain? How does it end lives so easily?

I *reach* to her, and the shock of her pain as we join makes it hard to remember what I must do: ease her agony, see why she hurts.

I soothe her pain, take it onto myself to diffuse it as much as I can and still retain the ability to think. Then I look closer, deeper, inside her.

Her blood is flooded with things that aren't usually there—components of cells, cells that are dead and dying all over her body. Why do they die?

Focus: on one damaged cell. Something is happening—something that isn't typical for a healthy cell. The whole cell is producing more

146

and more of a new protein, one that isn't usually there, at a furious rate. The cell is scavenging itself for amino acids, the building blocks of protein; it is destroying its essential components and then the cell wall, until finally the cell bursts.

This accelerated protein production is being repeated everywhere, almost like every cell in the body has turned into a tumor that grows and grows until the cell destroys itself.

Now that I see what is happening, can I target a cell and heal it?

I focus on one cell, where the protein production is just gearing up: send healing waves to block the protein production—to stop the process. And it works! I can stop it and heal the cell.

But while I've healed one cell, thousands—tens of thousands— more have died. It's spreading faster than I have any hope of healing.

And cells burst—releasing toxins into the blood, toxins that travel to all the organs.

Pain . . . organ failure . . . death.

Megan is gone: a little girl has died. So much pain, hers and mine.

The grim day goes on. We ease their pain as best we can and hold their hands as they die, but I'm filled with the same mad fury as Cepta that we are so helpless against this. Is that really all we can do? I'm obsessed with doing anything I can to help them, but even if I try with someone whose illness isn't as advanced as Megan's, I can't stop it by healing individual cells. It accelerates and spreads too fast.

And still more people are brought in; more are sick. More die.

Another dying man cries out in pain, and I kneel beside him. His name is Jason. I know him, of course I do. Despite how short a time I've been here, I know all of them, from the inside—from evening joinings. He's a chemist with a quirky sense of humor. Even at a time like this, he likes to grow impractical things, like flowers—ones you can't eat.

When I *reach* out to him, I'm plunged into his pain, like I have been into each of the others'. And this one more is too much—his pain, and mine, almost take my will away.

I'm weeping.

This is your moment, Xander says to me; his words in my mind

147

are fierce. *Work out the answer to your question. Why do so very few survive this—how do they survive? What makes the course of this different for them? If you find the answer, you can save him.* There is such conviction in his words that I start to believe it myself—that this is something I can do.

Jason's pain is so intense it's taking over; it's strangling his aura even before there are enough toxins in his bloodstream to kill him. His life energy is almost gone.

Is it just an increased ability to withstand pain that has some survive? If you can live long enough, can the process somehow be reversed? I doubt it could be anything as simple as that, yet . . .

I release Jason and *reach* out, far and wide, finding a startled Beatriz first. I explain, and she helps me gather other survivors. And this time when I join with Jason, they are there to help.

The shock of his pain is like diving into the sun. I couldn't manage this alone anymore, but together we plunge him into the cool, dark depths of his mind—helping him to release much of his pain.

We ease his passing. But he still dies.

CHAPTER 21

CALLIE

NO ONE HAS TOLD ME WHAT IS HAPPENING IN AGES, and I'm going crazy with worry. Shay said there was an epidemic here, one that can kill: has it swept through the whole of Community? Is everyone dying right now while I worry on a sofa with a cat?

The last time Shay checked on me, she told me to stay here, and I said I would. She's afraid I'll catch it, get sick like the others. She didn't say it, but I could tell—she was afraid I might have already caught it.

I feel well enough. Can I go there, see what is happening—maybe help? Or will I get sick if I do?

No. That won't happen.

The thought is there in my mind without me thinking it, like it came from someone else, another voice. Not other-me, but my own self that has been hiding away for so long that I don't seem to know how to consciously access my own thoughts, my own memories, anymore. But there are moments like this when I seem to know things, even though how or why I know them isn't clear. All I can do is trust that it is right.

I open the door. Funny how I can see where it is now: it must have been one of the blocks Shay said Cepta put in my mind so I couldn't see what was right there, in front of me. Is that like not being able to see past the edge of the world?

I'm scared of where I'm going, and my steps get slower as I walk. I'm not scared that it'll get me, but of seeing other people ill, maybe dying.

There is no one walking around, no one I can see through the windows of their houses. The library is empty. I open the door of the research center and listen, but there is no sound. And I marvel at simple things—like opening these doors—that I couldn't do before.

Are they in the hall where we had dinner last night?

I hesitate outside it, then open the door partway, stand there and try to take in what is happening.

There are people lying on the floor. Some are still, unmoving, bloody eyes staring straight ahead. Some are crying and screaming in pain. And in the midst of it all are Cepta and Shay, trying to help them. Xander is here too, but standing back, and it is his eyes that find me first. He walks to the door.

I feel his mind brush against mine, and his eyes widen.

"Callie?" he says.

"Yes. Shay helped me; I know who I really am now," I say, and he smiles, touches my hand.

"You shouldn't have come here. You don't need to see this. Go back."

I shake my head. "I can't stay alone while this is happening. I want to help."

"Aren't you afraid you'll catch it?"

"No. Should I be?"

He tilts his head to one side, like he's thinking about what to say. "No," he finally says. "You're immune."

CHAPTER 22

SHAY

I'M IN A FURY when I look up and see Callie standing in the doorway with Xander, because I'm so scared for her.

I told you to stay where you were! Please go; maybe it's not too late.

She shakes her head and says she's immune—how could she know that?—and that she wants to help. And when I don't seem convinced, she tells me Xander confirmed it. I can't work out what this means, that he knows she is immune when she's been here, in Community, all along—a place that hasn't been touched by the epidemic before. But I can't think about that right now. What is happening is taking all my concentration.

With Beatriz and the other survivors, near and far, helping now, I can go on. I join with one of the ill, then another; we ease their passing but can't stop them from dying. Joined as we are, I am the conduit for the others, and every time it happens, I feel each death keenly. It is like I'm dying myself. Despair grows inside me as it happens again and again, and I have to fight to make myself still try to help the next person. And each time I join with another soul, I delve deeper and deeper inside them, looking for something—anything—that might help.

What about the darkness I've sensed inside me—what I'd thought might shield the antimatter that is still detected in survivors, but hidden? I start to look for this in the dying. None of them have it.

Could this be it, the reason some live and some die?

I need to look for this in another survivor. I shy away from trying with Xander and instead ask Cepta if I can join fully with her, see if she has this darkness inside her. She doesn't understand and doesn't want to do it, but finally says she will try anything that might help one of her people.

We join. She isn't what she has appeared to be in many ways, but I try not to see, to pry; it's not why I'm here. Deep within her, I finally find it—a darkness that I can sense but not truly see or feel: she has it too. This is the thing that makes us survivors; it must be. This is what they lack.

I look across the room: Callie is holding hands with the sick too. Though she can't ease pain the way we can, it still helps. She's still well: I pray she's right, that she's immune like she said.

And Xander confirmed it? But how could he know?

Cepta, how long has Callie been here?

What? I don't know. Maybe six months.

Not a year?

No, not even close. Why are you asking me this? Did what you found inside me show you a way to help my people? Then do it!

Those who are left—the sick, the dying—I check them all. Not one of them has this darkness inside them. They're all going to die, and there is nothing I can do.

Persey is one of the last to fall ill. Her eyes are wide, frightened, full of pain. I drop to my knees next to her bed and take her hand.

She holds it tight as another wave of pain passes through her.

"Help me," she whispers. "Please."

Cepta is here too, and no matter her views on Persey usurping her place with Xander, her eyes are full of pity, and rage that we can't do anything. My strength is almost gone, but I can't let her die in this much pain. Like so many times before, I join with Persey, dive into the sun of her pain—I ask Beatriz and the others to shield me from it as much as they can so I can see more clearly . . .

There is no darkness inside Persey; I checked before, so I know this already. Yet . . .

Where does it come from? Is it already there in those who will survive . . . or is it made?

If it is made, then *how*?

Everything in our bodies is made by transcribing a section of DNA to RNA—basically, making a readable copy of a gene—and then translating the RNA to make a protein. Even though every cell we are made up of carries all our genetic information in our DNA, genes aren't always active—so hair doesn't grow bone, and bone doesn't grow hair. Cells are differentiated. But this process has been subverted in this illness: infected cells are forced to overproduce a new protein until it kills them.

Could there be something deep inside the genetic code that *makes* what saved me and the other survivors? We still got sick, so it couldn't have been there to begin with, but maybe it is activated by this illness?

I'm so deep within Persey now that even with the others trying to shield me, her pain is taking away my ability to think. Still I try to find something, anything, that is different between my DNA and hers. . . .

Is there—could it be—*here*? These repeating sequences of DNA inside me. Junk DNA, geneticists call it: *junk* because it doesn't seem to code for protein or have any function they can identify, other than maybe structural—and even that they're not sure of. We both have large numbers of repeating sections of junk DNA, but . . . some stretches of them are completely different.

Is this it? I need to compare DNA in more of those who fall ill and more survivors to know for sure. But if it is, can this be altered inside her, the same way I changed my hair, to change the course of the disease?

But I'm too late. She dies.

Persey was the last to die. Within a day, all of Community who were here, except three who didn't come down with it and so must be immune, are dead. The only others left are me, Cepta, Callie, and Xander.

Cepta—the one who controlled all in this place for so long—seems to have started to lose it.

She whispers in my mind. *Didn't you notice who he sent away with Beatriz? His favorites. Those he wanted to save.*

What?

The ones who left with Beatriz and Elena—all his favorites. Sent to safety. And poor Persey wasn't even one of them.

"Cepta, dear woman," Xander says, and holds out his arms. Trembling, she goes to his embrace. Her rambling thoughts calm.

Callie goes to Anna, and she and many of the people who live below come to help us. Those who served us—the immune—now outnumber us greatly. How will this change things?

Pyres are built for the dead, and I'm worried for Callie, but she says she'll be all right to stay, to see the fire. That now that she knows about Jenna, it won't scare her the way it did before. A torch is cast, and soon the flames dance.

I'm exhausted beyond imagining, and yet . . .

How did Xander and Cepta think staying isolated here would keep everyone safe from the epidemic? It was always going to find them eventually—especially when other people kept coming, drawn by the resources they have in this place. Even without Jenna around to spread this thing, people who are ill are still contagious to those they come in contact with.

And either Xander lied or Cepta did: how long has Callie lived here? Xander said she's been here the whole year since she's been missing, but then how did he know she is immune?

As we watch the pyres, I both feel the disappointment in Xander's mind and see it in his aura. It turns out that the members of his Community weren't that special after all. Most were scientists and engineers; they were carefully picked by Xander for their brains and skills. But at the end, they were people—human, like the rest of us— and so they were mortal. Most died; some few were immune; there were no survivors, not today. That's not unexpected, as surviving is

154

so rare and there were only about eighty Community members here, but Xander somehow thought his followers would find a way to survive—as if they could *think* their way out of dying.

With Persey I'd felt I might have been on the edge of working something out, something that could have helped—but I was too late.

Always too late.

CHAPTER 23

CALLIE

SHAY IS SLUMPED DOWN ON THE SOFA, not moving—barely even making the effort to breathe—but she's not asleep either. Chamberlain butts against her hand, and she hardly stirs.

"Tea?" I say, and she slowly turns her eyes to me and blinks as if she's having trouble understanding what I said. Then she nods.

I go to make it. Things have changed. Today it is Shay who needs Chamberlain, and she needs me too. Even though I'm desperately sad for all that has happened and how she feels, it gives me a warm feeling inside that somebody needs *me* and not the other way around.

I bring the tea in, put it on the table, half push her upright until she helps and sits up herself.

"Thank you, Callie," she says. Chamberlain sees a lap available and jumps onto her, plonks his front paws against her chest and headbutts her chin. She half smiles, gives in and strokes him. "Oh, to be a cat," she says.

"Drink that. It'll make you feel better."

She turns and looks at me properly now, seeing me and not some horror remembered from earlier. She smiles. "I'm so glad you're all right."

"I'm sorry I scared you earlier by going to the great hall."

"It's okay. I didn't know you were immune. How did you know?"

"I don't know how; I just did."

"Can you remember ever having been around the epidemic before?"

I shake my head, and now I'm the one cast back to the horror in the hall: I'd have remembered *that*, wouldn't I? I shudder and push it out of my mind.

"But Xander knew you were immune," Shay says.

"Yes. And that I know now that I'm really Callie, not Lara."

She leans down over her tea, in her hands now. "I don't always know what I should or shouldn't say, what you know, what you remember. If hearing something might freak you out or be useful or good to know, even if it hurts."

"So that must mean you're thinking of telling me something."

"Yes. But I might have to touch your mind, see if there are blocks that'll stop you from being able to deal with it."

I swallow. I'm scared, but I want to *know*—to fill in more of the blanks inside of me. "Go on. Do it."

She sips her tea, looks at me carefully as if searching for an answer. "Do you know who Xander is to you?" she says, finally.

I'm puzzled. "What do you mean?"

"Well, do you know who he is to me?"

"Cepta said he's your father."

"Yes, that's right." She nods at me encouragingly, and I'm thinking about Xander and how he is with me, and contrasting that with how he is with other people, and there is some strand of memory tied up with him and me—and a tickle in my mind. I sense that Shay is there, inside me, gentle and soothing—taking away barriers, taking away blocks.

I frown. "Is he . . . I mean, I think he's my father too. Isn't he?" My head is whirling with knowing this—and realizing that somehow I always knew it; it was just hidden. I put the two things together and open my eyes wider.

157

"Does that mean that you're my sister?"

Shay smiles. "Yes. I told you that the first time I met you, but I'm not surprised you don't remember; you weren't very well then. I'm your sister. Half sister, that is. We had different mothers."

Mothers. And now my thoughts are going somewhere *else*, to a fractured image in my mind: dark hair, long and straight like mine. A quick smile, good-night kisses on my cheek. And all at once, it comes into closer focus, and I can see her clearly: *Mum*. And I'm hit with *pain* and *homesickness* and *wanting* her to hug me so much that I can barely stand it. And then there is my brother too, who'd tickle me and chase me around the house, and I'd run away screeching until Mum told us to be quiet, that the neighbors would call social services if I didn't stop screaming like that. There are tears hot on my cheeks.

Shay turns toward me; her hand is on my shoulder, and she is my sister but one I don't know—at least, not like I know Mum and Kai. But she is the closest thing I have to someone who is mine, and when I finally turn to her, her arms go around me. We squish Chamberlain between us a little, but he doesn't seem to mind.

And, as if she misses them as much as I do, Shay cries too.

CHAPTER 24

SHAY

"I FELT YOU WERE CLOSE TO SOMETHING," Xander says. "When you were joined with Persey, you seemed to have something almost figured out." He's all curiosity and wanting to *know*; no sadness for Persey, a young girl who loved him. Misguided she might have been, but she did. It was all through her thoughts even as she died.

"I might have been onto something," I say. "I'm not sure if it was real or just me hoping."

"Tell me. Maybe we can work it out together," he says, but I hesitate, not wanting to go there. He takes my hand. "There are more people who can be saved." And he is passionate about this. He desperately wants to help people survive . . .

And then, all at once, it is there—a realization, one I'm surprised I didn't reach before:

He wants there to be more survivors.

And I'm not sure what this means—when or how it started, or if it even matters now.

"Shay?" he prompts.

"All right," I say. "Remember when my hair regrew after it was burned off in that fire? I made it grow back straight, not curly—and what I did wasn't just acting on my hair itself, on the protein that makes it curl or grow straight. It was more than that."

"What did you do?"

"I'll show you—it's easier that way." His mind touches mine and I go back in time, remember what I did. I replay it for him, careful to keep my shields up at the same time so he only sees what I want him to see—as if that isn't enough—and as he relives it with me, incredulity takes over his aura.

"You changed your *genes*?" he says. "You reprogrammed the actual code in your cells to make your hair grow this way?"

"Yes."

"That's amazing," he says, and thoughts flicker through him too fast to follow—all the things that could be done. "This is true evolution, Shay: the moment humans can decide for themselves how they will change." His excitement and desire to know how to do this, to try it for himself, make his own blocks almost come undone, and I'm seeing him more clearly than I have before.

"But is that a good thing? To be able to decide how we evolve?" I say, and I want to feel his clarity, his certainty—not this doubt that clouds me inside.

"Straight hair doesn't hurt anyone, does it?"

"Well, no; I guess not. But I didn't think it through. I didn't really even know what I was doing then."

"You could save lives. Think about it, Shay. This could open a whole new world of medicine. If you could master this and apply it to others, you could potentially cure a range of genetic inherited conditions—maybe even metabolic diseases, like diabetes."

And I can't argue with what he's saying, yet I'm still uneasy thinking about this. Where would it stop if we could do these things? Are there boundaries in what we can do—what we *should* do?

"But for now, let's go back to the epidemic," Xander says. "How does this apply?"

"I'm not sure of this, not at all. But there were differences in junk DNA—marked differences—between Persey and myself. If this is what is different between survivors and those who die, if we can work out exactly what part of it is important to survival and track the genes involved—then it might be possible to change them."

"Using existing medical technology to effect genetic changes isn't impossible," he says. "But it would take time—more time than an ill person can spare. Do you think you could change genes in somebody else too?"

I shrug. "I don't know. I feel it should be possible to do it to another person if I'm joined with them; I'm not sure that I know how."

"You could try."

I tilt my head, look at him, considering. "Why me? I've explained it to you now. Why can't you try it?"

"I don't seem to have the same instinct for healing that you do."

And another realization, insight, into this man who is my father: maybe healing requires caring for others more than yourself. And he doesn't, does he? I'm sad for him. He cares for Callie—I know he does—but not enough. And maybe he cares a little for me too, but still . . .

Not enough.

I shake my head. "I don't think I can do it. I can't face it; do you understand? Joining with people who are dying, trying to save them, and failing. I can't go through it again."

"Rest, Shay. There will be another day. Think how you would have felt if Callie had been ill and you could have saved her, but didn't know how because you didn't develop the skills when you had the chance?"

"Callie's immune. And how *did* you know that, anyway? Cepta said Callie's only been here for maybe six months, but didn't you say she's been here all along—the whole year and a few months now since she's been missing? And this is a place that until recently the flu had never been."

There are ripples in his aura; he's annoyed but trying not to be.

"You misremember," he says. "I said I took Callie to Cepta to begin with, and that is true, but it wasn't here. I brought Callie here when the epidemic started to take hold; we went through infected areas on the way and she was fine, so it seemed likely she was immune."

I'm looking at him, and his words are reasonable—yet . . . There is doubt still, inside me.

"Was Callie on Shetland?" I ask.

"For a time. Not in the research institute; I have a house there—as you know, since you stayed there yourself."

"Did she know Jenna there?"

He's perplexed. "Why are you still so interested in Jenna?" I'm not sure what to say, and he looks at me for a moment, shakes his head. "Look. No matter what you may think, I care about Callie. If there is something you've worked out about her illness, tell me."

I pause, thinking, not sure at first what to tell him when so much of what he says seems slippery with half truths. But she is his daughter, after all. Maybe there is something he knows that will help me figure this out.

"I'm not sure her illness is an illness," I say, finally.

"What do you mean?"

"She seems to have some strange sort of tie to Jenna. She knew how Jenna died. Exactly. She couldn't have been with her, so how did she know? That's the nightmare she's been having."

"What? That doesn't make sense. Maybe she heard about it and made it up in her imaginings."

"No, it can't be that. Jenna shared her memory with me of when her physical body was destroyed in fire; Callie's nightmare was too like what really happened to be anything other than Jenna's actual memory. And I don't understand it either, but there's something there—something that connects Callie to Jenna, as if each of them is tangled up somehow with the other. And I don't think Cepta suppressing these memories—or nightmares, or whatever they are—has been helpful. Once Callie accepted it for what it was, she's been more or less fine."

"I just don't see how . . ."

"No. But it is what it is, however improbable."

"Cepta was doing her best with Callie."

"Oh? Or maybe she was holding on to Callie and her so-called illness, to hold on to you."

There is a flash of anger through his aura now, and I've only said what I thought, but maybe I've gone too far.

He quickly suppresses his anger. "You spend too much time thinking about the wrong things. Enough deflection, Shay. You need to focus on how to save someone from the epidemic, and then give it another try."

I cross my arms. "It's too late. Everybody who could catch it here has died."

"We'll find someone; there are places out there where this epidemic is still spreading, still killing people. What if you could help them—don't you want to?"

I shake my head. "It's not that I don't want to; I just *can't*." I get up, walk out, cutting off the conversation. I'm uneasy—and not completely sure why. If there is a chance, however small, that I could find a way to do this, shouldn't I try?

But how many more souls will I cradle and then lose?

I *can't* face it. Not again.

I walk back to the house, to Callie. Is she really better, or am I kidding myself? I remind myself what I came here to do: find Callie and take her home. But I have to be sure she is okay before we can try to leave this place.

Cepta is leaning against a tree in the path ahead of me, not moving, and when I suddenly notice her standing there, I jump.

We need to be vigilant, she whispers in my mind.

Why? What do you mean?

She looks both ways, as if scared someone may be listening.

Watch for the others. They'll come here soon. You'll see.

CHAPTER 25

CALLIE

THE SMOKE FROM THE PYRES hangs in the still air the next morning. No trace of breeze comes to chase it away.

Shay sleeps on, exhaustion so heavy on her that I leave her in peace.

I need to get away from the heaviness, into the trees.

Chamberlain follows me out the door. I close it quietly behind us and walk at first, then as the air starts to feel a little clearer, run. We go the opposite way from the camps of the others; they've had pyres there too.

I *have* to see it. I have to see the edge. Now that Cepta's not in my mind, will it still be there?

I race around the trees to the clearing and stop, panting, full of disappointment. The world still ends. I was so hoping I could step past this place, with the other things I can see and remember now, but no.

I lean against a tree, then sit on the ground. Chamberlain sits next to me.

There's a butterfly dancing in the sunlight; Chamberlain suddenly launches himself into the air but misses, and I laugh.

The butterfly goes a little higher but stays in Chamberlain's sight, almost like it is taunting him to have another go.

Then the butterfly flies ahead and vanishes where the world ends.

Chamberlain leaps after him—and he vanishes too. My stomach flips. Is he gone?

I call him, and a moment later, his head peeks back through—and it's weird: a disembodied head out of nothing.

Hand shaking, I reach out, touch him. Scratch his ear, stroke his head and down his back.

My hand vanishes too. I'm startled and yank it back. I try to do it again—to push my hand out—but now it won't go. There isn't a physical wall I can feel, but when I'm looking at it and at my hand, I can't force through it.

Butterflies and cats don't vanish and then reappear. Somehow there is a world beyond this place; there must be—one that I can't see.

I stand up and try to step into it, a bemused Chamberlain watching. Again and again I try, but there is something that won't let me step into nothing.

Annoyed, I'm about to head back—when I hear something.

Distant voices? And footsteps. It seems to be coming from the nothing. I listen, and the sounds are getting gradually louder. Whoever it is seems to be getting closer.

Chamberlain went into the nothing and came back again. Whoever I can hear is coming this way.

I'm scared. Who is it? Should I run back, tell somebody? Hide?

I step deeper into the trees to watch.

The sounds get closer. Finally somebody steps out of nothing into the clearing where I was a moment ago, and then another person and another follow.

I'm relieved. I recognize them. They're Community. The ones that left with the girl Shay called Beatriz a while ago. Are they all coming back?

No, not all. There are ten of them; there were more than that who left. And Beatriz isn't with them.

I stay hidden, watch them walk back to Community, wondering why they have come back here now.

Does the epidemic still hang in the air with the smoke?

If it does, they shouldn't have returned. They'll get sick too.

PART 4

PLANETARY EVOLUTION

All things must live and die,
even stars: the death of ancient stars
ejected complex new elements.
They combined and formed our
planets. And so, life uses death
for its own purposes.

—Xander, *Multiverse Manifesto*

QUARANTINE

CHAPTER 1

FREJA

THERE IS WARMTH, COMFORT. Peace. I wake slowly, and even when consciousness begins to find me, I don't rush it. My eyes stay closed.

Breathing—even, close, behind me. There is the weight of an arm across me, a hand curling around my stomach.

It's Kai.

Is this real?

If it's a dream, I don't want to wake up. I want to stay here forever.

But no matter how much I want it, I can't find sleep again, and I begin to awaken more and more. I start to feel overwhelmingly like I must move, stretch, change my position a little, like there is no way I can stay completely still any longer—but I don't want to wake him.

I'm afraid what will happen if I do.

Last night when I kissed Kai, I wasn't thinking. I wasn't planning what would be the best thing to say or do; instead my feelings for Kai were out in the open, not hidden away like they should have been.

And he held me, kissed me back, comforted me. And promised he would stay while I slept, that I'd be safe.

But the more I wake up, the more I panic inside. It was everything that happened when we were captured that made me so stupid. Being terrified what SAR would do if they worked out I was a survivor. My ill-thought-out escape plan. That soldier—I shiver in disgust inside when I think of him, his filthy hands and filthier thoughts. But the thing that sickens me more than anyone or anything else is *me*.

I lashed out at the soldier, hurt him. I may have been protecting myself, but I'd promised myself I would never, ever hurt anyone like that.

It makes what they think about survivors true.

It makes what they think about *me* true. I'm *other*. I'm different from them in ways they can never accept.

If I can't accept myself, how could anybody else?

And that wasn't all. The gun—on the ground. I took it. I had to use it, or he would have hurt me—hurt Kai too. I try to force the image of the soldier's bloody body out of my mind.

Was it all of that—fear, shock, and pain together—that made me do the other thing I'd promised myself I would never, ever do again? There was a night in the woods, ages ago now, when Kai and I were so close to crossing beyond the line of friendship, and he said no. *Never again*, I'd told myself then. If anything is ever going to happen between us, it has to come from him.

I squeeze my eyes shut tight to stop the tears from escaping. I broke both promises to myself. I used my mind to hurt, and I kissed Kai.

What will happen now?

Will he open his eyes, see me, and regret that it is me in his arms, not Shay?

And it's even worse. I never told him what she asked me to—that she was only leaving him to try to find his sister.

But she hurt him; she kept hurting him! He's my friend; I was only protecting him.

I didn't tell him, but it wasn't to make this happen. It wasn't.

I deny it to myself, but there is enough doubt casting shadows inside to torture me.

And anyway, last night changes things, doesn't it? Because I didn't tell him what she said, this, now—being in Kai's arms—is the worst betrayal. One he could never forgive if he knew what I've done.

There is only one way forward for Kai and me. I *have* to tell him the truth.

But apart from that, even if he isn't thinking of Shay anymore—and if he is here and now—will he still think that I'm not the one, not for him? He doesn't love me; I know this. He can't hide his aura, even if he wanted to: it's all there. He likes me, I know this. There is a degree of care and concern—like what you feel for a *friend*. A word that now feels like a curse.

If Kai wakes and I see his regret, part of me will die.

And so I stay still, to prolong now, to make this moment last as long as it can.

CHAPTER 2

KAI

WHEN I WAKE UP, FREJA IS HERE, still and warm in my arms, and for a moment, I almost panic. This wasn't supposed to happen.

How did this happen?

She stirs; she must sense I'm awake in that way she has—that all survivors have.

"Hi," she says. She turns a little, faces me, and her eyes—they're not like they usually are. They're naked. They're full. And she's here with me now, and part of me is convinced that is all that matters.

"Hi," I say back.

Then she's troubled. "There's something—some*one*—we have to talk about."

I shake my head. "No. You're wrong about that. Shay is gone from my life; I know she is. I could never trust her again."

She considers my words; her face has more peace than it did before. And I wonder: did I say this because it is true, or because Freja needed to hear it?

Even *if*. Even if I can accept I'll never see Shay again—it doesn't change how I feel.

But how I feel is more and more a confused mess inside.

I'm about to say something else—I don't even know what—when Freja shakes her head.

"No," she says. "Don't say it. Whatever it is. This isn't tomorrow or the day after. This is *now*. This is all it needs to be."

Before my words can be found, she kisses me, and she's right.

This is all that there is, and all that there needs to be.

CHAPTER 3

FREJA

WHEN I WAKE AGAIN KAI ISN'T HERE, and I start to panic, start to sit up. I want to *run*, but I don't know to where. Then I hear sounds—water running, movement in the small kitchen next door. I settle back down where I am in this warm place to stay quiet and think.

I was going to tell him. I was. But he interrupted me; he didn't want to talk about Shay. He said it was over.

And he kissed me back. He didn't have to. He'd had more time to think about whether it was something he wanted to do or not, and he did. A smile curves on my lips.

Like I've conjured him up he opens the door, two cups in his hands.

"The pantry is mostly empty or spoiled, but I did find some tea. The power is out, but the gas is still on, so I used the stove. It's black, though."

I sit up against the pillows.

"Black tea is perfect. Thank you." I feel weird, shy, like I'm being unnaturally polite and not how I should be with him. I have to get this right, I have to, but thinking it isn't helping. I take the cup from him, not raising my eyes enough to meet his.

He sits in the chair next to the bed.

"So," he says.

"So," I answer. "This is weird."

"It is, a little. Are you okay?" I sit up a bit more and turn to face him, and I'm scared of what he's asking and why.

"What do you mean?"

"Well, it's just all that happened yesterday, and then this."

I frown. "This?" I look at him again, then realize what I'd missed, and grin. "No way. *Seriously?*"

"What?"

"You're having a crisis of conscience. You're worried you've taken advantage of poor defenseless me at a weak moment, aren't you?"

"Have I?"

"I'm not poor or defenseless or weak. I make my own decisions."

"Yes, I know that. But—"

"No but. Nothing to worry about, Mr. Knight in Shining Armor. Maybe I was taking advantage of *you*."

"Oh, really?"

"Sure. I played maiden in distress and appealed to your protective side." I fall back, a hand raised dramatically to my brow. "Oh, he-elp. He-elp."

He laughs, and I know I've gotten it right. We're all right. Relief floods through me.

"What happens next?" he says.

"Well. My lips are a bit tired and possibly bruised, so no more kissing for the foreseeable, if you don't mind. But perhaps there are a few more somewhat important things we should work out."

"Well, yes. Such as, is SAR off our trail, or do we need to run?"

"A good question. Even if they somehow manage to trail us, where do we run to?"

"Lefty all but admitted they're wanted. We could go to the authorities, tell them where to find SAR."

"I'm not convinced that's a good idea for me as a survivor, though."

"Perhaps not." Kai leans back, thinking. "Now that I know from Lefty that it wasn't Callie who was with us before, finding my sister, or finding out what happened to her"—pain crosses his face—"is at the top of my list."

"Find Callie—how? Where do you start to look?"

"By finding Alex, or Xander, or whatever you want to call him. It's got to be him: either she'll be with him, or he'll know where she is or what happened to her."

"And what else is on the list?"

"I want the world to know what Alex has done," Kai says, and the anger and hate he has for this man are plain on his face and in the way he says his words, even without seeing the black in his aura. "Alex isn't the saint he's always held himself out to be, that most people accept. He deliberately caused this epidemic, didn't he? SAR backed that up. And he's a survivor too. He may have an obituary, but he's alive and well, and he has to pay for what he's done."

"All right. How about we find a way to tell the authorities about Alex and his role with SAR? Tell them where SAR can be found too— or at least where we last saw them. SAR is also hunting for Alex, so if the authorities set out to find them, they may also find Alex, and vice versa. And, as you said, finding Alex may lead you to your sister."

"But Freja, you were right. How can we go to the authorities? You're still a survivor. Still wanted for murder."

I scowl. "I'm not a murderer," I say, but then hear the lie. I didn't kill that policeman in London I'm wanted for, but what about the soldier last night? The gun, the blood, his body are in my mind again, and this time I can't push it away. We left too fast to be sure—but somehow I am. He's dead. I *am* a murderer. I look down, hiding my eyes.

Kai takes my hand. "That was self-defense," he says. "But they aren't necessarily going to take our word on that. *I* need to go to the authorities. You don't."

Panic starts rising inside me again. Is he trying to get rid of me after all? Is it because of what happened last night? But I look into his eyes, study his aura, and that's not it. There is only concern there, and it warms me.

"You can't get rid of me so easily. But whether it is you or both of us, how can this be done? Who can we tell?"

"As a starting point, I think we should try to contact my mother."

"Remind me again how she figures into things."

"She's a doctor, and a scientist—an epidemiologist. She was on the original task force looking for a cure and a way to control the epidemic. She should know who to go to with what we know. Assuming she believes me now."

"Why wouldn't she?"

"The last time I saw her and told her about the particle accelerator and the real cause of the illness, she couldn't accept it. I'm hoping she knows that is true by now, that she should have believed me before—that should make her listen to me now."

"Where is she?"

"Last time I spoke to her was when I was in Glasgow—the week before we met. She was still in Newcastle then."

"So then the next thing we should do is go to Newcastle."

"We?"

I pretend to look at something in my hand. "My schedule is pretty open: I could probably fit in a trip to Newcastle . . . let's see . . . after breakfast?"

"I don't think you should come with me. It isn't safe."

"What—shall I hang around here instead, and wait for SAR to turn up? No thanks."

"I don't want you to take any more risks for me."

"I know. But face it, Kai. Nowhere is safe right now, not for me. And I want to help."

He's uncomfortable. "You're right. I know you are. It's just . . ." He shakes his head and shrugs. "Let me think."

He pauses a moment, and I manage to resist the impulse to see what he is thinking. Then he meets my eyes. "How about this? Maybe I could get in touch with Mum, see if I can get her to meet us somewhere on our own. And not tell her you'll be there or who you are."

Relieved he hasn't decided to try to stash me somewhere—not that

176

he could—I nod. "Sounds like a plan. But get in touch—how? There's no power here, so no internet. How about phone lines?"

"I tried it before. The line here is dead."

"So then. We find another car and head south, toward Newcastle. Try to stay out of sight and to find internet or a phone to contact your mum along the way. Deal?"

Kai is looking back at me, considering what I said. He finally nods. "Deal."

CHAPTER 4

KAI

WE DO BETTER THAN A CAR: later that day we break into an auto shop up the road, and there I see what I was hoping for at last—a decent bike. I find the keys inside the door on a hook, and away we go. And with no traffic, no one manning the speed cameras, no traffic police, we go fast.

Freja pulls at my arm just as I hear it myself; there is a low sound and something approaching on the horizon. I brake, and we pull in under some trees. Soon it is close enough to see and hear that it is a helicopter. I glance at Freja and know what she's thinking: could it be SAR, come looking for us?

But it doesn't home in on us or seem to be checking the highway; it crosses it instead and moves on, off to business of its own. Without discussion we get off the bike to wait a little, in case it doubles back.

Freja's crazy hair—the red grown out more, the blond catching the afternoon sun—is more of a mess than usual from the wind on the back of the bike, and I reach out a hand without thinking, start to comb it loosely with my fingers. She tilts her head a little, and then we're kissing.

This not-thinking thing seems to be working well; I don't want to mess it up.

We somehow *fit*—her height close enough to mine—but not just that way. . .

No, Kai, no thinking.

Soon we're heading back up the road again. She leans into me as the bike corners, and here in this moment, I can imagine I'm happy. There is the not thinking, the sunshine, the open road. The bike and the beautiful girl.

Given enough time, maybe imagined happiness could start to feel like the real thing.

CHAPTER 5

FREJA

WE SEE THE SMOKE IN THE DISTANCE before anything else. We stash the bike, go closer on foot to investigate. It drifts lazily on the breeze from a chimney in a farmhouse. It looks so ordinary, like we've stepped back into the world as it was before the epidemic. But we're still in the quarantine zone, so it's likely either survivors—though not being very careful to stay hidden if they are—or the immune, or army.

I pull on Kai's arm to draw him deeper into the trees. "Let me see if I can work out who is there," I say in a low voice, and he nods.

I *reach*.

There's a dog in a front room, dozing in front of the fireplace, too warm, too lazy to move. He finally stirs, and I watch through his eyes. There's a man in a chair, a book in his hands; I can see a faint *I* for *immune* tattooed on his hand. He's old, maybe seventy at least—white hair at his temples. The dog turns his head at a noise, jumps up, tail wagging, and goes through a door into a kitchen. There is a woman there, younger by perhaps thirty years. She's taking something out of an AGA cooker that is making the dog drool even as she nudges him away: a roast chicken? They've got power—there is a microwave with a red blinking clock. She reaches into it to take something out and turns it off right away. I watch her until she takes off the oven mitts and I can see her hand: she's immune too.

I cast about the house, overgrown gardens, outbuildings. There are chickens, a few cows, and that is it. No other people.

I withdraw, come back to myself. "There are two adults, both with immune tattoos, in the house—no one else," I say. "They've got power; there might be a phone or internet?" Kai doesn't say anything; he's looking at me uneasily. "What?"

"Your eyes. They changed."

"That's what happens when you *reach*. Haven't you seen that before with Shay?"

The words are out before I can call them back, stop myself from saying her name.

He hesitates, then shakes his head. "No. At least, never up close like that. I remember once Shay asked me if her eyes had changed, and I thought I saw something but wasn't sure."

"What was it like? In my eyes?" I'm curious, because even though I've caught glimpses of this with other survivors' eyes, I've never seen my own do that. When I *reach* out like that, I lose all sense of myself.

"It's hard to explain; the definition between the pupil and the iris is lost. Like, you know when someone focuses in close and their pupils get smaller? And then if they focus into the distance, they get bigger? It's like that, but almost like it's back and forth so fast all you see is a blur of the black of your pupils swirling in your eyes."

And now I'm looking into Kai's normal eyes with mine—the ones that can be weird and do things eyes shouldn't be able to do—and trying to imagine what it would feel like, to see something like that in someone close to you.

"So, what do you think?" I say. "Is it totally awful?"

Kai shakes his head. "Just something to get used to. It goes with the rest of you, like your stripy hair." He grins and reaches and pulls my hair, and he's kidding around now, but I know: it *is* weird for him. He's uneasy, as much as he tries to pretend that he isn't.

I'm different. Other.

And I always will be.

CHAPTER 6

KAI

FREJA KNOCKS ON THE DOOR and then steps back, next to me.

There's barking inside, and then the sounds of locks clinking, and the door opens. It's the old man Freja described as we walked here, and he's holding a shotgun, and it is pointed at us. Behind him stands the woman, her hand holding the dog's collar; despite the gun and growling dog, she looks scared.

"What do you want?" the man says.

I hold my hands out, show they are empty. "We don't mean you any harm. We need some help."

"Help? Doesn't everyone these days." He lowers the gun a little. "What sort of help?"

"Information. A telephone or the internet if possible." The smell of food is coming out the door, and it's all I can do not to drool.

"And I expect you're hungry." He snorts.

"A little," I admit.

"It may be that we need some help too—a different sort. Around the farm. Maybe we can make a deal?"

Hard labor is what they're after. Maybe they're taking advantage of our situation, but it feels good using my muscles until I'm exhausted, until I can't think. There are so many things not to think about.

Callie.

Shay.

Alex too, but the second he flits through my mind, I find more energy until finally the old man, Angus, comes out.

"Haven't you had enough, lad?"

Angus and his daughter—Maureen—are both immune, as Freja had seen from their tattoos. They are all that is left of their friends and family.

They chose to come back here, into the zone—to return to their farm. Home. They were discouraged, prevented really, from doing so at first. But the zones have broken down enough that after a while there was no one there to stop them.

The news they told us at lunch was almost enough to take my appetite. The epidemic continued its relentless march while we were cut off from what was happening. Maybe not as fast as it once did. There's a whisper inside that Shay had said Callie-who-wasn't-Callie was the real carrier. So with her gone, it's spreading the traditional way: person-to-person contact. It's slower, so the progression has slowed down too.

But Angus and Maureen had another theory. They said it's due to the survivors are being rounded up, *dealt with*. Stopped from spreading death.

I held Freja's hand tight under the table.

Our story, worked out on the way to their front door, was that Freja had been trapped far into the zone, that I'd gone to find her— that we're both immune. That the reason she hasn't gotten an immune tattoo is because she was in the center of the epidemic, where there is no authority. But this meant there was nothing either of us could say to defend survivors. Or else they'd be suspicious of Freja.

Back inside, Freja droops against my shoulder.

"Tired?"

"Yes. I've been weeding. So many weeds!"

Angus raises an eyebrow. "Kai is a better worker than you are." He nods at me.

"I'm not made for manual labor," Freja says.

"You did all right for one not used to it," Maureen says, in a grudging tone. "Anyway, Dad has something he wants to say."

He clears his throat, pours everyone a glass of wine. The way he handles the bottle, I can tell: it's precious.

"Something to ask, more like," he says.

I exchange a glance with Freja.

"Now hear me out before you say anything. I know you've got places you want to go, things to do. But the world out there isn't the same. Why don't you stay with us? I can't manage the work anymore. And we're sick of each other's company." He glances at his daughter.

He asks us to think about it and not reply yet, and there is a part of me wondering about what he says. What if isolated places like this are soon all that is left in the UK? Or maybe even the world. Maybe there is nothing to be done beyond getting through it, surviving.

Staying here wouldn't be so bad. With Freja.

Working so hard I can't think.

"I'm sorry. We can't do that," Freja says. Her words are stiff. "And now that we've done as you've asked today, can we use the internet?"

Angus exchanges a glance with his daughter. There is guilt on his face.

"Well now. It does work, or at least it did the last time we tried. But . . ."

"But what?"

"The generator. We're almost out of fuel. We can't waste it on the computer."

CHAPTER 7

FREJA

"THEY TRICKED US!" I'm furious.

"Not exactly. Well, maybe a little."

"You know they did."

It's the next morning and we're bouncing up the road in a dilapidated truck, empty cans in the back: ones we must fill with fuel for the farm before they'll let us turn on their computer. And from the sounds of things, everywhere with fuel in a reasonable stretch of miles that was easy to find they've already found.

"Let's double back and pick up your bike. What if we can't find any gas and run out?"

Kai hesitates, then nods. He turns around at the junction, leaves me in the truck while he goes on foot to where we stashed the bike.

"Let's just leave now," I say when he gets back. "Let's go to Newcastle and look for your mum—not worry about trying to contact her first."

He shakes his head. "We haven't got much fuel left in the bike either. We wouldn't get far."

I help him heave the bike into the back with the empty cans.

"So how about we drive as far as we can in the truck, then leave it and continue on the bike?"

"What would they do to find fuel without their truck?"

"They're going to have to get used to not having any at some point if supplies aren't being replenished. Why not sooner instead of later?"

"That's a bit cold. He's an old man, Freja."

"I don't trust him. There's something in his aura—he just *feels* wrong."

"Is that because of what they said about survivors?"

"No!" Then honesty makes me add: "Well, not entirely."

"It's what they've been told—that survivors spread the epidemic. They don't know any different."

"Well, they're both immune anyway, aren't they? So even if I were a carrier, why should they care? The only people around out here are immune—everyone else has left or died. It's not just that, and you know it. They find the very idea of someone living and breathing and being that different from them abhorrent. And if they knew what I was, they'd feel the same about me."

"Maybe if they got to know you and then you told them you are a survivor, explained how they've got things wrong, they'd understand."

"And maybe Angus would get out his shotgun again."

Kai has nothing to say to that, and we continue on in silence. He didn't have to say it out loud earlier; I could tell there was part of him that thought staying there with them on that farm wouldn't be such a bad thing. He'd be tempted if he didn't still need to try to find his sister and mum, and get revenge against Alex. And considering the state of the world and the options available, it's kind of hard to argue: at least on a farm, chances are, we wouldn't starve.

But I could never, ever do it—not with how they'd feel about me if they found out what I am. And how long could I hide it?

I glance at Kai as he drives. Sometimes he seems like the right fit, as if he were made just for me: *the one*—whatever that means. And sometimes I don't know who he is.

I sigh. No, that's not it. It's more that he doesn't know who I am—that's what is bothering me, isn't it? Kai is constant, steady. You really do know where you are with him.

It's me who is the problem: different, *other*.

Not quite human, like Kirkland-Smith said.

Kai nudges my shoulder with his. "You okay?"

"Sure. Fine."

"Could you get out the map Angus gave us? I can't remember the next turn."

I unfold it. Angus has marked places in red that have been checked and have no fuel, villages where they've already been and siphoned what they could from abandoned cars. They'd debated the best place to try that was within the reach of this truck, and decided the only place we could get to before running out of fuel was an abandoned air force base. Not too far away—but far enough that we don't have enough in the tank for a return trip if we don't find any. Angus hadn't tried it yet, not sure if there was anyone holed up in there. He said that it looked completely deserted, but that there were CCTV cameras that swiveled when you went up to it.

"Are we definite that going to the RAF base is a good plan?" I say.

"No, just the least bad idea. Are you sure you want to come with me?"

Kai had suggested before that I could hide some distance away and wait for him, but there is something about letting him out of my sight—no. I can't do it. Even though they're not likely to be as crazy as SAR, anyone in the air force might still want to lock me up if they work out what I am, or if they realize I'm wanted for murder in London. And maybe Kai, as well, if they've linked my escape from London to him by now. And didn't he say he broke out of jail a while back in Scotland too?

I shake my head. "This is crazy, but if you're going there, then so am I. If it isn't deserted, I'll be able to tell. Besides, have you got any other ideas?"

"Apart from keep going until we run out of fuel? No."

I peer at the map. "Okay, it's the next left."

After a while there are signs directing us to the base, and I put the map away. We're driving through lush, green countryside. Farms and fields are overgrown, abandoned. With the people gone, it is a riot of rich life, left to grow as it will without any restraint.

Just how I'd like to be.

CHAPTER 8

KAI

"HOW DO I LOOK?" FREJA ASKS, and pirouettes, wearing a truly appalling sun hat. It's wide-brimmed and covered in bright-pink flowers. Yesterday Maureen had insisted she wear it while working in the garden. Freja is too pale to handle the sun and so had a ready excuse for needing to take it along with us today.

"Awesome, oh yes," I say. "It suits you perfectly."

She punches me, hard, in the arm.

"Ouch!" I rub my arm.

I've got a more respectable baseball cap on, found near Angus's back door when no one was looking. It's not as big and floppy as Freja's but should do the job if I'm careful not to turn toward the cameras. It would have been hard to explain just why we needed hats to hide from CCTV—assuming anyone is monitoring it, that is. We're both wanted by the authorities, and somehow I get the sense this is the sort of thing it'd be best not to mention to Angus.

Not that he thinks anything of getting us to steal fuel from any available source. I don't imagine that dead people much care if you siphon their tank dry, but to be fair, an air force base might be different: the government isn't always that willing to share, whether they need it themselves or not.

"Okay, now let me do my thing and see if I can sense if anyone is around the place," Freja says. This time she closes her eyes. Did she do that so I couldn't see them go weird like the last time? I feel a twinge of guilt. It did bother me a little, and it's hard to hide things from her.

A few minutes pass, and then a few more. Just as I'm wondering what is taking so long, she opens her eyes and frowns. "I'm unsure what is going on. I thought at first that I might have sensed a few auras—or one at least, anyway—that could have meant one or more people were there. But when I looked closer, I couldn't find anyone. Then I had a good check around the place using insects, a bird, even a mouse. I didn't see any people. The grass is overgrown, and the whole place looks deserted."

"Why do you say it *could* have meant people? What else could an aura be, apart from human?"

"It could also have been a cat; sometimes I sense them like that—but I couldn't find a cat anywhere. It might have run off, though. There is also one other possibility."

"What's that?"

"It could be a survivor, one who sensed me and is blocking so I can't find them. Or someone like you, who isn't a survivor but knows how to block—but that's not very likely, since it isn't easy to learn and they'd need a survivor to teach them."

"What do you think we should do?"

"Check it out. From what I've sensed and seen, I don't think there is any sort of military presence."

"You could be wrong."

"Yes." She shrugs. "But it might have just been a cat. And if there is a survivor there, or someone taught by a survivor, even if they are military, I don't think they'd be against us."

"Okay then." I adjust the angle of my baseball cap to cover my face more. "Onward."

191

We walk up to the entrance; we left the truck parked down the road a little. There's one of those bars that lifts up to allow cars through when someone in a guard booth pushes a button.

"Don't look up," Freja says, "but Angus was right: there is a camera on the side of the building next to the fence that is swiveling to follow us. Someone must be in there watching."

"Unless it works automatically with motion sensors?"

"Maybe."

"There doesn't seem to be a bell to ring. Should we knock?"

"It's probably best to appear nonthreatening," Freja says. "Or at least as nonthreatening as we can look with hats carefully shielding our faces from the cameras."

"Hello?" I call out. We wait a few moments; nothing happens. "Shall we?"

I tug at the bar that blocks the road to see if it is one we can move out of the way manually, but it won't budge.

We bend down to go underneath it.

The place has an abandoned feeling. Grass that is probably usually kept at a precision length is overgrown; weeds are taking over flower beds. There are a few empty vehicles behind the building by the entrance—they might have some gas we can siphon, but we're hoping for bigger stores than that. A road leads to a hangar and airfields beyond. Some other buildings are in a clump the other way.

"I wonder if jet fuel would do the trick?" Freja says. "They must have supplies for the airfield."

"Maybe, but I'm not sure what that'd do to Angus's generator!"

"Let's look through the place and make sure no one is here."

We knock on the door of the building by the fence first. I call out hello again, try the handle. Locked. I'm looking for a rock to break in when Freja nudges me and points. There's a small open window. "I should be able to get through that," she says.

I give her a lift up, and she squeezes through, opens the door a moment later. She flicks a switch. No power.

We go in, check offices, a boardroom, a small kitchen, bathrooms. All appear dusty and deserted.

We step out the door and start down the road to the clump of buildings opposite the airfield.

Then there's a vague pressure in my mind.

A prickling feeling on the back of my neck.

I *push* back and feel whatever it is retreat—but not before I sense a feeling of puzzlement before it is completely withdrawn.

"Freja? I think someone just tried to jump into my head. I pushed them out."

She stops walking for a moment, closes her eyes. Opens them again a moment later. "I can't sense anyone. I'm guessing it is a survivor who has worked out I'm a survivor too and you aren't, and so tried to find out who we are through you. They wouldn't know you can detect and block them. I'll see if anyone answers a hail."

She's quiet again for a moment.

"I still can't sense anyone, and whoever it is won't answer."

"Why do you think they are hiding from us?"

"I don't know. Maybe they're scared? Survivors get hunted. They're being cautious."

"Or maybe they want to check us out before they attack."

"I can't believe that. Let's see if we can find them."

We start to walk toward one building, but then I stop. "No. This isn't where they are," I say.

She looks at me oddly. "Okay then, Einstein, how do you know that?"

"There was a weird sort of sense of relief I could feel when we started walking toward it."

"Shall we try the next one, then?" We continue on to the next building, a larger one. "Don't look up. There are more cameras on this one," she says.

There's a sudden increase of pressure on my mind, and I flinch and push the stranger out. "Someone tried again," I say. "Harder this time. I think we should check this building—I get the feeling they don't want us to go there."

"It's weird that you are catching a sense of what they think. Maybe whoever it is doesn't quite know what they are doing—either they're new at being a survivor, or they haven't been around many people to have had much practice. You could let them into your mind, introduce yourself?" She looks annoyed that her attempts to contact whoever it is are coming up with nothing.

"Not likely. What if they're not friendly?"

She looks contrite. "Sorry, you're right. If you let them in, you have no defense."

Her words float around in my mind as we're walking up the path to the door. *No defense?*

Shay and Freja are the only ones I've ever let into my mind by choice, and that was with trust. Does that mean that if I let somebody into my mind, they can control me or do whatever damage they want? Like the time Shay sent me to sleep: I couldn't stop that from happening.

I knock on the door, call out, "Hello?"

We wait a moment, then try the handle. It's not locked, and I'm surprised.

"Maybe whoever it is *wants* us to go through this door, but I was sure they didn't want us to come this way," I say. "Let's have a look around outside instead?"

We walk around the building. Something moves to the side, and I turn quickly—oh. "Look," I say to Freja.

A black cat with a white nose and socks stares at us intently from under a tree.

"Could that be all it was all along? A cat?" I ask her.

She shakes her head, then walks up to the cat slowly, bending down, hand outstretched. It looks at her, then runs away.

"It couldn't have just been that cat," she says. "For a start that was a well-fed cat with a shiny coat, so either it is a hell of a mouser, or someone is looking after it. And I've never heard of anyone being *reached* out to by a cat. *Reaching to* a cat is one thing, but the other way would be something else entirely." She frowns. "Yet I can't seem to reach *that* cat, which is odd: perhaps someone is blocking me."

"What next?"

We look around us. The overgrown lawn behind the building slopes down; there's a low concrete structure below us.

194

"What's that?" Freja says, pointing to it.

"Looks like an outbuilding or something?"

We walk down to it and around, and on the other side of the concrete, there are stairs. They go down, cut deep into the earth. The concrete juts out from the ground around the stairs.

"It could be some sort of bunker, maybe?" I say.

We hesitate at the top of the stairs, then start down them. The air temperature drops with every step, and a shiver goes up my back.

There is a serious door at the bottom.

"I'm guessing we'll never be able to break into this one," Freja says.

Just as we're wondering what to do next, the door opens.

CHAPTER 9

FREJA

A GIRL PEERS OUT AT US—maybe fourteen or fifteen years old. She has dark hair and eyes, and the bright aura of a survivor.

"Azra! I told you not to open the door!" a boy says, peering around her shoulder. A few years younger than she is, and he's a survivor too.

"No one wearing a hat like *that* could possibly be dangerous," she answers, an upturned eyebrow at the flowery monstrosity on my head. I take it off.

"Hi. I'm Freja, and this is Kai."

"What do you want?" the boy demands.

The girl gives him an impatient look. "I'm Azra, and this rude boy is Wilf."

Hi, Azra; hi, Wilf, I say silently while Kai says hello out loud.

"You blocked me. How'd you do that?" Wilf says to Kai.

"Easy-peasy, once you know how."

Wilf's eyes are wide.

"Now that we're all nicely introduced, what exactly *do* you want?" Azra asks.

"Well, we actually came here looking for fuel. We weren't sure if the cameras meant someone was watching the place still—so I wore this," I say, and waggle the hat. "To stay incognito."

"It's just us," Wilf says. "I worked out how to use the cameras! I was watching you the whole time."

Now Azra glares at him: is it because he said they were on their own? And I reassure her. *It's okay, as you said—we're not dangerous.*

"You two are here by yourselves?" Kai asks, concern in his voice.

"So what? We're fine," Azra says. *I'd be even finer completely alone*, she adds in an aside to me with another impatient look at Wilf. And I'm pleased she's talking to me like this now. "You might as well come in," she says out loud, then turns and goes back through the door.

"Come on! I'll show you. It's really cool," Wilf says, and we follow him in, down more stairs with dim lights on the walls—they have power? Well obviously, they must, to operate the cameras. At the bottom of the stairs, we go through another heavy door.

And it *is* cool: it looks like a control room, like something out of a spy movie.

"What is this place?" Kai asks.

"A bunker! You know, so in the event of war or nuclear fallout or something, the command from the base could hide away in here and direct stuff from underground."

"Did the air force just abandon it?"

"Most of them cleared out of the base when the epidemic got close," Azra says. "Some of them came here instead, but they died in this bunker—they must have been sick before they got in and locked the doors."

"Azra thinks they are ghosts," Wilf says.

"I do not!" she says sharply. "Anyway, one of them must have realized they were dying and tried to leave—we found a body up above. He left it unlocked. The others died down here."

There is a flash through her mind of the two of them moving the bodies. They couldn't get them up all the stairs, but there's some sort of back emergency exit. They put them out there and locked it. The doors all seal, but no wonder she thinks there are ghosts.

I do not.

Survivors hear the dead: we can't help it.

And there is a shock of pain and fear and something else inside her.

You mean . . . I'm not . . . going crazy?

No. Definitely not.

She's so prickly on the outside, but she's just hiding, covering up—being the older one who decides things so Wilf doesn't have to. Like I used to with my little sister. An involuntary wave of sympathy flows from me to her, and this time she doesn't push it away. And at the same time, I'm hiding a little part of me inside, where she won't see it—one that is shaken deep down. It's *this* feeling—talking to another survivor, using our minds. I've missed it *so much*. I'd felt like I was pining for some sort of deeper connection with Kai, but was it actually this I've been missing all along?

"How did the two of you end up in here on your own?" Kai says.

"The usual," Azra says. "Everyone died or left. We both got sick but didn't die. I ran away from the authorities—while there were still any here to run away from. Eventually I found Wilf and Merlin hiding on the base. Wilf's dad was in the air force."

"Merlin?"

"The cat," Azra says, and gestures to where he's been watching us from a high shelf, green eyes blinking. He meowed when she said his name but doesn't look inclined to get any closer.

"So then you moved in here?"

"It seemed logical. We're hidden. If we lock the doors, nobody can get in. There are endless supplies." She shrugs like it was no big deal, but it *was*. The traces I caught of what they found here . . . I shake my head.

You're a smart girl. Brave.

Don't forget gorgeous and amazing. She says it sarcastically, but I can tell she's pleased, that it's been a long time since anyone has said anything nice to her—too long. Not sure how she'd react, I stop myself from hugging her.

Wilf grabs Kai's arm and wants to give him a tour. Azra and I trail behind, still having a silent conversation all our own as we go. There are rooms to sleep in and supplies, like Azra said, of long-life food and water that stretch on and on in a storeroom full of high shelves. Not quite endless, but they'd last a good long while if they were meant to keep the air force command going through a war or nuclear attack.

There is power—some special system built into the place—but they don't know what runs it. There is no power in the surrounding towns and villages.

They're not sure, but there may be supplies of gasoline on the base; Wilf says they used to fill up here, that he thinks he knows where it was kept.

And there are also actual working computers. They have internet.

CHAPTER 10

KAI

FIRST THINGS FIRST. We explain to Azra and Wilf what we need to do—find a way to contact my mum in Newcastle.

Azra shakes her head. "She may have been doing research in Newcastle a while ago, but I doubt she is still there. Pretty much all the government stuff shifted west and south when the zones started breaking down. They'd have been too far from power and supplies there."

"Not enough bunkers," Wilf chimes in.

I shake my head. "I didn't think of that. How will we find her?"

"The old-fashioned way?" Wilf says, and opens a search box. "What's her name?"

Freja and I exchange a glance: it can't hurt to try. "Dr. Sonja Tanzer," I say.

I'm not expecting anything recent, so I'm surprised when a link to a research center set up to study the epidemic comes up. We click through another page.

Assuming this is correct, she's in Welshpool—in Wales. I curse under my breath, trying to work out how long it will take to get there, and how much gas we'll need.

"Can we contact her?" Freja says. "By email or something?"

"I can't do it directly," I say. "The last time we spoke, some sort of SWAT team swooped down on me twenty minutes later."

"Cool!" Wilf says.

"It really wasn't cool at the time." My stomach twists, remembering how one of them, whoever they were, went up in flames for no reason. Spontaneous combustion isn't something you want to witness, but if it hadn't been for the fire, it was unlikely I would have managed to get away.

"How about we make up a profile to contact her, one that isn't traceable to any of us?" Freja says.

"I've got about a dozen identities online," Azra says. "Wilf probably more. We can't be ourselves online either."

We talk it through and after a while come up with a plan, which begins with me emailing Mum—but not directly to any personal email address. Instead, we'll send a message through the Contact Us link on the center website.

It seems odd with everything going on that a thing like this is still in place. They wouldn't expect me to contact her that way. I hope. And I'll email as if I'm Bryson—a man who was infected and must have died soon after I left Newcastle. He was there the last time I was with Mum; there are things only the three of us would know. She'll work out that it's me, won't she? Again, I hope.

I fiddle the words around back and forth, and finally come up with this:

Dear Dr. Tanzer,

I'm sure you'll remember me: I'm Bryson, from the temporary base we set up in Newcastle during the initial outbreaks. I recall our day out in Newcastle very well; that girl we met left a mark on me, for sure. I'm being transferred to Cardiff and was hoping we could catch up on my way past?

And then I give an email address Wilf set up for this purpose.

"So this girl cut his arm and infected him, and he took off his biohazard suit because he knew that was it for him?" Freja says.

"Yes. Just the three of us were there. I suppose Bryson could have told somebody about it? But I doubt anybody he could have told would have lived through the outbreak. And if anyone is monitoring these messages, hopefully they won't know anything about Bryson or what happened to him. Everything was chaotic there then. Assuming anyone is even bothering to monitor Mum or trying to trace me anymore."

All we can do now is wait and see if she answers.

Next we check the news. What has been happening in the world while we've been away from any contact?

And it's much like Angus and Maureen said. It looks like quarantine measures are finally holding, at least in some places; there are areas of the UK that are still free of the epidemic.

But so very few of them. Most of Wales is all right. Ireland never really got hit—just stray cases and small outbreaks. There are odd pockets free of it here and there in southern England, and some islands, down south and in Scotland also. I remember Shay's friend Iona—the one who helped me find Shay when she was ill. Her family farm was cut off and the roads blocked. Are they still okay? I have no way of finding out.

We watch a news bulletin from BBC Wales: the main source of news now. The sense of optimism seems to be getting stronger. Despite the devastation in most of the country, hope seems to be returning.

Maybe the country can recover.

"Out loud, please," Freja says.

"Where does that leave us?" Azra says. "Not you," she says to me. She gestures at Freja and Wilf. "Us survivors. No one wants us."

Even though she is the one who asked them to speak out loud, now I can tell Freja is talking to them silently. Not that I'm not used to it whenever survivors are around.

Like she notices my reaction, Freja shakes her head. "Sorry. I slipped back to talking like that without realizing. I was telling them that there are groups of survivors in places. There was Patrick and the others, a group we were with for a while—I could try to contact them again; maybe we could get them to meet up with you two? There were a few teenagers, the rest adults—they were fine when we left them. Last time we saw them, they were thinking of traveling north to join another group of survivors in Scotland."

As she says that, I wonder: is the group in Scotland part of Alex's bunch—Multiverse? Is he at the center of these survivor groups—did he contact Patrick's group about joining together?

Maybe Patrick would know where Alex is.

"Do you know how to get in touch with them?" I ask.

"I think so. I didn't use the dark net Patrick set up, so I don't know how to contact them there, but I could try the website where I met JJ ages ago. It's got secret forums. Maybe he still checks it. Do you want me to try?" Freja asks the question out loud, but I can tell it is really aimed at Azra and Wilf, not me.

Azra shrugs. "I don't know. Maybe." She's being casual about it, like she doesn't care, but she must want to be with other people—and she should be. She can't stay alone with Wilf in a bunker underground forever, no matter how long the supplies might last. But what if it *is* that Multiverse crowd?

"I'm not sure about this. What if that website you met JJ on is being monitored now?" I'm giving Freja a let's-talk-about-this look.

She raises an eyebrow, and I know what she means—what she is asking permission for—and as much as I don't like it, I nod.

Is something wrong? she asks me, silently.

Maybe. We need to talk about this first.

All right.

"Maybe we should think about this for a while," I say out loud. "How about in the meantime we try to find that fuel?"

CHAPTER 11

FREJA

WILF WAS RIGHT ABOUT THE LOCATION of gas supplies on the base, and he even knew where the keys were kept. He's had a lot of time on his hands to explore.

Kai fetches the truck while we work out the emergency release for the boom gate so he can drive it onto the base. Now that we know it is just Wilf and Azra who monitor the cameras, at last I can be out in the fresh air without that appalling hat.

And I wonder why we're even doing this—getting fuel for the tanks in the back of Angus's truck. We've found what we need here: internet and supplies. Surely we're not going to take this truck back to Angus? Maybe this is just Kai's way of distracting us from attempting to contact other survivors—if we even can.

I can't see what his problem with it is, anyway. He was always a bit funny about being with that group of survivors—even though I could tell he liked and trusted Patrick.

But he doesn't like being the different one.

Who does?

When Kai drives the truck through the gate, Wilf and I get in the front with him, and Wilf directs Kai to the pumps. Azra went back to the bunker, saying something about making dinner.

There's no power on the base generally, just in the bunker. Filling the tanks is slow without it; it's a matter of siphoning small amounts and then transferring to the tanks. Wilf is soon bored and wanders off.

"Alone at last," Kai says, heaving a full tank onto the back of the truck, then getting an empty one to replace it.

"Why are we doing this? You're not still thinking we'll take them back to the farm—or are these supplies for us?"

"We can't leave them stranded without fuel or a truck—so yes, it needs to go back."

"Aren't other things more important?"

He meets my eyes. "Yes and no."

"Hmmm. And now is your chance to talk like you said you wanted to. What was bothering you earlier, Kai?"

"Lots of things: the state of the world, my family—and their whereabouts—kids like Azra and Wilf left on their own. We can't leave them here like this; what do we do?"

"It's not for us to decide, Kai. Look at all the two of them have managed so far." His eyebrows are going up, and I'm shaking my head. "I'm not saying we shouldn't offer help. Just don't be surprised if it is refused."

"They're not exactly adults. Should they decide what to do?"

"The world has changed."

"Don't I know it. Just because they're survivors doesn't mean they know what's what at their age."

"I didn't say that it did. But—"

"I just get the feeling you think anyone who is a survivor is vastly superior to everybody else. Like suddenly a twelve-year-old can make grown-up decisions."

"I never said anything of the kind! But you don't know how it is to be as they are. How would you know what's right for them better than they do?"

There's a pause, an uncomfortable one.

"Look, Kai. I really think the best thing we can do for them is get them to hook up with Patrick's group or another like it. I think once they've thought about it some more, that is what they'll want to do."

"What if Patrick and the others are with Multiverse and Alex?"

"We don't *know* that they are."

"We do know there was a mysterious group in Scotland that contacted them, asked them to go there and join up."

"Scotland is a big place."

"Survivors are, what—one in fifty thousand, something like that? What was the population of Scotland? How many groups could there actually be?"

I frown. "Math isn't my thing. Anyway, apart from Alex, nobody else we met in Multiverse was a survivor—that doesn't exactly make a *group*."

"Shay, Elena, and Beatriz have joined them, though." Kai manages to say their names without wincing, either visibly or internally, and despite my irritation at this conversation, I still notice this. I'm relieved he can say her name without it being a big thing.

"They did, but that was well after Patrick was communicating with whoever it was."

"I just have a bad feeling about contacting them. Aren't there any other options for Azra and Wilf?"

"Like what? Turn them in to the authorities and hope they've given up on the institutionalization or murder of survivors? I don't think so."

The last tank is full now, and Kai heaves it onto the back of the truck with the others.

"What now, then?" Kai says.

"If you want to take the truck back to the farm, go ahead. I'll wait here; I don't want to leave them."

Kai wants to get going instead of having dinner, and Azra packs some food for him. I manage to get her to hold back Wilf while I walk out to the truck with Kai. The bike is full of gas too, for his return, and he's managed to squeeze it back on the truck with the tanks.

"Well. Okay, bye, then," Kai says. "I'll be back tomorrow."

He stands there, a bit awkward—shifting from one foot to the other. Is he that impatient to get away from me?

"Kai?"

He turns toward me, and there is something else there, in his aura—some worry he hasn't shared.

I slip my hand around his back to tug him closer, and all at once he hugs me tight like he doesn't want to let go.

"Make sure you're still here when I get back," he whispers into my hair.

"You do have a history of losing girls," I say, surprised that I dare. "But don't worry; I'm hard to get rid of." And without waiting to see if he reacts to what I said, I kiss him, and he kisses me back until the world melts away.

A moment later I watch him disappear up the road, confused how I can feel one way one moment and another the next.

Is something wrong? It's Azra. She's standing in the shadow of the building behind me.

I don't know.

Nice kiss.

You were watching?

Not much to do here but watch things. She's sort of teasing and wistful at once.

We need to get you away from here before Wilf seems like a good option.

She shudders. *As much as I like the brat—and don't tell him I said that—that'll SO never happen.*

Over a dinner of tasteless reconstituted long-life spaghetti and meat sauce, we three have a meeting to talk about what Azra and Wilf should do. Wilf has some interesting suggestions, like traveling to the coast, building a boat, and sailing around the world. But eventually we get around to the option I'd raised earlier: contacting other survivors and maybe thinking about joining them.

And it's unanimous: they want to try.

Doing this when Kai isn't here feels wrong: I know he won't like it. But for so long now, we've been on *his* quests: first, to find Shay; now, his sister, and dealing with Alex. I've gone along—I've been there for him. I did everything I could to help and protect him on the way. Even though he maybe wouldn't agree with me not telling him what Shay said if he knew about it, I'm still certain it was the best way to help him. My friend.

Maybe now he's something more, even though I'm not sure quite what that *something more* may be.

Or may become.

Just the same: this is one time he doesn't get a vote. It is all about Azra and Wilf.

Back on the computer, first we check the email address Kai gave to his mum to reply to. There's a message! It says to call the switchboard and ask for her assistant to set something up.

Given that a dead guy emailed her and she is reacting like this, maybe she worked out it is Kai. Maybe she thinks doing it through a switchboard and assistant means no one will take notice?

Next, I find the forum I met JJ on before, all that time ago. He was the first survivor I found anywhere, online or in person, and I remember how amazing it felt to know: I'm not the only one. I'm not alone.

I log in. I'm surprised to see that I have a load of unread messages: they're all from JJ. Until recently he messaged every few days. They are variations on a theme but mostly asking if I'm okay, and I feel guilty that I didn't think to contact him before and am only doing it now because I need help.

The last one he sent was over a week ago. Is that because he's given up on me? Or maybe something has happened to him. I hope he's okay.

I bite my lip, then type this: Hi, JJ, sorry haven't been in touch. I'm fine. How're things with you? And I sign it using my online name, the one he first knew me by: Dineke. There's a pang inside when I see it on the screen again. It was my sister's name.

Until I found JJ, I'd thought I was even more different—and more

208

alone—than she ever had been, even before she killed herself. That's why I used her name.

Finding JJ then had made me find hope.

And all we can do now is wait, see if he answers. If he doesn't, we'll have to try other ways to contact survivor groups. But it's risky to search online for survivors when being one is so dangerous; anyone you find that way could be something entirely different from how they portray themselves—they could be survivor hunters. Or the authorities. Perhaps they are one and the same; it certainly was that way with SAR.

Come on, JJ, we need you.

Well, they do: Azra and Wilf. I'm good; it's me and Kai against the world as usual, isn't it?

But somehow that seems lonelier now than it did before.

CHAPTER 12

KAI

THE MILES GO BY, and since I'm trapped in the truck, there's finally nothing to stop me from thinking: Freja, and that kiss. I *had* to kiss her. I wanted to.

But I still have this feeling like I'm doing wrong—like I'm cheating on Shay—and that's completely crazy. She left me: she lost the right to say who I do or don't kiss.

Yet it's not quite as simple as that, is it? It's me who feels this way—who feels totally messed up in the head. Maybe it's not so much that I feel like I'm cheating on Shay but more that I feel like I'm cheating myself, and worse: if I feel this way, then I'm cheating Freja too. And that doesn't make any kind of sense.

Anyway, I'm sure Freja has Angus and Maureen wrong: they're good, decent, salt-of-the-earth type people. They've believed what the authorities have told them—they've had no reason not to—but they'll listen to sense. And they'd definitely want to help Azra and

Wilf. They've lost their family, children, grandchildren. They need each other.

By the time I get to the farm, I've made a decision: I will sound them out about taking those two in. I'll be careful what I say until I sense their reaction, but there is no doubt at all in my mind: it is the perfect solution for everyone.

It makes far more sense than trying to ship them hundreds of miles away, even to a good guy like Patrick. Anyway, I'm not convinced he hasn't made some connections—with Multiverse and Alex—that he'll later regret.

Even though it's dark and very late now, by the time I pull in front of the farm, Angus is outside, waiting. He must have heard the truck approaching.

I wave a greeting and open the door, get out and stretch my stiff arms and legs.

"It's a bit late, lad. Have you got good news for us?"

"The tanks are full."

He clasps my shoulder. "Excellent! From the base?"

"Yes. And there's more there if you should need it."

He's peering at the truck. "Where's Freja?"

"Well, we've found somewhere we can get online, so she stayed, and I'm heading back in the morning. I'm sorry, but we're moving on."

"I see." The disappointment in his voice is strong. "Well, come inside. Maureen's up too; she's making tea."

The kitchen is warm—wood burns in the stove. Maureen is in her dressing gown; she smiles when she sees me, but her smile falters when her dad tells her what I said, that we're not going to stay.

She shakes her head at Angus. "The two of us rattling around here on our own isn't so good."

"It's you I worry about, girl. I'm not likely to hang around for too many more years. You can't run this place on your own. Even if you could, you shouldn't be alone."

"Would you be open to other options?" I ask. "There may be something, well, someone. I mean . . ."

"What is it? Spit it out," Angus says.

"We found a couple of kids who are on their own. They need somewhere to go."

"Really?" Maureen's face brightens. "How old are they?"

"There is a boy about twelve. A girl fifteen, I think."

"Brother and sister? Immunity often runs in families—just us two in our family were immune, though." A shadow falls across her face: thinking of her own children.

"No, they're not related."

"How'd they end up on their own? Why didn't they leave with the other immune families when they were cleared out?"

I hesitate, unsure what to say—but I started, so . . . "Well, they're not immune."

Angus frowns. "How on earth did they manage not to catch it? It was everywhere around here."

Maureen makes the leap before I can decide what to say next. "Do you mean . . . are they survivors?" She must read the answer on my face. Her eyes go wide with shock, dismay.

"Listen to me, please," I say. "They're just kids who need help. Normal kids who need a hug and a hot meal now and then."

"Survivors aren't normal," Angus says.

"They're not exactly like us, if that's what you mean. But they're decent kids—I've met them, I know. And I do know this: survivors aren't carriers."

"That's not what they say—them on TV. The reporters and doctors and government officials," Angus says. "Why should we believe you?"

"I've known survivors to be around people and not pass it on. What the officials are saying isn't true."

"Even if that is so—and I'm not saying it is—there are all the other things that are wrong with them. And anyway, they're illegal. We're not harboring criminals."

"They're *kids*. They haven't done anything wrong; it's not their fault they got sick and didn't die. Look, this isn't something you have to do; it's just that they need help—and you need help too. I thought it was a good idea."

"You thought wrong. I think you'd better leave."

I stare back at Angus's closed, angry face, and I'm bewildered. How could I have gotten things so very wrong? As I head for the door, I can hear Maureen pleading with her dad to listen to me, to take a chance. The desperation in her to have children in the house is painful to hear; it's greater than her fear of survivors. But he's not having it.

I start to unload the bike from the back of the truck; Angus comes outside again. His face is like thunder.

"It makes sense to me now, what you said—that you've *known* survivors. That Freja is one of them, isn't she? That's why she never had the tattoo. You lied to us, and you brought her into our home."

He says it like she's a poisonous snake.

I don't answer him. I start the bike and head up the road.

As I go, I'm replaying what happened, the things he said, and I'm stunned. Even Maureen. The thought of survivors horrified her; she might have been willing to take them in, but only because having no children horrifies her even more.

How can they be so prejudiced about people they don't know, that they know nothing about?

CHAPTER 13

FREJA

I WAKE IN THE NIGHT, not sure why. Sleep doesn't usually desert me, no matter what is on my mind.

I stretch, trying to get comfortable in an unfamiliar bed, but I feel *wrong*. Is it the weight of the earth above? I'm not a rabbit or a mole; it's weird to be underground.

I'll go outside for some fresh air, a short walk. That's what I need.

I get up and put on clothes Azra found for me for tomorrow in the endless air force supplies tucked away in this place: men's trousers and a shirt, standard military issue. It fits okay with a belt, and anything different to wear—anything *clean*—is a good thing.

I hesitate halfway up the stairs, then go back down to check the computer first. Merlin the cat's green eyes glitter as he watches me suspiciously from across the room. He still won't come up close to me, like he's judging me and what I've done.

I know it hasn't been that long since we messaged JJ, just a matter of hours. It's unlikely that, even if he *is* still checking the forum, he's been online in the meantime. But I can't stop myself.

I log in to the website forum, and when it loads, there's a red *1* by Messages. I click on it—it's from JJ.

Hey there Dineke, how're things? What color is your hair these days? We miss you. I miss you.

And the weight I'd felt before, that I thought was the earth above, is gone.

I breathe in deeply and check the time: he only sent that ten minutes ago. Maybe he can't sleep either.

I'm good and kind of tiger-striped. How are you? Where are you?

I wait, tapping my fingers, hoping he is still there. A message pings in.

I love all cats, but especially tigers. I'm me: I'm always good. Where—well. You'll just have to guess. Is your friend still with you?

It sounds like he doesn't want to answer on this forum; he's not sure if he can trust it. So I won't either. And by "friend" he must mean Kai. Yes. I mean, usually—he's doing something—not right now.

Is he okay?

I hesitate. Yes. I think so.

I've met his ex. Well, at a distance. So I know you found her, that they split.

And now I know where he is: Kai was right. If JJ has met Shay, he must be with Multiverse. I'm surprised that these two parts of my life have somehow joined up. And yet I'm also not surprised at the same time: they're survivors. They need each other.

Is she all right? And what do you mean—at a distance?

She seems to be. We can do amazing things these days: come. Find out for yourself.

He's being deliberately vague. Is he being cautious still, or is he teasing me by hinting at details? Have they worked out a new way to communicate from far away? Maybe he isn't with Multiverse, then. Maybe they're just in contact. And I'm longing to know what they can do—longing to be there, to experience it. I shake my head. Focus, Freja, on why you are here.

I've got some new friends. They need help, somewhere to go.

There's a pause. He's thinking about what I said.

Will they fit in?

He means—are they survivors?

Yes. Absolutely. Would you like to meet them?

Of course. Any friend of yours is a friend of mine. Especially if you are coming too?

And now I feel it even more strongly—the *longing*. To be with more people like me. Not JJ, not like that—but just part of this whole collective of minds that connect and share things that cannot be shared any other way.

But what about Kai?

I don't know about that, I answer, finally.

Well, we'll have to think about how to do this, one way or the other. How/where. I'll get back to you.

Okay.

I really do miss you. But you're probably all taken care of where you are.

He wants to know what has happened with me and Kai, now that Shay is out of the picture. And I don't know what to say honestly, and am not sure I'd be honest if I did know.

No comment, I type at last. He can read into that what he will.

Ah, I see! Is there still a chance for me and you?

No comment!!!

Don't stress, just let me take my crumbs of hope where I can. Take care. I'll get back to you soon.

I sit there, staring at the blank screen for ages after he signs off.

What is wrong with me? I want one thing, then another. I don't understand myself, so how could anybody else?

The only person who ever really understood me was my sister, Dineke.

I wish I could be with her.

The pain and longing to be close to her is never far away. It fills me, and my tears start to fall.

CHAPTER 14

KAI

FREJA LOOKS UP WHEN I COME IN, surprise on her face. "You're back early," she says.

"I came straight back."

"Why?"

"You were right."

"Excellent! What about?"

"Angus and Maureen."

Freja looks at me closely, then swears under her breath. "You told them, didn't you? About Azra and Wilf."

"I didn't give any details about who they are or exactly where they are or even confirm *what* they are, but I think they worked it out. And Angus guessed about you too."

"How could you?" She's angry. "We've got to get out of here, *now*—all of us."

"Isn't that a little paranoid?" I say, but it was this same unease that made me speed through the night despite how tired I am.

"No."

"Maureen was trying to convince her dad to listen to me, to consider taking them; they might have come around if I'd waited. Even if not, I can't believe they'd do anything to put kids in danger." But even as I say it, I'm not sure, and now I feel even more sick in my stomach. "But okay. Just in case, let's move."

Freja defocuses, and I know she's talking to Wilf and Azra that way, in their heads. There are footsteps, and then the two of them come rushing in.

Neither objects to going, leaving this place that has been a home of sorts. They seem excited, not scared.

"How do we all go on one bike?" Wilf asks.

"We can't," I say. "And even if we could, it wouldn't be safe for me to ride it after being awake all night."

"There's got to be an abandoned car around here somewhere," Freja says. "And we need some tanks—extra gas."

Freja makes a list of what we need to take with us. Azra tells Wilf to erase the CCTV recordings before we go. Then she goes looking for Merlin. We all scatter to gather the things we need. Wilf knows a place with a car and runs to show me.

And all the time, I'm seeing the accusation in Freja's eyes. *Please* let this be okay.

CHAPTER 15

FREJA

I STUDY THE DASHBOARD, then put the key in the ignition.

"You do know how to drive, don't you?" Kai says.

"Ish," I answer. "I mean, I had a provisional license and took a few lessons. It'll be fine; there's no traffic anyway."

"Can I drive?" Wilf demands.

"No!" Azra and I say in unison.

With a few hints from Kai on the gears, I manage to get the car off the base, through the nearby village, and onto a main road.

"I didn't get a chance to tell you before, Kai. There was an email back from your mother."

"There was? What did she say?"

"The gist of it was yes, she'd like to meet, and she said to call her assistant via the switchboard to set it up."

"Really? Interesting."

"I wonder if that is because she's afraid her phone is being monitored, but through her assistant maybe not?"

"I hope so."

"So, all we need is to get down that way and find a cell phone network or a working landline."

"Are we heading to Wales? All of us?" Wilf says.

"I don't know, do you both want to come?" I say. "We'll talk when we stop, once we're far enough away from here. For now, Kai—you better get some sleep. The next driving shift is yours."

I glance at him moments later. He's so exhausted he's out: sound asleep.

I'm getting the rhythm of the car better now. He didn't say what route we should take, so I randomly head south-ish, staying on quiet roads where I feel safer. It's not like highways should be a problem for me, since there's no traffic. But I don't care; I've never driven on one before.

The two in the back seat both have headphones on; they're listening to music, but there will be nowhere to charge their phones once the batteries die.

It's my first quiet moment to think since Kai got back, and no matter how annoyed I was with him earlier, I have to take some responsibility for this. I should have guessed he was thinking of taking those two to the farm; I should have talked to him more, not let him go until he understood—or at least promised not to say anything.

Somehow he still doesn't completely understand what it is like to be a survivor—to be the ones everyone fears and hates. You'd think, with first Shay and then me, he'd know how dangerous the world can be for us. Yet he still believes most people will behave decently if you give them a chance.

Like how he believes that of me.

It's part of why I love him, so how can I complain about it now?

I sigh, the pain and guilt twisting inside me at the lies about Shay that I've told Kai—but it's far too late to say anything now. He'd never trust me again.

CHAPTER 16

KAI

GROGGY, I OPEN MY EYES, not sure how much time has passed. The car is bumping along off-road—is that what woke me?

"What's going on?" I say.

"We sensed something coming in the sky," Azra says. Freja brings the car to a shuddering stop now, under the cover of trees by a field.

A group of helicopters appears in the distance—three of them. Big military ones.

"They're heading for the base. Aren't they?" Wilf's voice is small now. "Are they looking for us?"

"There's no way to know," Freja answers. "They might be; it's in that direction. Or they might be doing something completely different that has nothing to do with us."

"Wilf, did you erase all the CCTV recordings?" Azra says.

"Yes, of course I did! Just like you told me to."

"Good."

"Oh."

"What do you mean, *oh*?"

"I didn't turn them off. They'd have filmed us as we left."

"Wilf!" Azra says, and we all turn to look at him.

"You didn't tell me to turn them off, did you? Nobody did!"

"No, but isn't it obvious?" she says, and punches him in the arm.

"Ouch! That hurt!"

"Stop it, you two!" Freja says. "There's no point in arguing about that now. Where were the cameras that were on?"

Wilf runs through them, and we fall silent. There's no doubt at all that the four of us will be on them—this car too.

"Maybe they won't think to check them, or know where to find them in the bunker," Azra says. "It's okay, Wilf."

She touches his hand, but he yanks it away. "If you're being nice to me, things must be really bad. I'm sorry. It's my fault, isn't it?"

I sigh. "No, it isn't. It's mine. Completely mine. I shouldn't have said anything about you to anyone, but I did. If anyone is looking for you, that is the only reason."

No one denies it, but Freja's hand reaches out, lightly touches mine, and I reach back for hers and hold it tight.

I'm sorry, I say to her, silently.

I know. It's okay. Just always do what I say in the future.

Really? Always? I don't know about that.

Like right now, give me a hug.

I reach out, pull her toward me, wrap my arms around her, and kiss her.

"Stop it!" Wilf makes gagging noises.

I pull away from Freja. "Right. Yes, okay then. Any more helicopters on the horizon?"

The three of them agree: nothing else is approaching.

"Should we get going?" I say. "It must be my turn to drive. There's just one thing."

"What's that?"

"Where the hell are we?"

CHAPTER 17

FREJA

WE'RE ON A HIGHWAY now that Kai is driving, and the miles fly past. We'll have to get rid of this car soon; if they've found that CCTV, they'll know what we're driving.

Azra and Wilf are asleep behind us. His head has slipped onto her shoulder. They're like brother and sister—they fight all the time, like Dineke and I did when we were younger. My little sister could drive me crazy, endlessly hanging around me, wanting attention all the time and never shutting up—like Wilf does to Azra. But I'd do anything to argue with her again.

I should try to sleep. I close my eyes, but my thoughts are traveling. I'm keeping a feel out all around us; I'm anxious even though there is nobody anywhere near—no one alive, that is.

The anxiety comes from the feeling that we're going the wrong way. That's it, isn't it? Not so much because of specific dangers of heading south, even though they are there. The farther south we go, the more likely we are to find people—army, air force, immune groups to start with—and then to hit quarantine boundaries. Boundaries that protect people who don't know what it means to watch those you care about get sick and die.

Or even worse: to get sick and survive.

But if we turn around, if we go north, we could head for Scotland—to Patrick and JJ, I tell myself, but they aren't all that is there. There is also Alex and his strange ways and his group, Multiverse. Shay, too, and what could that mean for Kai and me? I don't know, and I don't want to find out either.

But I still feel it deep in my bones: we're going the wrong way.

"Kai?" I whisper.

"Yeah?"

"I'm scared. For me, for them." I glance in the mirror to check: they're still asleep behind us. "And you too."

His hand slips off the gearshift to mine, gives it a light touch.

"I know, Freja. But I've got an idea to handle at least part of that."

CHAPTER 18

KAI

WE HIDE THE CAR IN SHADOWS, approach the rest of the way on foot.

"There's no one either in or near his house. It's clear," Freja whispers.

We find the key where Patrick always kept it, hidden outside. It's funny how he could be so careful about online security and leave his house key under a plant pot.

I unlock the door, and we step in. "It seems so long since we've been here," I say.

"Since we disappeared in the night," Freja says. "We never said goodbye." She sighs. I touch her shoulder.

Wilf flicks a switch on the wall. "There's no power, but you'll never guess what."

"What?" I say.

"I've got a signal." He waves his phone around, the screen light dancing around him.

"Be careful: we can't charge anything," Azra says. "When it's dead, it's dead."

"That's right. No games—essential use only," Freja adds.

"That all depends on what you think is *essential*," Wilf says.

"Maybe I should confiscate yours," Azra says.

"I'd like to see you try."

"Hang on a sec," I say. "Are these phones registered to either of you? If they are, you shouldn't use them."

"No." Azra hesitates. "We found them in the bunker."

"They belong to ghosts." Wilf's word for the soldiers who died there. "There was no phone signal there; we just used them to put music on."

"I don't know," Freja says. "Do you think anyone would check the numbers?"

"Seems unlikely with the mess everywhere that anybody could be bothered," I say.

"But if those helicopters were going there looking for us, and if they find the bunker and bodies, they could work out who they are and that their phones are missing?"

"Paranoia aplenty."

"Yep. But you said you'd listen to me in the future in areas of paranoia," Freja says.

"True."

"But we do need to call your mum tomorrow during office hours, so we'll have to use one of them then. Hopefully it'll be all right."

"Are we spending the night here before we go to Wales?" Wilf says. "What's left of the night, that is."

Freja and I exchange a glance. "Well, thing is," I say, "it might be safer for you to wait here while we go."

"What? Are you dumping us?" Azra demands.

"No, we're not dumping you. But in case the authorities are hunting for all of us together, it might be safer to split up. I'm going to go and see my mum, then come back here."

They both look at Freja, and even I can see their words not said out loud hanging in the silence: *Don't leave us on our own.*

226

"I don't know yet if I can go," Freja says. "We'll have to see where they are meeting. I can't cross roadblocks; they might be scanning for survivors."

Freja sighs, looks down. *I still think I should go with you, no matter what,* she whispers inside me.

I know. But you can't risk getting scanned. And I know you don't want to leave these two. I understand that—it's the right thing to do.

Then why does it feel so wrong?

I slip an arm around Freja; she leans her head against my shoulder.

Anyway, I'm not deciding yet, she says. *We'll see.*

"What if you don't come back?" Azra says to me.

"I will, I promise," I say. But we all know it is a promise I might not be able to keep.

CHAPTER 19

FREJA

ONCE EVERYONE IS ASLEEP, I slip Azra's phone out of her room—she's a deeper sleeper than Wilf—and walk silently down the stairs, then out the front door.

It's almost dawn. The world is still, hushed, as if it is watching and listening.

I walk down the lane. There's a bench farther along at a bus shelter, though I'm sure buses haven't run here for a long while. And when they did, they wouldn't have come to such an out-of-the-way place very often.

Even so, I *reach* out all around me to make sure: I'm alone. No people.

Phone on: good—there is still a signal.

Quickly I go to the forum and log in; there's a load of unread messages, one every few hours. JJ has been trying to catch me online. They all say some variation of hello: Hi gorgeous. Hey beautiful. Hello sexy.

Is this why I didn't do this with Kai watching? He knows I'm not into JJ, not that way, but he wouldn't like it all the same. There was always an animosity between them, since the time they first met, when JJ knocked him out by attacking his aura. That was before I'd taught Kai how to block psychic attacks. At the time, however misguided, JJ thought he was protecting the group of survivors he was part of. He did apologize for that—eventually—but Kai hasn't let go of that grudge.

I click on the latest one, sent about an hour and a half ago. **Darling girl, are you all right? Answer me.**

I answer: **I'm here now, are you?** I don't expect him to be unless he hasn't slept all night. **We've been on a bit of a trip about the place. Sorry I couldn't answer before.**

I wait, click "refresh." Wait some more. The sun is just peeking above the trees now, and I glance back down the lane, the way I came. I don't think anyone will wake up—they've only been asleep a few hours, and we're all exhausted—but I *reach* back behind me anyway to check. All still asleep.

I stretch, settle on the bench, and soon start to doze off a little myself. A bird chirps loudly, and I jump awake. Hit "refresh."

There is a message from JJ, sent just a few minutes before: **Hello? Are you still there?**

Yes! Are you?

Yes—at last we are online at the same time. So have you been off on a little vacation?

Something like that. It was rather spontaneous. As in, we had no choice. Will he understand that?

Seemed like a good idea at the time?

Exactly.

Where are you?

At the house of our mutual friend, where I last saw you. He should be able to work out we're at Patrick's.

Ah, lovely.

My new friends I told you about are here too.

Perhaps we can work something out, get together again? We could come and meet you partway, perhaps?

That'd be great. Only I'm not sure if I'll be going.

There's a long pause. Is he thinking or talking to someone else—Patrick, maybe? Hopefully not Xander. I want to tell JJ not to mention this to Xander, but I don't know how to get that across without saying too much. What would Xander say if he knew I might be coming? He'd be wondering about Kai—if he's coming with me.

I'm wondering that too.

But I'd so love to see you. Would pleading help?

I don't know; give it a try?

I'm dying to see you! I'm practically . . . desperate!

Some things never change.

But some do: change your mind.

You never know your luck. I hesitate, thinking how to phrase what I need to say. Then go for: Could we make it a surprise party? Though maybe you should let our mutual friend know, since we're staying at his house. But no one else.

There's a short pause. Who doesn't love a surprise?

I'm not sure when I'll get back online. Nowhere to recharge. So don't worry if you don't hear from me.

As usual, you ask the impossible.

I've got to go. I need to conserve battery.

All right. xxxxx

I hesitate. One x—on the cheek.

Ooooh, saucy!

Not *that* cheek. Bye.

I quickly log off, and then go to Kai's mum's work website to get the phone number for the switchboard. That'll be all I was doing if anyone notices I took the phone. Then I switch it off.

The sun is climbing a little higher into the sky, but clouds are pulling in, and I shiver. I hope JJ got that I want him to keep all this from Xander and anyone else, for now at least. And that if he did understand, he actually does it. Somehow I think he will.

Eventually I'll have to face Xander again—I know this somehow; I *feel* it, inside. But until then I'd rather he didn't know I'm coming.

Am I going to go with them, or is this just for Azra and Wilf? I don't know. I don't feel sure of much of anything anymore.

CHAPTER 20

KAI

IT'S 9 A.M., AT LAST: I can try calling the switchboard at a time of day somebody is likely to be there.

"I'm not sure you should make this call yourself, Kai," Freja says. "Just in case calls *are* monitored, and somebody recognizes your voice."

"I'll do it!" Wilf says. "Azra can't—a girl can't sound like a man."

"I don't know," I say. "Can you sound older? Calm and businesslike?"

"Let's do it pretend," Wilf says. He mimes a fake phone in his hand. "Ring ring." He raises his eyebrows at Freja.

"Hello?" she says.

"Good morning. May I please speak to Dr. Sonja Tanzer's assistant?" He trips over her name a little.

"May I ask who is calling?"

"Bryson."

"What was Bryson's first name?" I say. "Should he give a full name?"

"I don't know. If he's in the army, wouldn't he just say his rank or something?"

"What was his rank?"

I frown, trying to remember. "There was a lot going on at the time. I'm not sure."

"Just make up a first name. You don't want them to look into the real Bryson and find out he's dead, anyway."

"Good point."

"David Bryson. There you go."

Wilf practices it a few times, switching the wording around, until we all judge he is good to go.

I dial the number and hand him the phone—he holds it close to me so I can hear but first gives a mad grin. *Stay calm, Wilf!* I think at him, and he crosses his eyes. What *are* we doing?

It rings, again and again. I wonder if we should hang up, try again later.

Then there is a click. "UK and World Health Organization Epidemic Research Initiative. Good morning."

"Hello, this is David Bryson. Please connect me with Dr. Sonja Tanzer's assistant."

"One moment, please."

There is silence, then another phone ringing. A man answers.

"My name is Bryson. Sonja said to call you to set up a meeting?"

"One moment." There's a pause. "Ah yes, she left a note. She's on fieldwork this week but said that since you're traveling down, you might want to meet her at one of the collection centers? She's in Chester. If you can be there today or tomorrow, she suggested you might like to join her for her evening walk at six p.m."

I give Wilf a thumbs-up and mouth *today*.

The assistant gives more details. He says to go to the center reception and ask for her, but I'm guessing that is because Mum told him to say this, to cover up what she really meant. I know just where she'll be. But I write it down anyway.

Wilf says goodbye, clicks "end call."

"Good job!" I say, and we high-five.

"What on earth is a collection center?" Freja asks.

I shrug. "Who knows?"

Freja is on the computer.

"Chester is outside the zone boundary," she says. "I'm coming with you."

CHAPTER 21

FREJA

"IT'S ONLY A FEW HOURS AWAY," Kai says. "We'll be back tonight, I promise."

"Call if you have to, but only if it's important." I brandish Wilf's phone; they've got Azra's. "Don't wear the battery down on that one; keep it off unless you need it."

Azra rolls her eyes. "We won't. *I* won't let him," she says, and tucks the phone into her pocket with a pointed look at Wilf.

We'll be back on a bike today; one of Patrick's was tucked away in his garage. They must have used the four-wheel drive when they left—there were only five of them after we were gone. We siphon some gas from the car to top up the bike, then tuck the car out of sight in the garage.

"We can't use this car anymore in case they saw it on the CCTV. We'll have to find another one," Kai says.

I reply with something noncommittal. Maybe JJ will come; maybe that issue will be sorted out for us. But I haven't told Kai about that possibility yet. I want to get today over with first, not distract him from this meeting with his mum. But maybe I'm just putting it off because I know he won't like it.

Kai said it'll take two hours to get there. We're racing down the deserted highway; I'm *reaching* now and then—ahead and all around us—making sure we won't meet anyone in the road or in the air. All is quiet.

He slows as we near Chester. We'd talked this backward and forward and finally agreed to stash me and the bike outside the town walls somewhere. Then Kai will go in the rest of the way on foot, keeping in touch mentally.

I'm relieved not to be meeting Kai's mum—and not because it might be risky if anyone sees me and works out who I am. Even though it's completely trivial in the face of everything else, the thought of meeting his mother makes me feel queasy. I bet she could just look at the two of us, have that psychic mum thing, and be all disapproving.

Kai pulls into a backstreet, slows, and stops. "Is there anyone around?" he says.

I *reach* out again; but like everywhere we've come past, there is no one at home. It's got the unlived, unloved feel so many places we come to have these days. Everyone has either died or run away. The grass is long, yards overgrown, and plants wilted with no one to water them.

"No one is around," I say. "So, let's give this a try?"

Ever since JJ hinted at having met Shay at a distance, I've wondered: how far away can Kai go before we lose contact? I've always assumed it only works at very short range, since I can't touch someone's mind from much of a distance at all. But can I stay with him if we establish contact while we're close? We came early to check.

Kai hesitates, the reluctance he always has to let anyone—even me—touch his mind still there. But he nods. "Come on in," he says.

CHAPTER 22

KAI

THE LIGHT TOUCH OF FREJA'S MIND IS ON MINE.

Okay, away you go, then, she says. *Let's see how far you can get before we lose this connection.*

Freja stays with the bike while I walk on, for five minutes, ten.

Still with me? I say.

Yes. I don't think we could establish a link at this distance, but I can hold one we've already made. Stay where you are, and I'll catch up.

I wait for Freja. I'd given her a few quick lessons on the bike before we set out today, to make sure she could use it if she has to—and she's going slowly but doing well. Just as I think that, she almost falls over with it when she stops next to me. I grab the handlebars to steady it while she gets off.

"I'm glad you know Chester," she says. "I'd be lost."

"Yes, I know it pretty well. I wonder if Mum somehow managed to engineer being here, specifically? I know just the stretch of the wall she likes to walk along—we've been here several times. I'm sure she'll be there."

We get as close as we can without being in sight of the wall, then Freja's touch is back in my mind.

Far enough for you? I say, and Freja nods. She gives me a quick hug that we both wish could be longer. *Now tuck yourself away. I'll be back* soon.

You'd better be.

If anything worries you, or anything happens to me, just take off. Get the bike and go, I say. *I mean it!*

I know.

You have to—for Azra and Wilf. Right?

Right.

She looks lost, scared, but for me and not for her. *It'll be all right.* I give her a swift kiss. *Don't talk to me too much once I'm there. I'm not good at multitasking.*

I know. You're a dude.

Brat.

I walk to the end of the road and glance back to check on Freja. She has hidden herself and the bike away between a house and a camper van that was parked there; I can't see her at all. Good.

Another corner, a few minutes walking, and I can see it: the ancient wall. It stretches around Chester, almost all of it walkable.

You still there? I say.

You bet.

Can you sense anyone around me?

There's a pause.

No. But it might be a bit too far away to tell for sure. I'll let you know if I do.

I walk along the inside of the wall, below it, so I can cover ground faster. I'm still ten minutes early but unlikely to be first: Mum is always early—she's one of those people who think on time is late. I bet she's already there waiting.

I pass another section of the wall.

Nearly there, I think.

Good luck, Kai. I hope it goes well. Freja isn't sure that it will. I'm not either, but I'm also as desperate to see Mum, to know she is okay, as I'm sure she is me.

I'm approaching the stretch that is her favorite spot of the wall: there are views all around. It's too open to risk going up there, but just beyond it are stairs down. That is where I go.

I see her before she sees me. She's pacing back and forth in a small area in the shadow of the wall.

And I walk faster now until I'm almost running. She turns and sees me and does the same. Then her arms are around me, tight.

They feel thinner than they were. I pull away a little to look at her, still surprised somehow that I'm taller than she is, even though I have been for ages. She's always been such a larger-than-life figure in my mind that it doesn't seem right.

I touch her hair.

"More gray, I know," she says. "The world—and *you*—have done that."

"Sorry." There's a bench off to the side. She draws me to it, and we sit there. She holds my hand like she will never let it go.

"What is with all this subterfuge, *Bryson*?" She stresses the name. "I told you before, I'm sure we can get you out of whatever trouble you are in if you just come to me."

"You might be wrong there, and there are things I have to tell you. How much time have you got before you're missed?"

She sighs. "Not long, maybe twenty or thirty minutes. Is that long enough to convince you to stay?"

"No."

"Say what you have to say, and we'll see. But first I have something to tell you. You were right about the antimatter cause of the epidemic. I'm sorry I didn't take you more seriously before."

"The authorities know this now?"

"Yes. And that survivors carry antimatter."

"That may be so, but they don't spread the epidemic." She raises an eyebrow. "I've been around them and others who haven't been sick—they don't get infected."

"We need to study them more to be sure, but we still have trouble

238

finding survivors to study. This collection center and others like it are places we are testing the immune to screen for survivors who've slipped through, and we're taking samples from the dead to study. All to try to make more sense of this epidemic."

"Alex was behind it all—the particle accelerator at Shetland. He *has* to be brought to justice."

Her eyes open wider.

"Alex *has* met justice, Kai. Whether he deserved it or not is not for me to say. He died."

"When?"

"In a fire, at a survivor research facility—"

"That was faked somehow. He didn't die there. I've seen him since then."

She frowns. "There have been reliable reports—"

"You didn't believe me before when I told you about antimatter causing the epidemic. Believe me now. He had an arrangement with SAR, the Special Alternatives Regiment of the army. They were deliberately engineering a weapon in a secret lab in the Shetland Islands, and it got out."

Her eyes move from my face to something over my shoulder, and I turn.

There is movement behind me, a man stepping forward around the corner. He's not in uniform, but he *is* one just the same—he has that army look. I spring up from the bench, ready to run.

"Please, Kai, wait," Mum says, just as I hear *Run!* from Freja in my mind, and I pause, caught between the two pleas.

"This is a friend of mine," Mum says. "I want you to talk to him. No one else is here. Tell him just what you told me."

"I thought you'd have realized this was to be private."

"I did. But I trust him. Kai, this is Rohan. He's been assigned to investigate the epidemic. This is your chance to tell someone in authority what you want to say."

He holds his hands forward, shows he is unarmed, and walks toward us. "Kai. I'm pleased to meet you, though concerned. Your mother is breaching protocol and taking me with her."

My eyes are going between his and hers, and finally I sigh. All I can do right now is trust in her, even as I can feel Freja's fear, which is making it hard to do so.

"Do you know about SAR's role in the epidemic?" I say.

He inclines his head.

"First I've heard of this," Mum says. She glares at Rohan—is she annoyed he has withheld this from her?

"Do you know the identity of the scientist who directed the project?" I say.

"We've only determined aliases at this point."

"It's Dr. Alexander Cross."

His eyes turn to Mum. "Your ex-husband?"

"So Kai says. He's reported to have died, though Kai denies that. You have to know—he's always hated Alex. I'm not sure you can take anything he says about him as unbiased."

"How do you know he was involved?" Rohan says to me.

"Not just involved—he ran the whole show. Alex said so; he admitted it. He made out like he was really trying to find a cure for cancer, and then the epidemic accidentally got out, but I find that hard to believe."

Rohan asks for more details, and I give them, but part of me is also aware that Freja is coming closer. I'm silently urging her to turn around, to go back, while trying to answer his questions at the same time.

"Do you know where he is now?" Rohan asks.

"Somewhere in Scotland. He's with a cultlike science group called Multiverse. He's their leader."

"What?" Mum says. "I've heard of them; I think I even talked about it with Alex some time ago. He never said he had anything to do with them."

"He wouldn't. His role was kept secret. They know him as Xander."

"Multiverse? I've heard something about them recently," Rohan says, and frowns, shakes his head as if trying to jog his memory into place. "Yet Dr. Cross passed extensive security checks before doing some work for us. It was while working for us that he unfortunately perished in a fire—or so I've been told."

"That's what he *wants* you to think. Alex was a survivor—both of that fire and of the epidemic."

"What?" Mum is shocked.

"That's right: he's a survivor. And SAR is also searching for Alex. They blame him for everything that happened, and for them taking the fall."

"We have been looking for the SAR lieutenant too," Rohan says. "We may be close to moving in on him."

"Kirkland-Smith? I spoke to him as well."

A raised eyebrow. "You get around a bit."

"He's been hunting survivors, murdering them."

"I see." He exchanges a glance with Mum. "We're trying to come to grips with the survivor problem ourselves."

"What is that supposed to mean?"

"Calm down, Kai," he says. "We aren't like SAR: we are locating and identifying all survivors we can, true, but only to take them into protective custody—both to protect them and to protect others from them. So long as they don't resist, they're absolutely fine."

"But you've got everything so wrong. They're not to blame for the epidemic: it's SAR and Alex. And SAR is after Alex too—if you find one, you may find the other."

Kai! It's Freja, her presence more intense in my mind now; she must have come even closer. Alarm radiates from her. *Get out of there—now. They lied. There are three approaching left, and two right. Run!*

I spring up, go—run.

Mum is calling my name. Rohan takes up the chase, but he is too old and slow, and I pull away. Freja tells me where to go to get to her and the bike—she's brought it with her—and how to dodge the others who are coming and running toward me now too. Did Rohan tell them to come after a while, so we could talk before they took me?

I reach Freja, clamber onto the bike with her, and we go.

CHAPTER 23

FREJA

WE DON'T STOP FOR MANY MILES. I'm *reaching* the whole time, nudging Kai which way to go to elude those who follow, until finally I can't sense anyone at all anymore: we've lost them. I signal Kai to pull in for a break.

He gets off the bike, stretches. "I can't believe it," Kai says, a haunted look in his eyes. "I can't believe she set me up: my own mother."

"Maybe she didn't. Maybe as far as she knew, it was just this Rohan, and he is the one who betrayed her and did it?"

He pauses, thinking. "Yeah. That could be—in fact, that's more likely. Thank you."

"I was there with you the whole time, listening; I heard everything that was said. Do you think they believed you?"

"I don't know. I did what I could."

"So much risk, and all to talk to closed minds." I shake my head, scowl. "You heard what he said: the *survivor problem*." I spit the words out. "He didn't seem that bothered that Kirkland-Smith is happily murdering people, not if they're survivors. Like it's one way to deal with a pest problem, as if we are rats. He might prefer traps, but poison works too."

Kai reaches for me, but I shake him off, too angry to be held by anyone, even him. "Let's get going: as far from them as we can."

CHAPTER 24

KAI

I CAN'T THINK, can't talk anymore. Just ride.

Was all that a waste of time? I hope not, but I'm not convinced that Rohan would act on anything I said.

Mum—well, maybe. She knows some things I told her were true now, like antimatter being the cause, about SAR and the research lab too—things she didn't know before that were confirmed by Rohan.

There's a twist in my stomach when the implications fall into place. Maybe Mum is in trouble with them now? For setting up this meeting with me, even though she told Rohan. And because now she knows things not everybody knows: knowledge that might be dangerous.

Freja is silent too.

The bike's tank is getting low; we stop in a village to look for gas. Even though Freja tells me she keeps *reaching* all around and hasn't found anyone trailing us, we're both jumpy, nervous.

I find an abandoned car with some gas in the tank and start to siphon some out, accidentally getting some of the foul stuff in my mouth. I'm gagging and spitting when Freja calls out to me, alarm all through her voice.

The phone is in her hand. "There's a missed call from Wilf and Azra." She curses. "I muted it when I was coming up closer with the bike and forgot to take it off silent."

She calls them while I finish the job with the gas as fast as I can, fear coursing through me.

"There's no answer now," she says. "And they knew to only call in an emergency."

We get back on the bike and go, as fast as we can and still hold the road. Freja nudges me mentally, and I stop a bit later so she can try the phone again. Nothing.

When we get within a few miles of Patrick's house, I want to keep going, to race straight there, but Freja talks sense, makes me hold back. We leave the bike behind some trees and go in slowly, quietly, on foot. She says she is *reaching* as we go, and we are both sick to our stomachs at what we might find.

CHAPTER 25

FREJA

WE ARE CLOSE TO THE HOUSE WHEN I SENSE THEM. I pull Kai's hand, and we step back into the trees.

What is it? he says.

There are men around the house. Hiding in the woods. An ambush waiting for us, maybe?

But what about Azra and Wilf? Can you find them?

I'm still trying; I have been all along! I snap, tears in my eyes: I *reach* out and hail them again and again, but there is nothing in return. *They're not answering me, Kai.*

We stand there, uncertain what to do next.

Then there's a small sound behind us, and we spin around. Kai's fists are ready, but it's Wilf.

His face is ash-white, but he looks unhurt. He must have either seen or sensed that we are here and come to us, but his mind is closed.

I hold out a hand, go to him. Put my arms around his stiff body.

Wilf? It's okay, it's me. Let me in. Where's Azra?

At first he stays still, silent. Then when he finally leans his head against my shoulder and his mind opens to mine, I almost fall back from the shock of it.

Azra wouldn't let him use the phone, and he was bored, exploring the woods, trying to climb the tallest tree he could find.

Then they came. Soldiers. He saw it in their minds—that they'd tracked the car, the one from the air force. They'd worked out we had it from the CCTV, and it had a tracker on it, and they followed its signal here.

Azra told him to stay still and quiet in his tree. She made him promise.

And then she tried to run.

They shot her. In the back as she ran. They just shot her, and I see it all in his mind—the jerky slow motion of it as she fell to the ground. She tried to crawl away, and they shot her again.

Wilf saw it all from high in his tree, and now I do too. He's been up there since, afraid to move, until we got here.

In every way that counts—and more besides—she was his sister, and he watched her die.

She told me to stay in the tree. I just stayed in the tree.

You did the right thing, just like she said. I soothe him, hold him, rock him in my arms like a small child while he cries—silently—too scared to make any noise at all.

Then I let Kai lead us away. He carries Wilf. Merlin appears from the woods and follows us. We get to the bike, somehow get the three of us and a cat on it, and go in the other direction.

Azra was fifteen, barely more than a child. She was a survivor who *resisted* being taken into custody—she ran. They didn't try to chase and catch her, did they? No. She resisted, so they shot her.

The whole time we bounce up the road, these things all bounce through my mind, as if I'm thinking about this or making a choice. But the truth is: *I already know.*

The *survivor problem.*

The different, the damned.

Even as Kai takes us away from this cursed place, I know it. There can be no *us*, not anymore. There never really was, if I'm honest. How could there be?

The barriers between us in this world are too complete and profound.

And it's not just the end for us.

This is the end for me too.

As I was—I can never be again.

When we finally stop, exhausted, for the night, I try to explain to Kai that we—Wilf and I—have to go on without him.

I can tell he understands, at least a little, but he says he can't let us go on our own. That it's too dangerous.

But being me is *always* dangerous; it always will be, and he can't change that.

I tell him we'll talk again in the morning.

CHAPTER 26

KAI

IT'S LIKE SOME SORT OF BAD DREAM, but I'm awake. They've gone; they're really gone—Freja and Wilf. The bike with them. They even took the damn cat.

I don't know how long it has been since they left. I could try to follow them. I'm at turns angry and worried that she didn't let me at least see them safely to wherever she thinks they need to go. But if she doesn't want to be found, she'll block me at every step. Besides, they could be miles away by now on the bike. Assuming they haven't fallen off it—she barely knows how to ride the thing, and now I add that worry to the list.

What happened to Azra . . . I shudder. Freja showed me Wilf's memory, and it won't leave my thoughts.

But *why* did that make Freja feel she had to leave me behind? I don't understand.

I know something else now though. I cared for her; I really did. But this isn't like when Shay left me—when my guts were ripped out from the inside. I didn't love Freja. Maybe she knew this, and that is part of the reason she left.

But I still needed her. Now there is no one to think of besides myself, and that is something I don't want to do. *Can't* do.

I feel empty, lost. I have since Shay left, but Freja—and then Azra and Wilf—distracted me from the pain. Now part of me wants to just give up, to curl up alone in a dark room somewhere. Or better yet: find a cliff and jump, or crash a car into a wall at maximum speed.

Thinking like this isn't helping.

I start walking. I hesitate at a crossroads: north or south?

North: Freja and Wilf, Xander and Shay. Maybe even Callie.

South: Mum. And also Rohan.

I don't know whether Callie is really that way—that she is anywhere.

As for Shay and Freja, well, maybe, just maybe, it's about time I stop chasing after girls who've decided to leave me.

And we've got some unfinished business, Rohan and I. I have to tell him about Azra. Maybe then he'll see how wrong they are about how they are handling the *survivor problem*—it can only push us all further apart.

Like it has me and Freja.

I head south.

PART 5

CHEMICAL EVOLUTION

Extreme heat and pressure within
early stars forced the creation of
elements—from the initial few to all the
naturally occurring elements we have
today. Yet now we can create elements;
we call them artificial, but once they
are made, they are real enough.
Why not direct other stages
of evolution? It is inevitable.

—Xander, *Multiverse Manifesto*

QUARANTINE

CHAPTER 1

CALLIE

I RUN BACK TO OUR HOUSE in Community and yank the door open.

Shay is curled up on the sofa. She hasn't really moved much since almost everybody died.

She sits up, alarm crossing her face. "What's wrong?"

"They're back," I say, gasping for air.

"Who?"

"Some of the ones from Community that traveled away with Beatriz and Elena. I saw them walk in from the edge."

Shay's eyes are wide with shock. She didn't know they were coming, then. She shakes her head, gets to her feet, even though I can tell she's still really tired.

"Can I ask you something?" I say, knowing I should leave it, that other things are important to her right now, but I can't help myself.

"Of course, but make it fast."

"The edge of the world is still there. Shouldn't I be able to see through it now? Are there still blocks in my mind?"

She is walking to the door. "I don't know; I couldn't see any, but that you still see it that way suggests there must be. I've got to go talk to Xander now; we'll have another look later, okay?"

The door swings shut behind her.

CHAPTER 2

SHAY

I COULD HAIL XANDER BEFORE I GET THERE, but I want to see his face, his aura, and judge him with my eyes as well as my mind. There's no chance he didn't know they were on their way. He always knows what is going on. Xander is the puppet master; his people dangle from strings in his hands. How could he have them come back here after so many have already died? We've burned the bodies, but does the sickness still hang in the air of this place?

We couldn't save *anyone*. There were a few immune, but every single person who got sick died. He was disappointed. There was something in his thoughts about it, after Persey's death. He suspected that if we could try a few more times, we'd be able to work out how to save someone. But we ran out of patients.

He wouldn't have told them to come back, so they could get sick and I could try to heal them? Even as the thought forms, I'm pushing it away: he couldn't do that, not to them, surely? These are his followers. He cares about them; I know he does. He wouldn't risk them like that.

Would he?

And then there's me. I'm his daughter. Does he care enough about me not to put me through that again, the pain of trying and failing to save each one—experiencing each death as if it is my own?

No. He doesn't. He's said as much before, and it hurts to know this. I'm not even sure why. He's never been any kind of father to me. It wasn't his fault before, but he knows who I am now, and he still wouldn't save me from that pain.

If that is so, would he care enough about them to keep them away when coming here may mean they'll die?

Even as I can't believe he could do this to us all deliberately, I'm sick with distrust and fear. I *have* to ask him straight out if he has done this; it's the only way to know.

I've started to work myself up to confront him about it, but when I arrive, I don't need to bother. Cepta is there already, and she is furious enough for two.

He holds up his hands, and she's quelled so instantly he must have attacked her aura. "Listen to me, both of you. Some of them are ill; they were already. They've come home to die."

CHAPTER 3

CALLIE

THEY ARE TAKEN TO THE HALL when they fall ill—the place where all of Community, except for me, used to have dinner. After dinner in this same place, they'd join together, minds linked—something I've never experienced, but from what I understand, it is like being so close that they are part of each other forever. But before this group arrived, most of their friends had already died, here, in this same place. Was being so close in life why they couldn't stay away? Maybe they had to be together again—in death.

Cepta has me fetch blankets, and I run back and forth with what I can find. There isn't much available: a lot of them were wrapped around the bodies that were burned on the pyres. Soon the hall looks like a hospital again, beds made on the floor, but there aren't any doctors or medicine—there is just Shay.

Shay is next to a woman. Shay's eyes are weirded out like they go sometimes, and I know not to speak to her. But a moment later, her eyes come back to the way they usually are—they are shiny with tears. The woman is still now, quiet, blood in her open, blank eyes.

"Shay?" I say, and she turns her head slowly toward me.

"Callie. You shouldn't be here." Her voice is a faint whisper, her skin so pale that rings of darkness under her eyes stand out like bruises. She blinks, and I'm grateful for that movement, the only thing that shows her eyes aren't just as open and blank as those of the woman who died.

"Where else can I be right now?" I say, and it's true, but the horror around me is so complete that I want to run away.

A ghost of a smile crosses her face. Shay's hand moves as if to go to mine, then falls back. I reach forward instead and grip hers.

"What can I do to help?"

As I speak, there are cries of pain behind us. A man. Aristotle. I recognize him, like I do all the others—even though until recently I was kept isolated. I knew them by sight, heard their names when they spoke to each other. He's big, a wall of muscle that would tower over me if he could stand again, but now he is crying. Shay moves slowly toward him.

"Shay? Can I help?"

She answers without turning. "Where has Cepta gone? Find her and tell her to come back; I need her. Then put cool cloths on foreheads. Hold hands."

She's at Aristotle's side. Somehow her face is more alive than it was a moment before. She says something low to him, takes his hand. And then her eyes go weird again. His pain eases. I can see this instantly, but Shay shrinks further in on herself like she is being crushed.

I wish I could help her in a way that matters, help take their pain so she doesn't bear it alone. I'm not a survivor, but Cepta is; Xander too. They should be here—why aren't they helping?

I dash out the door.

Xander's house is closest. I try there first. I knock, afraid not to. Then call out, open the door. No one is here.

I run toward Cepta's house, and I'm nearly there when I hear voices: they're outside, by the front of her house. They are out of sight

257

behind trees. I can feel the discord before I hear it in their voices, and I hesitate, not sure I should interrupt.

"You know I'm right. This is the path, the way we must take." It's Xander.

I feel a light touch on my mind—it's Cepta. So tuned in to me, as she always has been, she must have felt my approach. She identifies that it is me, then withdraws. She doesn't say anything to Xander to tell him I'm there, and I know I should step forward, make myself known, but I stay still and silent. Listening.

"Your people are dying." Cepta's voice is anguished.

"Yes. We search for the truth, for pure knowledge, all of us. No matter how hard it is, this is what they must do." His voice isn't sad like hers, and I'm first shocked, then curious. What knowledge does he seek?

"Callie?" It's Xander. He's noticed I'm here now, and I step forward, hoping he didn't realize I'd been listening.

"Shay sent me. She needs help."

They are looking at each other; there is a brief silence. I know they are talking inside their heads.

"I'll go," Cepta says. "In a minute," she adds, and nods at me. Dismissed.

I run back to the hall. "Cepta is coming," I say, but Shay is with Aristotle still and doesn't hear what I say.

But there is a boy I can see to: Jamar.

He's a few years older than me; we've never spoken. His face is twisted in pain. A cool cloth, Shay said?

I find the bowl and the cloth and kneel beside him, place it on his forehead gently. His eyes focus on mine. There is surprise there. He wasn't here when Shay got the rules changed, made it so Community could talk to me.

"Hi," I say.

He swallows; a wave of pain crosses his face. "Hi," he answers, a whisper. Like he's afraid Cepta will hear.

"It's okay, you're allowed to talk to me now."

I take his hand, and as another wave of pain crosses him, he grips onto it. So much pain, his and everyone else's. So much death. Community always seemed to me to be a place that was content to be on its own, one that couldn't be bothered with the rest of the world. It seems wrong this could spread among them like this—as if they were ordinary. Even more ordinary than me.

Has it reached other branches of Community? Jamar and the others had been to the farm, and now I'm scared for them too.

I can't stop myself from asking. "Is the sickness at the farm?"

He shakes his head no, then gasps as that slight movement hurts.

"I don't understand. If it isn't there, then why did you get sick?"

He winces. "Aristotle said we had to come back. We met some people on the way. We must have caught it from them."

"When?"

"A day ago." His whole body shudders, caught in spasms of pain, and I grip his hand tight.

But it isn't enough.

I can never do enough.

CHAPTER 4

SHAY

I'M INSIDE ARISTOTLE'S MIND, lost in his pain. I'm trying to take it from him and can no longer tell if it is his, or mine.

Cepta is back now. She joins with us, and her help eases the pain enough that I can continue my search inside him—deeper, closer into the coiled strands of his DNA.

And just like Persey, and the last few who died, he is missing some sections of junk DNA that I have. I convince Cepta to let me look inside her again, and her junk DNA is almost identical to mine. There must be some link between these differences and what is happening to Aristotle now; I can feel it.

But I don't know how to fix it, or if it can be fixed, or what to do. I'm as helpless as I was before.

I ask Cepta what she makes of it, but she doesn't answer. She's distracted, deep in Aristotle's mind. Even as he is about to die, she is trying to learn something from him, and he is somehow resisting, and I'm both puzzled and angry and can't follow her thoughts.

And then he is gone.

The link between the three of us is broken with his death, and I open my eyes. My vision is defocused, split. It wavers, and then two become one again.

Cepta has moved on to a woman behind us.

Callie is holding a boy's hand; he's crying out, and there are tears in her eyes. I frown. What was his name? Jamar—yes, Jamar. His hair—that's how I remembered him. It sticks out in odd tufts.

Like my hair did when it was growing back after the fire. I changed my hair—changed my DNA.

I don't walk. He's on the floor, like Aristotle's body. Easier to crawl.

Callie protests. "You can't do this anymore," she says. She's right, but how can I stop? He'll die screaming in pain if I don't help him right now.

I ease her away and take her place by his side.

I smile at Jamar, hold his eyes and *reach* out to him. We are joined, inside.

Now there are others in my mind to help. Beatriz has linked them together and found me again. They ease his pain, and I focus deeper inside. Cells, DNA, junk DNA—but like all those who die, he is missing the sequences that I have, that Cepta has.

But what does it actually *do*?

With Beatriz shielding me, now I can think.

Go back to basics.

Genes in DNA code for RNA; DNA is transcribed to RNA, making a messenger that can be translated into protein—the stuff we are made of, head to toe, is all produced this way.

But junk DNA doesn't do this—it doesn't code for any known genes. It's thought to be structural—purpose or purposes largely unknown. Hence called junk.

How do differences in junk DNA change whether someone lives or dies?

I don't know.

But die he does: Jamar, and then another, and another.

Until finally they are all gone. I lie down among them, as still as they are, on the ground. Callie tries to raise me, but I can't even open my eyes. I hear her footsteps; she's gone. Cepta too. I'm alone with the dead.

What use am I as a healer? Everyone dies, and as each one slips away in a kaleidoscope of fear and agony, they take part of me with them. Soon nothing will be left behind but an exhausted shell, one that has almost stopped feeling anything at all. I wish it would stop completely and take away the pain of the dead—their last thoughts and memories. But the only way that can happen is if I die too.

It wouldn't be much of a step for me to take now, crossing the line between living and dying. My fatigue is absolute, and with it comes cold, deep and numbing. A cold that settles into my bones, makes them stiff—awkward. As if the parts of me that move don't coordinate anymore—instead they drag what they are joined to along.

The tiredness and cold are one and the same—I can't tell them apart. I can't heal myself. I'm lying still. Quiet. I can't move or I'll shatter.

Callie is back now, Xander with her. I vaguely feel him gather me up. He carries me out of the hall of death.

The night air is chill, and I shiver.

I blank out again, and when I come back to myself, I'm in my bed, alone with Callie. She is the one who comforts me now.

My thoughts are thick and slow, but sleep won't come: *too tired to sleep* sounds ridiculous, but it's exactly what I am.

Why didn't I run away, refuse to try again? I never made a choice—it was thrust upon me.

Xander—he's my father, but that feels remote and disconnected from who or what I am. He thinks this duty is mine. That it falls on me even as it is killing me.

Because death isn't just when the last breath is taken and the heart stops beating, when the last synapses in the brain fire and then thought is gone. There are other ways to die—slowly, but just as sure.

When hope is gone, there is nothing left.

CHAPTER 5

CALLIE

I'M FLYING. *An island spreads out below me—it's dead and dark. Something has happened here, something bad.*

But there is also something—someone—good: Kai, my brother, and Shay, my friend. They are both there below me, walking across the blackened landscape.

Shay's mind touches mine, seeks me out—wants to know if I'm okay to do this. And I'm not, but somehow when we find the place, the burned-out barn, I know I have to do it anyway.

Still linked with Shay, I slip through the crack in the rock and travel down, down, down . . . into nightmare.

I force my eyes open to end the dream, but it's still there. I'm both me, in this bed, and somebody else in another place—one that holds nothing but terror. Gradually it fades, but my heart is still beating fast, body tense, poised as if to run.

Another dream that is not a dream. She has a name, one I know now: *Jenna*.

I can't stay still, and I sit up, get out of bed. I want Shay, but I can't wake her. I can't. Not after what she's been through. But maybe if I can just see her, I'll feel better.

I follow the walls in the darkness from my room to her bedroom door: it's open? But I closed it last night. I peer inside, then go closer to confirm with my hands what my eyes strain to see. Her bed is empty.

I switch on a hall light and then quickly check the rest of our small house. She's not here.

I'm worried. Where could she be? Just a few hours ago, she was too tired to even speak.

I open the front door to the chill and dark. It must be cloudy. I can't see any stars. I can hardly make out the dark shapes of the trees beyond the house.

There is a thump next to me and, still freaked from my dream, I almost scream. But it's only Chamberlain. Did he jump down from the roof? I bend to pet him.

"Do you know where Shay is?" I say. He turns his head, eyes glinting green—they seem to reflect the thin light from the door. And then he starts walking down the path.

I hesitate, goose bumps on my back and neck. Did he actually understand what I said? I follow him.

Shay sits alone in the dark by the pyres—the almost dark, as there are flickers and sparks from still-smoldering fire. Chamberlain is by her feet, giving me a look that seems to wonder how I ever doubted him.

"Shay?"

She is so still. I go closer, take her hand—it's ice cold.

"It isn't good to be here," I say. "Come home with me."

"I don't understand," she says, voice faint.

"What?"

"Why they died and I didn't. I got sick, but I didn't die." Her voice is wistful, like she wishes she could join them.

"I didn't even get sick."

"Lucky. It's not fun, before or after." She turns to me, puts a cold hand on the side of my face. "Immune," she says.

"Yes."

She frowns. "Could that be an answer? So obvious to check, and yet . . ."

"Check? What?"

"Callie, is it okay if I look inside of you? I need someone who is immune to check how they are different from or the same as those who die and those who survive." Her voice is stronger now.

"Then will you go to sleep?"

"Yes. At least, I'll try."

"All right, then. Go on."

Shay's mind joins with mine. I can feel even more strongly now how exhausted she is, and I'm worried.

Never mind, she whispers inside. *This won't take long.*

But it does. When she is finally finished, she is even weaker, and I have to help her back to our house, and into her bed.

CHAPTER 6

SHAY

I KNOW THAT IF I DON'T SLEEP SOON, I'll be no good to anybody.

But later that same morning, I'm still lying in my bed, eyes open. I can't leave it alone: how does it all fit together?

I'd found a hidden darkness, deep inside me. I thought this shielded any antimatter hidden away, that this was why I survived.

But it's not as simple as that.

Those who survive have repeating sections of junk DNA that those who die lack. I've confirmed this now with Aristotle, Jason, others. Though my group of survivors is limited, true: just Cepta and me.

And then I had to know, to see what is the case with the immune—like Callie. And she didn't have those sections of junk DNA either. There didn't seem to be *anything* different between her and those who get sick and die! I spent ages looking and found nothing—just the usual small variations you get between different people, the variations that make them different from each other. If one of them somehow made this difference between life and death, I have no way to know which it was.

What else can I do?

Maybe . . . I need to see someone who isn't immune, isn't sick, and doesn't have the repeating DNA survivors have—and see what is different between them and someone who is sick? Or even better, how they change if they become ill.

But of course I could never do that: take a healthy person and expose them to the epidemic to see what happens.

Shay? It's Xander again.

I consider ignoring him, but what is the point? He'll know I'm awake.

Yes?

Not asleep?

I should be. I can't. Things keep turning over and over in my mind.

A sign of genius.

I don't think so; if I don't sleep soon, I'll cease to function completely.

Perhaps talking things through will make it come easier.

Maybe.

I'll come to you.

He cuts off then, not leaving me a chance to say yes or no. I sigh. I'm not sure I'm up to verbal sparring with Xander right now, keeping things hidden that should stay hidden. Maybe he knows that, and that is why he insists on now.

I haul myself out of bed, walk into the front room. Callie looks up from her book, and a disapproving look crosses her face.

I sigh. "I know, I know!" I sit next to her. "I can't sleep. And Xander is coming over." She holds my hand. I feel like we've reversed roles, big and little sister, and it makes me feel warm inside that she cares. I study her, aware suddenly that I've been neglecting her and forgetting why I'm here—to make her well. To take her home.

Another healing task where I'm failing.

We hear Xander approach.

"Shall I stay or go?" Callie says.

"Up to you."

The door opens.

"I'll go."

CHAPTER 7

CALLIE

I CUP ONE HAND ON THE ROUGH BARK OF A TREE near the edge, stretch out my arm—use my body weight to swing forward. Weight and then momentum turn me in a spin toward the other side of the tree. My mind is blank; I've made it that way as much as I can. I have no purpose. No thought.

Chamberlain leans his head sideways, watching, whiskers twitching. He's puzzled, I think, as to why when I spin from one side, I then stop dead. As if I hit a wall—one that isn't there in the usual sense, but I can't move beyond it into the nothingness.

Defeated once again, I drop to the ground. Chamberlain rubs his head against my hand until I reach and pet him, scratch his head, behind his ears. He drops beside me, warm against my leg.

Before everyone started dying, Shay had told me that there were walls in my mind, that she'd taken them down as much as she could. I can't ask her to check again now, to see if she's missed anything, not with what she's been through. Yet if they are all gone, then why can't I move beyond the edge of the world?

I *know* the world doesn't really end here. I know Chamberlain has stepped beyond and come back again, that other Community members have appeared from the nothing to come home again—to come home to die.

So it isn't that I'm fooled—I truly believe there is a world beyond this place, that I should be able to step through to it.

But I still can't do it. And I can't see it either.

What is really stopping me? Why can't I leave?

I sit on the ground, against the tree. Something still isn't right with me; I know it isn't. I'm so much better since Shay has been here, but something—someone—is still there, just out of my sight in much the same way that the rest of the real world is just out of my sight from this place.

Jenna.

She's still with me, in the shadows, around my edges. I can feel her presence. Hear her whispering inside me. She's been quiet, waiting for something. I don't know what.

She comes in my dreams, content with that for now. But I can feel her impatience growing.

She wants out.

CHAPTER 8

SHAY

"SO, THERE ARE GENETIC DIFFERENCES between those who survive and everyone else—both the immune and those who die from the epidemic," Xander says.

"Yes."

"Interesting. Why do you think this is?"

I tilt my head, look back at him. "Why do you ask *why*, rather than *what does it do* so we can try to work out how to stop it?"

"Changes in the genetic code of a species over time: what do they mean?"

"Changes can be from environmental and other pressures; mutations that are random are then perpetuated if they give a survival advantage."

"Yet ninety-five percent don't survive this epidemic. It's like it's going the other way."

"Unless these genetic differences are just random. Until the epidemic hit, they didn't mean anything."

"Do you believe that?"

"I don't know." I try to focus closely and fail. I lean back, eyes closed. Sleep is coming for me at last, no matter what either of us may want, and my thoughts are floating the way they do before you nod off, random fragments and images flickering through my mind. How'd we end up having junk DNA that most people don't? DNA that makes us survive?

I open my eyes again. "How can you get wholesale repeating sections of DNA in some people and not others? Random mutation here and there couldn't do that. It's almost like . . . it was done on purpose."

He's thinking. "The best gene splicing and editing technology we have now probably couldn't do that. Even assuming it could be done, and even if the changes could be made in germ cells so they'd be passed on to offspring, it would take generations to distribute it in the population like it is. If you go back long enough ago to distribute an applied change through the population, that technology wasn't even dreamed of then."

"All this talking about *why* is very interesting, but isn't the whole point to try to come up with a way to stop people from getting sick, stop them from dying? All I can see is that the immune and those who die lack these sequences—assuming that what I've seen in the small sample sizes is the same for everybody. So maybe we can predict who will survive if they get sick after being exposed to the epidemic, but that isn't going to help anybody else. And me adding a chunk of DNA to somebody to save them isn't something I think is possible. It's not like when I made my hair straight—that was a tiny adjustment to a gene that was already there. I can't create whole repeating sections of DNA from nothing. And we still have no way to predict who will be immune."

"You need subjects who haven't been exposed to the epidemic—to study the differences further and, once you know if they are immune or not, to compare more closely between immune and non-immune subjects."

"No."

"No?" He's surprised I'm objecting to the obvious next step—

the one I'd realized myself earlier—but *no no no*. I'm not experimenting on healthy people, not like that. It's wrong. Besides, all I need right now is to sleep.

I close my eyes and slip into black.

CHAPTER 9

CALLIE

BY THE TIME I GET BACK TO THE HOUSE, Shay is fast asleep. She's on the sofa, a blanket around her. Did she fall asleep midsentence?

Xander is still there, on a chair across the room. He's got a certain look Cepta used to have sometimes, one I'd learned meant *do not interrupt, no matter what.* He's thinking.

Then his eyes weird out, and I know he's gone; his mind is off doing whatever it is that survivors can do. The house could burn down and I doubt he'd notice.

CHAPTER 10

SHAY

I WAKE UP IN THE MIDDLE OF THE NIGHT and stretch. The fatigue has been reduced, but it's not gone, though I must have slept a good ten hours at least. My head is pounding.

Tea. That's what I need.

When I open my door, there's a faint light down the hall. Callie's door is partway open. I look in, and her eyes look back at mine.

"You're awake?" she says.

"So are you. Tea?"

She gets up, and we walk to the kettle together.

"I know why I'm awake: because I slept all day long. How about you?"

She shrugs. "I don't know. Funny dreams."

"Funny, but not funny?"

"Yeah." There is a shadow across her aura. What is it?

We make our drinks, go to the sofa. There's something niggling at me, something about Callie—there was something I was supposed to do . . . and then I remember: the edge of the world.

"You mentioned you wanted me to see if there are other blocks in your mind."

"Yes," she says, and she's being truthful, but there is something else too. Something she's keeping close.

"Do you want me to look for blocks now?" I ask, and she nods.

I close my eyes—not that it is necessary to do so, but it seems easier when I'm still tired—and *reach* out, touch Callie's mind.

I've already removed some blocks before. There were ones that stopped her from being herself, others that made it so she couldn't break certain rules, like where she could go around Community. Shouldn't being able to see how to leave this place be the same sort of thing? But all the superficial, obvious ones are gone. What else could there be?

Gently, I sift through her memory of going to what she calls the edge of the world. When we went there together a while ago, I saw through her eyes how the world disappears, but I still can't understand why she sees it this way. I search closer and closer, but I can't detect any psychic barriers. If they are there, they are so deep I can't find them.

I let her go, open my eyes, shake my head. "I couldn't find anything. I'm sorry."

"So, I guess I'm just crazy, then."

"No! Of course not. Just because I can't find something doesn't mean it isn't there. I'll think about it. Maybe if we actually go there and I try again, I might find something?"

"Okay," she says.

"Is there something else that is worrying you?"

"No. Well, not really."

"Not really?"

Callie looks down so she's not meeting my eye. She shakes her head.

"Maybe I can help if you tell me?"

She sighs. "It's . . . well, it's Jenna."

I'm startled. "Jenna? What about her? Ah. Is it that nightmare—have you been having it again?"

"The burning one? No."

275

"Something else?"

"Yes. I've dreamed about her a few times."

"You haven't woken up screaming."

"No. I don't seem to do that anymore; not since I know who I am, and who she is. But it's awful."

"Tell me."

"It's like I'm flying through the air. It's at night, but there's enough light to see, like the sky isn't quite dark even though the sun is gone. You're there, with my brother, walking across an island. It's like it's all been in a disaster or something; everything is blackened, burned."

I'm listening to Callie's words, but they're drawing me back to my memory of Shetland. The wasteland after the fires.

"And then there's what looks like a burned-out barn," Callie says. "There is a crack inside it that I can make myself thin enough to flow through. And then I fly down and down, and it's awful." She shudders. "There's skeletons, and you can see their eye sockets. Usually I wake up about then."

The hair is standing up on my back, my neck, and I shiver.

She looks up now and meets my eyes. "What's wrong, Shay?"

"That's all real—it happened. I was there."

"I don't understand. How do I dream about things that I didn't see myself? Why?"

I take her hand. "I don't know."

"I'm crazy. That's it, isn't it?" She says the words with a bit of a wobble in the middle, like she's trying to face something.

"No, you're not!"

"Sure. These things that happen in my head are all very reasonable and rational."

"Look, it's not like you're making things up and thinking they are real. Somehow you know things that actually happened to Jenna, as if you have her memories. I don't understand how, or why, but it's real. You're. Not. Crazy. All right?" I nudge her shoulder. "All right?" I say again.

"All right." She gives me a small smile.

I reach out, hug her, and she hugs me back.

"Thank you," she says.

"I'm sorry I haven't been there for you much lately."

"It's okay," she says, but it really isn't—she spends too much time alone for a thirteen-year-old—especially one who appears to be channeling a dead girl.

CHAPTER 11

CALLIE

SHAY GOES BACK TO SLEEP, but I can't.

Jenna is in the shadows. She knows I'm alone.

I've spent a lot of time trying to hold her away, to pretend she's not there—because if I accept she's real, doesn't that prove that I can't tell the difference between things that exist and those that are only in my mind?

But Shay said I'm not crazy. That Jenna was real, that things she's shared with me actually happened.

If I'm not crazy, then what does it mean?

Maybe I don't have to slip to unconsciousness and wait for Jenna to reach out to me in a dream. Maybe I can reach out to *her*.

"Jenna?"

She's happy—that's understating what she feels. Her mind joins with mine in overwhelming joy.

I see so many things. She's excited and shows one memory after another, until we get to the day she first found Mum in Newcastle.

I see through her eyes, savor the memory—watching Mum. I feel Jenna's joy and my own to see her again.

I want to leave this place and go to her—to Mum. I have to find the way to get beyond the edge.

Jenna's approval fills me.

But all of the things she shows me are from when Jenna thought she was me.

"Who was Jenna as herself?" I ask her, and there is quiet. She's withdrawing, and then she's gone.

CHAPTER 12

SHAY

AS SOON AS I'M AWAKE THE NEXT DAY, Xander is there.

"Are you feeling better?" he asks.

I shrug. "Physically, yes."

"I'm sorry the last days have taken so much out of you."

I turn to him, surprised.

"I do know that they did, and I'm sorry. But you can see how important it is. Maybe you can find a way to change the course of the illness. You seem to have a particular knack for healing work, one that I don't share. If you figure this out and then if you could teach others how to do it too? Think how many lives we could save."

"I'm not saying it isn't a good cause. I'm just not convinced there is anything we can do."

"Just because a problem is hard doesn't mean it isn't worth tackling. Solutions often hide, but they will be there, presenting themselves when you least expect it—usually when you're thinking or doing something else."

And this brings my mind to another problem: Callie. I know I have reason to be cautious with what I tell Xander, yet he may know something that I could use to help her.

"Speaking of which . . ."

"Yes?"

"Callie. She's been having more nightmares."

"Do you want me to get Cepta to—"

"No! Whatever it was you were going to suggest—no. She's okay; she's not freaking out or anything. It's what Callie has been dreaming about that concerns me."

"This is more Cepta's area."

"I'm not so sure about that. Callie has been dreaming about Jenna."

"I don't understand this obsession she seems to have with that girl."

"It isn't that. She's been dreaming things that she'd have no way of knowing, things that happened to Jenna when I was there, so I know they are true. It's like there's some sort of link between them, tangling their memories together. I don't understand it at all."

"Isn't Jenna gone now? Didn't you say she was destroyed in that bomb blast?"

"Yes. At least, I was sure of it at the time. And if somehow I was wrong, I can't believe Jenna wouldn't come to me. If there was any way she could reach me—she would. And she hasn't."

He has that faraway look, thinking, and I don't interrupt. Finally his eyes focus back on mine. "Assume for a moment that you were wrong and Jenna did survive. How could she communicate with Callie? Only survivors could see and hear Jenna, and if she were here, you would see her too."

"That's true."

"So if Jenna as she was can't be here, and she couldn't communicate with Callie anywhere regardless, then she must be in existence somewhere else and as something else. What is she? Where is she? Why is it only Callie who is aware of her?"

"I don't know. They're not together in the same time and place in any way I can understand—how could they be? Yet somehow they are."

"If it is true, it is outside our understanding with the laws of physics as we know them: two people—or one person and an entity of some sort—tangled together. At a distance. Spooky action at a distance?"

Now I'm really startled. He's quoting Einstein's criticism of quantum physics—that entangled quantum particles that instantly influence each other no matter how far apart they are break the rules of relativity. My head is spinning. "Do you really think that is in operation here?"

"No. I'm just pointing out that the perceived impossibility of something is often explained when you understand the rules more fully." He tilts his head to one side, looking at me closely until I'm struggling not to squirm. "How about a psychological explanation? If there is a link, could it instead be between you and Callie? You are the one with memories of Jenna: perhaps you are projecting them onto Callie."

That hadn't occurred to me. But then I shake my head. "No, that can't be it. Callie was having nightmares about Jenna before I got here."

"Hmmm. True. There must be another explanation. No idea what it is at the moment, though."

"Don't dismiss a problem just because it's hard. There'll be a solution in there, somewhere—you'll probably see it when you least expect it."

He smiles to hear me saying his words back at him. "I'll think about it some more," he says, and I know he will; he's intrigued by a question he can't answer. "But before I go, there is something I came to tell you."

"What's that?"

"Prepare the spare room: a guest will be arriving soon."

CHAPTER 13

CALLIE

I'M RESTLESS. Even though the flames of the pyres are finally out, I feel as though the smoke still lingers and stains this place.

I have to get away from Community, and there is only one place to go.

My feet know the way, and I hurry until, at last, I sit by the edge, *willing* myself to see beyond it. Jenna creeps back, closer.

She isn't anything I can see either, just something—someone—I can sense without seeing. Like the world out there that can't be seen, but I still know it's there.

If I can communicate with Jenna, then there must be a way to move beyond this place too.

Jenna shows me her memory again: of Mum's face. And my tears fall.

I hold out my hands. What if Mum were right there, in the nothing? Could I step forward and reach out—hug her? Feel her arms wrap around me and hug back?

No. But I don't know why.

There's a faint sound in the distance—a mechanical thing in the sky—the helicopter? I thought I heard it go off hours ago. I sit and listen, and it's coming closer, but I can only see it in the sky when it crosses this boundary.

It stirs up the air, the dust. I wish it could clear the cobwebs in my mind.

CHAPTER 14

SHAY

SHAY, YOUR GUEST WILL BE WITH YOU SOON. *Come to the field above. We're landing.*

I frown, uneasy. I asked him before who it was and try again now, but he's not answering. There's a vague sense of amusement from him, and then he is gone.

I step out of the house just as Callie returns from her walk.

"Where are you going?" she says.

"To the landing area. Xander says he's bringing a guest."

"Can I come?"

"I don't know who it is, or whether this is good or bad."

"I'll come," she says, and there is a ripple through her aura, one that says she has to come and look out for me. And even though things should probably be the other way around, I'm glad she's coming.

We walk out under gray skies together. The helicopter has landed, the blades going around and around stirring up the trees and long grasses.

Who has he brought?

If I could make it be whoever I want, it would be Kai. And then my wishing and longing for him are so strong that I almost can't make my feet go on.

It can't be him, can it? Just because I want it to be Kai won't make it happen.

I want to know, but I don't want to know *yet*. Until I know it isn't him, there is always a chance, however small, that it could be.

But I force myself to *reach* out to the helicopter—to see if Kai's familiar pattern of energy is there.

No. Disappointment rips through me. I knew it was beyond unlikely; it shouldn't hit me so hard.

Yet it shows I'm still alive. That somehow, I still know how to hope. At least a little.

So, who is it going to be, then? I *reach* again. Whoever it is, I'm registering a mix of strong emotions—fear, anger—mostly being quelled by Xander, but they're giving him a good fight. A guest? I don't think so. Whoever it is doesn't want to be here.

The helicopter door opens; Xander emerges. He helps—a mixture of helping and dragging—someone else out the door. It's a girl with blond hair. He takes her arm, and he laughs; she's giving him some cheek, I can tell from here.

I look at her, and my stomach flips. Is it . . .

No. It couldn't be, could it?

And I'm scared and angry, but there is another rush of longing through me all at once too. I don't know whether to run toward them or away.

I look again.

It really is her; it is. *Iona.*

"Who is she?" Callie says, forgotten at my side.

Iona is looking at me, then looking again—much like I have been with her. Xander lets go of her arm.

"Shay? Shay!" Iona shrieks and runs toward me, and I run to her, and then her arms are around me, mine around her, and so many emotions are rising inside me now that I can't speak.

How is she here? Why? Xander brought her: to be a subject. Didn't he? And I'm furious and scared at once, that he could play with her life like this.

Will she catch it?

She's pulling away now, looking at me with some trace of fear in her eyes too.

Because I'm a survivor, is that it? Pain passes through me.

"Despite what you may have heard, I'm not contagious—survivors don't carry the epidemic," I say. "You believe me, don't you?"

"Yes, yes; of course I do,"Iona says, her eyes searching my face. "It really is still *you*, though, no matter how you've changed. Isn't it, Shay?"

"Yes. I'm still me. But the epidemic has been here, just a day ago. You shouldn't be here; it isn't safe."

"Tell that to Mr. Ego."

"What happened?"

Xander has caught up with Iona now, stands behind her. "I brought her along for a visit. I thought you'd be happy to see each other?"

"Take her home, Xander. Do it now."

"No."

You bastard.

I've been called worse.

The wind swirls, the helicopter blades still going behind us; someone—one of the few immune here, untouched by the epidemic—is walking toward it to deal with it for Xander. If I could fly the damn thing, I'd knock both him and Xander over and run for it with Callie and Iona.

I can still taste smoke at the back of my throat from the pyres, the bodies. The least we can do is take Iona out of the open air, to our house—a place no one has been sick.

"Come on, let's get you inside." I turn my back on Xander. "Breathe through a sleeve or something," I say to Iona.

"Will that help?"

"I don't know."

I rush her to our house, Callie with us. We get inside, shut the door, and I race around the place, closing all the windows. I'm so scared for Iona I can hardly think.

But then she stops me and takes my hand.

"Shay. I'm so sorry about your mum,"she says, and I burst into tears.

CHAPTER 15

CALLIE

"LET'S SEE IF I HAVE THIS STRAIGHT," Iona says. "This place we're at that you call Community is part of Multiverse. And you're Callie—Kai's sister? The one he and Shay were looking for?"

"Yes."

"Wow. And Mr. Ego, who is also known as *Xander*, is the head of Multiverse. And not only is he your dad, he's also Shay's dad. And she's run off to have words with him now about bringing me here." Iona shakes her head. "Really? This is all true?"

I nod.

"Where is Kai?"

"I don't know. Shay doesn't either." I'm uncomfortable with all these questions, not sure what she might ask next, so I ask some of my own. "Where did you come from? And how did you end up here?"

"Our family farm, along with some neighbors', has been barricaded off since the epidemic began; we've managed to stay clear of it. I was working in the fields with my brothers. We heard this helicopter come—it landed half on our veg garden, thanks very much. Mum'll be furious." Then pain crosses her face, as if she realizes her own departure will be harder for her mum to deal with.

"Anyway, my brother went running for his shotgun, when he just fell over. My other brother too. It was like they passed out, bang, just like that."

"They're okay?"

"Mr. Ego said he put them to sleep, that they'd wake up in a few hours."

"And then what happened?"

"He invited me for a ride. And it was like I couldn't say no, couldn't stop myself from stepping forward, getting in."

"He's like that."

"Huh. But he wouldn't tell me why he came there in the first place, where we were going, and even though I couldn't do anything about it, I was really angry."

"Believe me: I know how that feels."

"And then we landed here, and I saw Shay. But I still don't understand *why* I'm here. Shay obviously didn't know anything about me coming either."

I'm looking at her, this Iona. Shay introduced her as *my best friend* before she ran off to Xander, after telling me to fill Iona in on things. And I'd felt something like jealousy when Shay said that thing about Iona being Shay's best friend, as if Iona was going to take my place with Shay. But why did Xander bring her if she might get sick?

Then I'm remembering the things I overheard that he said to Cepta—she was upset, but he said they had to pursue this knowledge, something like that. But I truly don't understand what it means.

"I don't know," is all I say. "Maybe Shay does. Or maybe Xander will tell her."

CHAPTER 16

SHAY

"HOW COULD YOU BRING HER HERE?!" I'm so furious my hands are pushing at his chest, shoving him, without any thought.

"You needed a subject to test who hasn't been exposed to the epidemic. I brought you one."

"And you just randomly picked my best friend?"

"Shay, it was a practical, obvious solution. There are very few people available in Scotland who aren't either immune or dead: this group wasn't too far away."

"How did you even know about Iona?"

"From my computer—on Shetland. I saw the communications between you and Iona on her blog."

"So *you* were why it was compromised. Does that mean it was you who sent people to Iona's friend's place? The one Kai was going to go to?"

"Yes, but he never showed."

"Why were you trying to find him? It's not like you get along."

"No. But we were trying to find you, a known survivor. He seemed the best link. We didn't know at that point that you were at the air force facility. Likewise, we also helped Freja get away from the authorities in London, but she disappeared with Kai before we could contact her."

I shake my head, pushing out the questions, my wanting to know things that don't matter right now when only one thing does—Iona.

"How could you bring Iona here? The epidemic has been here just a day ago. She might get sick. How could you just casually risk someone's life like that?"

Not just anyone: Iona. Someone I care about.

"Don't waste time."

"What?"

"In case she gets sick, don't waste time. Here is your chance to investigate someone who is well, and then see what happens if they get sick."

My hand is a fist and taking a swing at him before I know what I'm doing, but he easily catches it in his hand. He's half laughing, then serious. "Don't push your luck, Shay."

I stare at him: he's my father, and he does these things? And it's not just what he has done that hurts. It's that he has done it to *me*, to someone I care about.

I back away from Xander, and I run.

CHAPTER 17

CALLIE

SHAY BURSTS BACK INTO THE HOUSE. Her eyes are wild.

"What's wrong?"

"He—I—I can't . . ."

"Sit down," Iona says. "Breathe. Then explain."

Shay nods, sits down across from us. Calms herself, her breathing, but her eyes are full of horror and pain.

And guilt.

"I'm so sorry, Iona. It's my fault you've been caught up in this."

"No, it isn't. It's Mr. Ego's fault. So what is he up to?"

A half smile. "Good nickname, by the way, though maybe it's more accurate to say he thinks he is God."

"So then, what is our deluded demigod up to?"

"Trying to work out how to cure the epidemic."

"It's hard to argue with that."

"You're a subject."

"Not so good."

Shay starts to explain about how everyone who lived here got sick, and how she was trying to save them—the way she can join with people, take their pain. That she saw differences in the DNA of survivors.

"Whoa. You can seriously look at somebody's DNA, kind of inside of them?"

"Yes. And survivors have extra DNA that no one else has."

"Do I have it?"

"I don't know. I can check. But only about one in fifty thousand who get sick survive." Shay's face is a misery.

"I still don't understand why he brought me here."

"About one in twenty are immune. If you're not immune, I can see how you change from before being ill and during the process of becoming ill—see if there is a way to bias what is happening toward survival. I haven't done that before. I've only seen people when they are already really sick."

"So he actually *wants* me to be infected? Deluded demigod is too good for him." She says a string of swears, not all I'm sure I've heard, and while I've been listening to Shay explain these things to Iona, I'm beginning to understand some things I didn't before. And remembering things I heard. Horror is growing inside of me.

"Shay? Jamar told me some things when he was sick."

"What's that?"

"He said no one was sick at the farm. That they were told to come back here, and some people met them on the way before they got here—he thinks that's who they caught it from."

"*What?*"

"Who's Jamar?" Iona says.

"There was a group of about ten who were away when the illness struck," I say. "Xander said they were already sick. That they came home to die."

"That's not what Jamar told me."

"Xander deliberately brought them here? I mean, I'd wondered at the time, but he convinced me—and Cepta too—no. He lied, and we believed him."

"Xander is a deluded demigod megalomaniac murderer: double

D, double *M*," Iona says, and then adds more swear words. "Though maybe I'll be a survivor, and he's out of luck?" she adds.

"You could be. Or you could be immune."

"One in twenty chance of immunity: not the greatest odds. Though if I had a one in twenty chance of winning the lottery, I'd think it was worth a shot. Not so keen on one in fifty thousand."

"I don't know how to tell if someone will be immune or not. But do you want to know if you might be a survivor if you get sick? Though I don't have to do any of what he wants me to do. We could just do what we like tonight and see what happens tomorrow."

"Tempting—just to be able to waggle our middle fingers at him. But is there a chance that if I'm not immune, you could do something about it if I get sick?"

"Maybe; I don't know. I haven't managed it before." Shay's head drops to her hands.

"I bet if there is a way, you'll find it," I say.

Shay looks up, a half smile there, but it falls away. "Thank you, Callie. But all I've done so far is fail." She turns to Iona. "So. Do you want to know if you could be a survivor?"

CHAPTER 18

SHAY

IONA IS NERVOUS, and there isn't much that scares her.

"What do you have to do? Does it hurt?"

"No. All I'm going to do is join with your mind, then have a look at your DNA and anything else I can find. If it looks as though you're likely to be a survivor based on that, I might compare your DNA to Callie's too: is that okay, Callie?"

"Of course."

"So, here we are: the perfect sample group for you to poke around in," Iona says. "An immune, a survivor, and me: the great unknown. What do you mean, exactly, by joining with my mind? Is it like a Vulcan mind-meld?"

"I don't know, maybe. You'd have to ask Spock."

"Really, it's okay," Callie says. "Xander would have been doing it before to make you get on the helicopter and stuff—it didn't hurt, did it?"

"You mean you could make me do stuff too?" Iona says to me.

"I could. But I won't."

"All right. Go. But you'll stop if I ask you to?"

"Of course."

Iona is sitting straight upright in her seat, rigid.

"Maybe try to relax a bit? Just lean back, close your eyes. Be comfortable. This may take a while. Remember to breathe." I'm saying that as much to myself as to her. As close as we were before, we'll be closer now. Will she be like Kai, and hate that I can do this?

I *reach* out.

Hi, Iona.

She's startled. "Shay?" she says out loud. Not that I can hear her—when I'm *reaching* out like this, my physical awareness of myself and my surroundings vanishes—but I can see it inside her that she has done so.

You can talk out loud if you want to, but you can also say it in your head and I'll still hear it.

Shay. This is weird.

Yep. Sorry, I'm the Mistress of Extreme Weirdness now. And I let her see my feelings, not just me seeing hers.

How lonely that must be. She takes my hand, squeezes—again, not something I can feel physically, just through Iona's mind.

If you hold my hand now, I can't feel it. I'm just in my mind, not in my body while I do this.

Mega-weird. Sorry. Go on, do whatever it is.

Just leaving a light touch on her thoughts, her mind, in case she wants me to stop, I *reach*: further inside, blood, cells, particles, waves. I spin around within her, not wanting to look close enough to know. But that's why I'm here, isn't it?

I force myself to focus on Iona's DNA. And they're not there—the repeating junk DNA sequences I have, and Cepta has—they're not there. Chances were small, but I'd still hoped. If we're right about how this works, then if Iona gets sick, she won't survive. Is there any chance she hasn't been exposed to it coming here, where others have died so recently? Could it pass her by?

But that's not the end of the question: she could still be one of the five percent who are immune.

I study closer and deeper along every strand of her DNA, every gene, every protein. I join with Callie too, to see if there is anything I've missed that is different about her.

Maybe—just maybe—there is something about the actual structure of some of the DNA that is different in Callie? The way it is packed together or something? But I'm not sure.

Finally, I can't put this off any longer.

I withdraw, open my eyes. Iona's meet mine.

"Give it to me straight," she says.

"Okay. If we're right about how this all works—going by your DNA—you won't survive if you fall ill. All we can do is hope that you are immune."

CHAPTER 19

CALLIE

WE FOUND SOME POPCORN and got Anna in the kitchen to make special unhealthy treats. We're staying up all night. Because, as Iona said, if this could be her last night, she might as well enjoy it.

"Are you sure there isn't something to drink?" Iona says.

"Sorry," Shay says. "It's not really the Multiverse way. Though there is something else I could do: I can boost your serotonin. You'll feel amazing."

"Leave that for when I get sick."

"*If.*"

"I think Cepta has some wine," I say.

"Really?" Shay says, surprised. "Should we invite her?"

"Who is Cepta?" Iona asks.

"She was—well, I guess she still is—the Speaker for this branch of Community," Shay says. "Like, she's in charge when Xander isn't here. But they haven't been getting along that great."

"Sounds like a good reason to invite her," Iona says.

"Callie? Do you mind?"

I hesitate. "No," I say, even though I do. "But can you have wine, Shay? When you might have to be joining minds and healing and all that later?"

"No problem; I can metabolize it out of my system in a blink if I need to."

"No hangovers?" Iona says.

"No chance."

"Okay, let's invite her!"

Shay's eyes weird out, and Iona's do in a different way: she hasn't seen that before.

"What's with Shay's eyes?" Iona says.

"It means she's *reaching* somewhere, to talk to somebody or something. She was like that the whole time she was joined with you."

"Wow."

Shay's eyes go back to normal. She frowns. "Cepta isn't answering. Maybe we should check on her? She hasn't been quite right since— well. Since so many people died." Her eyes flash to Iona with a *sorry* for having mentioned that.

"I'll go," I say.

"Are you sure, Callie?"

"Yes."

"I'll keep contact so I'll know if you want me to come, all right?"

I nod and open the door, step outside. It's dark already. So much of the day passed us by with Shay and Iona joined, me waiting. If Iona is infected already, that was hours of the time gone by until she gets sick—it's usually about a day; isn't that what Shay said? I'm sure they want to talk alone for a while, without me there, and I walk the long way around to Cepta's. I can feel a trace of Shay there, in my mind, listening in case I need help. Unlike when Cepta used to do it, it is comforting.

There is a faint, flickering light in Cepta's bedroom window. I knock, but she doesn't answer, and finally I open the door, look in. There is no one in the front room. I step in, peer into the small kitchen: empty.

Her bedroom door is open. It's never open; she always leaves it closed, and I'm curious. She'd have noticed I'm here by now for sure if she was in there.

I peer around the bedroom door, then—startled—take a step back. She's sitting on her bed, cross-legged. Still.

I look closer: her eyes are wide-open and weirded out. She's joined with somebody or *reaching* somewhere. She can't tell I'm here.

Her room is grander than other bedrooms I've seen in Community, where everything is simple and functional. The bed is bigger, and it's got pretty, filmy curtains that hang down from the ceiling and drape around it. The window is open, and the curtains wave slightly in the faint breeze, nearly catching the candle on the bedside table. I tiptoe in, watching her eyes, and blow out the candle—hoping she'll just think the wind did it or something, and I won't have to explain why I was creeping around her room.

Back in the kitchen, I open the refrigerator: inside it is a bottle of wine. *Sauvignon Blanc*, the label says. Is that any good? There are some others in a box in a cupboard, though not as many as I remember seeing once before when I was fetching Cepta's lunch. I hurry, scared now she'll hear me. I keep the cold one and replace the bottle in the fridge with one from the box and creep back out. My heart is beating fast.

Shay must notice. *Is everything okay, Callie?* she asks in my mind.

Yes. I've got a bottle of wine. I'm coming back now.

CHAPTER 20

SHAY

"AH, SHE'S A LIGHTWEIGHT," Iona says. She winks and nods at Callie, fast asleep in her chair after the half a glass we let her have.

We're on the sofa, holding hands in the dark room. The moon shines through the window.

"How does it feel to have a little sister?" she says.

"Strange. It was always just Mum and me." Pain presses into my chest again, and it's a moment before I can speak. And Iona knows—and waits. It's like we're joined even though we aren't right now: we understand each other. It's so good to see her, to talk to her. But what if . . .

No. I push that thought—of what might happen to her because she was brought here—firmly away. We agreed: tonight is for us. Not Xander, not the epidemic—just us.

"Tell me about Kai," Iona says. "What happened there?"

"He did everything he could to find me. And when he did—well.

I was an idiot. I didn't believe some things he told me about Xander; he didn't believe some things I told him about his sister. I decided to go with Xander to find Callie, and here I am."

"And Kai didn't go with you? Why not?"

"For a start, it's a long story—but he didn't believe that Callie was still alive. And I couldn't tell him why I left, because he wouldn't listen."

"Sounds like he's stubborn."

"Yes, he is; and he has a temper too. But it was fair enough in this case. He was also really upset I hadn't told him that Xander is my father. He was right; I should have." I sigh deeply. "But anyway, I'm still hoping. I asked a friend of his to tell him why I left. I hope she did."

"Aye. To hope," Iona says, and clinks her glass against mine.

"How are you feeling?" I ask her, unable to stop myself.

"Happy to be with you, scared, angry at that double *D*, double *M* you call Dad."

"I never call him that!"

"Well, you know what I mean."

"What I meant was, how are you *feeling*? You know, physically and stuff."

She shrugs, not answering, and cold fear creeps inside me. "Tell me," I insist.

"Well, I've got a small headache. It's probably the wine."

Her aura shines in the dark, all that she is now, all that she has been—and will be, for however much time she has. And shadows are there: faint patches still, but beginning to darken and spread. She has a headache, yes, but that's not all. "Are you aching a bit inside too?"

"I guess so." She sighs, looks down. "It's nothing I can't ignore."

She wants to pretend it isn't there, isn't happening, but what if I can help? "Let me check you out from the inside."

She sighs, puts her glass down on the table. "Looks like the party is over." Her eyes meet mine. There is fear in her aura, but she's trying to hide it. "Whatever happens, I'm glad I saw you again."

"Me too." *But I so wish you'd never come.* The pain she will feel will overwhelm me. It was bad enough with someone I only knew for weeks; what will it be like with Iona?

I have to fight to hold on to *hope*: without it I can only fail, as I have over and over again. But how?

Iona's eyes echo the fear she tries to hide. I can fake it for Iona— then maybe it'll feel real.

"We can do this; I know we can. We'll get through this together. All right?"

She gives a little nod.

"All right?" I say again, louder this time.

"Right! Now do what you have to do. Let me know if I can help."

"You lie down—be comfortable." I get up, and she pulls her feet up on the sofa. I tuck a pillow under her head; she winces a little. I sit on the floor next to her. She puts her arm around me lightly.

"Okay. I'm ready," she says.

I *reach* inside Iona.

I had no doubt, not really. But it's still a kick in the guts to see it inside of her. It's started.

CHAPTER 21

CALLIE

I'M TRAVELING THROUGH MEMORIES *from long ago: a Christmas, Kai holding me up to put an angel on the top of the tree. A trip to the beach with him and Mum. The day he gave me the dolphin necklace.*

And it's lovely, so lovely it takes me a while to realize that it isn't me who wanted to see these things: it's Jenna.

I separate her wishes from mine.

Jenna, why are you here with me?

She doesn't know why, but there is something she does know, something she doesn't want to tell me.

Please. I have to understand.

She hesitates. She gets why I need to know, but she's scared.

We can do it together, she/I think.

Everything shifts and changes: we're with Shay? And we're with Chamberlain. Shay is crying; Jenna is there. They're on a bed, wrapped around each other.

Someone shouts: Get out of the house! *in my/Jenna's mind, Shay's too. We tell Shay Kai is there, is coming.*

Shay gets up, scoops up Chamberlain, runs out of the house, rips the door open.

Sees Kai running toward her.

And . . . what is falling from the sky?

I/Jenna wrap myself around Shay and Chamberlain—covering them—just before the bomb hits.

LIGHT

SOUND

PAIN

Then a scream reverberates in my ears that isn't in this memory/dream.

I open my eyes, heart pounding wildly, unsure at first if it is me that is screaming. But then the room comes into focus.

Shay is there, sitting on the floor next to Iona.

It's Iona: she's crying out in pain.

CHAPTER 22

SHAY

I'M SHIELDING IONA'S PAIN AS MUCH AS I CAN while still focusing inside of her. Her agony doubles within me: there is the actual pain, and the pain of it being *hers*.

And this time I see how it happens—from the beginning.

Whatever triggers this illness—is it the dark light lingering from those who were sick? It acts like a catalyst, triggering the repeating sections of junk DNA inside of her: genes that are never normally active kick into gear and are transcribed again and again, until the cell is flooded with RNA copies. At the same time, these are translated to make a new protein—the one I'd found in dying cells before. The protein-making machinery of an infected cell is taken over, goes faster and faster, and it's like a cascade: a few drops become a waterfall. It is happening everywhere, and her cells are starting to die.

But how do I stop it? I can't. Failure faces me: it's ugly.

I'm in Iona's mind still; I can't not be—I have to be there for her in all the ways that I can.

You said you could do something—do it! she says.

But I don't know how.

There's a wave of agony inside her that I buffer as much as I can. It subsides to a degree. *Think: what did you do? You got sick. How did you stop it inside of you?*

I didn't do anything. It just happened.

Another wave takes her again, and her thought and reason are lost for seconds, then return.

And I can't take her pain: I want to run, to hide, to *stop*. But it's not just the physical pain. It's remembering Mum dying and trying to help her—to show her how to compartmentalize the pain. To put it away like I'd done. She couldn't do it.

Maybe there is something in that?

Another wave magnifies Iona's pain, precious seconds lost.

Iona, listen to me. Look in my mind at what I show you. Put the pain away. Put it in a drawer and shut it.

I show her what I mean, and she's visualizing, trying to do as I said.

It won't fit in a drawer. She's crying.

Something bigger, then—a whole house.

There is another wave. I'm not sure how much longer she can withstand this.

I have to hang on to *hope*. Think, Shay. I got sick, just like Iona is—this out-of-control cascade must have been happening within me too, just like it is to Iona now. Why did it stop in me? If it is because of this extra DNA I've got, what did it do?

Maybe it wasn't just putting the pain away, it was having somewhere to put it too—not just the visualization of an imagined room or building but a real place.

The dark shadow—buffer, whatever it is—inside of me. The one that I can sense? Is that it? Is that what this extra DNA I have codes for?

I can't change Iona's DNA like that—there is no way that I know of to transfer DNA from me to her, no way to create it from nothing inside of her.

I have to look more closely at what it might have made inside of me.

Iona? You're on your own, just for a moment. I love you.

307

I let go of Iona's mind and *reach* deep inside myself. Further, deeper, beyond where I've gone before: I fight to see it more clearly, but it is trying to see that which can't be seen.

Maybe . . . it is like staring at an aura: I have to *unlook* to see.

And I have it more clearly now. Deep inside me: a dark shield. This is the drawer, or house, or whatever physical symbol you want—this is what hides the pain. This is what Iona needs.

If Iona can't make her own, can I share mine? It doesn't seem to have physical size or quantity in the way ordinary things do. It is both nothing and everything. Tiny and immense.

I can try to channel it. The way I can use particles as waves. Waves of dark healing this time, from me to Iona.

Don't let me be too late. I *reach* back to Iona. There is just a whisper, a bare spark, of who she is inside of her still. She's alive. Barely, but she's alive.

Increased hope and urgency give me strength I didn't know I had. I sense Cepta is there now too, and Beatriz. Everyone is joining together, even Xander. Together, they help me channel this dark wave to Iona.

I'm urging Iona to join in, to fight, to hide the pain away where it can never hurt her again.

And then, all at once, her pain is gone.

CHAPTER 23

CALLIE

THERE IS NOTHING WORSE THAN WAITING, watching, not being able to do anything.

I hope I did the right thing, bringing Cepta to help Shay.

Shay and Cepta suddenly slump down. Shay is crying as if her heart will break. Iona is still and pale on the sofa behind them.

Oh no, no . . .

I reach out to Shay, to take her hand.

"You did everything you could."

She looks up at me, shakes her head. "She's alive. She's just asleep. She survived."

Cepta sits up a little. Her face is as pale as Shay's. "Good thing too. I want to have a word with her about drinking my favorite wine."

CHAPTER 24

SHAY

I WATCH IONA SLEEP. Callie says I need to sleep too, and I know she's right, but I'm afraid that if I don't stay here with Iona, something will happen. She'll slip away, or when I wake up, I'll find this was all something my fevered imagination came up with, and she really died.

So I watch her, and I think.

If Iona hadn't made me go back to when I was sick, to how I stuffed the pain away like that, I don't think I'd have been able to work it out. She helped save her own life. I couldn't see how to move DNA to her, but doing it this way—the dark waves, the dark matter—did the same thing. I checked afterward, and the DNA I have, that survivors have—Iona has it now too. They must go together.

And what about Mum? If I had known how back then, could I have saved her? Maybe. There is no way to know, and I wish so much that I could travel back in time, that I could take what I know now, and save her.

Xander hails me, but I refuse to talk to him. He's exultant. I feel it before I push him out of my mind. He'll think he was right to do everything that he did—that I was able to save Iona proves it to be so.

But she could have died. Now that she's survived, will she be changed forever, like I am? If so, she might not thank us for that. And how could Xander risk her life like that? Does he know how much she means to me?

Maybe . . . he does. Maybe that is why he brought her: to motivate me to push, and push harder. To find a way to go beyond my limits.

Mum was right: there *is* a wrongness inside of him. He lies; he justifies the lies; he manipulates and hurts the people around him.

When we talked about Mum before, Xander made it seem like she left him because he was different—because he was a survivor. He made me feel like there was no chance for me and Kai, that if Mum were still here, she'd feel the same about me as she did about him. That she'd feel this wrongness inside of me too.

But how she felt about him wasn't just because he's a survivor, was it? I'm different now from when she knew me, but I'm *nothing* like Xander.

There's a sense of easing within me—a letting go. Thinking about Mum will always hurt. I'll always miss her. But if she were here, she'd still love me, no matter what. That I'm a survivor and all the weirdness that goes along with it could never change that. I'm sure of it now. It was only because of Xander that I'd questioned this: he made me question *her*. And that makes me even angrier.

And what about Kai? We *could* work things out. At least if we couldn't, it wouldn't just be because of what I am—we're not doomed by that one thing alone.

Kai warned me about Xander too. I should have listened.

One thing I do know: it's time. Callie, Iona, and me—we've got to get out of here.

PART 6

STELLAR EVOLUTION

Chaotic first elements and particles dispersed from the big bang; they condensed and developed into the stars we see at night. And so evolution continues to take the simple and make it more complex—much like we have become.

—Xander, *Multiverse Manifesto*

QUARANTINE

CHAPTER 1

FREJA

WHEN JJ HAILS ME, I'M SO STARTLED that at first I don't answer.

He tries again: *Freja? Is that you?*

Yes! It's me; where are you? I cast out to feel for his location, but find nothing. I'm puzzled. He'd have to be nearby to talk like this, so where is he?

Not so. I've gotten help with projection. Other voices join in now; some introduce themselves—Beatriz, Elena—while others are old friends—Patrick, Zohra.

I was worried when I didn't hear from you again, JJ says. *We've been trying to hail you for days; you must have just gotten within range.*

Where are you?

Scotland, on a remote farm. Where are you?

Just past Carlisle. Heading north, toward you. I almost cry, the relief is *so* strong: I didn't know how I was going to find them. Instead, they've found me.

Freja? You don't seem yourself. Is something wrong?

Yes, I say, but then I can't find the words. Instead, I show them: Azra's death, as witnessed by Wilf. And we're all together now. They're comforting me, and it's so beautiful to be together like this again that this time the tears do come.

Beautiful? I like to think I'm more handsome, JJ says, and gives me a mental hug. *What can we do to help?*

I want to join you. And bring Wilf.

What about Kai?

He's not with us anymore. I hide how I slipped away with Wilf as Kai slept; that isn't something I want to broadcast to everyone. *I need to be with you, with people who are like me. Wilf does too.*

People like me: I know that includes Xander and his Multiverse. There was that day so long ago now that I met Xander; we were in the same car when we raced to the airfield to escape SAR, just us and a driver. We talked during that long drive. I'd been suspicious of him—the way Kai felt about him, it was hard not to be—but I understand so much more now. So many of the things he said were right. We don't belong with the rest of the world. They will never accept us.

Hang on a sec, I just need to check something, JJ says. He's back a moment later. *Stay where you are. One of us will come and get you.*

CHAPTER 2

CALLIE

CEPTA IS IN MY MIND. Fully. I sit up in bed, too startled to protest or try to resist.

She's soothing, easing my fear, but with her own feelings and words, not by changing how I am inside like she used to. Then there is a rush of thought and feeling from her to me, too fast to make real sense. And then—and then she says *goodbye*. And she's gone.

I hesitate, wanting to wake Shay, to ask her what this might mean. I'm scared Cepta has done something to me again, even though I don't truly think she has. At least, not in the way she has done before. But Shay was awake a day, a night, and another day. She only slumped asleep next to Iona a few hours ago. She's exhausted; I can't disturb her.

Cepta said goodbye? And the way she said it—like it was a final, forever thing. Where could she be going?

I don't understand, but I feel . . . different. Somehow lighter, freer.

I settle back down to go to sleep. Whatever has happened, it doesn't feel like a bad thing. It can wait until the morning.

CHAPTER 3

SHAY

A NARROW FLAME FLICKERS AND WAVERS, beckons me forward to climb into bed. Dread is heavy, but I step toward it. Rest is here. Rest, rest . . .

There are filmy curtains all around—like a princess's bed. I push them aside. A bed so soft and warm, how can it feel so chilling? I should run, I know it, but there is no strength, no way to resist. Rest, rest . . .

I lower myself, lie down. The curtains close around me. The candle that called me is here; there are others too, casting thin pools of light in darkness. The curtains wave gently as I close my eyes. Rest, rest . . .

But it's all a lie, a trap. I can't open my eyes, but I can still see: the candles catch the edges of the curtains, the bed linens. Flames march prettily up the fabric as it burns, curls.

This soft bed is a pyre: a thing for the dead, not the living. But I still live, breathe.

Just.

The heat and pain is fierce, and I'm screaming.

Then the screaming is real, but it's not my voice—it's not in my ears either—it's in my mind. Fatigue is so heavy on me it's like I'm trapped under a mountain, and I have to force myself to stir.

I smell smoke.

I struggle out of bed, to the front room. Iona is standing at the open front door, holding on to the doorframe as if she'll fall if she lets go. Callie steps out of her room now too.

Iona turns. "There's a fire," she says, her voice no more than a whisper. "I see the glow—the colors. And around the stars?" Awe ripples through her aura; she's not sure what is real and what isn't—what she sees with the new eyes of a survivor.

But I can't help her right now. "Wait here," I say to Iona. With Callie at my heels, I run across Community. A house is on fire, well alight. Others are there already, forming a chain—with buckets of water—but it's futile. All they can do is stop it from spreading to the trees and houses around it.

It's Cepta's house.

I'm *reaching* for her now and calling her name out loud—Xander is too—but there is nothing.

No reply.

Her pretty bed, like a princess's?

Her candles.

Her pyre.

CHAPTER 4

KAI

I WALK UP TO THE SENTRY POINT at Chester slowly, hands out where they can see them. They don't notice me for a while—slackers. But when they do, it's all guns and attention.

"Stop! Stay where you are! Hands up!" one of them shouts.

I stop, put my hands over my head, and wait while they work out what to do.

Finally two of them come up to me in full biohazard suits.

"State your name and why you are here," one of them says.

"I'm Kai Tanzer. I'm immune, so you don't need the suits." I start to lower my hand to show my tattoo, but the movement alarms them. Their guns are now raised, and I put my hand back up.

"Don't move! What is your business?"

"I'm hoping that Dr. Sonja Tanzer—my mother—is still here? If not, I'd like to speak to Rohan."

"Rohan?" They exchange a glance.

"I don't know his full name. My mother introduced him as Rohan."

One of them talks into a radio, then I'm gestured forward.

I'm marched, armed soldiers all around, into the walled city.

CHAPTER 5

FREJA

WILF'S EYES ARE ROUND WHEN I TELL HIM that they're coming to get us in a helicopter tomorrow. "We're going up in it?"

"Yes." And I'm pleased he is showing excitement at the thought. He's barely spoken these last few days.

"Cool. Who's coming? Is it your friend you told me about?"

"No, JJ can't fly the helicopter. The pilot is Xander—the head of Multiverse."

"Tell me again what that means."

"Well, from what I understand, they are a group of mostly scientists. Some of them are survivors. JJ says they've been working on how to stop the epidemic, and lots of other projects."

We leave the bike nearby, and walk the rest of the way to a cricket pitch. Merlin follows behind, still keeping his distance from me. JJ picked the pitch as the best place near us for the helicopter to land, and asked me to have a look now—to make sure it's clear. We check for signs of life on the way.

There is nothing; this village is dead. Like so many other places.

One more day. Then we can leave it behind.

CHAPTER 6

CALLIE

WE BURY CEPTA'S BODY—what is left of it—later that day. Xander insists on being the one who wraps her in a blanket and carries her to her grave. Shay watches as he does so, a questioning look in her eye. We stand by it now. Shovelfuls of dirt are cast into a dark hole until all sight of her is gone under the earth. Xander has her gold necklace wrapped tight around his hand.

I feel sick about how she died. There has been so much death already—so many bodies for the pyres—but she was still *alive*. So many times I've dreamed Jenna's death by fire, when she died the first time. The pain and fear are there in my memory, and I can hardly hold it back enough not to scream.

"Why did this happen?" I say to Shay. "Was it an accident? She had candles, those curtains. The other night I saw them waving around and blew out her candle. If only I'd checked on her last night."

Shay's arm tucks around mine. "This isn't your fault, Callie. I promise."

"But was she just careless, or . . . ?" I can't put it into words. She said goodbye, like it was forever. And it was.

Xander turns and joins our conversation now. "Cepta was never careless; everything that she did was thought out and deliberate." And I agree this was the Cepta I knew, at least before the epidemic came here.

"Do you mean she did it on purpose?" I can't *not* ask, even though I'm scared of what he will say.

"Cepta couldn't live when so many of her people have died," Xander says. "With so much going on, perhaps she didn't get the support she needed from the rest of us." He shakes his head. "I just can't believe she's gone." And there is raw pain in his voice. "Why is she gone?" He almost sounds puzzled.

"She said goodbye to me," I say. "I didn't know what she meant. I should have known! Maybe I could have stopped her."

Xander's eyes are intent on me now. "When was this?" he asks me.

"I don't know. It was in the night. She was in my mind and said goodbye. Then I went back to sleep. When I woke up, her house was already on fire."

"You didn't know; how could you?" Shay says, and gathers me closer to her.

"We didn't always get along, but—I can't believe she's . . ." My words are choked, and now my tears are falling.

Cepta was meant to help me, and I don't think she always did. Sometimes she could be mean. But she was *always* there.

Not anymore.

CHAPTER 7

SHAY

I TAKE CALLIE BACK TO OUR HOUSE. The things I have to say to Xander now need to be said alone.

Iona is still on the sofa where we put her before Cepta's burial. She's so pale.

"How are you feeling?" I ask her. "Any better?"

"I don't know. Shaky, weak. Can barely stand. My head is weird; everything looks wrong." Her eyes are cast down as if she can't bear to look around her. Can't bear to look at *me*.

"It's the way things are with survivors, I promise. It's normal. You'll feel better soon."

"You call this normal? Huh." Her eyes are starting to close again. Soon she's asleep.

I tuck Callie onto a chair with Chamberlain. "I'll be back soon," I say, and head out the door.

We need to leave—Iona, me, Callie. I don't care if I have to put Callie to sleep to get her over the edge of the world that she sees. But

Iona—she's too weak. We'll have to wait for her to regain enough strength, to know how to use her mind and how to shield it. Otherwise she'll broadcast to everyone when we go.

But we're still here now, and I can't leave this alone: *I have to know.* What really happened to Cepta?

I walk back toward Cepta's grave: will Xander still be there? He's not, but I find him nearby—staring at the remnants of her house.

He's calling her name, projecting silently over and over again. *Cepta! Where are you?* And there is such pain in his aura, his words, that despite everything, it tears into me and my hand is drawn to his arm, to comfort him, but then—I see it, and my hand falls back to my side. He is searching for her, but not as she was.

He glances toward me, acknowledges my presence, but says nothing.

"Others have died by fire—other survivors, I mean, like those who died at the RAF institute," I say. "They didn't become like Jenna. Did you think Cepta would?"

"I wasn't sure. But why would that happen only to Jenna?"

"I don't know. Lucky that she was the only one, or the epidemic might be across the planet by now."

"Yes, of course. But I don't understand, and I don't like not understanding anything." He's frowning. "Maybe it's something about the contained fire being more intense, or the construction of the room itself." He's thinking out loud now; I can see that—speaking as if he's forgotten I'm here. Dread grows inside me as the implications of what he is saying take hold.

"Do you mean the room where Jenna died?"

"It was like the quiet room we have here—the construction—one survivors can't penetrate with their minds."

"Why would they have had a quiet room on Shetland? Jenna was the only survivor there then. How would they have known how to make it or what it could do?"

"It was a chance discovery. The density and materials needed for the walls in a room that could contain an intense, closed fire turned out to be the same as a quiet room. It was on Shetland that I worked out that it blocked survivors' minds."

"But you told me that Jenna didn't die like that. That that was what she said, but you told me—you told all of us—that she was mentally unstable, that she made it up. That she died in the underground fires and explosions that followed the oil reservoir accident at Sullom Voe."

His eyes are on me, aware now of what I've said, what he's let slip. Will he still try to deny it?

"The disaster actually began at the particle accelerator," he says. "Shutdown procedures weren't put in place like they should have been when something went wrong. Probably because people were dead, or dying, from the epidemic—from Jenna. The underground explosions from the accelerator caused the oil reservoir fires."

I process that. "So the Sullom Voe accident was a cover story?"

"The government knows what really happened now. They're not saying."

"Anyway, that's not the point: stop trying to deflect. You lied about how Jenna died."

"She was dangerous, Shay. Very. We had no choice. We didn't know it would turn her into a contagion."

I turn my head, careful to keep my thoughts shielded, but there is nothing I can do to stop the horror I'm feeling from rippling through my aura.

"You lied. You deliberately burned her in a fire—burned her alive. What she went through . . ." I shudder.

"We're not—*I'm* not—monsters. There was a colorless, odorless gas containing a knockout drug released in the room first. If what you say is true, it didn't work. She must have processed the drug out of her system, a skill I didn't know survivors possessed. Until you showed me it could be done."

I believe that when he says it, but how many other things have I believed until he later admits the lie?

"Even if that is so: what gives you the right to decide who lives, who dies?"

"She was a danger to herself and others. It was the right thing to do at the time." And he completely believes what he says.

"What about Cepta? Was she a danger to herself or others?"

324

"Obviously. Since she killed herself. Such a senseless waste of a beautiful mind." His aura ripples with sadness, and despite everything, there is still a part of me that wants to believe him. He always has such conviction, certainty, in all that he says and does. It would be so *easy* to follow him.

Like Cepta did.

I shield my thoughts carefully. Did something change between them? Did she question him about the death of her people, maybe even oppose him?

Or maybe she didn't. Maybe she did what he said to the end: to *her* end. Another one of his experiments.

He lied about how Jenna died. Who can say what is the truth about Cepta's death? That dream I had—was it a dream, or was I joined with her in my sleep?—there was no sign of Xander there, but in the dream I was scared, trapped. There's no way it was a *choice* to be there. And then he deliberately handled her body himself, so I didn't come into contact with her, couldn't sense her last moments.

Cepta could be cruel—to Callie, to others who weren't members of her Community. Some of her views I found hard to accept. But she *fought* with everything she was in order to try to save her people. I'm sure she'd have given her own life if it could have saved them.

And now, Xander wants everyone to believe she *has* given her life—but she hasn't saved anyone.

No. It can't be. She wouldn't waste her life like that in aid of Xander's schemes. I'm sure of it in my core. It's not who she was.

I'm shielding carefully, watching Xander. Somehow I always *want* to believe him, to give him the benefit of any doubt, no matter how small. The reasons for this I can hardly understand myself. Is it because he's my father that I think he should be more like me? Is it just this way he has—that he has with everyone—and the utter conviction of his own beliefs? Or maybe he has been subtle enough to adjust my aura, my mind, to influence my thoughts without me even knowing.

No matter the reasons—*enough*. I'll never believe anything he says, ever again.

I shake my head. Push him out. Walk away.

CHAPTER 8

KAI

ONE OF MY ARMED ESCORTS TAPS ON A DOOR. It's opened from within.

They salute. "Major General, sir!" And Rohan looks up from a desk. *Major general?* I don't know much about rank, but I get that a major general is right up there. Why would he even be *here*, at this little post in Chester?

"Ah, Kai; there you are." Rohan gestures at the guard. "You can go."

"Major General," I say, and nod.

"Have a seat," he says, and I sit in a chair opposite his desk. "I must say, I'm surprised to see you again. You seemed quite keen to get away from us the last time we met."

"I wasn't expecting soldiers—or you either, for that matter."

"No, I suppose not. Your mother didn't know they were there either. She was furious with me." A rueful smile. "Though they wouldn't have moved in without my signal, which was precipitated by you making a run for it."

"Is my mother still here?"

"No. She's moved on to another center." He doesn't say where.

"Am I under arrest or something?"

He tilts his head to one side. "You should be, but I haven't decided yet. Why are you here? Let's talk about it. But first there are a few things I want to tell you."

"I'm listening."

"First of all, I want to thank you. We've had confirmation in various ways that Dr. Alexander Cross is indeed still alive, and we've linked him conclusively with Shetland. We might not have done that if you hadn't put us on his trail."

"What are you going to do about it?"

"We're working on that. We don't know his exact location, though several sources suggest Scotland. There are a few known Multiverse sites there to check, though I expect they have others we don't know about. We're assembling a team from across all the armed forces—soldiers, air force, navy—also police. They are all immune, like I am, and can travel into the zones safely without biohazard suits. And we're going to go there to look for him. If he will cooperate, there is some hope that he may know how to stop the epidemic. In any event, he has charges to answer."

They believed me? They're actually going to go after Alex? I feel like I've been holding my breath—waiting for something that wouldn't happen no matter how I wished that it would—and now, it has. A tightness inside of me lets go.

But what about Freja? Shay? And Shay's friends: Beatriz, Elena, Patrick and JJ too, if they've met up. What does this mean for them? I *have* to go with them. "I'm immune. I want to be part of this."

"You're not trained. You are, in fact, wanted for a variety of reasons by the police and other authorities."

"I can help you."

"How?"

"Partly because I know Alex; I know how he thinks. But more importantly, do you understand how survivors can get into your mind, learn what they want to know, maybe take control of you? Or worse."

He inclines his head. "We have some knowledge of this, though it is difficult to isolate the truth from all the wild stories."

"I can block them so they can't control me or interfere with what I do. I can get to Alex without him being able to stop me with the use of his mind; I've already done this with him. I can help you get close to him."

"How do you block survivors? Could you train others how to do this?"

"A survivor taught me: it's about visualizing and enforcing barriers in your mind. I could explain what I do, but I'm pretty sure you'd need a survivor to help you learn how to do it—it took me a while to manage it."

He's leaning back in his chair, thinking.

"Even if only you can do it, that could be useful."

"There is something I need from you in return."

"Oh? I'm not in the business of making deals. But tell me what it is, and we'll see."

"Alex deserves whatever you want to do with him—chuck him in jail and throw away the key, at very least. But the rest of them? Other survivors who have fled to Scotland to be safe? They're *not* in the same category. They had nothing to do with what happened in Shetland. They're innocent people who got sick and survived: none of anything that has happened is their fault."

"And?"

"You have to promise not to hurt them."

Rohan stares back at me a long moment, and I don't interrupt whatever is going on in his head.

Finally he sighs. "Kai, it would be easy to make promises to you that can't be kept. I won't do that. I don't know what we'll encounter, or what means we'll have to use to achieve our objectives. But I will say this: we would never take a life unless there was no other way."

And I believe he means what he says. But what about Azra?

"You said as much the last time we spoke. But that isn't what I've seen since then. This is the real reason I came here today: to tell you what is going on out there."

And I tell him exactly what happened to her, a fifteen-year-old girl, whose only crime as a survivor was to run. Shot in the back.

His face is grave. "I will personally see that an investigation is launched into this. If what you say is true, there will be consequences for those responsible. And I give you my word: no life, survivor or otherwise, will be taken unless unavoidable. I'll ensure this message is reinforced to all personnel."

Is that good enough?

I have no choice. And if I'm there, maybe I can stop things from going the wrong way.

He holds out his hand. I take it in mine.

But as we are shaking hands, I'm still remembering Azra.

CHAPTER 9

FREJA

FREJA? A mind touches mine; it's Xander. I recognize the feel of him right away. He's distinctive both in person and this way—his voice is unique.

Yes, it's me.

I'll be there in five minutes or so. Still all clear?

Yes. No signs of life.

We'll have to go right away. There have been aircraft reported going east-west.

Air force?

Don't know. Better to avoid being sighted.

We wait in the shade of some trees at one end of the cricket pitch. Soon we can hear the helicopter, then we see it.

It seems to hover in midair above us a moment, then descends slowly. The blades kick up dust and leaves in the long grass as it lands.

A door starts to open, and I can feel Xander's impatience to get going now.

Wilf, standing next to me, is holding Merlin in a tight grip. That cat doesn't like the looks of our mode of transportation, and neither does Wilf. "Isn't he going to stop it so we can get on?"

"No, but it's all right. The rotor blades are higher than they look—they'll be well over our heads."

"Are you sure?"

"Yes," I say. "Come on." I touch his mind lightly and reassure him as much as I can as we walk under the blades, bent down because Wilf wants us to be. He's not the same boy he was before. He was never fearful, not like this. He's lost his spark.

Xander steps out now. "Freja. Lovely to see you again," he says, smiling like he always knew he would. "And this must be Wilf."

"Hi," Wilf says awkwardly.

Xander gives him and Merlin a hand up, shows him where to sit, in the front, and settles me just behind. He checks that we're belted in correctly, then gets into his seat next to Wilf.

"Do you want to learn how to fly?" he says to him.

"Can I?"

"Sure. I'm our only pilot; it'd be handy if someone else could help me out sometimes." Xander starts a commentary of all things helicopter as we take off. Soon Wilf has forgotten his fear. He's entranced.

Are you? Xander thinks.

I jump. I hadn't been aware my thoughts were so transparent. *I don't know how I feel about much of anything at the moment,* I answer, truthfully.

You've done the right thing, he says. *Bringing Wilf, yourself. There are so few of us. We have to look after each other.*

There will always be few of us. We'll always be different.

Being different can be a good thing. But in time there will be more of us, and fewer of them.

If only that could be true. It's us or them, isn't it? I sigh.

Listen to me, Freja. I have a plan; I need someone to help me. You may be the one.

He tells it to me, step by step. And it is both cruel and beautiful at once—the way nature often is.

The way I begin to see it must be.

CHAPTER 10

CALLIE

"**DINNER IS HERE,**" I **SAY.** Shay and I help Anna set our plates and things out on the table, and then Anna leaves. We haven't gone back to eating as a group in the hall—the place so many people died. There are so few of us now anyway that we'd barely fill the head table.

Iona stays curled up on the sofa.

"Iona? Will you join us?" Shay says.

"I'm not hungry."

"You have to eat. Come on, I can help you up."

Iona shakes her head, and Shay goes and kneels next to her. "Or I can bring it to you here?"

She doesn't answer. Her eyes close, then open again a moment later. She looks at Shay. "Don't talk to me like that."

Shay sighs. "You can feel better if you want to. I can show you how. But it's hard to do it by talking; it's easier to show you in your mind."

"I don't want that. I don't want any of this."

"I know. I'm sorry."

"I don't feel like myself anymore."

"You're still Iona, just like I'm still Shay. It's weird getting used to things, but—"

"No."

"No?"

"I'm not getting used to this." Her eyes are closed again.

Shay exchanges a look with me, gets up. "Let me know if you change your mind and I'll bring you something."

There's no answer.

Shay's worried; I can feel it and see it. I shut the door between us and Iona.

"Is she going to be okay?" I whisper.

"I think so. She just needs time, but . . ."

"But what?"

She half smiles. "Quicker would be better just now, that's all. How're you?"

I shrug my shoulders. "I still can't believe Cepta killed herself."

"If she did."

"What do you mean?" I look at her more closely, and I may not be a survivor, but sometimes I can see things that are unsaid too. "You know something: what is it?"

"Maybe. I'm not sure I should tell you."

"Why? Don't you trust me?"

"Yes! Of course I do; it's not that. It's just that it might be better for you if you don't know right now."

I think about what she said and the way she said it. "Do you think I can't handle knowing whatever it is, is that it? What could be worse than thinking she killed herself and none of us did anything to stop her?"

Shay sighs. "No, Callie; that's not what I meant at all. You're made of stronger stuff than I think any of us realized. I'm sorry, I shouldn't have said anything. Is it okay if we leave this for now? I promise I'll tell you everything when I can. Don't say anything about this to anybody, okay?"

"Sure," I say, but I'm annoyed and don't hide it.

Shay tries to get Iona to eat something later, but she refuses, says she's too tired, that she just wants to sleep.

Shay is tired too, and I feel guilty for getting snippy with her after everything that has happened.

I take her hand, and she gives me a hug.

"Go to sleep too," I say. "Now."

She smiles. "Yes, Miss Bossy Boots. Right away."

The house is soon dark, silent, but I can't sleep. Too many things are spinning through my mind.

With Cepta there are only three possibilities. Either it was an accident, though Xander said it couldn't be, or it was suicide—but now Shay has implied it wasn't—or . . . somebody killed her.

Who would do that? Why?

Jenna whispers inside me; she knows, she says. *Watch.*

And it's like one of the dreams she has with me, but I'm awake. She shows me the fire, the first one, when she was locked in a room and the wall started to glow. I want to pull away from this memory, but she won't let me. And for the first time, I see her *after* the fire, as she saw herself: cool, dark. A form only survivors could see. She doesn't even have that anymore now.

And she shows me what happened afterward: everywhere she went, death followed. She was the contagion.

But I still don't understand what this has to do with Cepta.

Jenna is still there, wanting me to work things out; I can feel her impatience.

Cepta was a survivor like Jenna was. She died in a fire too.

Wait a minute: would that make her into another contagion? If someone killed Cepta, maybe they wanted to make another contagion, like Jenna. But *why* would anybody do that on purpose?

That would spread the epidemic everywhere she went! Who in their right mind would want that?

CHAPTER 11

SHAY

THE NEXT MORNING IONA WON'T EVEN ANSWER ME.

She's half-asleep, half-awake—this I can see from her aura—and she hears me, at least at some level, but she doesn't stir. Whether she won't or can't, I can't tell.

I sigh. She is so pale, so thin. Won't eat. Won't talk. She's getting weaker, and I'm scared both for her and for us. We need to get out of here *soon*: I feel it, deep in my gut.

I try to remember how I adjusted when I first became a survivor. I may not have stopped eating and talking, but there was a time when it was all very hard to take.

And sometimes it still is.

Of course, back then I had Kai with me. There couldn't have been a better reason to want to get well in a hurry. And Jenna was there too, though she was masquerading as Callie then. She helped me even though I refused to accept that she existed for a long time.

"Iona? Please. I need you. I need you to get better: I need you to *want* to." I stroke her hair, hope she can hear and understand what I'm saying.

Callie comes in the front door. "Did you hear the helicopter?"

"Hmmm?" I turn as her words sink in. "No, I didn't. There was a helicopter?"

"You were both asleep. I went up to look. A woman—a young one—a boy, and a cat got out of it with Xander."

"Do you know who they are?"

"No. I didn't recognize them."

My stomach churns. What next? More sick people to heal who will lie still and silent like Iona?

Maybe I should leave this alone, but when has that ever stopped me? *Xander?* I hail him.

Yes?

Who was in the chopper?

Come by my house and find out. We'll be there in a few minutes.

Do you have to play these games?

He's amused. *Yes. Bring Callie with you.*

We hear voices before we see them; they're outside Xander's place.

And there is something familiar about one of the voices—a woman's, or a girl's. I *reach* out just as they round the corner, and my jaw drops.

"*Freja?* Is that really you?"

"Shay." She smiles, holds out her hands, and gives me one of those London double-cheek-kiss greetings, and the whole time my thoughts are spinning around. Did she come here to find us? I'd asked Freja to tell Kai to come after Callie and me: does Freja being here mean Kai is nearby too? I can't stop myself from *reaching* out all around, hunting for Kai, but there is no sign of him.

I want—*need*—to speak to Freja, to ask her these things, but with Xander so close, I don't dare, even silently.

I'm so distracted it takes a moment to notice the boy who stands to one side, a little behind Freja. He's about twelve or so and has the aura of a survivor, but his is muted, damped down. He is introduced as Wilf and mumbles hello.

"Callie?" Xander says. "Could you show Wilf around?"

She visibly bristles. "Sent away so the grown-ups can talk? Fine," she says. "Come on."

She marches off. Wilf is looking at Freja: a silent conversation? Then he trails after Callie.

"You're probably wondering why I'm here," Freja says. "I decided I made a mistake. I should have come with you to start with. I belong with my own kind."

There's something hidden behind what she says, but I don't want to look too closely, in case it draws Xander's attention to it too.

"Tell Shay what made you sure of this choice now," Xander says. "Better yet, show her."

There's a shadow of sadness, anger too, through her aura. "There was a girl with Wilf, a few years older—named Azra," Freja says. "The air force tracked them. Wilf was hiding up a tree, and they didn't find him, but this is what he saw." And she shows me Wilf's memory—is this the reason he was sent away with Callie, so he wouldn't see us living it now? Azra runs; I recoil as she is shot in the back. She tries to crawl away and is shot again.

Tears rise in my eyes.

There is no life for us in their world, Xander says to us both, silently. *Not anymore. We have to make the world our own.*

Callie and Wilf return. Freja and Wilf are moving into one of the many houses emptied by the epidemic, and Xander enlists some of the others to help them find what they need.

Before they go to settle in, Freja whispers silently, only to me: *Let's talk tonight. I'll call when I'm alone.*

The rest of the day passes slowly. Iona is just the same. Callie is moody, keeping to herself. Please, Freja: have good news for us. I need help.

I need Kai.

Hope that has been so hard to hang on to is there inside me now—stronger than before.

At last Freja hails me. She says Wilf is asleep, and to come to their house. I slip out in the dark, watchful, but don't see or sense anybody on the way.

She's watching. The door opens as I reach it.

She hugs me properly this time, and I hug her back. She draws me into the small kitchen; a black-and-white cat runs in past our ankles. She tries to shoo him out but then gives up and shuts the door. We sit down, and the cat meows, then jumps on my lap.

Freja laughs. "That's Wilf's cat—Merlin is his name. He likes you better than me."

"I'm so glad you're here, Freja."

"It's good to see you. Are you all right?"

"Not really. No. So much has been happening. But tell me first: is what you said before the real reason you're here?"

"What do you think?"

"I don't think, I *hope*: that you had a reason for wanting to talk to me late at night like this."

"Yes. We've got our secrets, haven't we? And you did what we didn't think was possible: you found Callie. Now we've got to work out how to get her home."

"So you came here to find us?"

"Of course."

I almost collapse with relief. Does that mean Kai is waiting somewhere for us to bring Callie to him? I hope it too much to say the words out loud. But there isn't just Callie and Kai to consider now. "Things have gotten more complicated—with Xander."

"I'm not surprised. What is up with him, anyway?" she says. "All this stuff he's been going on about today: making the world our own, like we can take over or something."

I shake my head. "I know. And there's more."

"Tell me about him. Tell me everything that's been going on."

"Some of this is just guesswork. But you know how he told us at that air hangar before we left that he'd been involved in trying to find a cure for cancer in Shetland? Not so."

"Then what was it all about—developing a weapon?"

"No, at least not from his point of view. He was already a survivor. I think everything he's done all along has been to try to create more survivors. And that's not all. He's been deliberately bringing his own people into an epidemic area so they'd catch it, hoping I could work out how to cure them. Playing with their lives. So many died. And, just recently, I think he murdered someone—Cepta. She was the Speaker of this Community, in charge when Xander wasn't here. I think he's been experimenting, trying to work out how to create another contagion—to spread the epidemic farther. To get rid of most people and just cure the ones he wants to live: that's how he wants to make the world his own."

She asks me how I've worked all this out, and I tell her everything I can. It's such a relief, at last, to share my suspicions—to not carry them alone—and the more I say the words out loud, the more I can see the truth within them.

"That's all just . . . wow. Hard to believe." Freja shakes her head. "What do you think we should do?"

"We've got to get out of here, and tell everybody we can, as soon as possible; we have to find a way to stop Xander from trying again to create another contagion. But there is a problem: my friend Iona."

"Is that the girl Xander told me you cured? He showed me how you did it—that somehow channeling the dark waves transferred DNA and saved her. It was awesome."

"Well, thanks. Iona doesn't think so, though; she's been trying to reject what has happened to her. She's too weak to travel. But I'm not sure I can risk keeping this to myself much longer, even if we can't leave yet."

"What are you thinking of?"

"Contacting Beatriz, Elena, and the other survivors. You know some of them, don't you? JJ and Patrick?"

"Yes, and Zohra and a few more. Could you hail them long-distance without Xander knowing?"

"I'm not sure; maybe."

"Even if you could, are you sure of them all? Would they be on your side, or Xander's?"

339

My eyes are widening. "Are you serious? Could anybody think what he wants to do is right?" But even as I say it, I'm not so sure. And what if they don't believe me? Either way, someone might tell Xander. Can we take this risk?

"Look, it's late. Get some sleep. We'll both think and work out what to do. Talk again tomorrow?"

I go to ease Merlin off my knees, assuming he's asleep, as he's been so still, but now I see that his eyes are wide-open. He jumps down, and Freja goes to hug me again, but Merlin gets in the way. I want to ask her everything about Kai: how is he? Where is he? But something holds me back. What if he can't forgive me for not believing that Xander had been a survivor for a long time—and for not telling him that Xander is my father? What if it is only his sister he wants to find?

I can't bring myself to ask her, in case the answer is one I can't bear.

CHAPTER 12

KAI

ROHAN'S AIDE HANDS ME THE TELEPHONE. "Dr. Tanzer is on the line," he says, and leaves the office, shuts the door.

"Hi, Mum."

"Kai, thank God. Are you all right?"

"Yes, I'm fine."

"You're with Rohan?"

"Yes. You didn't tell me he's a major general."

"We might have gotten to that if you hadn't run off so quickly. But I'm sorry about the other soldiers being there that day. I didn't know about them."

I know she didn't, but trust a major general and what do you expect? But I don't say it. He seems to be a pretty cool guy, considering it all; anyway, Mum and I need to make peace.

"Let's just move beyond all that now. It's all right. There's something else I have to tell you. He's told me you know about this force he's putting together to go to Scotland to find Alex. I'm going with them." I'd asked him if I could be the one to tell her.

"You're *what*?"

"Don't freak out. Please. I've gotten insights into Alex. It makes sense for me to go."

There's a pause, a long one. "Be careful," she says at last. And I can feel all the things she doesn't say in those two words—that she hates it, and she's scared something will happen to me, but she's accepting that I have to do this. And those two words almost make me come undone in a way that a whole long argument wouldn't have.

"I will, I promise."

"*Ich hab dich lieb.*"

"Love you too."

Things move quickly that day. There are arrivals by the hour: army, navy, air force, all from different branches of this and that—all immune.

Rohan has me address the group of almost a hundred that have arrived by that evening: to explain how survivors can influence your mind, how I've learned to block them. Just in case it might help.

We're moving north tomorrow.

CHAPTER 13

FREJA

I SLIP BACK INTO MY ROOM.

"How'd it go?"

I'm startled, spin around. Xander stands there in the dark.

And it's so hard to know what to say, what not to say. What is right and what isn't right have gotten tangled and lost inside of me.

He knows. He comes closer, takes my hand, holds it gently in his like it is a precious thing.

"Doing the right thing is often the most difficult path to take," he says. "But you do know what is right—for us and everyone like us. Don't you?"

And the doubt eases inside. I nod.

He smiles. "Tell me."

And I do tell him, everything Shay said, even though it means that his smile is soon gone. It tears into me to know how much this betrayal is hurting him. How much Shay is hurting him. That's what she does, isn't it? She betrays those closest to her. First Kai, now her father. She doesn't deserve either of them.

"Shay intends to leave, to tell outsiders our plans?" he says. "Are you sure?"

"Yes. There is no doubt."

"Let me see—every word," he says. He joins with my mind and sees the whole conversation I had with Shay, not just the words but every nuance of feeling in her aura as she said them as well.

"Ah, Shay," he says, his voice heavy with sadness. "First your mother, now you. I'd so hoped you'd be different—that being a survivor made you one of us. But I was wrong."

"You can't trust her," I say. "Not anymore."

"No. I can see that now."

"You have to stop her." And the *pain* of what Shay would do fills both of us. It's such a waste of what she could have had with him, as his daughter.

But then his smile returns. "Thank you for doing this for me, Freja. And I've just had the most wonderful idea: Shay's life *will* have meaning. She'll be the beacon to lead us out into the world." He holds me closer. "And you will be by my side."

CHAPTER 14

CALLIE

THERE ARE TOO MANY THINGS jostling around in my mind, and sleep leaves me early. There's a barely-there brightness at the window. It's almost dawn.

Can what I saw with Jenna actually be true? Was it what happened to her in the fire that made her into a contagion?

She was burned alive: like Cepta.

I still can't understand why someone would want to do this. And who could it be? There's only one answer, one possibility, isn't there?

Xander.

Jenna's feelings—approval for me, hate for Xander that is pure and strong—vibrate inside of me.

I need to talk to Shay, but she's been so distracted, so worried about Iona . . . I don't want to wake her this early. I lie in bed with everything churning through my mind until finally I decide, that's it. I will talk to her. I can't leave this.

I get up, stretch. I'll make her tea to apologize for the early-morning wake-up call.

I walk through the front room to the kitchen. Iona is still asleep on the sofa, which she's claimed as her place. Shay is right to worry. The water and snacks we'd left next to her haven't been touched. She's so pale, so still, that I reverse my steps. Go close to her, then closer, until I can see the faint movement: she's breathing.

"Iona?" I say her name softly. "Would you like some tea?"

She stirs but doesn't answer.

I make three cups anyway, leave one next to Iona with extra sugar in it, just in case she does drink it—it might help her.

I knock lightly on Shay's door and open it.

Her bed is empty.

CHAPTER 15

SHAY

I'M SHIVERING. There's heavy dew on the grass. Cold drops flick up on my ankles and bare legs from my sandals as I walk across Community to the research center. I hold my arms closer around myself.

There are red and pink streaks across the sky from the early sun—dramatic slashes of color that defy rather than blend into black cloud. With the eyes of a survivor, not even a sunrise is a simple thing anymore. And what is that saying? Red sky in morning, shepherds take warning?

Freja?

Still she doesn't answer. She'd hailed me from my sleep earlier, said she'd found something interesting in the research center, to meet her there, and then—nothing.

What could it mean?

I *reach* out around me as I walk, but all I find is a sleeping consciousness here and there, including in Xander's house. He's sound asleep. That makes me breathe easier.

Merlin is in front of the door to the research center. His eyes are wide, his fur ruffled as if he's had a fright—his aura too. I bend to pet him, and he meows an urgent story. My misgivings multiply. What has him so freaked out?

I *reach* again for Freja: there's nothing. Has something happened to her?

When I open the door, Merlin gets in my way, almost trips me up, and I have to shoo him away to go through and close it before he can follow.

I walk down the hall.

Freja?

Still she doesn't answer, and I can't sense her anywhere either. Unless she is deliberately blocking me—which wouldn't make sense, since she's the one who asked me to come. The only place I know that would stop me from sensing her at close range is the quiet room: the room Cepta put Beatriz in a while back to see if she could find a way to *reach* outside of it. She couldn't, and if Beatriz couldn't, then I'm willing to bet no one can. Could Freja be in there?

Down the hall, down some stairs, around a corner—I remember the way. The lights turn themselves on for me as I go, and switch off behind me again.

Finally I reach the hall with the quiet room, but have I taken a wrong turn? It looks different. There's been work done on the walls or something?

I walk along the hall, and there it is, in the midst of the changes—the door to the quiet room. It's ajar.

Freja?

Still she doesn't answer.

I walk up to the door, push it open a bit more to look inside. It's empty.

Then something slams into me from behind and pushes me into the room.

I sprawl on the floor, scramble up, turn, rush to the door—

It bangs shut.

348

CHAPTER 16

KAI

A HAND IS PUSHING MY SHOULDER, a voice saying to wake up.

"What?" I say, still half-asleep.

"The major general requests your presence at an interrogation. Get up. Hurry."

I throw on some clothes, and then, rubbing my eyes as we go, I'm led to a small room with a glass wall on one side.

"You can sit there and listen. They can't see you."

I sit down. Through the glass is a soldier I haven't met, with Rohan next to him. And opposite them is . . . Lieutenant Kirkland-Smith. *No way.* Somehow they've gotten their hands on that nasty piece of work, the one who tried to kill Shay and would have killed Freja given half the chance? The other half of the equation behind what happened at Shetland?

". . . have to know what you're dealing with," Kirkland-Smith is saying.

"We've got a pretty good idea," the other soldier says—he's doing the talking. Rohan sits and listens.

"Survivors aren't human, not like you and me. They're dangerous. They can't be allowed to live."

"We know now that they aren't carriers of the epidemic, that that belief was false."

"That isn't what I mean."

"So, explain: what do you mean, then?"

"When we moved in on Alex Cross at his Northumberland house we had a SAR prototype bomber to deal with the survivors. But one of them knocked it out of the sky. It crashed, killing those on board."

"And how did they do this?"

"There was no antiaircraft fire, no weapons of any sort. One of them did something—however they do these things, with their mind—and the pilot and copilot's hands froze on the controls. They couldn't move."

I'm not sure Rohan believes him, but I was there. I saw it happen. It was that girl, wasn't it? Beatriz. A child. She just looked at the plane—and it fell out of the sky.

"At your arrest earlier today, you said you had vital information that you would only give directly to our command. Is that all you have to say?"

"No. There's more. I know where Alexander Cross is hiding. We tracked him at last. If you hadn't interfered—well. Let's say your problem would have been gone by now."

"Where is he, then?"

"In Scotland."

"Be more specific."

"I'll take you."

"Tell us."

"No."

Afterward there's a tap on the door, and Rohan comes in.

"Can't you inject him with something to make him tell you?" I say. "Or twist his fingernails off or something?"

"Bloodthirsty, you are. No, we've decided to play his game, at least for now. He knows Alex; he might be useful."

"He wants to find survivors and kill them all."

"He seems to have some . . . issues, for sure."

"What did you think about what he said—about the bomber?"

He shrugs. "Sounds like nonsense?" he says, but he says it like a question. He wants to know what I think.

"I was there. It crashed. I couldn't say how it happened for sure, though. But just think about it for a moment. If a survivor could do such a thing, and a bomber was sent there to kill them all—you couldn't argue much more strongly for self-defense."

"True. Yet this is alarming from a military point of view, to think someone could do that. Just one person is all you need—no large guns or other equipment. How do we guard against that?"

"Easy. Keep them on your side."

CHAPTER 17

FREJA

I FEEL WEIRDLY ON FIRE MYSELF. Every nerve and fiber of me is tingling. Fear, excitement, dread are all mixed up, churning inside of me.

Shay will be our beacon to the world, Xander said. I knew what he meant: he explained it all when he confided in me about his plans. We need another contagion, made in fire—to cleanse the planet. To make it ours.

And I'm part of this?

It's appalling, cruel . . .

Necessary.

I can't sit still; I can't . . .

Everything that is happening—that is going to happen—to Shay is her fault. Isn't it?

I need *something*. . . . I don't even know what it is.

Yes, I do. I need to see Xander.

I'm about to hail him, but someone beats me to it.

Freja? The split second when I think it might be Xander turns to disappointment: it's JJ.

Hi, JJ.

How're things? Are you settling in there—or perhaps you'd like to come and visit us? It'd be good to see you.

No! I mean, I'm happy here.

How's Wilf holding up?

Wilf's name brings a twinge of guilt. I haven't seen much of him since we got here. I haven't tried.

All right, I think.

Freja? Is everything okay?

Yes! Everything is amazing! I love being here—with Xander.

Ah. I see. Is that how things are?

Honestly, JJ. Not like that. He's just so . . . And words fail me.

So old? So silver-haired?

Stop it.

Sorry. Just want to know that you're okay. Is anything going on over there?

No. What do you mean?

Nothing. Let me know if you need anything.

Sure. I've got to go.

I push JJ out of my mind.

That was a weird conversation. Has Xander considered what he will tell the other survivors? Of course—he must have. He's Xander.

I try hailing him now, but get the mental equivalent of a busy signal. He can't talk now; he's doing something else.

Too wound up to sit still, I head out the door—to get out of these four walls.

I have to talk to Shay.

CHAPTER 18

CALLIE

WHEN I FIND WILF, he is hanging from his knees upside down on a low branch of a tree.

"Have you seen Shay?" I say. "I'm looking for her."

"I saw her early this morning."

"Where?"

He swings himself up so he is sitting upright on the branch, then climbs down to stand next to me.

"I'll show you."

We walk across Community. "I was in that tree," he says, and points at the one that overlooks the library and research center. I've climbed up there myself before. It's a good spot to watch the comings and goings of this place.

There's a pang inside when I remember: that was the first time I saw Shay. I didn't know who she was then, that she's my sister. It's not that long ago, but it's like my life and all the things in it have changed completely since then—mostly because of her.

"I was high up in the branches, out of sight," Wilf says. "It was very early; I'd been watching the sun come up." I must give him a questioning look. "Merlin woke me up, and I couldn't get back to sleep. I feel safe in trees. Anyway, I saw Shay walk across below me and then go through that door." He's pointing at the research center.

We walk over to the door. I turn the handle, but it won't open. I'm shocked. I've never, ever come across a locked door in Community before. I didn't even know they could be locked.

"Was anybody with her? Did anyone follow her in?"

"No. Well, Merlin tried to, but she didn't let him. And Freja went in a while before Shay did—it wasn't quite light yet then."

Freja? The one who seems always to be with Xander since she got here? Now I'm feeling sick inside. What has happened to Shay? She wouldn't stay in there of her own choice; I know it. She'd be with Iona and me.

"What's wrong?" Wilf says.

"Nothing."

"You can't lie to me, you know. I'm a survivor. I can see how worried you are. Why don't you ask Freja? Though she's not always easy to find." I feel there is something behind what he says, and now I'm wondering why he's really climbing trees in the middle of the night.

"Are you all right?" I say.

"Did they tell you about me?"

"No. What do you mean?"

He hesitates. "I saw some bad stuff."

"You don't have to say if you don't want to."

"I don't. Then Freja brought me here to the land of weird."

I almost laugh. "Good description. You don't want to be here?"

"I've got nowhere else to be. But I don't think we should have left like we did, sneaking out on Kai like that."

"You know Kai?" My eyes are wide now. "How is he? When did you see him? Where?"

"Whoa with all the questions! I take it you know him too?"

"He's my brother."

355

"Small world—I didn't know. He wanted to come with us, at least to make sure we got here okay. But Freja said he couldn't, because he's not a survivor."

Disappointment crushes through me. He's not here; he doesn't know where we are. "I'm not a survivor either."

"Er . . . sorry. I didn't mean anything by that. Freja's weird about it, is all."

"It's all right," I say, even though it isn't. "Look. If it's okay, could you not mention to Freja that we've been talking about all this and that I've been looking for Shay?"

Curiosity crosses his face, then he shrugs. "Sure. Why not?"

I make excuses, then walk away.

Despite what he said, I'm not sure of Wilf, that he won't say anything. What will happen if he does?

If they know I'm asking questions, poking around, I'm sure they'll mess with my mind again like Cepta used to, until I don't ask any more questions. Maybe I won't remember Shay; maybe I won't even know my own name again.

Shay can't help me. Iona won't even move. There is no one here who can do anything about this but me, but what can I do alone?

I can't even leave to get help!

I kick a tree, and then I'm hopping because my toes hurt. I'm so . . . useless!

Though I haven't gone to the edge of the world lately.

I have to *try*.

I go back to our house, try to rouse Iona, and then give up. One thing I do know is this: she needs to have water even if nothing else. I pull her up half sitting, drip water into her mouth for a while, then let her slide back down again. She seems to almost wake up, and then she's gone again. I make sure she has food, water in reach, then pack some for myself but only a small amount—anything else would raise suspicions if I'm seen.

Chamberlain watches while I rush around, then follows me out the door.

I walk toward the gardens and, once out of sight of Community, go the long way around the perimeter to the place where the path disappears. The wind is picking up, the sky darkening.

I sit down on the path and stare at the place where it leads to nothing. Take a pebble and throw it. It disappears, and Chamberlain dashes after it. He disappears too.

I can sense Jenna's presence, feel that she's *willing* me to leave, to look for help for Shay. But trying to go past this point has never worked before: why should it now?

Think things through, Callie. *Think.*

Fact: the world doesn't really end.

Fact: my senses say that it does.

Guess: Cepta put this into my mind—a block, Shay called this kind of thing. It was so deep that Shay couldn't find it.

Fact: Cepta is gone. She said goodbye.

I lie back on the ground and close my eyes. That night there'd been a rush of thought and feeling from Cepta—so much that I couldn't follow it, as if it were all tangled in a knot. I try to remember, to think back to that moment. She was telling me something, I'm sure of it—to be free. I'd sensed that more as a feeling than an understanding at the time.

But when I look here, the world still ends. If it was Cepta who put a block in my mind, how could something from her mind live on beyond her in mine?

There's a faint nudge from Jenna—reminding me she is there. Well, Jenna died, and somehow she's still around in my mind, so it can happen.

Guess: the world ends because I still think that it does. I have to *unthink* it.

Jenna, can you help me?

I imagine her as she saw herself, a form of darkness. I stand up, hold out my hand as if I were taking hers in mine. Chamberlain is back now from pebble chasing and looks up at me.

"Let's get out of here, okay?" I say, and he seems to agree.

I gesture at the disappearing path, take a step forward, another . . .

Focusing on Jenna, on her darkness against the foggy whiteness where the world ends . . .

Chamberlain is at my feet, walking along beside us. The wind is whipping my hair around my face, and I use my other hand to hold it.

Okay, this is it. This is the moment.

Jenna being with me is an impossible thing. The world ending is an impossible thing. Let one cancel out the other—*now*.

The world shimmers, and the white fog dissolves in the wind.

We walk down the path together.

CHAPTER 19

SHAY

"**LET ME OUT!**" I bang on the door again uselessly. It's thick, strong, and only unlocks from the other side.

I've lost all sense of time. I'm thirsty, my voice is hoarse from yelling, and my arms ache from banging on the door, but I can't stop myself from doing it.

Then my eyes catch movement in the window: it's Freja.

"You tricked me! And locked me in here. Why?"

Is there regret on her face? She moves out of view, and then—there is a clicking noise.

"Sorry about that, Shay." It's Freja's disembodied voice.

"But why?"

"You were going to go against Xander, against all survivors. We had no choice. You know Xander is right: this is the only way. Survivors need to seize the world and save it."

Her words are sinking in even as I want to push them away. I'm shaking with fear. There is only one way survivors can seize the world. The epidemic has to eliminate everyone else.

If Xander wants another contagion like Jenna to spread the epidemic far and wide, then he needs a survivor to burn in fire. It didn't work with Cepta; her house wasn't a closed system. But now he has me trapped here, in a quiet room—one that is built like the room Jenna died in.

Xander—my father—could he really plan to do this? To burn me alive?

And Freja: I *trusted* her.

"How could you do this to me?" I say.

"Me? What about you? You're the one who betrays those who care about you time and again. First Kai, then Xander and all of us."

"What? You know why I left Kai—to find his sister."

"But you still left him—for the second time. And there were too many secrets between you. He'll never forgive you for that." And as Freja speaks, I'm starting to get a suspicion, a realization, one that tears into me inside.

"You never told him, did you? You never gave him my message."

"No. You should thank me, Shay. You could never have reconciled with Kai even if he did forgive you—you're too different from him now. Like I am. There was no way for it to work. It's easier this way than having to say goodbye again later."

I'm slumped down on the floor now, arms around myself. Kai doesn't know why I left him. Freja never told him I went to find Callie. And that's not all. That means he's not out there somewhere, waiting or coming for us, is he? The hope I'd found when I saw Freja here—no. It was false.

"How could you do that to Kai? I thought you were his friend."

"And that's why I didn't tell him."

Whatever twisted logic she might have applied in that case, it's nothing compared to pushing me in here to be burned alive for Xander's scheme. Why?

There can only be one answer as to who is behind this now.

"What has Xander done to you, Freja?"

"What do you mean?"

"Don't you know how to protect yourself, how to block? He's good at it; I'll give him that. At manipulating people, getting them to do what he wants. Don't let him use you!"

"He's not! I make my own decisions."

"You may think that, but fight against him, Freja. Why did you even come to talk to me now? You must be having doubts inside about what you've done—what he wants to do. Push him out! Think for yourself!"

"No. *No*, you're wrong! Anyway, this is all your own fault. If you hadn't betrayed Xander—and Kai—none of this would have happened. Poor Shay. I understand better than you think how hard all this is for you. You see, after you were gone, Kai needed a shoulder to cry on. So did I, for other reasons. We needed each other."

A shoulder to cry on . . . They needed each other? What is she saying? I try to push the words out, but I can't.

"We were together—Kai and me."

"I don't believe you!"

"It's true. We became very close."

Her words are burning inside me, and I can't see her aura or *reach* her mind. I can't taste the truth of what she says in any way—but despite that, I know. I just know, like acid burns and knives stab. She's telling the truth this time.

"So you see, I understand how hard it was to be so close to Kai, and then to leave him. I had to do it too—leave him behind—so I could have forgiven you for that. But I can't forgive what you were planning to do to Xander, to all survivors."

And then the mike clicks off. She's gone.

How could I have trusted her? How could I have been so *stupid*, telling her everything that I did?

She was Kai's friend—I trusted his judgment—but that's not the only reason. If I'm honest, it was also because I was so desperate for help, to confide in somebody after so long going it alone. Xander may have twisted and manipulated her thoroughly, but he couldn't have succeeded at that unless she agreed with him, at least on some level. She really thinks it's them or us: normals or survivors.

361

And with everything else, there are four words going over and over in my mind: She didn't tell Kai. She didn't tell Kai. She didn't tell Kai . . .

And she said they were *together*. What does that mean? Did he hold her, kiss her? Did she do *more*—what I'd promised Kai on Shetland and didn't deliver? Who could blame him? She was there, gorgeous, available. He thought I'd betrayed him, that he didn't owe me anything.

But still I howl silently inside. I loved him—I still do—so much. How could he betray that? Didn't he feel the same? I thought he did, but if he did, even if he thought he'd never see me again, *how could he?* Maybe I was wrong about him—about *us*—from the beginning.

There's a core of hurt and pain so deep inside me it threatens to pull me in and drown all that I am. I'm too sad to move; too sad to even cry. I can barely convince myself to breathe.

CHAPTER 20

KAI

"NO, NO, NO. WHY ARE YOU HERE?" Despite what I'm saying, I'm still smiling as I give Mum a hug. We're in the middle of chaos— people and equipment rushing all around us—but this is a moment to hold on to.

"I got myself attached to the medical contingent," she says. "Pulled a few strings. Immune doctors are in short supply."

"You don't know what we might find."

"Neither do you."

No. But maybe I've got a better idea what Alex is capable of, though I keep that to myself.

We're assigned to aircraft, belted in. There are just over a hundred of us now. All serious, quiet. All immune—tattooed—and taken from various forces, like Rohan said. It's not a standard military operation with everyone mixed up like this. Even I can see that. They've had to go everywhere they could to find enough immune personnel to go on this mission.

We take off at dusk. We're going to land at a deserted airfield suggested by Kirkland-Smith—one that is far enough from our target for us not to be heard or spotted in the air.

What then?

Then. I hope.

CHAPTER 21

FREJA

XANDER HAILS ME. *Callie is missing.* He's not happy.

What? Where could she be?

I have some other things to attend to. See if you can find her.

He's cut off now. Gone.

Where could Callie have gotten to?

I *reach* out, all around, but don't feel her presence. Of course, she's not a survivor, so unless she is near, there is nothing much to feel—it's hard to find non-survivors this way unless you know them very well, and I don't.

I focus on Callie—use her to push thoughts of Shay, and the crazy things she said, out of my mind.

Xander said Callie couldn't leave Community, that she's blocked mentally to prevent her from doing so, but there are only so many places she could be here.

The weather is drawing in: great.

I start at one end of Community and walk the length and breadth of it, sending my senses out for her, using my eyes too, but there's no sign of her.

I keep looking, afraid to stop. Afraid to tell Xander that I've failed.

CHAPTER 22

CALLIE

ADMIT IT, CALLIE, IF ONLY TO YOURSELF. You were so convinced you wouldn't actually be able to leave Community that anything approaching a plan for after didn't really enter your head.

Rain pelts down in heavy drops so hard they sting. Chamberlain has vanished; he probably ran home for a warm dry bed, and it's hard to blame him. I can't decide whether to huddle under a tree or keep walking.

By now somebody must have noticed I'm missing. Should I get off the path in case they come this way looking for me?

Or maybe no one has noticed. Without Shay there, I'm not sure anyone would have a clue where I should be.

I find a knot of determination, deep inside. Shay did so much for me. I have to get help for her—I have to.

I walk on through the rain. After what must be a few miles, the path leads to a road. There is thunder and lightning. Should I get away from the tall trees at the sides of the road? I don't know if it's better to be on the road or under the trees, and so I go for ease of walking: the road.

Another crash of thunder sounds, and the sky lights up. And this time when it does, I can see something ahead, on or near the road. Some dim lights and dark shapes in the rain.

Friend or enemy? I don't know. I stand there, not sure what to do.

Then I see movement ahead. Someone is walking toward me on the road.

"Is that Callie?" a voice calls out. Anyone who knows who I am must be linked with Community. I'm poised to run when there is a touch on my mind.

It's okay, Callie. It's Beatriz. Elena is here too, and some other friends. We've come to help.

There's reassurance, but the usual sort; no one is messing around with my brain.

Help is what Shay needs. They were her friends when they arrived, weren't they?

I walk forward in the rain. As I get closer, I see the dark shapes are a truck and a van. A light flashes briefly in the night. I see a flashlight in the hand of the figure I saw. It isn't Beatriz, but a man, one I haven't met.

He's soaked like I am. "Crappy weather or what?" he says. "I'm JJ. Come on, let's get out of this."

I follow him to the van, where the back door opens. And there are Elena, Beatriz, a few people I don't know—and Chamberlain.

I'm pulled inside, wrapped in a blanket. Chamberlain is warm and dry already.

"A cat always finds the best place to be," Beatriz says, and strokes him. "He found us, and that's how we found you."

"Why are you here?"

"We're worried," JJ says. "Shay isn't answering hails. Freja is sounding weird. Xander was already known to be weird. So we've come to investigate."

"Callie, do you know what's happening?" Beatriz says.

"Yes, some of it at least. But it's not easy to believe."

"There's a lot of that going around," JJ says. "Tell us anyway."

So I do. First I go back in time and tell them that Jenna was the contagion who spread the epidemic so fast, that she'd been a survivor and was made that way in fire. That Xander wants there to be another contagion—I don't say this is what Jenna thinks; I'm not sure they're ready to hear about her, or what I could say about her even if they are. And that Shay went missing, that she was last seen going into the research center—and now it's locked.

"She must be in the quiet room," Beatriz says. "That's why she can't hear us, or answer."

"So let's put things together," the other man says—Patrick, he'd said his name was. "Xander wants to make a new contagion from a survivor. Shay is locked up in a quiet room. He must be planning to use her. His own daughter?" He shakes his head.

"I don't understand," Elena says. "Why would he want to do this?"

"He's like Freja," I say. "He thinks you're all better than everyone else."

"He wants everyone to die—is that it?" Patrick says. "And then survivors will be all that are left."

"And immune," I say.

JJ is shaking his head. "I can't believe Freja could be involved in this," he says, but the others seem to be having less trouble with it.

"There's other news," Patrick says. "There's a force heading this way. We're not sure who they are or what they want. We've been monitoring them from a distance. But they seem to be making their way to the same place we're going."

"You mean to Community?" I say.

"Yes."

CHAPTER 23

SHAY

TIME HAS STOPPED. It's like when I was in the hospital room at the air force base, in solitary. There is nothing to mark it. I could have been here for hours or days; I can't tell. There's nothing to eat or to drink, and no bathroom. Being a survivor has its advantages. I *reach* inside, recycle my body's water, find unused fat and muscle, and break them down for nutrients to keep up my strength in case I need it.

There have been noises, for what feels like hours: things being moved, banged, hammered maybe, all muted through these walls. The glass in the door is covered now. Something is being built around this room, and I'm afraid I know what it could be. This quiet room is being converted to a fire room.

Then finally there is a click: the sound system.

"Shay?" Xander's voice is in my room.

I consider not answering him, but—no. I want to hear it from him—my father—in his own voice, his own words.

"Why am I a prisoner?"

"You planned to betray me." His voice positively drips with sadness.

I say something rude, something with four letters—and then embellish it with a few more.

"It's said to be a sign of intelligence: knowing when and how to swear." He's amused. "In any event, you're so smart I expect you've got this all figured out."

"Let's see. An enclosed room. An intense fire. Another contagion to clear the world for survivors. That's it, isn't it?"

"Yes. You shall be the shining beacon of your people."

"You're crazy. You're not *my people*, and I don't give a damn that you're my father—it doesn't make any difference. You've completely lost it."

This time he laughs out loud. "Is it crazy to want to save the world? Is it crazy to want to cure the infection that is humanity across the surface of our planet, and stop the destruction and pollution supposedly rational people are inflicting on it daily? Is it crazy to want to end war and suffering and starvation?"

"No, but it all depends how you want to fix these things."

"The only way. We'll clear the world, select who to save—we know how now, thanks to you and Iona. We'll start with a selected few in Multiverse."

And it's like it was with Freja before. I don't need to see his aura to know: he believes this. Fervently. That it is the only way.

Who's to say he isn't right about part of it—that the infection of humanity, as he calls it, won't self-destruct, ruin the planet, destroy each other? Even without his ability to manipulate me mentally because of this room, his ability to make things seem reasonable is astonishing.

But he isn't reasonable. He isn't making any sort of sense: kill billions of people and save just a few? How can he even begin to justify that?

And despite the absolute misery I've been in—I don't want to die. Every breath I take is precious, and it is *mine*. The more we talk, the longer I may live.

"Was that what you were doing from the beginning, at Shetland? Trying to make more people like yourself—more survivors?"

371

"Of course. Though I didn't have any idea how fast this epidemic would spread, with Jenna's help. And it soon will again—with yours. We're finally directing evolution, not just experiencing it."

"No. I'll stop my own heart from beating before the fire. If I'm already dead, it won't work."

"I don't believe you." His voice is sure. "Until the very last second of your life, you'll fight to hold on to it. But just in case you are tempted to do so, to save yourself the pain: if you fail to become what we want, the next try will be with Iona. After that, Beatriz. After that, Elena."

So maybe he does understand me better than I think. And I'm starting to understand more about him too.

"Did you deliberately bring the epidemic to Community? Did you arrange for infected people to come and spread it?"

"A sad necessity—to find a cure, you needed people who were sick."

"And it didn't work at first. So then you brought more of them back from the farm and made sure they were exposed and got sick. Didn't you?"

"You needed more patients to work things out. Iona too. You've shown us the way, at last. But enough of your questions, Shay. There is something I want to ask you."

"Oh? What is that?"

"I'm still curious about the connection Callie seems to have with Jenna, about how it works. Has she said any more about it?"

This I wasn't expecting.

"No. Why do you want to know that now?"

"You know me better than that."

"I know you can't stand not understanding something."

"Exactly."

"Why ask me? Ask Callie. She'll explain it better than I can."

There's a pause, and my mind leaps: he's asking me instead of her. Does that mean . . . she isn't there?

"Oh, *well done*, Callie. Has she worked out how to leave, is that it? If you can't find her, you can't ask her." And now I'm the one who is laughing. "I never told her about you, Xander, so if she left, then Callie must have figured you out all by herself—or maybe Jenna filled her in? Callie must have thought it was a good time to get the hell out of here."

There's a click: microphone off.

CHAPTER 24

KAI

AFTER THE FLIGHT AND A DRIVE comes the walk. It's raining, but I don't care—what I hate is that Kirkland-Smith is leading the way. What if he's taking us on a wild goose chase while some of his friends do his dirty work? Rohan knows my fears, but he says he has scouts all over the area and beyond: that he's sure we're going where we want to be.

We stop, set up a camp of sorts in the dark and wet. We're within a few miles of our target, he says. Tomorrow morning, we move in.

I'm settling down to sleep when something brushes against my mind. Automatically I push it out.

I rush to Rohan's tent in the rain and get let in. "Someone knows we are here," I start to say to Rohan, but then my words trail away. His eyes have gone . . . weird.

"Kai? This is Beatriz," he says, and it's his voice but eerily doesn't sound like him. "Please let me talk to you."

"Not in my mind. Can we meet? Are you nearby?"

There's a pause.

"Yes. Walk left down the road by yourself. I'll make sure no one follows you."

"Yes, fine. Let him go."

Rohan shakes his head, a confused look on his face, and then he . . . falls asleep.

I slip back outside into the rain. I walk to the road and turn left, while part of me wonders if I'm walking into a trap—if I should have told somebody before I left.

But I'm guessing if I tried, they'd just take an unexpected nap too.

And Beatriz, that little girl—she was Shay's friend. I know she was.

I keep walking. Just as I'm wondering how much farther it might be, someone rushes out of the darkness toward me, someone with long dark hair . . . blue eyes . . .

I blink and blink again in the dim light and can't believe—I can't—it can't be . . .

She's taller than I remember—can it really be?

"Kai!"

Callie rushes into my arms, and I hold her close. I'm choking with tears, touching her hair, looking in her eyes, then holding her close again. "Callie? It's really you?"

"Yes. It really is."

"Kai?" Another voice calls out: it's JJ. "Come on. Let's get out of the rain and have a chat."

A few minutes later, JJ's group and I drive up the road, then walk together to the sentry. I go first to tell the sentry to take the group to Rohan.

We'll join them soon, but Callie and I have something else we need to do first.

"Mum? It's me, Kai." I peer into her darkened tent, flashlight in hand.

She sits up, half-asleep, rubs her eyes. "Is something wrong?"

"Yes, but something is also very right. Can we come in?"

"*We?* Who is it? Wait, let me get dressed," she starts to say, but

Callie has had enough of waiting and pushes past me, rushes to kneel next to Mum.

Mum raises a hand to her cheek, looks at me, shakes her head. "I'm still asleep. Is that it? I'm dreaming?"

"No. You're awake. I promise," I say.

"Callie?" she says. And then there are tears on her face and her arms are around Callie, and she's saying things in German and then remembering Callie's German isn't so good and going back to English.

I step away, leave them to have this moment alone. Now there are tears in my eyes again too.

A few minutes later, I go back, and clear my throat. "Sorry, but there are things happening tonight that can't wait. We're wanted."

Soon we are all in Rohan's command tent: me, Rohan, Callie—Mum wrapped tightly around her like she'll never let go—and JJ, Beatriz, Elena, Patrick, Zohra. Apart from Rohan and my family, survivors all.

Patrick begins. "We've talked everything through and have decided we have to tell you the truth about what may happen. We have to work together to stop it." And he lays it all out: how the epidemic can be spread rapidly by a contagion; that Xander—Alex Cross—knows how to create one from a survivor, and they're afraid he plans to do so imminently with Shay. And when he explains how this could be done, the fear and pain for Shay that hit me almost make me stop breathing.

"We have to go there—now," I say.

"That isn't the obvious answer: we could be too late," Rohan says, and he hesitates, doesn't fill in the blank: that they could aim whatever weapons they have on this one place to stop this, and end Shay's life at the same time.

"These are innocent lives: Shay, Freja, Iona, others," Patrick says. "We need to stop Xander, yes. But are we any better than him if we disregard them in pursuit of our goals?"

"I'm not sure about Freja being innocent, though," Callie says. "It looked like she was involved in trapping Shay."

I stare at her, shocked. "But *why* would she do that?"

"I can't believe that of Freja," JJ mutters. "I *can't*."

"We have the better position if they don't know we're here,"

Patrick says to Rohan. "But they're survivors. As soon as they notice something is up, they can see where you are. We can try to block them, but there are too many of you to be sure it would work."

"Even assuming we manage to get close before they notice we're there, how do we know we will be in time?" Rohan says. "That he won't act before we can stop him, even if he doesn't see us coming?"

"We need someone on the inside," Callie says.

"Who is there that we can trust?" Beatriz asks.

"Well, there's Iona—but last I saw, she was unconscious. And maybe Wilf."

CHAPTER 25

FREJA

JJ HAILS ME AGAIN, and I consider not answering. But he persists, annoying like a skeeter buzzing in my ear.

What? I finally snap.

Nice—when here I am, missing you. How are you, Freja?

Annoyed, I wonder why he's asking me the same thing he asked me the last time, almost like he's checking up on me.

Or checking up on what is going on here?

Then I realize what I should have the last time we spoke. He's not using others for projection: it is JJ, and only JJ. I don't answer him further. I push him out of my mind, then block him completely.

That he could hail me without help with projection from others means he's close by—how close, I'm not sure. I cast out with my mind to see if I can locate him, and for a moment, there is a brief sense of *something*—not just one survivor, a whole group of them?—which then vanishes. As if JJ is blocking me back now.

And that's not all. There are spots of consciousness beyond JJ—

dim and hard to detect, but they're there. A large number of people, none of them survivors.

They're not too far away if I can sense them like this. I could try to locate them more precisely with animals, birds, insects in the surrounding woods, *reaching* to them and using their eyes, but I'm scared—too scared to handle this on my own.

Where is Xander?

I *reach* out and find him underground in the research center.

He doesn't answer me. I run to warn him.

CHAPTER 26

CALLIE

BEATRIZ ASKS IF SHE CAN PEER INTO MY MIND to understand the layout of Community, and then she will try to contact Wilf and Iona. She touches my mind lightly. It seems weird that this girl so much younger than me can do this thing that I can never learn.

I visualize Community, the whole layout, with emphasis on the location of the research center. Vaguely I sense she is projecting this to everyone else and that most of them are leaving, rushing to go there now. Then she asks me to show her the house we lived in.

Still in contact with my mind, she *reaches* out for Iona.

Iona? Iona! Beatriz has found her; she calls her name again and again. There's a sense of someone being startled awake, then slipping back to unconsciousness.

She's not well at all, Beatriz says, an aside to me.

Iona is starting to wake up a bit more; still Beatriz calls her name.

Go away, Iona says, finally answering.

I'm Beatriz, a friend of Shay's. Let me help you.

No. Don't want help. Don't want to be like this.

Stop thinking only of yourself! Shay is being held prisoner. If you don't help us, she may die. Callie is here too. Tell her what's happened, Beatriz says to me. And so in a rush, I explain it all—everything—with Beatriz channeling my words to Iona. Bit by bit Iona is becoming more aware, and by turns frightened and angry.

Can I really help? How? I can't even sit up.

You can, but first we have to help you. Please. Let us in.

There's silence a moment. *Oh, what the hell. Go on, then. Do what you have to do.*

Beatriz lets my mind go now. A few minutes later, she opens her eyes. "We've joined together to heal Iona, but she'll still be weak for a while. Maybe too weak to help."

"How about Wilf?"

"Isn't he Freja's friend?"

"Yes, but he's Kai's friend too. He wasn't happy with how Freja was handling things. If we tell him more, I think he'll help us."

There's silence for a moment: they must be talking about it.

"Yes, we'll try Wilf," Beatriz says, and joins with me again. It seems funny she's the one doing this.

What, because I'm eight years old? she says. *I'm better at this than the rest of them.*

I describe Wilf, and she *reaches* out, casts around. I tell her where his house is, but he's not there. I picture Merlin, his cat, and she finds him curled up in the grass under a tree. *Try up in the tree,* I suggest.

Finally, she finds Wilf: high up in the branches, overlooking the research center and library.

Wilf? Hi. My name is Beatriz. You don't know me, but Callie is a friend—she's here too.

Callie? Are you there? Everybody has been looking for you. Have you left the land of the weird?

Yes. For good reason: I needed to get help. Listen to what has been going on. We tell him everything: Shay a prisoner; Freja and Xander behind it; what we are afraid they plan to do.

Should be surprised but I'm not, not with Xander involved. A mental snort. Wilf seems to have figured him out quicker than most. *What can I do?*

For now, just stay where you are and keep watch. Tell us if you see anything.

How about what I already saw? Freja ran into the center really fast a moment ago.

Do you know why?

No. She looked really rattled, though.

There's a pause; a quick conversation, some angry faces.

JJ may have let something slip to Freja, Beatriz says. *She might have worked out that we're here.*

There was also something going on in there earlier, Wilf says. *I don't know what. Materials moved in and out. Like they're building something. But everyone else has left now—it's just Xander and Freja.*

And Shay.

Wait. Someone is coming. I don't know her. She's walking really slow, like she's sick or something.

Show us.

He visualizes what he can see.

It's Iona? Beatriz says. *Quick, everyone: shield her so they won't know she's coming. Maybe there is something she can do.*

Iona tries the door. It opens.

Freja unlocked it before, Wilf says. *She was in such a hurry she must have forgotten to lock it again.*

Iona goes through the door. Merlin runs from the grass behind her and just slips through with her before it shuts.

CHAPTER 27

SHAY

THE NOISE OUTSIDE MY ROOM—construction, probably, but I don't want to think what they've been building—stopped a while ago.

Surely turning this into a fire room would take a while? Wouldn't there be equipment and tech that Xander needs to get a hold of and assemble? Someone might miss me and come looking before it's ready?

But then I'm remembering what I saw when I first came here—yesterday morning or the morning before or whenever it was. There were already changes.

He's been planning this for a while. Hasn't he? Even though he did the *experiment* with Cepta, he'd already worked out it probably wasn't going to be enough doing it that way. Maybe she was arguing with his methods, or maybe he just killed her to tick all the boxes on his scientific method.

It's too quiet, too still; quiet like the dead. My voice is raw. I can't scream anymore. Hum—yes. I start humming a song I heard online back in Killin, before the world changed. What was it called? I can't remember—it was by Tusks. I know I liked it, meant to download it but never got the chance. I focus on the words inside my head, on humming the tune just to hear something, anything.

Then there is a clunk.

I stop humming and sit up abruptly. That didn't sound like the mike coming on this time.

It's . . . the lock to the door?

It opens, and there is Xander.

"I thought we should say goodbye properly," he says.

I fling an attack at his aura; he easily deflects it.

He's a good foot taller and much stronger than me, but I have nothing to lose—a cliché, but it fits the here and now. I spring forward to grab his legs, almost manage to make him topple over. But then he backs out through the door and pulls me to my feet in the hall. He has me in some sort of lock hold. I can't move at all.

Before he has a chance to say anything else, there is the thud of footsteps, coming this way—Freja rushes toward us. She's radiating alarm.

"What is it?" Xander says, his voice calm.

"JJ is nearby," she says, gasping. "I'm guessing some of the others may be too."

I'm not in the quiet room anymore. I fling my mind outward: *JJ? Beatriz?*

"I wonder if they reasoned out what is the next logical step for us to take?" Xander says. "Do they want to witness the moment everything changes for us, or do they want to try to stop evolution?" His eyes weird out; he's *reaching*, then they clear. "If they want to try to stop this, then they will be too late. They are too far away."

Shay, are you all right? It's Beatriz. I project to her what is happening, here, now.

"That's not all!" Freja says. "There are others approaching too. Many of them—they're not survivors—some kind of force? I don't know who they are."

"Interesting." Xander's eyes defocus, then return to normal. "It's Kirkland-Smith and friends. We're probably surrounded."

Kirkland-Smith? SAR? Another surge of fear rushes through me and joins the others.

No, it's okay. He's not in charge, Beatriz says to me. *He just showed them how to get here.*

Them?

Armed forces; they've come to arrest Xander. Kai is with them.

Kai. He . . . he's coming here? They're here to arrest Xander?

Xander shrugs. "It doesn't matter. I've seen where they are. They're rushing toward us now, but they will be too late." He leans down, kisses my forehead. "I do love you, Shay. Remember that, no matter what happens. Unfortunately, we can't delay this any longer."

This isn't love, I spit at him in his mind, with all the fury I can gather, but his aura is steadfast, determined. He will do what he will, no matter what I say—convinced he is right in all things.

"There are controls." He tells Freja what to do as he holds me. I struggle uselessly. There is a rush of warmth near us: the new walls around the quiet room are igniting. It must be well shielded to contain the fire, but we feel it begin through the open door.

Adrenaline and panic give me more strength. I fight against Xander with all that I am, but I still can't get away.

He's maneuvering me to the open door. Then there's a black-and-white streak that launches itself at Xander—Merlin? His claws rake Xander's arm and Xander falters, shaking Merlin off. I renew my efforts.

But then he kicks Merlin across the room—I gasp, winded, feeling his boot as if it is me he kicked—and now he's pulled me in front of the door. I can feel the heat even more. My mind is going back to the other time I almost died in fire. The *pain*.

That time, Xander saved me.

Please, please, please don't do this to me. And tears are running down my face.

He turns at a sound: footsteps. Someone else is coming down the hall toward us. Can it really be too late to stop this?

Yes.

Xander turns. He flings me away from him.

But . . . the wrong way? Out into the hall, and into Freja, not the converted quiet room. Instead he goes into it himself, hitting the door control on his way in.

Freja screams, launches herself at the door, and tries to release the lock, but it won't. There must be a fail-safe to keep it locked when the fire has begun.

There is an increased rush and roar of flames now that the door is closed. Freja howls, falls to her knees, pounding on the door with her fists.

"Shay? Thank God." Iona grabs me; her arms wrap around me. It was Iona we heard coming? Merlin limps over to us. He's all right too. He's giving me one of those superior looks cats can give—one that says I should have listened to him from the beginning.

"Is that Freja?" Iona asks me.

"Yes."

"Xander is where?"

I gesture. "In there."

We hear the flames. We hear his screams.

Not for long.

Iona pulls Freja to her feet, faces her. Freja's face is wild.

Iona takes a swing; her fist connects. Freja crumples back down to the floor.

Iona stands above her, shaking her hand out like she hurt it.

"That. That's what happens if you try to hurt my friend."

CHAPTER 28

KAI

WE ALL CONVERGE on the place that Callie calls Community. The hotheads among us want to rush in with guns blazing, but Rohan listens to Beatriz and the others about what has gone down: that Shay is alive; that Xander took her place and may be a contagion by now—but that he's in a sealed room and can't get out as long as they don't blow anything up.

So Rohan reins them in.

Callie shows us the way when we get to the research center. We rush down a hall to the quiet room. I see Freja first. She's on the floor, crying, and I go to her, to help her. She seems to have a black eye. But she pushes me away.

And then when I look up, I see Shay. Iona is there too, arms around her. Shay's eyes are on me, open wide. Full of pain.

There is this . . . space between us, even as I want to run to her. Then others are here, investigating the room where Alex is supposed to have died—survivors, and soldiers too—making sure there really are no cracks, no exits, no way out.

Someone says it had to be made that way, completely sealed, or it wouldn't have worked—that as Alex is now, he won't be able to open a door or do anything to get out.

And with all the noise and people around us, all I can do is look at Shay, across the room.

PART 7

COSMIC EVOLUTION

Imagine nothing: it is both the biggest and the smallest concept that the mind can encompass. Then came the big bang! Space, time, matter, and energy were all created in that one event. From nothing. One event, and one only, that came before everything. Or so they say . . .

—Xander, *Multiverse Manifesto*

CHAPTER 1

SHAY

IT IS SOME TIME LATER before I can bring myself to see Xander again. I have to do this. I have to be the one to tell him.

Until now, I've stayed away.

Survivors—JJ, Patrick, Zohra, a few others that have joined us now—have been guarding him in turn. The normals can't even see that he exists in there, sealed in his room with his own ashes. They take our word for it that he can never be allowed to get out—the consequences that this would have. But as he is, he'll go on forever, won't he? We won't. This risk can't go on and on. We can't allow it.

They've built a double lock structure around the fire room where he died. Patrick unlocks the first door, and I step through. It seals behind me. I stare at the second door—the one to the room where I was imprisoned, where I thought I was going to die. And I'm nervous, scared, even though I know he's no threat to me now. He could make normals sick. He could make them burn, like Jenna did before. But not a survivor like me.

He can't touch me, I remind myself, and knock. I don't know why. They release the door remotely, and I open it.

And inside is a form of darkness—like Jenna once was. Cool and soothing to my eyes.

Shay. I hoped you'd come. Xander is pleased to see me, and I have no idea how I feel about that.

"You thought you'd thought of everything, didn't you? The thing you missed was how to get out of here."

When I built it, I thought you'd be the one inside, and I would be here to let you out. Afterward, when it was me, I was completely certain the armed forces would attack with their weapons and accidentally break me out at the same time.

"You knew they were coming? I mean, before Freja told you?"

Of course. How is Freja?

"In a secure mental facility. She's really lost it." And I know she's ill, that I should feel sorry for her, but with all the trouble she caused—and pain—it's hard.

Shame. She had a weak mind.

"A weakness you exploited. But you still failed. You didn't know Kai was coming, that Callie brought Beatriz and the other survivors and the armed forces together through Kai. That they would cooperate."

No. It's fair to say I was . . . astonished at that development. Cooperation, I mean! Of course, any daughter of mine would have to be resourceful. And how about you and Kai? How are things going?

I don't answer him. He can read into my silence whatever he wants. Kai and I have talked, but it hasn't been great. He accepts that I left to find his sister, that Freja should have told him and didn't. I accept that if it weren't for that fact, he wouldn't have gotten together with her.

But that doesn't mean I can forgive him.

Or Freja. I know her mental state—and her fear—drew her to Xander, made her susceptible to him. But not passing my message to Kai? There is no reason she could give for that that I could accept.

Perhaps I should try another question. How are things going out there in the real world?

"The epidemic is essentially over. You know how I couldn't detect

391

differences between the immune and those who die? We did a closer study, bigger samples. There are just a few base pair changes in the immune that alter the structure of their DNA slightly—enough to stop the cascade reaction that kills people. It's easy to change this in people—much easier than what I did to save Iona. We've been busy making everyone in at-risk areas immune. Also, the right wavelength of pure light destroys dark light, and can be used to decontaminate areas. This is why SAR's bomb destroyed Jenna. It was a prototype that used light. Light treatment also cures the sick if they are reached early enough." I don't say out loud that it is hard to see how the UK can ever recover to anything like it was—not when something like eighty percent of the total population have died. And he did this.

Impressive work, he says, and he means the science that has achieved this—not what we've chosen to do. He wanted the epidemic, didn't he?

And everyone else—how are they getting on with survivors?

"Mixed. In some places, they're still having to be imprisoned for their own safety—or so the wardens say. In other places, they're almost viewed as heroes by making people immune, healing them." I don't go into it, but that's what I've been doing. I needed something to throw myself into. Conferring immunity, yes, but also healing cancer patients, broken arms, sickly babies—the works. It turns out that stuff I read on auras was half-right: which said those with rainbow auras were healers and star people. There have been no signs of excessive twinkling, so I'll stick with healing.

Perhaps it is time for you to tell me why you're really here.

"We can't leave you like this forever."

Out of sympathy? I doubt it. What do they have planned?

"The light that cures—it should destroy too. They've been experimenting with portable pure light sources. One is on its way here."

I see. They've decided it's time for a more final solution.

"I'm not sure you should use those words. Maybe they fit better with what you were planning to do—to kill everyone on the planet, leaving only survivors?"

Trying to convince yourself I deserve it, are you? How long have I got?

"A few days until they get everything here and test it, I think."
That should be long enough.

I leave soon afterward. Xander didn't seem surprised when I told him. He sounded relieved, happy even. But who would want to be a dark shadow of themselves sealed alone in a room forever?

That should be long enough, he said.

He asked for a recorder, someone to come in and write down the things he dictates. I don't go back, but Patrick arranges it. Other survivors go in and transcribe it for him in shifts. Even though we're not sure if we should, it's hard to say no to someone's last request.

He calls it the *Multiverse Manifesto.*

That last day I spoke to him, I didn't ask the one question I desperately wanted answered. Was it because I'd never know if I should believe his answer?

Or maybe I was afraid.

The question was *why*: why did he, at the last possible moment, take my place in the fire?

Was it because he heard Iona's footsteps and thought that justice was coming to get him, that there would never be any escape for him as he was? Was it desperation that made him decide to become his own contagion?

Or maybe he did it to save me.

CHAPTER 2

CALLIE

TODAY IS THE DAY THAT MY FATHER WILL DIE.

Or will die again—like Jenna did.

I should probably care, at least a little, but I don't. Maybe sometime later after it is all over, I'll feel different. But Jenna is still so much a part of me. After all the things he did to her, it's hard to feel anything about him at all when her hate for him is so strong inside me.

And Jenna died again like he will, yet somehow she is here in my mind. We're still tangled together. Where will Xander go?

Jenna isn't sure, but she thinks he may come to the same place where she is. She says that's okay and that they're ready, waiting.

Where is that? Who is waiting?

She says if I close my eyes, drift into dreams, she can show me . . .

CHAPTER 3

JENNA

I TAKE CALLIE BACK TO THE DAY I LEFT EARTH. I was with Shay and Chamberlain, covering them completely.

Something fell from the sky above us.

I fought to protect Shay, not to run away and save myself.

There was terrible pain.

Burning . . .

Tearing . . .

Peace.

And then . . . absolute, complete joy. It was a level of happy I'd never felt before, being delivered from the worst imaginable pain and fear to the most chilled, blissed-out state. Being everywhere—among each scattered galaxy and its stars, near and distant—and nowhere—all the vast nothing between—at once. And being every *when* too. I experienced it all: from the big bang that started things, to the next one, and the next. And all the while, this universe, and all the others, soothed, cradled, accepted me. There was no judgment.

But no matter how far away I went from what I was, there were still things I had to set right.

Could Callie help—would she? I thought so. I *hoped* so. While I was still everywhere and every when, I *reached* out and back, found her, and claimed her as mine. Then we were linked even more closely than we were before, despite the blocks inside her mind. I knew she'd find a way if anyone could.

Reassembly came next. Every tiny speck of me was like a speeding car, heading for multiple collisions—at way beyond the maximum on a highway, or even the light of the stars in the sky. But even though it hurt as much as when I came apart before, I wasn't so scared. Now I knew what was happening.

When it was over, I drew a deep breath. Cold air flooded into my lungs, and I coughed.

I had lungs? I could feel cold?

I drew my arms around my shivering body and opened my eyes.

Where did I find myself, and where am I still?

It's a new world, a new place, and while everything is subtly different, it is also the same. It's like Earth but not Earth. They call the Earth I came from Earth-minus and this Earth-plus. They told me they are different versions of the same world. They are both in the same place and infinitely far apart—dimensionally speaking—and one is matter and the other antimatter. Which makes my head spin to think about.

I was taken into custody to start with. Traveling between paired matter and antimatter worlds as I did—as dark light, they explained—is illegal. But they soon understood it wasn't my fault, that Xander was behind everything that happened to me.

They released me, found me a place to live. And everyone here is like I was as a survivor: we talk with our minds, and can do all the things survivors can do. It's just normal.

I could be happy here, but I can't let go. I'm always watching, waiting to see what Xander will do, through Callie's eyes. We were and are still a pair: light and dark light, matter and antimatter, Earth-minus and Earth-plus—two sides of a coin that never see each other but each know the other is there.

Linked as we are, I try to help Callie when I can. It was hard at first; she resisted me, didn't believe I was real. But then Shay helped her accept who I am.

And now Xander might be coming here.

We're ready.

As soon as Xander arrives, the same way I did—traveling as dark light—he's taken into custody. He's charged with crimes against the multiverse. He seems happy about that.

There's a trial. It plays out on this Earth's version of TV.

I soon get bored with all the background information. Apparently for Xander to have a fair trial, he has to know it all. But I make myself watch and listen.

They explain how after each big bang, matter and antimatter don't destroy each other like they should because they are shielded from each other by dark matter. So every world—every universe too—is in pairs: a matter one and an antimatter one—all kept apart by dark matter.

Then a long time ago, before they made it illegal, the people who lived on this antimatter planet learned how to travel as dark light to their paired matter world: Earth-minus. When they arrived, all the early humans started to die. They'd brought dark light with them, and it triggered something that killed the Earth-minus people. And then the new arrivals to Earth-minus started getting sick and dying too. Normal light on Earth did the same thing to them; more slowly because it wasn't a pure light source, but they were dying.

They figured out this must be due to evolution. If you mix matter and antimatter together, the dark matter keeping our worlds apart will collapse the dimensions, and it'll trigger another big bang. This has happened time after time. It's like Earth-minus and Earth-plus used evolution to protect themselves: making us die if we went where we should never go.

But not surprisingly, the ones who traveled to Earth-minus didn't want to die. They messed around with their DNA. They did experiments with ancestors of cats first—that's why cats like Chamberlain and Merlin are so weird and clever and feel a little like mind-reading survivors. They've got DNA from Earth-plus in them too.

397

Then the travelers made hybrids of themselves with the early humans from Earth-minus, so they could survive the light on that Earth, which created people with shielding to survive dark light too—sort of like how dark matter shields matter and antimatter universes from each other. They figured out how to save early humans who weren't hybrids by putting mutations in their DNA to stop the process that made them die in dark light.

It turns out that when they first went to Earth-minus, they communicated with Earth-plus using entangled pairs—a person on one planet could communicate instantaneously with one on the other. Now I did listen carefully: this must be like me and Callie.

Eventually the hybrids regressed, lost technology, lost touch with this world and where they came from. Then this next part seems to be guesswork, but they think that without any dark light around on Earth-minus anymore, the mutations in the early humans weren't stable enough or something—and that over a very long time, their DNA started to revert to the way it had been before.

At this point Xander gets very excited. He said that's why some people are immune—they've got these introduced mutations still; most people die because they've reverted; and some very few, who are hybrids, start to get sick in the presence of dark light because of their Earth-minus heritage, but then this triggers their Earth-plus genes to make the dark shielding. They get better and also have these abilities awakened, like telepathy and stuff.

Whatever.

It all takes *forever*, but Xander is finally found guilty of crimes against the multiverse.

Weirdly, he still seems happy. He's allowed last words, and he says he's ecstatic—strange thing to say, in the circumstances—that he was right about how to travel to this world. He says that he's ecstatic to finally understand everything.

His punishment is dissolution—his atoms are scattered far and wide.

They say it is painless.

I'm disappointed about that last part.

CHAPTER 4

KAI

I KNOCK AND OPEN THE DOOR, LOOK IN. It's Callie's fourteenth birthday. She asked me to come, to bring cake, and I've got a massive chocolate fudge cake with candles.

"Hello?" I call out.

"We're in the kitchen," Mum says.

When I walk into the kitchen, Mum is there. Rohan. Wilf. And someone I didn't expect to see: Shay.

She's surprised too.

"I blocked her so she didn't sense you coming," Wilf says. He, Mum, and Rohan get up, leave the room.

It's just Callie, Shay, and me.

"I thought you weren't able to come," Shay says to me, and gives Callie a look. "This is a family thing. I'll go." She gets out of her chair, stands, poised to run.

"No. It's my birthday, and you're both staying," Callie says. "Anyway, I've had enough of this. You're my two favorite people, and you are both suffering, missing each other. It's beyond stupid. Work things out. *Now.*"

And I stand there, helpless. *Wanting* Shay more than I ever did, but knowing she always pushes me away.

CHAPTER 5

SHAY

CALLIE TAKES MY RIGHT HAND, Kai's left, and puts them together. We met because of her. We were parted because of her. Can she bring us together again?

I look up into Kai's eyes. Callie is right. No matter how I try to get him out of my head, my heart, I can't. He's always there. It's like a toothache in a tooth I can't pull. My traitor hand clings to his tight, and when it does, there is an answering light in his eyes.

I shake my head, fighting not to cry. "How can we forget everything that happened?" *The things we should have said, the lies that came between us.* "We can't go back to what we were."

"No," he says. "But maybe we can become something better." He raises my hand and presses it against his temple. "Come on. Come inside, and you'll see."

I feel rather than see Callie leave the room, shut the door. My eyes are closed. I can't breathe, can't think. I don't know what to do.

"Shay? Please."

And like the petals of a flower must open to the sun, I *reach* to Kai inside.

I'm crying. *I don't know if I can do this. I don't know if I can let go of the hurt and the pain.*

Shay? I love you. I've always loved you.

Is that enough?

It's all that I have, he says, and his tears are falling now too.

Kai is here, next to me. He is also here, in my mind. Then his lips are on mine, his body is against mine, and the answer is *yes*.

It is enough. It is all that there is.

CHAPTER 6

CALLIE

WILL I EVER TELL ANYONE about Jenna and Xander—explain it all?

I don't know. I don't know if knowing everything—no matter how happy it made Xander at the end—really helps.

Or even if it does, if anyone would believe me.

Anyway, I'm not sure if knowing that survivors are hybrids—that part of them comes from another planet, even if it is paired to this one—would be a good thing for Shay and the other survivors. Some people are still pretty weird about how different they are: imagine what they'd make of that?

Besides, even though she doesn't say it out loud, I know Shay somehow needs to believe that Xander did what he did to save her. And I know that isn't true.

Xander must have worked things out after finding out about the bond between Jenna and me—she had to be *somewhere*, but she'd vanished from our planet. He must have guessed that if he became like Jenna, eventually they'd destroy him like they did her, and he'd escape to another world. Though I'm not sure being dissolved was in his plans.

So I'll keep what Jenna showed me to myself.

But it seems comforting somehow to think that this Earth we live on found a way to protect itself—that we evolved in a way that would prevent us from triggering another big bang, either accidentally or on purpose. I hope that the changes survivors have been making in people now, to make them immune, don't affect that—even as I'm glad my mum, my brother, and I were all immune.

As for now, there is still something I have to do. Jenna and I need to say goodbye.

We're closer than I could ever be to anyone else—I know this. She even finally shared with me who she was before she ended up in Shetland. She'd been in one foster home after another. Some horrible things happened to her, and she ran away. Runaways and others from shelters were gathered up by Xander's followers and ended up as subjects in Shetland.

My memories of Shetland were hidden by Xander and Cepta so thoroughly that even though I know the truth now, it's foggy, like a movie I've watched instead of something that happened to me.

But I know I was there, with Jenna—that's where we met. We'd talk and hold each other in the night to stop being so scared. Even then it was like we'd always known each other—now I sort of understand why. When Jenna *reached* out to me, she was out of time—*every when*, she said—so it was kind of like she'd always been in my life.

Xander had been so sure I'd be a survivor like he is. He'd convinced me to sneak out and meet him that morning I went missing in Killin; then he'd convinced me Mum had said I was to go with him. I started to question this and ran off into the woods when we stopped for gas. That was when Shay saw me. But Xander found me on the road—he knew where I'd be. He was a survivor, after all.

And I was taken to Shetland, like Jenna was, to be experimented on.

And he was *so disappointed* when I wasn't a survivor, when I was immune instead—and most of all, that he was wrong. He shipped me off to Cepta to tinker with my mind so I'd forget it all.

I would have, if it hadn't been for Shay and Jenna.

Jenna and I have shared fear. Horror. Joy. And Jenna is still here, right now, just out of reach. She's always there.

Yet in her murmurs in my dreams, and near waking, Jenna agrees: it must be this way. We both know it's time. It's better for Jenna, better for me too. We can't live anything like normal lives, not tangled together the way we are.

Goodbye, she whispers.

"Goodbye, Jenna," I answer her. "I hope you will be happy now."

She pulls away. There's a sense of us both letting go, of solitude—one I can't remember having felt before. I panic and want to call her back.

But it's too late. She's gone.

I get out of bed, pull the curtains. The stars are bright in the sky. Is Jenna out there somewhere I can see?

There is silence, pure and true, in the night, in my mind. Shay taught me how to block survivors like Kai can. Now that Jenna is gone too, my mind is completely my own. For the first time in my whole life, *no one* can see my thoughts or make me think what they want.

I'm not sure who I am, completely alone like this—like pages no one can write on but me.

It's scary. It's lonely.

But it's also *amazing*.

ACKNOWLEDGMENTS

While writing this trilogy, I've been shamelessly stealing names from friends I've known a long time or met along the way. Thank you to the following for the names of their children, spouses, and/or pets:

Addy Farmer—for Henry, Wilf, Freya, Angus, and Persey (her cat)

Jo Wyton—for another Henry (they can share) and Merlin (her cat)

Sally Poyton—for Spike and Beatriz

Karen McKee—for Iona, Euan, and Duncan

Caroline Horn—for Azra

Thank you to my awesome agent, Caroline Sheldon; my lovely editors—Megan Larkin, Emily Sharratt, and Rosie McIntosh—and everyone at Orchard Books and Hachette Children's Group.

And thank you most of all to Graham, Banrock, and Scooby: cheers!